GHOST EATER

❦

Frederick Highland

THOMAS DUNNE BOOKS
ST. MARTIN'S PRESS ❧ NEW YORK

THOMAS DUNNE BOOKS.
An imprint of St. Martin's Press.

www.stmartins.com

Design by Susan Yang

Library of Congress Cataloging-in-Publication Data

Highland, Frederick, 1945-
    Ghost eater / Frederick Highland.—1st ed.
        p.   cm.
    ISBN 0-312-30671-7
    1. Indonesia—History—1798-1942—Fiction.   2. Search and rescue
operations—Fiction.   3. Sumatra (Indonesia)—Fiction.   4. Ship captains—
Fiction.   5. Missionaries—Fiction.   6. River boats—Fiction.   I. Title.

PS3558.I3645G48 2003
813'.54—dc21
                                                            2003049240

First Edition: September 2003

10   9   8   7   6   5   4   3   2   1

AMG
with love and appreciation

What is the meaning of these mysterious images? In order to answer this question we must remember the attendant tiger, the belief in which is prevalent throughout Sumatra. Many people are supposed to have an animal of this kind, whose woe and weal are inevitably bound up with those of his master. . . . Here the tiger is considered a sort of double and the fate of the two is closely intertwined.

— F. M. SCHNITGER, *Forgotten Kingdoms in Sumatra*

GHOST EATER

FROM THE JOURNAL OF CAPTAIN ULYSSES DRAKE VANDERS

ABOARD MERCHANT VESSEL *PHOENIX*

PORT OF KAOHSIUNG, FORMOSA, MARCH 31, 1911

"The Jolly Boat"

The hammering, the clattering, the brisk and charnel festivities of the salvage yard had only brought home the truth. I was treading the deck of a wooden corpse. I had no desire to winter over only to bury her in bleak Kaohsiung. I had no desire to toll the bell, like a dour sexton, for this fine old sailing vessel, perhaps the last three-masted barque in the South China Sea. So I wired Mr. Fairfield in Aberdeen once more, not that it would do me any good.

"Sell her, salvage her, or I'll damn well sink her in the harbor," was the message I had wired, and I was close to carrying out the third option. This reckoning was interrupted by my first officer.

"I've sent the fellow to your cabin, Captain."

"Whom have you sent, Mr. Radhakrishnan?" I tore my gaze from the dismal scene of shipyard cannibalism taking place across the harbor. My first officer has always been ginger about interrupting my musings, so I smiled to set him at ease.

"The man from the jolly boat, sir," he replied, referring, in sailor's lingo, to the covered funeral barges that deliver the departed, their coffins piled with offerings, from the city of the living to the City of the Dead at the other end of the bay. "I thought you were there—in your cabin, I mean—until the bosun pointed you out."

Putting my field glasses away, I stepped down from my lookout on the bowsprit and followed Mr. Radhakrishnan aft. *Phoenix* is a doughty merchantman of fifteen hundred tons, and I've made it my business to keep her seaworthy. The ship's canvas was laid out amidships, a half dozen of our diminishing crew scrubbing out mildew and stitching tears and rents with lively needles. She might never unfurl those sails again, but I would not have it said that Ulysses Drake Vanders let a ship in his care look like salvage, even if that was her fate. If she was headed for the ax and the saw, she would face her executioners looking trim and proud.

Passing the quarterdeck where the bosun was on duty, I looked over the side. The jolly boat was there, all right, bobbing on the tide, its fringed yellow canopy fraught with Chinese calligraphy and strung with red and gold streamers. Beneath the awning nestled two coffins of polished camphor wood. The effigies of the occupants were elaborately and fantastically carved on the lids, a bespectacled Asian man and a woman with billowing hair that framed her long, narrow features. Their hands were crossed on their chests, and each wore a crown in the shape of a bird rising from a nest of flames. The sides of the coffins had been decorated with a pattern of tropical leaves, enigmatic symbols, curious towers, and animals, among which I made out a playful elephant rearing on its hind legs. Marveling at this curious cargo, for these were unlike any Chinese caskets I had seen, I descended the gangway to my cabin.

The Chinaman who stood before my desk was a diminutive fellow. Scarcely five feet, he wore a farmer's straw hat whose broad brim hid his features almost to the chin. His black cotton pantaloons were tied at the ankles with strips of leather. A coolie's coarse black jacket completed his attire, except for an extravagant yellow silk sash with tasseled ends that he wore loosely about his waist, a symbol of his calling as ferryman of the dead. By way of greeting, he bowed formally, as if on a diplomatic mission of high consequence, and held out a black-lacquered box, a foot long and perhaps half that high. It bore no mark, but its surface was polished to a high sheen. My face was reflected in it like a dark flame.

"Who sent this gift?" I asked, taking it in my hands.

The Chinaman bowed once more.

"I don't think he can speak, sir," said my first officer. "He made his wishes known by signs."

The boatman pulled out of his jacket a calling card, creased and yellowed with age. Its lettering, written with a quick, decisive hand, had faded into a ghostly script.

I held the card up to the opaque light coming in from the stern windows. "Perhaps you can make more of it, Mr. Radhakrishnan. My eyes . . ."

Our mysterious messenger bowed once more and seemed about to take his leave when a glass display case mounted on the bulkhead caught his eye. Pinned to the green felt, the insect's wingspan was nearly six inches across. The predominant color of the wings was a translucent, almost cobalt blue, lined in black. From tip to tip were splashes of color like droplets of molten gold.

The old man lifted his hat to get a better look. Our eyes met in his reflection, and I felt a twinge of recognition, although I doubted if we had ever met before; if so, it had been long ago. Perhaps the impression was mutual, for I had the distinct impression he was trying to humor me, not in a way to give offense but almost with affection, as if appraising a grandchild who had learned to recite the lesson though did not understand its meaning. This look, at once warm and wise, was framed by a ghastly geography that explained why he had not removed his hat. He might have been a leper, for leprosy will do that to a face, but I suspected he had been the victim of misfortune. Deep ridges and crevices were scored from brow to chin, as if his features had been melted in sheets of flame, as if he had been cursed for looking upon that which should never be seen. But I saw neither self-pity nor despair in this riven mask. If he had walked through the fire, he had also found an oasis of serenity in the embers.

I could see that my first officer had caught a glimpse of the ferryman's terrible aspect as well. And was shaken by it. He drew our attention back to the specimen and, as he stepped forward to gain a better look at the butterfly, the messenger bowed and retired.

"Native to Sumatra, Mr. R. *Papilio aurensis*. The Golden Sura," I added, using the common name.

"Arabic characters, they seem."

"Malay legend has it that this is the final passage from the Koran. It was so beautiful that Muhammad wrote it on the wings of a butterfly."

"That's a fanciful notion, Captain."

"No more so than for *Aurensis* himself. It's his artifice for attracting a female. In all creatures, the illusions drive—although there was a time when I would have thought that idea ridiculous."

The young man's face clouded. "I suppose my illusion has been to think that I could climb my way to command by knowing the currents, the wind, and how much canvas to put on—as you did, Captain. But the *Phoenix* is one of the last of the three-masted merchantmen. I'm not likely to serve on another."

Mr. Radhakrishnan is a fine officer, alert, capable, but a worried one, a tall Indian with the soulful eyes of the god in his name, at least as the Hindu devotional prints portray Krishna. Originally from the Punjab, he had run off to sea, forsaking his Brahmin heritage. There is no going back for him. But the way ahead is obscure, seeing as he is about to marry a Chinese girl in Singapore, and the fate of the *Phoenix* is uncertain.

"A ship's officer will always benefit from knowledge of the elementals," I reassured him, "even in this brash new age of oil and electricity."

"I doubt, sir, if *Phoenix* will live to see oil and electricity—or even a coal-fired boiler, for that matter."

"Well, there you have it, Mr. R. That's why we pace the deck as Mr. Fairfield paces the boards of his office in Aberdeen. I can hear that rough thistle in his voice now: 'Should she be outfitted with steam?' he repeats to himself. 'If it's to be an engine, then what kind of engine is it to be?' And so he will dither back and forth in faraway Scotland, dragging his oft-mended boots, answering his questions with questions. '*Or* should I scrap her and be done with it?' He will lift his scrawny neck out of his starched collar like an aged tortoise, survey the bustling shipyard below his office window, and look for a sign, being the good Presbyterian that he is. So here we wait three quarters of a world away for a word from a man waiting for a sign."

I could see Mr. R. was amused by my little impersonation, and that it had served to lift some of the cloud from his mood. I placed my hand on his shoulder. "You're a fine young officer, Radhakrishnan," I reassured him. "I've recommended you for that new marine-engineering school in Hong Kong. Let's see where that gets us."

"Thank you, sir." Embarrassed, he returned his gaze to our friend *Aurensis.* Then he looked around. "The Chinaman, Captain. He's gone."

"Why, so he has."

"An outlandish fellow, sir. Did you see—"

"Yes, I saw. As curious as his cargo."

"Those two coffins in the boat, sir . . . The man was Asian, perhaps Chinese, but the woman—"

"What about her?"

"The woman looked European. Not Chinese. Definitely European. With a flame dancing over her head. Like a queen."

"Yes, European, now that you mention it. With a fiery crown."

After my first officer took his leave, I returned to the black-lacquered box. I had placed it on my desk next to my well-worn copy of Alfred Russel Wallace's *The Malay Archipelago*. I turned it around. It was perfectly joined on every side, and I soon realized it was a type of Chinese puzzle box. I held it up, shook it. It was light, but something rattled softly inside.

I turned on my desk lamp and, putting on my reading glasses, once more examined the Chinaman's card. I traced the faint impression of each letter with my finger. *It is finished.*

"It is finished," I whispered, picking up the box. As if awaiting that very phrase, the lid slid open. I smiled when I realized that my thumbs and forefingers were holding the box by its bottom corners. The placement must have released the hidden spring.

Inside, nestled in rice-stalk packing, was a porcelain bottle stopped with a cork, the rim sealed with red wax. I lifted it out of its nest. The vessel had been painted a deep blue and fired until the glaze crackled.

I held the bottle to the light. A river meandered around it. Lush ferns and palms lined its banks. Stands of bamboo and banyan canopies marked the beginning of the rain forest. Inquisitive eyes seemed to follow the progress of a riverboat that was drifting down the stream, half hidden among the leaves. On closer inspection, I saw that I had mistaken the wings of butterflies. Not miniature eyes but tiny butterflies flitted about the forest.

There was liquid in the bottle. I cut through the wax and pulled the stopper. Taking a cautious sniff, I plucked a sherry glass from the sideboard. The liquid poured the color of pale honey. Holding it up to the light, I brought the glass beneath my nose. The bouquet was unmistakably that of palm wine, mingled with the aroma of herbs—cardamom, saffron, perhaps—familiar but from long ago. Where? I drank.

The wine rose immediately to my head and then went outward, suffusing my limbs with delicious warmth. I closed my eyes, remembering where I had last tasted this liquor, remembering back across the years, remembering how steady the hand had been that held out the cup to me, and how desperate the circumstances. With a stab, her face rose before me: beautiful, tantalizing, terrible to behold.

I spoke her name. Even after all these years, speaking that name was like casting a spell that might bring some unknowable terror knocking on the door. Or some unknowable peace.

A moment later I had flung open the cabin door and was bounding along the starboard side of the ship. "Have you seen him, Mr. Hastings?" I called as I plunged past the quarterdeck, nearly bowling over the astonished bosun.

"Who, sir?"

Hands sliding down the rail, I raced to the bow. Leaning out on a stay, I scoured the harbor. Dozens of sampans, lighters, and high-sterned junks plied the choppy water, anxious attendants to the weathered merchant steamers. The coal trails of the steamers were like ghostly fingers against the pale blue sky.

Along the length of the shipyard piers, ships that once proudly bore canvas and drove before the wind—brigs and sloops and three-masted schooners—were tied together like so many irrelevant aristocrats awaiting the guillotine. In the three great dry docks, the ritual of revolution had commenced. Industrious teams cut down spars and lowered masts, hulls and keels were stripped of copper sheathing, while other crews scavenged ruthlessly for every bit of brass that glittered on the decks.

Of the jolly boat with the yellow canopy there was no trace. But I knew this ferryman of the dead was no apparition, though it had been many years since I had set eyes on the man known as Kung.

Returning to my cabin, I pulled an old leather-covered sea chest from the locker beneath my bunk and unlocked the lid. A whiff of camphor, must, and the abiding memories of old notebooks. I sat on the deck and went through the volumes, their pages stiff with age. Along the spine of each volume I had written the name of the ship and the year, beginning with my first voyage out of

U.S. coastal waters—*1866: The* Asia. I had not opened these pages for years. Then the book I sought was in my hand.

1875: The Lorelei.

I brought down the porcelain bottle and filled another glass. I opened the page, surprised at how lithe and leaping my penmanship was in those days. I lifted the glass to my lips once more and drank the sweet and bitter liquid down.

The bite of the liquor took my breath away.

"Satu palm wine," said Wallace with a toast. "It's the drink of disappointment. Builds courage, stamina, cauterizes the innards as it fortifies the spirit." He downed his jigger with gusto. "I admit I may have fermented it a tad too much," he said, making note of the sudden color in my face and the sweat on my brow. He pulled out two collecting jars from the bag. "We didn't nab *Parnassius fallax*. Still, we've had a fair catch this morning, my young friend. We've come away with some very nice little artistes." Two butterflies flicked their wings feebly as if in reply. *"Papilio memnon,"* he added, sticking the tip of his long nose against the glass. "And her muse, *Papilio coon.*" Using the handle of his net like a staff, he rose from his seat on the bole of a coconut palm and looked around with a lordly air.

The domain of Alfred Russel Wallace, renowned botanist and author of *The Malay Archipelago,* was a patch of jungle he had claimed as a preserve, for it teemed with the lepidoptera he most fancied. The fact that it also teemed with wild boar did not deter him. He considered them to be practically domesticated now that they had learned to supplement their natural diet on the garbage of Kuching.

At fifty-two, Wallace was an energetic man whose light blue

eyes reflected an uncurbed appetite for turning over rocks and leaves and discovering exotic worlds. A veteran of the East Indies, he had explored the Amazon basin in his youth, adventures he described vividly in his writings. He was not too fastidious about his person—he rarely remembered to trim his great mane of whitening hair and bushy beard—but he was an affable companion and mentor whose discerning observations, usually delivered at great length, were leavened with wry humor. Despite his exuberance, a shadow lingered, as of a great personal loss, that gave him a wistful air.

"Now, *Papilio coon,* Vanders," said the botanist, "is a prize. And I'm sure you will tell me why."

"She is the model for the mimicry of memnon in the other bottle you hold," I replied, aware that this was a quiz. "Coon is a beauty but distasteful to predatory birds. Memnon has adapted her cousin's brilliant streak of orange and even the shape of her tail to fool the same predators."

"There you are," he said with a wag of his voluble beard. "Could you ask better proof of *my* natural selection?" Provided he could still claim the possessive pronoun, Wallace didn't in the least mind that his friendly rival Charles Darwin had adopted his term for the mechanism of evolution. "In questions of biological adaptation, follow the food chain, Vanders. Who is eating what? Who is dining on whom? Now where did Peng get to?"

It seemed a natural association that his attention should swing to the cook, who often accompanied Wallace on his treks into the jungle. The problem was that Peng was terrified of the jungle and would bolt at the slightest provocation, real or imagined.

"I once tried using a Dayak as an assistant," Wallace had explained to me on our first collecting excursion some weeks ago. "They can find anything. But here's the rub. Dayaks find certain butterflies to be tasty treats and will pop the creatures in their mouth before you can say Jack Robinson. That's how I lost *Asty-*

anax perfidia. My Dayak got to him before I did. I'd been searching for a specimen for almost ten years. I wept, Vanders, I wept."

Peng's collecting net was spread out on a giant orchid plant. "Must have seen a python," Wallace mumbled. "Or a walking stick."

"It might have been that fellow over there." I pointed to a diminutive resident standing rather forlornly in the middle of the trail that led into the deeper recesses of the rain forest. The orang-utan's gold-and-copper-streaked hair fell from his arms like fringe from a buckskin jacket. He stood absolutely still, his round bearded chin jutting forward, leaning on his knuckles and observing us like a bemused scholar would some exotic fauna, which, to him, we were.

"The Old Man of the Forest," said Wallace, not without affection and even a trace of reverence. "I think he comes out sometimes to take notes. I sent one to Darwin some years ago. She was a spirited girl and bit him. This incident led to an exemplum of how human subjectivity can alter the writing of natural history. When Darwin's *Descent of Man* came out last year, he listed the chimpanzee and baboon as the closest relatives of *Homo sapiens,* pointedly giving short shrift to the orangutan, which probably has the best claim of all the anthropoids. Darwin's a good man to bear a grudge."

By the time Wallace had finished his discussion of the kindred behaviors that linked orangutans and humans, we had left the Borneo jungle the ape claims as its own and emerged along the muddy path of a fenced village. Many of the land Dayaks, particularly those who had been Christianized, had settled close to Kuching for the protection afforded by the White Rajah's guns. Their pagan brethren were more warlike, and keener to gather heads, now that they knew their traditional way of life was contested by a relentless enemy. The newcomers' houses, built on stilts over the river, had the look of ramshackle impermanence, and indeed their inhabitants were waiting to see which side would prevail. Smoke drifted up from the outdoor ovens. Only the children were out, it seemed, rolling around in the dirt as children will, chasing chickens and lording it over the pigs. As we settled in the two-man *prahu* we had beached at the edge of the village, I saw a European woman in a gray dress, with a white back-veiled topi, emerge from one of the huts on the shore. She waved, and I waved back.

"You wonder what brings them to the edge of the world," Wallace mused. "Women with Bibles."

Past the Dayak settlements, the canopy of the jungle opened up to a wide river vista. The thatched bungalows of the Europeans stood on the outskirts of the town, their verandas and windows open to catch what little breeze the location afforded, and that only during the monsoon. People meandered along the bamboo sidewalks, a recent innovation of Charles Brooke's chief of public works.

Kuching, the capital of Sarawak, occupied a crescent of the broad Sarawak River about a mile inland from the South China Sea. This little slice of northwestern Borneo had been ruled by Malay rajahs for centuries, before the English adventurer James Brooke arrived in 1839. Brooke's role in putting down an insurrection led the sultan of Brunei, whose rule extended over all of North Borneo, to an act of cunning generosity. He made Brooke rajah of Sarawak in the hope that he would lure the British to help the sultan thrash the pirates and oust his erstwhile enemies, the Dutch. The Indonesian trade was rich in gold, coffee, tea, spices, and diamonds, and the sultan was bedeviled by thieves and cutthroats, terms he applied with equal vitriol to buccaneers and Dutch East Indian officials. Some journalist had dubbed Sir James the "White Rajah," and it had stuck. James Brooke ruled Sarawak—perhaps he would have preferred the word "guided"—with paternal loftiness until his death in 1868. Except for outlaws and the heads of the Chinese tongs, whose powers he had tried to curb, his passing was mourned by all.

By 1875, the year I first visited Kuching, the rajah of Sarawak had become hereditary; Charles Johnson Brooke, James's nephew, was the second to bear the title. So successful had the Brooke line become that the little state of Sarawak had nearly quadrupled in size, and the once powerful sultan of Brunei had become little more than a resentful titleholder to lands that were administered by the English upstarts.

Kuching reflected this gain in renown. It was a bustling port, able to accommodate some forty merchant ships at a time. Most of them were sailing ships, their proud masts topping the blue sky, but here and there a steamer made its presence known with a belch of soot. As Wallace and I paddled into its wide expanse; the harbor was teeming with watercraft, cargo barges, and the graceful Malay outriggers known as *prahus*. Among the tall ships was the merchant sloop the *Siren,* to which I was attached as first mate, under the command of Captain Warner Kepple. The *Siren* had unloaded a cargo of foodstuffs and medicines from Singapore and was about to take on a load of antimony and pepper for the return trip when Captain Kepple was struck down with malarial fever. We had been stuck in stifling Kuching for three weeks, and not much outside my lepidoptera excursions with Wallace to relieve the tedium.

It didn't look like we would be shipping out anytime soon. The captain was in and out of the fever, and when he was delirious, his raving could be heard all over the ship. In his right mind, Kepple was a taciturn Dutchman, neither kindly nor cruel to his odd job crew, a mix of Malay, Filipino, and Lascar, with here and there the odd Chinese and Japanner, and even three Americans— one black, recently emancipated and new to the sea; and one Scots-Irish, a former whaler who knew his scrimshaw. I was Yankee number three, and all in all we were typical of an East Indies crew, which is to say, a mélange and a mystery.

"He turns forty-one this year." Wallace pointed to the Brooke bungalow, a sprawling native-style manse that took up most of a small island at the head of the Kuching anchorage. Brightly colored streamers drifted from flagpoles in a desultory breeze. The stairway from the guard tower at the water's edge to the bordered veranda was lined with bamboo torches chained with yellow ribbon, the color of royalty in the Malay states. Indian servants were moving tables onto the lawn and shaking out the linen.

"The doors are thrown open on the rajah's birthday," Wallace said, "from high to low. Quite a soiree. Which reminds me," he added. "I had breakfast with him yesterday or the day before. He expressed a keen interest in you and your background."

"Oh?"

"I pumped you up, naturally. Perhaps did you too much credit. He wanted to be sure that you attended the party tonight. He expressly wishes to meet you." Wallace cleared his throat. "That means he wants something. Be forewarned—the rajah usually gets what he wants."

⤚❧

A sprightly Chopin polonaise could just be heard lilting above the rumbling of Chinese drums and the resonant echo of Malay gongs. The melody may have seemed incongruous, drifting across the water in a remote harbor of the Malay Archipelago, but then every element of the rajah's birthday party made its contribution to marvel. An elegant catamaran with a gold-trimmed silk canopy, torches at the gunwales, made its round of the merchant ships, picking up European passengers and transporting them to Brooke's island dock. Arrayed before the landing were some fifty war canoes of the Sea Dayaks, former pirates who had become pirate hunters and the guardians of the Sarawak River estuary. Wearing feathered headdresses adorned with tiny cowries, they swayed back and forth chanting birthday salutes to their warlord and benefactor.

"The English rajahs of Sarawak have made it policy to win over their adversaries," Wallace shouted over the din, a bit too loudly since he was standing right next to me in the boat. "They've been damned good at it."

Once onshore, we followed the human stream up the path of crushed coral that led to Brooke House: Europeans in evening clothes and uniforms, Malay *datus* in head-hugging turbans, embroidered tunics, and tapered breeches. Arranged on the lawn before Brooke House were various entertainments. In one corner an Indonesian puppet theater enacted a scene from the *Mahabharata* to a bug-eyed medley of children—Ibans, Dayaks, Chinese, Malays, and Europeans. Another area had been cordoned off for a gamelan band and Balinese dancers, brought over expressly for the occasion. Behind the mansion, the smoke of roasting steer and goat rose in the sultry air. Two impeccably dressed Sikhs in red turbans and sashes ushered us inside. The reception hall was paneled in carved teak and lined with tribal war shields draped with the colors of Sarawak, a red-and-black cross surmounted by a crown on a field of yellow.

Despite tall ceilings and the broad palm-leaf fans swaying overhead, the air was close and mixed with scents of different cultures: the French perfumes of the European ladies; the clove, cinnamon, and musk scent favored by the Malays; and the more delicate orchid fragrances worn by the Chinese women. One of the Europeans, a handsome brunette with flowers woven into her hair, was at the piano finishing her Chopin to a patter of applause, mostly that of admiring men, including an Iban chief so elaborately tattooed that he appeared a walking tapestry. In a corner halfway across the room a knot of European women in blooming taffetas and crinolines surrounded a pale, ferocious blonde in a black evening dress. They did not applaud the pianist but rather waved their lacquered fans furiously as if banishing a bad odor.

"That chief with the boar tusks in his ears is Iban Buna," Wallace confided at my side. "He thinks that Chopin captured his soul in a previous life. He prevails on Miss Burdett-Couts to play the composer whenever he visits. He even tried to kidnap her once, and the piano, but Charles talked him out of it." He inclined his head to the women with the fans. "That group over there, standing as stalwartly as King Harold's doomed thanes at Hastings, are the companions of Lady Brooke, rani of Sarawak. See how they so jealousy guard her. None of them like Miss Burdett-Couts, the niece of the first rajah's benefactor. The Brookes owe the Burdett-Couts a great deal, and that is why Charles invited Irene to visit and see firsthand the thriving country her aunt once nursed through lean times. The rani likes her not at all. Then again, Charles likes the rani not at all and is shipping her back to England at the end of the month."

"Leaving Miss Burdett-Couts behind?"

"That's it. She and Charles get along famously. In fact, she's nearly minister-without-portfolio around here. And that's in spite of the fact that the rajah has a very dim opinion of white women in the tropics, and particularly in Sarawak. He believes they are too dangerous to have around. That's easy to understand when you know that it's Charles's policy to bring over single young men to make up his field residents and bureaucrats. Single young men with a world of ambition and no connections are quick to hire and easy to mold. They will also work for a pittance."

"And they can also fall into an abysm of loneliness," said the pianist, who had apparently caught part of Wallace's explanation. "Unless they are kept busy. Which Charles keeps 'em."

"Idle fingers do the devil's work, ma'am." Wallace winked at her, putting his lips to the tips of the lady's glove. As he bowed into the background, Miss Burdett-Couts took me by the arm and guided me across the floor in the direction of a colorful throng of people gathered about a short, stocky man in a plain brown suit. Engaged in animated conversation, he wore a royal yellow ribbon draped across his chest. So, I thought to myself, this must be Charles Brooke himself.

With this continental company off our bow, Miss Burdett-Couts and I sailed past the frosty island where Lady Brooke and her entourage cast forth frigid stares. "I don't mind them," my companion whispered in my ear. "That fellow over there, however, the Chinese rotundity with the braid and the black skullcap: him I mind."

"Trouble, I gather."

"That's Heng Kash, kingpin of the Kuching wharves, lord of the stevedores, and head of the Chinese tongs. His men burned Kuching to the ground thirteen years ago and nearly managed to kill Sir James Brooke. Charles wasn't in town for that event. He was serving as an agent up the headwaters of the Sedang, trying to stop a renegade Iban named Ranalang from collecting heads."

"It seems you're well informed on matters in Sarawak."

"Let's attribute that to family tradition. And an abiding interest in the remarkable Brookes. As for Charles—you may find him a bit coarse, although I prefer 'rough and ready.' He has spent half his life in the Sarawak bush, where Sir James sent him to test his mettle. He speaks Malay and thirty of the native dialects, not to mention French, Dutch, and Portuguese. The gift of tongues, among other qualities, makes him eminently suited for the job."

The man in the brown suit and the regal yellow sash looked up from his circle of Malay aristocrats and exchanged a swift glance with Miss Burdett-Couts. At the same moment a brass band in the adjoining room announced the evening's formal entertainment with a crash of cymbals and the blare of a British cavalry march. "Unfortunately," she said, moving me down the hall, "he has no sense of music except that which sets marching feet in motion."

The martial tune was summarily muffled as she closed the tall mahogany door on what appeared to be a combined study and office. Bookshelves lined the long room, crammed with reports and accounting ledgers and leather-bound books. Loose paper and portfolios spilled across a great desk adorned with the Sarawak coats of arms in gold filigree. The desk also held a microscope and a curious brass model of a steamship engine. From its perch in a corner, a sunbird with a brilliant orange breast regarded me with a cocked and suspicious eye. Opposite the presumptuous bird, a small long-nosed monkey made subdued growls as it restlessly circled its gilded cage. Despite the clutter and the menagerie, French doors opening onto a spacious veranda made the paneled office bright and airy.

My companion had already poured a whiskey from a decanter on the sideboard and held it out to me. Perhaps my hand shook slightly as I took the glass; it had been a long time since I had been so close to a beautiful woman with scented flowers in her hair.

"Make that two, Irene."

Charles Brooke stepped from a corner of the room as if he had been standing there all the time. I started at his sudden appearance.

"My uncle had a number of hidden doors built into the design," said Brooke, amused by my wonder. "One of these clever little entrances saved his life during an assassination attempt." He took his drink and nodded in the direction of the busy harbor. "You should have seen this place forty years ago, when Sir James first arrived—a few huts, a few canoes, and more crocodiles than people."

The thing that struck me most immediately about Charles Brooke was his extraordinary alertness, the tensile energy of a shrewd observer; a man to whom action was obviously second nature. There was nothing particularly distinctive in his appearance, certainly not in the face, the lower part of which was draped with a walrus mustache, and topped by a mop of unruly brown hair, slightly graying at the temples, that had been partially subdued by a dose of macassar oil. His eyes, when he turned them on you, sized you up in a glance. You could almost hear the hum of his calculations.

"That's your ship down there?" he asked, pointing at the sloop whose riding lights had just winked on. The sky, fiercely crimson but a moment ago, made way for the night like a genie slithering back to the magic lamp. "The *Siren,* out of Singapore but under Dutch registry. Captain Kepple is doing better, I take it?"

"He was resting easy when I left this evening, Your Highness. I think it's fair to say your physician, Dr. Deeds, has saved his life."

"You've been his first mate, let's see now, for six months." He downed the whiskey in one movement and set the glass on his desk. "By the way, highness me no Highnesses, nor Your Excellencies. My name is sufficient."

"As you wish, Mr. Brooke. Six months on the *Siren*. Prior to that, a year on the clipper *Standard*."

"And prior to that, a year on a French cutter out of Papeete, *L'Aiglette,* as a gunnery officer," Miss Burdett-Couts added, "but there the trail begins to thin out. Except to mention that you left America in 1866, the year following your Civil War."

"You know a good deal, it seems."

"Our mutual friend Alfred Wallace has been filling us in on your exploits," Brooke said.

"Although it's curious," the lady reflected, "that a young first lieutenant with a promising future in the United States Navy would have abandoned his career for—"

"For adventure, no doubt," the rajah interrupted.

"Yes, for adventure," I replied cautiously.

"Not that we are trying to pry into your motives," the lady added hastily.

"Many the young man who comes out to the Orient to seek his way in the world." Mr. Brooke said this with a gleam in his eye that seemed to say we were birds of a feather.

"Few can be trusted to succeed," Miss Burdett-Couts qualified. "Man or woman."

"You'll forgive me," I said, exceedingly nonplussed, "I fail to see where—"

"Where all of this is going." The rajah placed a hand on my shoulder. "To sound out a man is in my manner and my interest."

"The rajah has no small army of enemies, Mr. Vanders."

"Your past is of no significance, except to show that you are a fellow of some mettle."

At this point, my confusion was nearly complete, at odds with my suspicion, the show of a rajah's trust, and a lady's sweetly disarming smile.

"Yes, naturally, you're quite at sea." Miss Burdett-Couts picked up a paper from the desk, and handed it to Brooke, who passed it on to me.

"It's a letter from the Dutch governor in Batavia." The rajah bid me walk over to an immense wall map of the Malay Archipelago. "The island of Java, six hundred miles to the south of us, is, as you know, the last stronghold of Dutch power in Indonesia. Sarawak, since allied with England, has been erstwhile enemies of the Dutch and always competitors for trade in the region. But we cooperate, too, especially in matters of area security."

"This letter," I said, scanning the contents, "refers to a Christian mission on Sumatra."

"The sixth largest island in the world," said Brooke, running his finger around a spear-shaped landmass on the map. "Nominally under Dutch control, but really a patchwork of warring tribes, feudatory states, pirates."

"An uneasy population of Hindus, Muslims, Christians, headhunters, and animists," added the lady. "And ghostly ruins in the jungle that go back thousands of years."

"And containing the richest minerals, timber, and gold resources in the region," said Brooke. "It's uncertain that any one person or group or nation could ever control the place—the Dutch gave up trying a hundred years ago—but if anyone did, he would control the archipelago and the Far East trade that goes with it. Naturally, this would not be in the interest of Sarawak and her allies."

"And the Christian mission?"

"Light of the World, it's called. In Batak territory. The tribe is allied to the Dutch, also nominally." Brooke pointed to an area on the northern quarter of the island. "It can best be reached by water, up the Asahan River."

"What has this to do with me?"

"Two months ago, a party of tribesmen came out of the jungle bearing a troubling message from the reverend Noel Ames, the head of the mission. They had traveled overland to the Dutch administrative center at Palembang for weeks—harried and pursued, they claimed, by bloodthirsty spirits."

"You did say 'spirits.' "

"Baptism may be a cure for original sin, but it does not cure superstition."

"What did the missionary have to say in his letter?"

"I have not seen it," said Brooke. "It was addressed to the head of the Unity Church Mission in Palembang, Mrs. Bridgett Hannover. She oversees church operations in the Dutch East Indies, including Light of the World. The contents of the letter were serious enough that Mrs. Hannover exhorted the Dutch governor to take action. She also went to the British honorary consul at Palembang to see that he did."

"*That* gentleman," Miss Burdett-Couts said, lighting an oil lamp on the desk, "spoke to a businessman acting as the American chargé d'affaires in Sumatra. You see," she added with a throaty chuckle, "how little matters escalate."

"At length the Dutch governor-general at Batavia contacted us. Discreetly."

"Then the mission must be in considerable danger," I conjectured.

Miss Burdett-Couts opened the door to the veranda to catch some air. "We do know that the chief of the Bataks in northern Sumatra, Radjah Dulah, has had his hands full trying to put down a tribal incursion." She took my glass and walked back to the sideboard. "There are two other missionaries. One is Ames's wife, Susannah. The other is an American, Deborah Rand."

"You need someone who knows the territory," I said flatly, now that the gist had become clear.

"No one knows that territory," said Brooke. "At least no one who can captain a riverboat."

"You have a boat to do the job?"

"A seventy-foot stern-wheeler named *Lorelei*. She's waiting for you on Banka, an island off the Sumatra coast. You've seen service with steam-powered vessels?"

"I served aboard a side-wheeler during our Civil War. Briefly."

"I do have an interest in propulsion mechanisms." He patted the little brass engine on his desk. "In fact, it is my intention to add a steam-powered vessel or two to my navy. Naturally, an experienced officer would be an asset."

"The rajah is offering you a commission," said Miss Burdett-Couts encouragingly. "In the Sarawak navy."

I liked the way she pronounced "commission," as if it were flanked by standards flying gallantly in the wind and courageous men ready for duty.

"I don't really have a navy," Charles Brooke admitted. "But I am about to create one. I would like to call it the Royal Sarawak Navy, but Miss Burdett-Couts advises this might displease the sultan of Borneo, whose loyal vassal I remain."

"I have suggested that we substitute the word 'Regal.'" She smiled graciously as if she had chosen the word for me rather than for the rajah.

"And the *Lorelei* shall be my navy's first steam-powered vessel," the rajah confirmed more loudly than was necessary.

"When you bring her back safely from your mission." Miss Burdett-Couts said confidently, as if the mission were nearly done.

"Yes, do bring her back," said the rajah. "In one piece."

"How do our Dutch friends figure into all this?"

"The Dutch are too preoccupied with fortifying Palembang against another revolt in the south. Palembang is their last outpost of any size on Sumatra. If they lose that— Besides," he said, returning to the veranda, "the fate of British missionaries is the least of their concerns. But they will provide the boat and a squad of native soldiers to travel upriver with you."

"We don't know what has happened at Light of the World," said Brooke's beautiful minister-without-portfolio. "But we need someone to find out."

"And get the missionaries out, if there are any left to be got out," Brooke cautioned. "At least the effort must be made. I've struck a small bargain with the Dutch . . ."

Then, on the rajah's private veranda overlooking the Kuching harbor, and while congratulatory fireworks dazzled and exploded in the muggy air, Brooke told me about Rowan Fahey, Irish outlaw, pirate, opium smuggler, and gunrunner. The Dutch governor at Batavia wanted him badly. It just so happened that Mr. Fahey was biding his time at this very moment in the Kuching jail.

⤝⤞

"The rajah said that against me, did he?" asked Rowan Fahey with as much incredulity as the rhetorical nature of his question would allow. "Why, it's a wonder a man could commit that many crimes in a lifetime and never be apprehended by the finest constabularies in the seething Orient. And here is Rowan Fahey," he added with a touch of grim irony. "Hoosegowed in godforsaken Kuching for merely disturbing the peace."

The Kuching jail, a line of cells that ran along the rear wall of the constabulary, was as comfortable an accommodation, if one had to serve time, as one was to meet in the Orient. The cells were clean and provided with a stool, table, and lamp. Black-browed Rowan Fahey looked almost comfortable as he lolled on a rice-straw pallet and picked his teeth with a sliver of bamboo.

"The way I hear it, Mr. Fahey, your escapade had all of Chinatown in an uproar. When it was over, Canal Street was in a shambles, and a warehouse had been set ablaze."

"That was none of my doing!" Fahey swung off his cot to defend himself. He was somewhat over medium height and built, from his square shoulders down, for the prize ring. "It was the shipmates of that bosun from Liverpool what went on a rampage. I merely decked the fellow. For patriotic reasons," he added with satisfaction. Despite the menace in his movement, Fahey had the sweetly presuming countenance of a pockmarked choirboy, albeit one prone to gin and debauchery.

"And then took on half the crew of her majesty's cutter *Renown*."

"They cling together like bilge rats, do her majesty's sailors," Fahey said contemptuously. "Especially when they batten down on an Irishman. Besides, I had no quarrel with them, either collectively or individually. It was their captain, a certain Mr. Averil T. Claridge, I had words for."

"What harm did the captain do you?"

"Harm, sir?" Fahey had gone to the bars of his cell and was squeezing them as if they might be an adversary's neck. "Haven't the Claridges held sway in County Tyrone for the past three hundred years, ever since damned Billy Cromwell sent the pestilential and papist-hating hounds to bedevil my people? Wasn't it just forty years ago, at the worst of the great famine, that a Claridge burned my grandfather's cot above his head and ran the family off lands they had farmed since the druids?"

"This Captain Claridge was responsible?"

"A Claridge is a Claridge. The man who bears the name bears the brand of the name." He intoned this as if it were a dark biblical prophecy.

"Perhaps if you had been less in the mood for revenge, the rajah's custom agents never would have found the French carbines hidden under the deck planks of your sloop."

"Yes, well, the guns," said Fahey, looking up at me from under his brows. "There is the matter of the guns." His face went solemn as a headstone. "They framed me, wouldn't you guess it? Someone set me up in Brunei, where it's all a snake pit of Malay intrigue. I had dropped anchor to take an innocent load of dried fish and sea cucumbers to Keelung. I would have been there by now, had not a squall sprung up and changed my plans. But some things are appointed, strive against them as we will."

"According to your first mate, it wasn't a squall but the intent to drop off your contraband on the west coast of Sumatra that brought you this way. And you hove to in Kuching because you sprang a leak."

"You were wiser to put your faith in the devil than in the words of that Po Ying. There's a slopehead who's in the devil's employ. The man's victims litter the bottom of the archipelago." Fahey took on a look of earnest resolution. "Besides, it's my word against his. That still counts for something, doesn't it? I have confidence in you, sir."

"How is that?"

"Come now, sir." The smile, too, was broad and wide as a choirboy's, but not without an undercurrent of cunning. "It's clear to see from the cut of your canvas and the way of your speech that you're a ship-going American barrister come to plead my case. Besides, I feel that I know you already. Indeed, I have met you before. I have a knack for faces."

"We've never met, Mr. Fahey," I said cautiously. "I would have remembered."

Fahey snapped his fingers as if to summon his memory. "Mayhap it was in Boston. Or Philadelphia. Or San Francisco. I've been to those places. Half of America is filled with lawyers, and they are accounted to be the cunningest lot of devils who ever took over a docket. With their mother's milk, they learn the lies of Cicero. If anybody, you'll get me off this rap. It's appointed." He rolled his eyes heavenward.

"I've been appointed, Mr. Fahey. You've got that right. I've been appointed by the rajah to transport you in irons to Kota Baru on the island of Banka. But I just wanted to get a look at you myself before I signed on."

"Kota Baru is a Netherlandish stink hole!"

"That's where I hand you over to a Dutch escort from Batavia, Mr. Fahey. And get a river steamer in return."

"You've sold me down the river for a boat! That's *slavery,* sir." He shook his head in deep disappointment. "And here your country fought a bloody war to end that hateful practice."

"I know. I fought to set men free."

"There, a Union man. We're natural allies! You can see what I'm up against here, sir, and all on trumped-up charges."

"*That* you can sort out in a Dutch court."

"Dutch justice? And what is your name who means to hand me over to Dutch justice?"

"Ulysses Drake Vanders, former first mate of the *Siren* and now in the rajah's employ."

The Irishman's jaw dropped a yard. "Another Dutchman! Well, Ulysses Drake Vanders, take a good look at the man you've condemned to death. Dutch justice means to swing 'em high and then hold the trial."

"The Dutch are a tidy people," I observed.

>≈

I had just stowed my gear aboard the British cutter *Renown* when a launch pulled alongside bearing Alfred Russel Wallace and Irene Burdett-Couts. Captain Claridge, Rowan Fahey's nemesis, had agreed to make the run to Kota Baru for Rajah Brooke, an itinerary that fit into his primary mission anyway, namely to show the British flag and strike fear into the hearts of pirates. The Irish felon had been brought aboard a few hours earlier and deposited in the brig, where a Scots marine stood guard over him, as much to dissuade the crew from having another go at him as to prevent his escape.

Claridge made his cabin available to us for a brief farewell. It was a snug and tidy berth with a Persian carpet on the floor, a Queen Anne's desk beneath the stern windows, and beside it, a brass telescope on a tripod. This instrument looked out over the harbor, busy as ever despite the fearsome heat. There being little in the way of wind, two merchantmen were being towed around the bend of the river by a line of flat-bottomed pole boats. The *Renown* was next in the queue.

"Mr. Brooke wanted you to have these," said Wallace, placing a canvas satchel on a chair. "Books."

"And here are your letters to the Dutch officials," said the rajah's beautiful plenipotentiary with a smile of approval that raised me practically to the rank of admiral. "I can't tell you how deeply Mr. Brooke appreciates your acceptance of this command. He has every confidence in you. Everything has been arranged with *Siren*'s master. Captain Kepple is, as you know, pulling out of the worst of the fever and should be on his feet in a week or so. The rajah is making allowances for six weeks, on the outside, for you to complete your mission on the Asahan River. It's now the second of October. The northern Sumatra monsoon begins in earnest in November, and you must get off the river before it floods. When you steam back into Kuching with the *Lorelei,* there will be an opportunity to discuss your future with the Regal Sarawak Navy— and other things." She lowered her long dark lashes when she spoke the last three words. I must confess my heart rose a beat or two.

"I think that ties up all the loose ends," I managed to say. We all stood for a moment in awkward silence.

"About Sumatra," said Alfred, clearing his throat.

"I appreciate the time you've taken with me, Alfred. I feel like I've been through a course on Sumatra geography and ethnology. I'll be bringing along your book."

"It was a long time since I last was there—1857. I got as far as the Kampar River, but I never went up the Asahan. What that part of the island holds will be for you to discover. Most of the northern interior is uncharted. I don't know anything about the missionary operation at Light of the World. Apparently, it got started about three years ago at the invitation of Radjah Dulah's late wife, who wished to encourage the Christian religion."

A youthful midshipman interrupted our farewell with the word that we were about to weigh anchor. On the quarterdeck, Irene wished me Godspeed, gave my hand a peremptory shake, and was down the ladder to the launch before I could thank her. Alfred drew me aside before he followed her. "There were certain things," he said guardedly, "certain aspects of my sojourn in Sumatra, that are difficult to explain. As a man of science, I should have shrugged off these events long ago. But since they happened to me, and since I do not doubt my own experience, they have left indelible impressions. The impressions went into field notes I made during my visit to Sumatra. I could never bring myself to include them in my book." He tapped the canvas bag. "The notes are in here. Make of them what you will." He looked at me, a face lined with the experience of thirty years of tramping about the world in all kinds of weather, sustained by boundless curiosity. "I hope you won't think the less of me for including them."

"I have always and will always treasure your friendship," I said, taking his hand warmly. "If there is something I could bring back for you . . ."

The lines of experience lifted. "A specimen? But no—there is little likelihood—"

"Tell me, Alfred."

"Only on Sumatra will you find *Papilio aurensis,* the Golden Sura. She is described in my field notes. Rare, passing rare . . ." His gaze drifted off across the river, and for a moment he was lost in reverie. "But it was not meant for me to bring her back," he said regretfully.

"I'll find your Golden Sura, Alfred, count on it."

The launch swung around in the muddy water of the Kuching harbor, its engine humming, the only boat in the rajah's small fleet powered by steam. Wallace waved his floppy field hat, and Irene

Burdett-Couts placed her fingers to her lips and held them over her heart. Or so it seemed.

Could she have actually blown me a kiss? I asked myself as I whistled my way back to the captain's cabin to claim my gear. The first thing I did was open the oilskin portfolio she had provided me. I ran through the official papers, made out in duplicate and duly signed in Charles Brooke's impatient hand. There was something pressed between the pages. It fell into my hand. It was a dried blossom of English clover, four lucky leaves on its still-greenish stem.

Some moments later I had joined Captain Claridge, at his invitation, on the poop deck. The thatch-and-red-tile roofs of the Kuching wharves were receding in the distance.

I straddled the deck of the cutter and drew in lungfuls of the rich morning air as if it were tonic. And it was, for the name on the documents identified the bearer as "Captain Ulysses Drake Vanders." I was headed for my first command.

3

For three days the *Renown* skirted the coastline of northern Borneo as far as the Sambas River, two hundred miles east of Kuching, before she turned and struck for the deeper waters of the archipelago and the windward passage to Banka Island. Throughout the patrol, the crew kept an eagle eye for pirates, since that was part of Captain Claridge's mission, but the buccaneers didn't show their colors, and indeed pirates had been but a minor trouble since Sir James Brooke subdued them twenty years before. The *Renown* was made for this kind of work, a sleek cutter of three hundred tons, rigged for speed. With a shallow draft, a cutter can dart in and out of the estuaries where the Chinese bandits and seagoing Dayaks make their lairs. It's a fugitive coastline, in both senses, a shifting geography of mangrove swamps and mudflats and beaches bright as gold dust constantly being refined and re-defined by storm and tide. Outside of the outlaws, there are a few native fishing villages tucked in along the coast, but they have all the permanence of gypsy caravans. Their inhabitants harvest the wilder creatures of the archipelago, for the shores and seas of this endless Eden constitute one of the great hatcheries of the planet. And one of its great slaughterhouses.

It happens without warning. The sky is suddenly filled with raucous gulls and terns and white-tipped gannets driven to a frenzy by what they see below. Flying fish leap into the air in dazzling terror. Beneath our keel, the water has been stained blood pink by a great bloom of shrimp. In this vast drift of tiny crustaceans, shoals of red mackerel and Indies shad skim the surface, their scales glinting in the sunlight as they dive and roll, driven to an ecstasy of feeding. Hawksbills and majestic green turtles snap among them, their shells shimmering beneath the water like plates of imperial jade. Behind them glide in the great predators, gangs of makos and tiger sharks, their fearsome dorsals cutting through the bloom, sweeping down upon the others like Mongol hordes, tearing and thrashing left and right, and churning the water into a rusty crimson foam. The birds descend at last, like starving churls on the pickings of the fat lords' feast. They rise up one by one, torn morsels dangling from their beaks, until the surface is still again, the frenzy bled out, the marauders vanished.

The lesson of this natural spectacle was not to be lost as the *Renown* turned in to the rolling chasms of the open sea and the stiff buffets of the windward passage, for I was not the solitary witness. It was Alfred Wallace who had awakened me to the relatedness of all things in the natural world, dependencies and associations based more often than not on clever disguises, sly ruses, and coy subterfuges, and all with one aim: the propagation and survival of species. However, it was left to Captain Claridge to cast the natural scheme into a broader cosmic net, his Yorkshire vowels rising and falling with the waves, his spoon poised over a bowl brimming with seafood chowder. His was a fierce gaze framed by a fiercer mane of white hair. That gaze burrowed into each of us as he searched restlessly about the table.

"And that is where the Creator has tipped his own hand. He is in love with his palette but not with the things he has created," he intoned. "For what is the conclusion of this grand self-amusement but beautiful mouths to feed on each other? And evolution? Mr. Darwin has brought us to the brink but will not look over the precipice. Mark you, boys! Even if adaptation is the design, the Genius has set the table for Mr. Reaper. And Mr. Reaper is not particular about what he eats."

If the captain's aim was to make us weep like walruses for the plump oysters and crimson prawns on our plates, he did not succeed. The *Renown*'s officers ate with the hearty relish of English sailors while their commanding officer brooded like Ezekiel at a Babylonian feast. He had the pockmarked pallor of the austerities, like one who had walked out of a thunderbolt. Even his hair looked like a tangle of Saint Elmo's fire, and his sunken eyes peered out, not unkindly, like melancholy hermits from their caves. A paternal prophet who presided over the mess with a delicate forbearance as his "boys" quietly elbowed each other for bread, gravy, and tangerines like urchins at a charity picnic.

"You've never been to Sumatra, I take it, Captain Vanders?" Claridge pushed his bowl away and handed the orderly his napkin. He pronounced the word "captain" as if it were a penance.

"This will be my first time, sir."

"I spent some time on that island, attached to the diplomatic mission at Palembang, in the fifties. The Dutch have turned the place into a miniature Amsterdam, minus the canals, but beyond the patches of plantations, all is wildness. Do you know what wildness is, Captain Vanders?"

"We Americans attach a certain sentimental longing and fear to wild places, sir."

"I'm not speaking of wilderness as such, Mr. Vanders. Some twenty miles to the west of Palembang is an area known as Pasembah. I say 'area,' for it was a thriving city some hundreds of years ago. The Malays consider it a place accursed. My guide would take me only to the outskirts and then squatted down to chew some betel nut. I don't think he expected to see me again, at least not alive.

"It took the rest of the morning for me to hack my way through the thickets, until I was standing on smooth paving stones, the foundation of a royal road that, for its straightness, might have

been built by Roman engineers. The road led to a wide stairway—
twenty men could have easily ascended it abreast. The steps were
like rows of crooked teeth, broken by roots as thick as pythons.

"At the top of the stairway was a sight I'll never forget. I could
still make out, amid the ruin of collapsed walls, the orderly plan of
the streets, for the city had once covered the entire valley floor. At
the center below me, at what must have been the town square, rose
a bewildering array of obelisks and pillars, jutting upward thirty feet
or more and teetering at different angles. Each pillar bore strange
glyphs, carved from the bottom to the height of about five feet. Each
pillar was topped with a carved face. Each face was individual,
though they all shared one common overwhelming woe. Like the
blind, they stared out into nothingness; like sufferers, they grimaced
in their pain. I can hardly describe to you the sense of sorrow and
foreboding that overtook me in this wild, windswept place with its
desolate guardians. That's when I saw the thing, boys."

The captain paused in his story to allow the orderly to pour
him a cup of tea. There was silence at the table. The dishes had
been carried off; glasses of claret and mugs of tea had replaced
them. Ensign Fury, the youngest of the group, looked on the face
of his captain as if he might burst into tears. Claridge's sad eyes
fell on each of us in turn as if he were testing our mettle for
prophecy.

"The creature was standing at the base of one of the pillars,
one arm stretched out as if tracing the symbols carved into the
stone. About four feet tall. Covered with hair except where it
thinned out on the breast and thighs. I knew it wasn't an orang-
utan or other primate. The creature had fully formed lips, a higher
brow, a more sharply defined chin. I stood absolutely still, but he
had sensed I was looking down on him. He slowly turned, his arm
still raised until it was pointing at me. We looked at each other
for the briefest moment—and then he was gone."

"You actually saw one of the man-apes," Ensign Fury whispered in wonder.

"I have no doubt. The Kubu tribesmen on Sumatra call them *gugus*—'wraiths.' The Malays have another name for them, the *anak*, the children of the forest. They don't treat them as children, though. They hunt them down and kill them. They are too much like ourselves."

"He ran off," I said, encouraging Claridge to continue his story.

"I am not nimble on land," he continued, "especially when it comes to climbing over stone walls. I had to abandon the chase. When I returned to the trail, the guide looked at me as if he had seen a ghost. Perhaps I was still trembling, for nothing in my experience had ever affected me so. How strange it was to see him in that ancient place, for the *anak* are never reported beyond the Barisan Mountains in the far north. It was if he had come to try and make sense of . . ."

"His descendants?" I offered.

"The Malay legends say that the ancient city at Pasembah was the work of the Rajo Alam, the Lords of the Winds. Their civilization once extended from Lake Toba, in the north of Sumatra, the length of the island. The legends say the Rajo Alam designed their cities, but it was their slaves, the *anak*, who built them. So perhaps the fellow I saw was visiting the handiwork of his ancestors. What were his feelings, do you think, as he traced the unreadable symbols in the stone? If he could feel in that way, if he could remember . . ."

The master of the *Renown*, his eyes fixed inwardly, did not wait on an answer. "There is wildness in all things, Captain Vanders. We emerge out of it, and we return to it. And what takes place between our birth and our return is a doomed struggle against it. There is a graveyard on the western coast of Sumatra, at a place called Bengkula, where we British tried over a century ago to establish a settlement. The settlement has vanished, but you can find the tombstones sticking out of the natural tangle. They bear neat little legends. 'Here lies Johnnie Rankins, son of so-and-so, and brother of so-and-so.' They came out here as laborers, carpenters, and masons, accountants and clerks. There are dozens of these stones at Bengkula. And not one boy beneath these stones saw his twenty-fifth year." Captain Claridge placed his white napkin on the table and rose abruptly. "This place you're going to, Captain, has no use for us." He turned to his first officer. "Mr. Morgan, I'll be waiting on the charts for the Banka Island channel." He bowed. "See to the watch, Ensign Fury. The rest of you gentlemen I bid good night."

Mr. Morgan followed the captain out while the rest of us stood in silence. We resumed our seats and looked at one another sheepishly, as young men will who share some guilty secret. At length, Lieutenant Frye, the second officer, cleared his throat. "The captain was not always like this."

"He bids us eat and be merry at table," said another. "I think it eases his loss."

"What loss is that?" I asked.

"Two years ago. He finally married after some forty years a bachelor. A beautiful girl from Dover, twenty years his junior. For a man who keeps much to himself, the engagement gave a buoyancy and lift to his stride. His intended was to join him in Singapore."

"The ship never made it." Frye let the words tumble out. "The captain's intended was on a packet boat. The packet passed into the Malacca Strait—and vanished."

"No trace at all?"

"Nothing. As if she never were."

"The captain resigned his commission and sailed the strait on his own, up and down, from shore to shore. He tacked about for a year looking for that Dover girl."

"He returned to the *Renown* after that," said Ensign Fury. "You can hear him pace the deck all night long. I do not think he sleeps."

Frye folded his napkin and rose. "How does one take vengeance on the sea?"

I lay in my bunk that night, watching the overhead lantern swing back and forth to the easy, comforting creak of the *Renown*'s timbers as she took the swells. Normally, that loveliest of motions is enough to sway me asleep, but the captain's tale of the man-ape of Pasembah and the vanished world of the Rajo Alam spun about in my head and led me to peruse the Sumatra journal with which Alfred Wallace had entrusted me, a quarto notebook with an ink-stained green chamois cover. Unlike the pages of his *Malay Archipelago*, so filled with keen observations about the natural and human worlds he encountered, these pages recorded a passage into the interior of his own soul as well as that of an immense island, and one that had profoundly unsettled him. I turned to the final entry, dated August 13, 1857.

> *Is it possible there are certain places in the world set apart from those ordinary appearances to which we attribute reality? Are there places, then, that body forth their own images and appearances? I believe this island called Sumatra has its own order of things. A simple Kubu tribesman who dines regularly on snakes and the flesh of crocodiles believes he will take on the cunning and strength of these animals when he goes into battle. And lo, he is a mighty warrior! Yet this same warrior will, should some wizard give him the evil eye, writhe in pain for a fortnight before he withers away.*
>
> *Perhaps I have seen what I should not . . . Perhaps that is why, even as I write, a tigress paces outside my bungalow, waiting . . . The simple tribesman could tell me what spirits I have offended, what gods I must appease to make them go away, what ablutions I must perform to be healed. He could tell me why the tigress stalks me, why I can hear her pad back and forth, hear her low snarl, smell the sharp odor of her spoor — and yet she is invisible to others. Yes, back and forth she pads, waiting. Shall I run*

outside to confront my terror or wait until she leaps through this open window? My whole being aches, sweat from my forehead drops on this page, but it is not the fever that racks me. My pistol is on the table before me as I write.

It is something else, a presence I can feel all about me, a presence I shall have done with at last when we sail down the river tomorrow to the sea. And then I shall have done with Sumatra. I shall have done with her illusions — even the sweetest visitor I ever had in my life — before she becomes the thing that pads back and forth in the dark outside . . .

Nothing followed. I closed the manuscript wondering why Wallace had wished me to read these very personal thoughts of a journey made so long ago. Perhaps he was trying to prepare the ground for me, a ground marked by a fever tiger and dark imaginings. These images became entangled in my dreams with those Claridge had conjured in his dinner ramble, and it was not long before I saw the man-ape myself, his long, hairy arm pointing to a graveyard on a hill overlooking a vast river. There were the young Englishmen of Bengkula, in disordered rows, some of the tombstones leaning, some fallen, and among those teetering monuments, I found my own.

Two days later the *Renown* glided into the harbor of Kota Baru in fair weather and with a jaunty breeze in her sails. On the northwestern tip of the island, the port was nearly enclosed by two thin peninsular arms whose headlands, cleared of foliage, held two artillery emplacements made of earthwork. Invisible across twelve miles of water known as the Sumatra Strait lay my next objective, as soon as I had handed over Fahey and claimed my ship: the east coast of one of the world's most tantalizing islands and, if I were to credit Captain Claridge's dark oracles, a perilous destination.

As for the town that Rowan Fahey had called a "Netherlandish stink hole," Kota Baru was like a score of other Dutch settlements that dotted the archipelago—settlements that protested, with the prim, obstinate order of red-tiled compounds, the exotic anarchy of the jungle that surrounded them. The island of Banka had seen palmier days when it was a busy tin-mining port. Some five years before, the bottom had fallen out of the metals market, and it looked as if the place had never recovered from the disappointment. Its former hopes were proclaimed by a three-story white-washed baroque hotel towering on a bluff above the harbor. Encircled by weathered gingerbread balconies and topped with Gothic spires, the building had all the pathos of an abandoned dowager whose lover had made off with her jewels. The wharf below was lined with tin-roofed warehouses, trading firms, and a customs office. A rind of orange road led to the town on the hill beyond, its slope dotted with plantations of banana, papaya, and pepper, and here and there the bamboo hut of a Malay laborer.

Outside of a few lateen-rigged fishing boats, the only ship in the harbor was a French merchant sloop of about three hundred tons. As if galled by the sight of the *Renown*'s Union Jack, her crew pointedly ignored us as they prepared to weigh anchor.

That was when I caught my first glimpse of the steamboat. The stern-wheeler that would soon be under my command was moored at the westernmost slip on the wharf, between a warehouse and the wooden railing that led up to the hotel on the bluff. Mr. Brooke had been right about her dimensions, some seventy feet from bow to stern and three decks high. On the second level, a white iron railing encircled a passenger deck. Perched above was the tall wheelhouse, with windows all around, and behind it a whaleboat swinging on davits.

Every ship has a character and spirit all her own, one gradually revealed to the sailor who keeps her company. First meetings can be deceiving. Even so, I looked on *Lorelei* with a little disappointment. She was not top of the line. She was of an earlier generation of saltwater steamboats, perhaps twenty years old, and therefore built prayerfully, broad-beamed for stability but with a shallow keel, for her makers had also intended her for river work. Despite these ambiguities of design, she looked trim and seaworthy, and one had to give her credit for simply surviving a punishing climate. Her decks and hull had recently been painted, and this bright white gown offered the hope that, though a spinster, she might yet charm a suitor or two. "*Lorelei,*" I said aloud, hoping I might be charmed. "*Lorelei.*"

Two hours after the cutter weighed anchor, I was treading up the hill to the muddy main street of the settlement, my prisoner clanking in irons morosely by my side and escorted by four grim marines under the command of Lieutenant Marsden. This was apparently a first command for the lieutenant as well, for he strode, saber on his shoulder, eyes riveted ahead, as if marching out to the hedgerows of Waterloo under the eyes of the Iron Duke. But there were few to appreciate his martial mien, except for a scattering of sullen Malays who turned down alleys as we approached, and a solitary pie dog that relieved itself against the porch post of a trade-goods store that didn't seem to have any goods to trade. We halted before a whitewashed cement building at the center of town, over which drooped, in humid resignation, the Dutch flag. "Where do I find the commandant?" I asked two shy Dutch women carrying boxes tied with red ribbons. They twirled their parasols in reply, heads down and hastening across the road.

Within, a dank room large enough to accommodate three desks and a holding cell in the rear, its bars made of bamboo. It was musty with the smell of tropical rot. Trails of green mold slithered down the cracks in the plaster. Two of the desks were empty but held yellowing cards announcing the imminent return of their officials. The man sitting on the third desk, in the middle of the floor, had gone the way of the town. His face was blotched and unshaven, and he had the look of someone who had just been rousted out of bed. Like black poppy seeds set in a dumpling, his eyes squinted at us. When awareness dawned, he slid off his perch and offered a florid salute.

Commandant Beets, as he introduced himself, was delighted to see us. Yes, he had heard about us and our mission. He offered drinks all around from a dirty gin bottle, which Marsden and I politely refused. Somewhere along the line of duty, Beets had lost his officer's tunic. He stood before us scratching his soiled undershirt, the other hand pulling his suspenders up from his knees. When I reminded him in halting Dutch that I had come to hand over the prisoner, he took on a look of some perplexity until, at length, giving a snap of his fingers, he said, "All guests must sign in." He slid over a thick ledger and handed me a pen.

Beets repeated the name "Rowan Fahey" to himself, and then,

seemingly satisfied, he pointed my prisoner into the holding cell, which he secured with the stem of an open iron padlock. Perhaps as an assurance that prisoners were not to be mistreated, he tried to pat Fahey on the head. The Irishman drew back and spat on the floor. In a sudden blaze of indignation, the commandant picked up a dry mop from the corner and heaved it at the prisoner with the admonition that felons dare not soil a good Dutch floor. He kicked Fahey's cage for good measure.

Lieutenant Marsden could hardly conceal his deep misgivings about the business, which both of us shared, but his job was done, and we shook hands. I bid him express my thanks to Captain Claridge. With a shake of his head, he took his place before his squad and marched back down the muddy street in a drizzle.

I turned to securing the release of the *Lorelei*. "Ach, the *Lorelei*!" Beets assured me she was mine and had been waiting for me. However, he said with a wink, her release would cost me.

"My papers say nothing about payment for her," I reminded him. "We have an exchange free and clear, the felon Fahey for *Lorelei* and armed escort."

"Oh, the soldiers are to board her, too?" he sputtered, pouring another dram of gin. Bidding me take a seat behind one of the empty desks, he methodically went through each paper I had brought, muttering to himself, "So, so, so," and hemming and hawing. After a painful delay, he tore a sheet from the ledger and began writing furiously. At length he handed me the paper with a flourish. "Not a guilder less."

The paper was filled with a bewildering array of figures, additions whose sums were subtracted from absurd products and quotients derived from impossible divisions.

"What am I to make of this, Commandant?" I asked him numbly.

"You are to make of this thirty thousand guilders. And not a guilder less," he repeated stubbornly. "You cannot board a sturdy Dutch girl and expect to pay nothing."

I looked at the shabby surroundings, a calendar on one wall, a faded portrait of Queen Wilhelmina on another, and a slate board that appeared to list a duty roster. I walked over to it and ran my finger down the line of names. "Where is Subaltern Hooft?"

"*I* am Subaltern Hooft," said the commandant, rising unsteadily to his feet and making a sort of salute.

"And Private Herkimer?"

He broke into an eager grin. "At your service, Kapitan."

"I see." It was all I could do to subdue my rising panic. "And where, then, is Commandant Beets?"

He thumped himself officiously on the chest with his gin bottle. "As you see him, *meenheer*."

I ran down Banka's main street as I had never run before. By the time I reached the end of the main pier, *Renown* was just edging around the lee shore of the harbor, her jib and spinnaker ballooning in the wind. I pulled off my tunic, stripped off my white shirt, and began waving it furiously over my head, jumping up and down on the dock and hallooing with all my might.

I heard a jingling of harness and the clatter of horses' hooves on the hilltop. The ship beyond my reach, I ran back up the hill. A troop of native horse soldiers had just pulled up with a field-gun caisson before the government building. One of them tried to stop me, but I pushed my way through. I practically bowled over a gangling officer with gilded epaulets and a mustache that drooped like a weeping willow.

"Who in the hell are *you*?" he asked in dismay. I was immediately aware that here I was, shirtless and disheveled, addressing the real commandant of Kota Baru.

"Captain Ulysses Vanders," I said, breathlessly slipping on my coat and simultaneously stuffing my shirt down my back. "Of the Regal Sarawak Navy. Commandant Beets?"

"The Regal Sarawak Navy? What the hell is that?" He removed his black felt hat and shook the raindrops from its spray of red ostrich feathers.

I went over to the desk where my papers lay scattered. I was aghast to see that the false commandant had dribbled gin all over them. As for the impostor, he was sitting at the other end of the jail from Fahey, rolling his eyes and mumbling in a strange tongue.

When I started to explain, Commandant Beets cut me off with a wave of his hand. The man in the cage with Fahey was a town disreputable named Sweelinck, the officer told me. Once a week, with tiresome regularity, Sweelinck beat his wife and children, then went after his neighbors. Once a week the commandant tossed Sweelinck in jail. There was no point in locking the jail or even posting a guard, since Sweelinck, once confined, honored the majesty of the law. Provided he was out of gin.

As for the commandant, he had been on some errand in the interior when word reached him that a sail had been sighted. He had raced back to town only to find—thundering generations of Jesus!—the ship was not the packet boat from Batavia he had been waiting for. It was only an Englisher cutter, damn all Englisher imperialists to hell.

"I'll join you in that toast!" cried Fahey from his cell.

"An Irisher!" cried Beets in reply. "What the hell is an Irisher doing in my jail?"

I started to explain again, but Beets brushed my papers aside. He had received no word from his superiors in Batavia regarding the receipt of a prisoner in exchange for a steamboat or the arrival of an officer from some outlandish navy in Sarawak. In fact, the packet boat from Batavia was three weeks overdue. He had been counting the days, since his replacement was supposed to be on it. And then he would be free of this godforsaken place in the middle of nowhere. The only visitor in the past week had been that French sloop off-loading cargo and several passengers bound for Java and Sumatra.

"You don't sound like an Englisher," he said. "But you arrived in an Englisher boat."

"I am an American, sir."

"What is an Amerikanisher doing in an Englisher boat, yet serving in something called the Sarawak navy?" His eyebrows rose in melodramatic suspicion. "Perhaps it is that you are a spy."

"Your Excellency!" Rowan Fahey jangled his manacles as he clung to the bars of his cell. "This is precisely the point I've been wanting to bring to your attention. The truth of the matter is that *I* am Captain Ulysses Vanders, and this man you've been talking to, a notorious scoundrel and scourge of the Pacific, is Rowan Fahey. At gunpoint, Fahey made me exchange clothes, took my papers, and tossed me in here with this fellow as daft and dangerous as a loon."

"Oh, so the master is the butler and the butler is the man!" Beets gerrymandered in English. "Then perhaps both of you are a pack of spies!" He walked over to the cage, reached through the bars, and pulled Sweelinck to his feet. "As you value your life, Sweelinck, who is the impostor here?"

Sweelinck's eyes roved from the commandant to me to Fahey, and then he pointed to himself.

"Yes, I know that, Sweelinck, but which of these two is the impostor of the other?"

The Dutch prisoner jabbed a finger at Fahey.

"All right, we're getting somewhere," said Beets. "Sweelinck may be out of his head, but he does know the false from the true." He picked up my papers again. "Vanders. That's a Dutch name. Where do your people come from, Vanders?"

"Leyden, sir."

"Do you have family in Leyden?"

"An old country relative, Commandant. A professor at the Oriental Institute. Julius Erasmus Vanders."

Beets tugged at his mustache. "You know Professor Julius?"

"Why, yes, a distant cousin. We've never actually met, but he and my father corresponded."

"Then you know of his daughter."

My mind raced back to a tintype the family had received sometime during the war years—1862, perhaps. Uncle Julius, as the children called him, was a stout, bespectacled man with a drinker's nose and a shock of white hair that looked as if it had been electrified. His arm rested paternally on the broad shoulder of a young girl who, to her misfortune, resembled him in every particular.

"Yes, Elsa Hortense Vanders, a great—soul."

"Yes, and a great beauty," Beets enthused. "We are engaged to be married. Seven years. Ever since I came out to the East Indies. But I'm going to Leyden to marry that girl, Vanders. As soon as that damned packet boat arrives." Commandant Beets's eyes now held a look of appreciation. "Why, Vanders, we are practically in the family way," he confirmed. "However, that changes nothing in the official sense. Accordingly, I must ask you to surrender your sidearm. Until I hear otherwise from Batavia, you and the Irisher are under arrest for being a nest of spies."

Rowan Fahey groaned in his cell, and Sweelinck stuck out his tongue.

><@

I had never thought to greet my first command under ship's arrest, or *"bootskerker,"* as Beets put it. He drove me in a buckboard down to the wharf with two of his native soldiers, reiterating that everything must wait on the packet boat from Batavia. Until then, *bootskerker*. The *Lorelei* was as good a place as any to keep an eye on me. A wavering in his glance suggested he might be considering other solutions for this "nest of spies." For the time being, I was allowed the run of the ship and permission to get a drink and a meal at the Prince William Hotel, provided my guards came along. Fahey remained in his cell with the terror of the town.

A chill of anticipation went straight through me as I stood on the quay and looked over my new command. Twenty feet above, a burnished brass plate on the wheelhouse bore the name *Lorelei* in bold lettering. Taking the gangway aft of the bow, I stepped on the deck for the first time. Twin anchors had been carefully stowed on either side of the foredeck. Sunk into the boards was an iron gun mount that might have once supported a small cannon, a six-pounder, perhaps. A gaping doorway led to the hold. Empty now, its cavernous space took up about two thirds of the ship's main deck and was fitted with a small galley on the starboard side, and a privy aft of a stairway that led to the passenger deck. I took this ladder two steps at a time. On the second level were four cabins, two to a side. I opened each one. They were identical in size and fittings and spacious enough for four cots, washstand and basin, and stowage lockers. My cabin was aft of these, right next to the stern-wheel. It was much smaller but had a writing desk and chair and a narrow bunk whose sides were framed with panels of mahogany carved with a coat of arms that showed a sword coming out of a cloud. On the starboard side, a ladder shot up to the steering deck. I had a good view of the wharves and the hotel from this height. The wheelhouse was a snuggery with a folding chart table and windows on three sides. I closed my eyes as I placed my hands on the polished oak wheel and listened to the soft, familiar creaks of a ship at mooring.

My silent communing with *Lorelei* was interrupted by an ominous clangor from deep within the ship's innards. Just as I stepped out of the wheelhouse, the smokestack erupted with a belch of soot. When the cloud of debris settled, I saw with horror that a fine layer of black ash had dusted my new uniform. Following the tattoo of metal upon metal, I clattered down to the main deck in a fit of indignation and ran the length of *Lorelei* to the engine room. Since the steamer was oceangoing, the bulk of the engine was housed below deck to protect it from salt spray. An open hatch led down to two huge condensers of Watt design. From these sprang a profusion of flywheels, connecting rods, and pistons that drove the great stern-wheel.

Climbing among this web of pipes and valves was a bony, barefoot fellow wearing a turban and stained canvas trousers. He was delightedly banging away at a fitting with a wrench nearly the size of his forearm.

"What are you doing down there?" I cried.

The noise stopped. The Indian peered up at me, his amber eyes as wide as egg whites. "Who is that up there calling me in English? Are you not a Dutchman?"

"I am not a Dutchman but an American. I am Captain Ulysses Vanders, and I am here to take command of this vessel."

The man's eyebrows shot up in consternation. Taking my hand, he swung out of the iron labyrinth below. "I am most terribly afraid I have got grease on your hand," he clucked apologetically, offering me an oily cloth.

"And soot on my uniform."

He started to dust me off with the cloth but thought better of it. He responded to my glower by coming to attention. "If Engineer Habab Kumar Devadatta is to be cashiered, then certainly he is most deserving of it," he said, mimicking the clipped tones of a soldier of the Raj. "However, I would like to say it for the record that I am most pleased to make your acquaintance, Captain Vanders. Long have I labored to make the *Lorelei* a fit vessel for her next master. And it is a pity that I will not be here to be of further service."

I could have sworn that a tear actually formed in the corner of his right eye, summoned, no doubt, to dampen my ire. This engine genie stood about five and a half feet, his dark complexion complicated by a layer of engine soot. His ears were long and rubbery and poked obstinately out of his turban. These were outmatched in size by an arched and impertinent nose. He seemed created to tend engines, a limber, agile man with broad hands and spidery fingers made for grasping and ratcheting. The quaintness of his appearance notwithstanding, he gave the impression of unshakable confidence, and his expression of regret was at once insincere and arrogant, since it was plain he did not expect to be let go. Oddly enough, I was inclined to agree with him.

"It seemed you knew I was coming," I said.

"Kota Baru is a town that lives on rumor, sir."

"Too bad some of it didn't run off on Commandant Beets."

The engineer's attitude eased slightly, and he offered a sly smile. "Commandant Beets is a species of man who hears and sees only what he wishes."

"There's truth in what you say," I replied, thinking of that tintype of Elsa Hortense Vanders.

"An American!" Devadatta grinned at the novelty of it with a solid parapet of white teeth. "Truly, you are the first American captain I have known. Captain Ulysses Vanders," he repeated, moving his lips as if tasting an exotic fruit. "An American bearing the name of the greatest sailor who ever lived. Lately, I have been having this dream. Of slipping the mooring and getting out of this infernal place. We fight our way past the Dutch guards and give them a sound drubbing. It is the beginning of the grand adventure for which my heart has been longing. And the one who leads us out of here is none other than Ulysses, bravest of all heroes and crafty as a *naga*."

"So you've read Homer," I said, wondering how much of this chronicle hadn't been dreamed up for my benefit.

"No, but I have read Mr. Bulfinch's *The Age of Fable*," he said excitedly. The Indian pulled out a tattered volume from a crate next to a sleeping mat rolled up in the corner. There wasn't much to his little space. Most of the engine room was taken up by stacks of hardwood fuel. There was a small work table with a vise and a toolbox. Over it hung a framed engraving of a radiant Indian deity tinted blue, dispensing rays of benediction tinted gold, upon a bevy of half-clad and adoring Hindu females tinted brown and red. Devadatta opened the book to the chapter that began the chronicle of the wily Greek sailor who took ten years to reach home. "I have read it twenty-seven times," Devadatta added proudly, tapping the page with his forefinger. "The former master of the *Lorelei,* he gave me these few books."

"Who was the former master?"

"A Hohenzollern, somewhat crazy. Perhaps you've already seen the crest carved into the captain's bunk? That belonged to Captain Von Fritz."

"I've seen the crest. What happened to the captain?"

"That, sir, is a very long story." Devadatta provided a brief biographical narrative about his own journey from his native Travancore to Calcutta, where he had served on delta riverboats. He taught himself all about engines and landed on the *Lorelei* two years before, when she had been bought from her British owners by an agent for the Dutch East Indies Company.

"We made almost seven knots all the way across the Indian Ocean down the Malacca Strait," he added with pride. "Maybe that's better than when she left Liverpool in 1852 for Bombay. In that place and in that year, this ship was born."

"So that's how she ended up in India."

"The *Lorelei* was built for the Indian service. She had a different name then. The *Deborah,* I think."

"She's a seasoned traveler."

"As are we all, sir." Devadatta's nod affirmed a maritime kinship.

I produced a small silk flag bearing the arms of Rajah Brooke. "We sail on the first vessel to fly this insignia—when we sail."

"This is a bonny flag," Devadatta said admiringly as he held it up. "But it is not the Stars and Stripes, I think."

"Not the Stars and Stripes. This is the flag of the Regal Sarawak Navy."

Devadatta shook his head as if this might or might not be relevant information. "When do we get under way?"

"I'm afraid those Dutch soldiers are outside to ensure we go nowhere at all."

"No doubt," he said ruefully, "Commandant Beets thinks you are a spy."

"Then you know the temperament of the man."

"I do, Captain. Because I am also suspected of being a spy."

I looked at him with surprise. "Then why aren't you in prison?"

"Because the commandant is a landsman, Captain. He thinks that any ship is a prison. Little does he know that my prison is my universe."

I stepped outside the engine room. My Dutch guards were sitting on the wharf, puffing on leaf tobacco. I stepped back and lowered my voice. "Tell me, if we were to get under way, how quickly could you get up steam?"

The Indian patted the engine casing. "She will fire up in twenty minutes on the captain's order." He looked at me slyly. "At any hour of day or night."

"I'm glad you have such confidence, Devadatta. To be honest, my acquaintance with steam-powered vessels has been slender. And not always amicable."

"You are a rope-and-canvas sailor, I can see. *Lorelei* will do her best to win your esteem. That I can assure you, Captain."

"That's good to know, Engineer Devadatta." With that, I allowed my growling stomach to lead me to the dining room of the Prince William Hotel, my guards in tow.

><

The Prince William's dining room took up most of the second floor of the hotel. I supposed it had been built during one of those speculative fevers that recurred every decade or so in the archipelago and left so many financially ruined corpses in their wake. The room offered a spectacular view of the harbor for fifty or more diners, but the tables were mostly empty, the linen faded. As for the local gentry lounging at the table next to mine, they were the disgruntled heirs of a vanishing legacy, a condition that they bemoaned loud and long amid a clutter of delft dishes, mugs of ale, flagons of wine, torn roasts of chicken, and clouds of Indies tobacco pouring from clay pipes.

The tradition went back three centuries, when the first Dutch trading vessels began navigating beyond the horn of Africa into the waters of the fabled Spice Islands. The Portuguese had beaten them to the lucrative spice trade, but the Dutch wasted no time in ousting their rivals by burning them out of Malacca in 1641. After that, the trading octopus known as the Dutch East Indies Company spread its tentacles from one Indonesian island to another, until it held a jealously guarded monopoly in nutmeg, cloves, and other commodities craved by Europeans that could be fed only by the unique markets under company control. The power of the company did not please rival European colonizers. The British in particular, after projecting power into India, saw their interests on a collision course with Holland.

The tide of history had turned for these men gathered at the table, and they knew it. Their plantations, mines, trading prerogatives, and privileged way of life were threatened not only by competition from without but by restive Malays who had once ruled fabled kingdoms and were eager to throw off the Dutch yoke. The men's talk was seasoned with a mix of resentment and nostalgia, with what-ifs and might-have-beens. The empire their forefathers had carved out with such maritime daring was now only an illusion. Someone—certainly not they—must be to blame.

"It wasn't the British who ruined us," said one of the burghers, aiming his clay pipe like a blunderbuss at the head of the man across from him. "It was Bonaparte."

"Ach, if we Dutch hadn't kicked the papist Spaniards in the pants, the French never would have heard of 'Liberty, Equality, Fraternity.'" The stout red-nosed speaker polished off a glass of claret with a trembling hand. "So for teaching them liberty, they took ours."

A fat trader with a pandanus fan concurred. With languid movements, he barely stirred the pall of blue tobacco smoke that enveloped them. "The Little Corporal brought his cannons to Amsterdam and made us a present of his brother Jerome."

"Mark it in your book. Eighteen-oh-five. The year the Frogs stabbed us in the back," said a sallow-faced man named Jock, jabbing his fork into a hayrick of boiled cabbage and hefting it to his lips. "And all because Boney's simpering brother wanted to be a king."

The claret drinker reached for a flagon. "Of someplace."

"Of any place." The smoker rapped the bowl of his pipe on a tray.

The cabbage eater stayed his fork. "So Boney gave our Holland to a nincompoop."

"The Dutch Indies was the icing on that cake." A man whose muttonchop whiskers curled from his cheeks like briars pulled thoughtfully on a meerschaum. "The French sent their own administrators out to the Indies."

"My father well remembers that time," said an old-timer, lifting his chin from a bowl of chowder. "The French came out to the Indies and took over the company. That was just the excuse the British were looking for; they took the Indies from the French."

"From there it was all disaster." The claret drinker's tone suggested a death in the family. "Even if the Englisher robbers did give us back our islands."

The old-timer's rheumy eyes flared with indignation. "But only after Stamford Raffles stole Singapore from right under our noses!"

"Our Malays were corrupted after that." The smoker sank his pipe into a tobacco pouch as if it were a cure for misery. "Nothing but trouble ever since."

"And declining profits," added Jock with a feeble twirl of his fan.

"And troubles in Sumatra." The claret drinker poured himself another, slopping some over the rim. "Now we've got this superstitious nonsense about the Ten Thousand Years and the end of the world or some such."

"Ten Thousand Excuses, you mean!" grumbled the mutton-chops. "It's another damned Malay trick to get out of work. The head overseer of my Sumatra plantation—my best man!—up and leaves me last week. 'Just where do you think you're going?' I ask him. 'I'm taking my family into the mountains,' he says. 'You've got a contract,' I say. He says to me, 'What good is a contract when these plains split in two and the fireballs fall from heaven?' "

The cabbage eater pushed away his empty plate and pulled a gold toothpick from a pocket in his waistcoat. "Damned Malay foolishness. It's because of the disturbances up north. Some tribe has gone on the rampage, burning villages, taking heads."

"They're all shitting their pants over in Palembang," said an eavesdropping waiter, speaking of the government center on Sumatra. "It's practically a state of siege."

"That Batak lord up north—what's his name?"

The old-timer looked upward as if the name were written on the frescoed ceiling high above. "Radjah Dulah. They call him so."

"Has his hands full," mumbled Jock.

"And there's talk of smallpox up there. That's another punishment from the gods."

The talk turned dismally to the effect it all would have on coffee exports. This led someone to reflect on the arrival of a British cutter that morning. The conversation veered to a discussion of foreign spies and how Commandant Beets was one to give them swift justice—an ominous note. I was glad that Charles Brooke's parsimony had excluded gold braid from my uniform, and that my guards waited discreetly outside the hotel. But it was as good a time as any to leave, even though I had scarcely touched my plate of fish and yams. I had lost my appetite completely.

On my way out, I passed three young couples playing bezique at one of the dining tables and talking gaily in French. I figured they had arrived on the French sloop we saw departing as *Renown* entered the harbor. The only other guest in that great dining room was a well-dressed Asian traveler in a French-tailored suit, studying a newspaper through his pince-nez. He nodded curtly as I left the hotel for my first night of ship's arrest.

>⊛

I had taken to keeping a journal our first night out of Kuching, so I busied myself that night in my procrustean cabin with recording the day's disheartening turn of events. At length I put down my pen and pushed away from the small writing desk. The room was stifling, and I might have slept topside except for the mosquitoes. There was a porthole, though, overlooking the stern-wheel, and I opened the cabin door for a cross breeze before I lowered the netting.

At some point, in a confused dream about Charles Brooke leading me down a long passageway by candlelight, a floorboard creaked, and there before me was Irene Burdett-Couts, holding my Navy Colt. She was aiming it straight at my forehead with an outstretched arm and a calculating eye. I felt the deadly coolness of the tip of its barrel on my brow.

"I wouldn't want to make any sudden noises or movements, Captain Vanders, sir."

I awoke to discover that this part of the dream had crossed the threshold of consciousness in earnest. Sure enough, the tip of a revolver was pointed against my forehead, but the voice held too deep a brogue to be that of Sarawak's lovely minister-without-portfolio.

"You wouldn't be fit for duty with a bullet in your brain, and besides, the detonation would have the hostiles down upon us."

"Fahey! What the devil?"

"Aye, it's me, all right." The Irishman made a low chuckle. "The prison hasn't been made that can hold Rowan Fahey. Getting Sweelinck to pick the lock took longer than I supposed, or I would have been here sooner. But he became more astute with tips from my hip flask. Studied locksmithing in Amsterdam, did Sweelinck."

I sat up slowly. The pistol was still pointed at my forehead. "What time is it, then?"

"Another two hours before dawn."

"And the guards?"

"Trussed up against the warehouse like chickens, all unharmed but for the lumps on their pates."

"You'll get all of us killed!" I swung out of the bunk. "And I'll thank you for my revolver."

"We'll be killed for sure if we stay in this Netherlandish stink hole," whispered Fahey. "And keep your voice down! As for the pistol, it is best kept in the hands of the new master of the *Lorelei*."

"Namely, Rowan Fahey."

"You can meditate on that fact while you're in the wheelhouse." He went back to the cabin door and looked out. "Your Lascar and I have stoked the boilers. Now we're going to slip our moorings. I think you'll find us all breathing easier once we've cleared the channel."

"You'd be of better service with a lantern on the bow. It's going to be difficult enough finding the harbor passage. No marker buoys, and there are shoals on either side."

"You might as well announce our exit," he argued. "Besides, the moon is nearly full—there should be enough light to make a run for it."

"And what of the Dutch artillery at the harbor entrance?"

"We'll just have to take that chance."

The patter of bare feet outside the cabin drew Fahey's attention.

"Don't shoot!" cried Devadatta, throwing up his hands. "What is going on here, sir? This man came in and ordered me around and—" He looked with misgiving at the pistol.

"It's all right, Devadatta. Mr. Fahey here is acting under my orders. It looks like you'll have your wish—we're going to make for open water."

A few moments later the Indian and the Irishman were each to a side of the stern-wheel, poling us out into the black water. In the wheelhouse, I waited some breathless minutes for Devadatta to get up steam. Then I felt the stern-wheel's arms shudder and begin to turn. Exhilarated at the sound of water pounding through the paddles, I set the steamboat's bow, using the dim outline of the headlands at either side of the harbor as a guide.

"Take a look!" Fahey cried up from the foredeck. I leaned out of the wheelhouse and shot a glance to the stern. Lights swarmed on the water—the hounds were giving chase. Torches flickered among the trees. It didn't take me long to figure out that Beets and his horseman had saddled up and were headed for the artillery forts on the headlands. Once those cannons were trained on us, the snare would be complete. The *Lorelei* continued to churn water, but I couldn't put on any speed until I was sure of the harbor channel. I could hear the reports of soldiers firing their rifles from the *banca* boats behind us. We had been less than ten minutes under way when Fahey signaled me with his lamp that I was in position to make a run for it.

"Tell the engineer to give me full steam," I called down to Fahey. Taking the lantern with him, he raced aft to the engine room. The *Lorelei* had idled for a minute when the hull suddenly shuddered and the wheel came to a jarring stop. So did my heart. We were dead in the water.

Footsteps bounded up from second deck, and Fahey leaned in to the wheelhouse, brandishing a rifle. "Your engineer says a connecting rod's frozen. He's working on it. I'll hold them off." He vanished, and I could hear him running down the second deck. With a sense of foreboding, I watched the torches draw closer to the headlands.

I waited in fitful silence, stepping outside to gauge the distance of the line of boats, closing in like a pack of demon-eyed wolves. A bullet whizzed by my ear, and I ducked back inside the wheelhouse. At that moment the *Lorelei*'s stern-wheel made a full revolution, stopped, and just as Fahey squeezed off a round to dismay our pursuers, took on new life with such pulse-pounding determination that the bow of the ship nearly lifted out of the water. We lurched ahead, and I kept her pointed directly for the stretch of gray water between the headlands. As we picked up speed, the lights of our pursuers fell away, but the headlands bristled with torchlit activity like hives of incendiary wasps. We were close enough that I could make out the mass of each fortification in the moonlight. As we pulled into the channel, a brilliant orange bloom flashed from the emplacement on our port side. The artillery shell shrieked overhead and landed about twenty yards ahead of us with a shiver of water like the breaching of a whale. The fort to our starboard echoed the challenge, but this time the trace of the shell was a high whistle far above us. It was followed by a detonation at the opposite fort that lit up the night sky and seemed to rock the very headland. Another explosion followed in its wake with a furious crimson glare.

Fahey pounded up the ladder and burst into the wheelhouse with all the jubilation of the newly saved and risen. "If this isn't a sight for sinners, Vanders—damned if Beets's gunners haven't gone and blown up one of their own forts. Three cheers for Dutch gunnery! Hip, hip . . ." Both of us gave hurrahs of victory as we shot through the harbor gap at full speed and churned into open water.

The headiness of our escape sustained us for a good half hour as we sought the deep water of the Sumatra Strait. Then the leaden uncertainty of our future began to weigh in. I was aware again, although by no overt act of Fahey's, that he had my old service revolver stuck in his belt and a Vickers rifle cradled in his arm. The uncertainty soured into bitter knowledge—I was a captain only in name, in charge of the wheel but empty of command.

"Time to hoist the Jolly Roger up our mast," said Fahey wryly, leaning out a wheelhouse window and looking up at a night sky whose fading stars heralded the coming of the dawn. "We're as free as men are ever likely to be."

"Aye, free to play the hare to the Dutch hound."

"I have no hankering after a Dutch gallows." He rubbed a chafed wrist. "And seeing as Sweelinck was kind enough to remove my bracelets, I have no hankering for another pair of those, either."

"So where does that leave us?" I asked miserably.

"There's a little cove I know of, north of Malacca, where a man might find some friends."

"Contrabanders and pirates, you mean."

The Irishman pulled his head back in. His voice was hard. "A pirate, you might know, is a poor man with the gall to act like a rich one."

"So you intend for me to head to the Malay coast?"

"Unless you can offer a more congenial destination."

I debated about whether to explain the nature of my mission and its urgency. I wasn't about to go back on my contract with Charles Brooke, and I wasn't about to cave in and give up my command. Not without a fight. For the moment, however, I was Fahey's captive, disarmed and outfoxed. There didn't seem to be any reason to withhold my objective from him, so I outlined the situation of the missionaries at Light of the World in dire terms.

I saw almost immediately that my appeal to sympathy was the wrong tack. "What a convoluted notion you have of the world, Vanders!" Fahey chuckled, looking on me like a hapless fool, but he was of a humor to play it out. "What's in it for me if we make this trek up the river?"

"I'll intercede with Rajah Brooke," I said lamely. "I'll tell him how you volunteered to save the missionaries even though it placed you in imminent danger. I can make a good case that Beets is a spy-crazy lunatic. Brooke knows how to reward a good deed done by a changed man." I knew I was making ludicrous sounds. "He can work out a better deal for you with the Dutch."

"Here's something fancy," he sneered. "Let me tell you something. You're lucky if the high and mighty Charles Brooke doesn't put a price on your head himself. At the very least, he'll turn you

over to Batavia in order to skirt an international incident. The
Hollanders aren't a mighty power anymore, but they have enough
to oust Mr. Brooke out of Sarawak if they were of a mind to. Put
this in your pipe, man—you've just heisted a Dutch flagship!" He
put his thumb and forefinger together. "A minuscule kind of flagship, it's true, but they'll hang you as high as if she were a ship o'
the line."

I looked at him with a bleak stare. "So what are you offering
me, Fahey, the opportunity to throw in my lot with your Malacca
friends?"

"Oooh, and wouldn't they give a bonny welcome to a captain
with such a fine steamboat," he said, slapping his thigh. "A boat
like this could slide and slither along waterways not dreamed of
by a frigate." He grabbed my shoulder in enthusiasm. "A man
might well make himself one of those rich pirates and a king like
Charles Brooke to boot. It has happened in this archipelago many
a time."

What a joker black fate had handed me for a card! A prisoner
in my charge had not only turned the tables on me but could offer
me a far better bargain than any I might find for him.

Fahey was laughing, as if to underscore my own recognition,
with tears at the corners of his eyes. "You're offering for me to
meander up some uncharted Sumatra river with you, and all in
search of some Protestant Jesus talkers who should have known
better to keep to their own kind and their own country. Who gives
a tinker's damn about them? And *you* will put in a good word
for me with the double-dealing White Rajah? Perhaps I am an
outlaw, Vanders, but that doesn't mean I've taken leave of my
wits!"

I was silent in my chagrin but then felt the slight, hopeful tug
of possibility. "Regardless of where we go, we've got enough fuel
on board to make it across the channel to Sumatra. There's a
fueling depot at the head of the Jambi River. With luck, we might
make it."

"And our Dutch friends?"

"You won't find a Dutchman north of Palembang these days. The depot is operated by a half-caste and his family. So I've been told."

Fahey reached for a hurricane lamp and lit the wick with a flint. Pulling down the charting table, he smoothed out a map of the Sumatra coastline. "The Jambi is due north about thirty miles." He tapped his finger on the map with finality. "Then north it is."

5

"Steer for the Jambi River, Captain Vanders."

Rowan Fahey rubbed a hand over the stubble on his face and yawned. We were more than midway across the strait, and already the east coast of Sumatra was a long gray possibility about a mile off our bow. The heart-pounding commotion, at least for the present, was over, we knew there was no ship in Kota Baru that could give us chase on the open sea. But it was only a matter of time before word was carried to Palembang, which was home port to at least one fast Dutch cutter. "After all this excitement, I'm going to turn in for two hours. Then I'll relieve you." He paused as he left the wheelhouse and said menacingly, "Oh, and if you get any heroic notions, know that I'm a light sleeper with an excitable nature. And I have all the guns."

I grasped the wheel more tightly as Fahey clomped down to the second deck. My stomach knotted with dread and indecision. As a result of my humiliation at Fahey's hands, my thoughts had turned to being infuriated with myself. My command and captaincy had slipped right through my fingers. I had lost my head back in Kota Baru. In an act of sudden abandonment and rashness, I hadn't taken the full measure of things. I had failed to reckon that by trying to escape Beets's injustice, I had turned myself into a renegade. Fahey had spoken the bald truth. At the very least,

I'd go up before an international board of inquiry. They would strip me of my officer's commission and blacklist me for service under any flag.

Somehow I would have to regain the upper hand. But even if I was able to make him my prisoner again, I would still have to prove to the world I was not a pirate.

It was then that the whole dynamic of my dilemma shifted in the lifting darkness. Fahey had turned in over an hour before. The Sumatra coast loomed ahead in rugged definition, the water in the strait smooth and still but moving with a swift southerly current. I heard the shout before the prow of the little *prahu* was right in front of me, about twenty yards off the starboard bow. I swung the wheel hard to port and called to Devadatta to cut the engine. Farther off to starboard, I heard a woman's plaintive cry.

Fahey appeared on the bow, holding a lantern out over the water. The boat reappeared like an apparition. Sitting forward was a European woman wearing a planter's straw hat, and behind her a Malay woman in a silk shawl. Both of them held on to the gunwales as the narrow native boat rocked in our wake. The boatman in the stern waved a long-bladed paddle over his head to gain our attention. How they had gotten themselves into the middle of the Sumatra Strait at night was a puzzle. I locked the wheel in place as I descended to the main deck.

"You *are* going up the Asahan?" The European woman's tone was querulous, almost quarrelsome. Coming without an introduction, it suggested that we had been shilly-shallying and had no right to keep her waiting. British manner, sure enough, but I was willing to wager she had spent some time in Australia, to judge by the accent. Fahey looked over at me with a long face, and I couldn't help but feel apprehension about how he might handle this dilemma. "Come now," cried the peevish one, "you are the captain of this vessel, aren't you?"

"I am the captain, madam," I said, stepping forward clumsily and lifting my cap, my mind racing on how I might turn this new twist to my advantage.

"Very well then, Captain . . ."

"Vanders." Devadatta reached out and grabbed the end of the boatman's paddle.

"Captain Vanders. American?"

"American."

As my engineer drew the dugout closer, the woman in the straw bonnet eyed me much as a heron with indigestion might observe an odd fish. She was, I guessed, about forty years of age, a plain-featured woman with broad hips and narrow shoulders who stood flat-footed in the *prahu* as if to challenge Atlas to move her. A spray of freckles played beneath a pert, uptilted nose. Her blue eyes had seen something of the world and told you so directly. "Perhaps, then, Captain Vanders, you can tell me if Providence has placed me in your hands. I must know if your ship is sailing north, at least as far as the Asahan River. If not, then we'll strike for Kota Baru."

"That might be entirely for the best," Fahey suggested.

"Speak up, sir," said the bonnet, turning with some ferocity on Fahey. "Who are you?"

"That's none of your—"

"This is Mr. Fahey," I cut in with sudden resolution. "First mate. We *are* bound for the Asahan. But how could you know?"

"Are you a Christian, Captain?" She looked up at me with a doubtful squint.

"My father raised his sons with the aid of a Bible," I said, remembering how sturdy a book it was, and well suited for knuckle whacking.

"A sly answer," said the woman in the bonnet. She held up her own tattered copy of the Scriptures as if to admonish me. "Yet I'll give a ready reply to your question. There were no ships at Palembang, so we hired a *prahu* and struck for the coast, hoping to hail a trader. The river mouth is wide, the tide swift, and our boatman lost his way in the dark. We prayed. And there you were. More than luck, I think, Captain."

"Luck it was," Fahey muttered at my side. "Damnedest luck."

"That's Sahar." She nodded to the Malay girl who sat behind her, head bowed and concealed by her shawl. "She assists my ministry at Palembang. And I didn't introduce myself, did I? Hannover. Mrs. Bridgett Hannover." She rubbed her forehead. "I'm afraid we haven't had much sleep. On the Asahan—my church has a mission there."

"Light of the World."

The women exchanged a quick glance. "You know of it?"

"Indeed I do, madam. For it's our destination."

"Then heaven be double praised!"

"Your fame precedes you, Mrs. Hannover."

"Oh, and how is that?"

"Why, I have come from Kuching. Your appeal for help got through to the Dutch and thence to Sarawak. Rajah Brooke speaks—most highly of you."

She wrinkled her nose as if there were a sudden odor. "If Charles Brooke has anything good to say about me, then I had better mend my ways."

"You do not approve of the rajah, I take it."

"The man is practically a pagan and an idolater. He has spent far too many years in the bush."

The missionary latched on to a carpet bag and held it up. A vexed Rowan Fahey looked on, caught in a paroxysm of indecision, rocking his weight from one foot to the other. Since he had been caught off guard by this development, I meant to keep him so.

"You are welcome aboard, Mrs. Hannover." I took the carpet bag. Devadatta unfolded a wooden ladder, and as the Englishwoman braced one foot on the step, I gave her my hand to swing her over the gunwale. "Both of you are welcome." I left Devadatta to help the Malay girl clamber aboard with a suitcase as I turned to the scowling Irishman. "Look lively there, Mr. Fahey. Show the ladies to a cabin. We can sort things out later in the morning. That's the port cabin, aft, Mr. Fahey."

The Malay girl put the suitcase at Fahey's feet. Giving me a black look, he hoisted the baggage to his shoulder and mounted the ladder to the second deck and the passenger cabins. Mrs. Hannover spoke in Malay to the man in the canoe. With a wave of his paddle, he drifted off into the darkness.

"I'm grateful to you, Mr. Vanders." The missionary offered a thin, abrupt smile that revealed her exhaustion.

I followed the ladies to the second deck and swung up to the wheelhouse. Devadatta had already scampered down to the engine room. No sooner were my hands on the wheel than I heard a piercing scream from the deck below. A moment later I was standing at the doorway of Mrs. Hannover's cabin, and for the second time that night, I witnessed an astonishing sight. The missionary had her arm around the trembling Malay girl. Fahey held the lantern high in one hand and my pistol in the other. On the floor of the cabin, seemingly oblivious to our presence, squatted a Chinese man, naked to the waist, his shaved head glistening as he bent over a tiny candle and some sticks spread helter-skelter on the floor. To add to his bizarre appearance, the fellow wore a Polynesian tattoo for a collar.

"*Permettez moi une explication,*" said a well-dressed Asian stepping out of the shadows. The pince-nez on the bridge of his nose flashed in the light of the lantern. "*Nous sommes vos prisoners, une condition que j'espére reveler à acheter les billets du passage.*"

A quick, hopeful gaze roved over us, from Fahey to Mrs. Hannover to me, but when no one made reply, the man's features fell with the hard truth that he was, alas, among barbarians.

"I suppose you might wish to consider us your prisoners," he labored in unaccustomed English, delivered with Gallic reluctance. "I do not know what the conventions are regarding the status of stowaways. However, I am hoping that you will consider us passengers more than happy to pay." He removed a wallet from the inside of his coat. "I can offer you twice, thrice, the normal passage rate, if you find that suitable. For both of us, of course. For my assistant, Master Kung, and for myself." He made a perfunctory bow. "I am Dr. Phan Dom Diem. Radjah Dulah has retained me as his personal physician."

"Physician to the lord of all the Bataks," I said, recognizing him as the man I had seen sitting alone in the Prince William Hotel. *"Il est un plaisir pour vous rencontrer."* I offered a slight bow as I returned his introduction.

"Voilà!" he answered, brightening. *"Ici parlez français!"*

"Je parle un peu de français." I smiled apologetically as I pressed my thumb and forefinger together.

"Un peu," he repeated like a man who saw the light receding. "Ah well." He sighed, preparing to shoulder once more the rude sack that was the language of the Angles. "The radjah has asked me to make haste. Thus my unconventional method of booking passage up the Asahan River."

"We'll sort all this out at the Jambi Station in the morning. See that the ladies are settled in cabin number two, Mr. Fahey."

Rebellion seethed in Fahey's look, but the sudden turn of events had complicated his plan. "So much for your damned official secrets," Fahey muttered in my ear as he hefted the suitcase. "All we need now is a booming brass band."

~∽

I spent the few hours that remained of this wrenching night at the helm, guiding *Lorelei* closer to the coast so that we could slip into Jambi Station at first light, refuel, and be quickly on our way.

I was in a turmoil of emotions made more keen by the unexpected appearance of four passengers, as bizarre a complication of strangers, it struck me, as fate ever brought together. And why they had been brought together on my boat I could only wonder— until I was forced again to the bleak and bitter fact that I had no boat and no command. From now on I would ever be casting glances over my shoulder, with an eye for the sail that would spell, at the least, my professional ruin and imprisonment. I could not bear the thought that I would have to make myself over again, if even fortunate in that chance. Ten long years it had taken me to resurrect myself from the living dead and build a sort of life among the unknown islands and archipelagoes of this world.

There was more to feed my disquiet. Despite the possession of recent charts, I was in unfamiliar territory, and the devious shapes that night and imagination make of hunched, gnarly mangrove and mazes of nibong palm were all the more unsettling because of it. On another level, equally unsettling, I had the distinct sense of being watched by some brooding power, as if my arrival had been anticipated but not welcomed. Perhaps it was the distant trumpeting of elephants or the sudden snarl of a jungle cat that held some teasing echo of my name. Perhaps I heard some message in the haunting cries of nightbirds. All these seeming portents mingled with the heady orchid odors carried on the breeze, so thick and honeyed they might drown the senses. This vast island looming to port side had mysteriously asserted its subtle menace and the exercise of its will, as a great khan behind an intricate screen might savor the wretched terror of any rash pretender dragged in chains before him. Yet as I kept my own baleful eye on Rowan Fahey—standing on the deck before me, staring into the darkness, a rifle cradled in his arms—I knew I must resist this and all surrenders. It was my command that had been taken, and I would have it back regardless of the cost.

As if to bolster my resolve, the wheel gave a sudden, willful tug to starboard. *Lorelei*'s sign, I took it, that we were one in our vow and our mission. We rounded a tangled headland, and Jambi Station swung into view, its dock and outbuildings silhouetted in the less sinister hues of dawn.

6

The sun was already above the tree line by the time Fahey, Devadatta, and I had secured the mooring at Jambi Station. The rickety dock led to the overgrown landing, a trail snaking through knee-high weeds to the station house. We had made our first stop on the Sumatra coast, although the "we" had turned out to be a much different set of voyagers than foreseen. Despite the lack of sleep, or because of it, I was restless and worried, especially as I listened to the faint stirrings in the cabins that told me our passengers had begun to rise. What would I do with them? And how would I gain control of my ship? I had no answer to these perplexities.

Set on low pilings above the swampland of the Jambi River, the station house was a rambling structure of a style unique to Sumatra. Given the long, graceful sweep of its carved gable, the building seemed, from a distance, like a brown thrush ready to soar into flight. Three outbuildings flanked the main house: the cookhouse, from which a plume of smoke curled in the muggy air; a storage shed; and a washing area, partly enclosed by woven bamboo walls. Above the enclosure rose a wooden tower with a tin catchment on top, the first bathhouse I had seen since leaving Kuching. I hastened toward it, carrying a towel and a shaving kit. In a clearing beside the dock, Devadatta had taken charge of two

Malay workmen, and together they pulled timber from a huge pyramid of split logs. A spent sow, her belly dragging the ground, and several scrawny hens rooted and pecked in the dirt. From somewhere in the dense forest beyond came the persistent yap of a dog.

Shaved, with the sleep dashed out of my eyes, I followed my nose to the main house, the aroma of curried chicken drawing me on. There I found Rowan Fahey already seated on a mat before a long table, working on a bowl of the steaming stuff. A Malay woman dressed in a one-piece sarong of many colors waved me inside with a smile filled with betel-blackened teeth. To dispel some of the smoke and gloom, I lifted the hinged nipa shutter that covered the solitary window in the building. *Lorelei* rested in her mooring across the clearing, beleaguered but no less defiant. Then I realized I was seeing what was inside of me. I glared at Fahey and swallowed my anger, knowing I would need a clear head if I were ever to get her back.

Fahey grunted a good morning as I sat across from him and began unwrapping one of the tarot cakes baked in banana leaf that had been heaped in the center of the table. "We've got to get rid of 'em," he whispered as the woman set a steaming bowl of rice before me.

"How do you propose to do that?"

"Why, leave the lot of 'em behind," he said between mouthfuls. "There's enough traffic between the Jambi and Palembang. They'll get picked up. Eventually."

"We can't just leave them here." I was glad to see how haggard he looked. I doubted if he had slept, and that made him at once more vulnerable and more dangerous, especially with my Colt tucked in his belt. "I won't leave them here."

"Well, we're not hauling them to Malacca, I can tell you that." A grin spread across his square jaw. "Or do you propose I put the lot of 'em out of their misery?"

There was no time to counter that sinister suggestion, for I heard the sound of women's voices. Mrs. Bridgett Hannover stepped inside, accompanied by Sahar. The missionary seemed in her element, nimbly sliding to the floor next to me, tucking her legs under her, and, after brief greetings and a briefer blessing, pulling in the plate of taro cakes. She wore a simple gray cotton frock with a black collar. She had removed her woven hat and wore her cinnamon hair up to get some relief from the heat. By contrast, Sahar was a kind of exotic vestal, her head draped in a deep purple veil edged with gold ribbon. She wore a short, slim-fitting Malay tunic, known as the *baju kurong,* which barely covered her midriff, and a long blue *kain* sarong. She was perhaps ten years Hannover's junior, lips full and sensual, nostrils delicately flared, with a fetching round birthmark below her left cheekbone. I guessed her to be a mixture of Malay and Arab and Indian ancestries. She lowered her glance as she entered, not so much for modesty, I thought, as to hide the milky stigmatism that discolored her right eye.

"Some things require explanation, Captain Vanders," the missionary said with a smile as our cook placed more coconut-shell bowls on the low table. "You know who I am, but you do not know why it is imperative that I travel up the Asahan with you."

"We are on the same errand, I take it."

She examined me beneath a lifted eyebrow. "Then you know what has happened at Light of the World?"

"It was a letter from your Reverend Ames that set our expedition in motion. So Mr. Brooke informs me."

"That letter." Hannover frowned. "A confusion of thought and a jumble of emotions. If it hadn't been for the handwriting, I never would have recognized the writer as Noel Ames. He is the soul of Light of the World—its center, a man of strength and self-possession. Before Noel and Susannah went up-country, there was no mission in all of northern Sumatra. He carried Christ to the Asahan."

"The self-possessed often become the self-absorbed," said Dr. Diem, inviting himself to the conversation and bowing as he entered. Following him was his assistant, Kung, who settled at the far side of the room.

"Or it may be he contracted a fever," Bridgett Hannover continued, nettled by the interruption.

Diem looked around for a chair. Finding none, he reluctantly settled on the pandanus mat beside Fahey. He had made no concession to the tropical heat—a cream-colored suit, a silk waistcoat, a black cravat tied meticulously at the throat.

Here's a tightly coiled spring, I remember thinking. There was an academic remoteness in his manner, an open and penetrating gaze that did not invite familiarity. He was light-skinned, the color of a hazelnut, and his hair was neatly parted and dressed low on his forehead. He had the languid, finely molded features of the Asian aristocrat, delicate, almost feminine. In all, he gave the impression of fastidiousness that could not help but make others in his company appear slightly disheveled in contrast, as if they had forgotten to tuck in a shirttail or pull up a stocking. My own shirt was squared away, I was relieved to note.

Diem lifted a wooden spoon to his lips, sniffed the rice gruel, and tasted it gingerly. "Perhaps you might let me take a look at that letter, Mrs. Hannover. I might be able to shed some light on the morbidity of your friend's mental state."

"Morbidity, Dr. Diem?" Hannover tried to control the irritation in her voice. "Perhaps this letter is none of your concern."

"I apologize!" Diem replied, his eyes widening at the recognition that he had been rude. "My studies in Paris centered on nervous disorders. Call it a clinician's curiosity. More often than not, this gets me into trouble." He offered a tentative, almost boyish smile.

"You are a long way from Paris, Dr. Diem," I said.

"We are all," Diem replied, looking around, "a long way from home, it would appear, Captain. My own people are Annamese. Radjah Dulah is an old family friend. This led to my appointment as physician to the radjah's family."

"Annam." Bridgett Hannover appeared to trace a map with her finger on the table. "A kingdom south of China."

"The Gulf of Tongkin," I added.

"Manchu China is due north—our erstwhile adversary."

"These days your Viet emperor had better look to his back," Fahey said, reaching past Diem for the plate of taro. "The French are already bringing over their furniture. All the way from Paris." He popped a ball of rice in his mouth.

"I leave those matters to the politicians. French medicine is what drew me to Paris. They lead the world in the study of nervous disorders and hysteria. You might say my sojourn with the radjah fulfills my practicum. His son, Prince Bandarak, suffers from some mental malady. The radjah thinks he is possessed of a demon."

"Noel Ames befriended the prince," said Bridgett Hannover. "And tried to help him."

"You haven't mentioned the American woman at the mission," I asked. "Deborah Rand."

"Deborah Rand?" Hannover replied, as if startled by the name. "I can only trust that God has kept her in his sight. And Susannah Ames."

Rowan Fahey reached for the bowl of mangoes. "Deborah Rand, was that the name?"

Hannover looked at him with new interest. "Do you know of her, Mr. Fahey?"

"It may be I heard of someone by that name in my rambles," he said, biting into the golden flesh of the fruit. "I hear many names. How does she look?"

Hannover clasped her hands before her and lowered her head as if it were an effort to recall. "Why, on the tall side, I suppose. From a missionary family. Connecticut or Rhode Island, I think. Although we learned of her through a relative in Hawaii."

"She has gray eyes." It was the first time Sahar had spoken, in a voice soft and low as a flute. "Like the eyes of a wolf."

"Where would you see a gray-eyed wolf in Sumatra?" Fahey chuckled at the idea.

"In a picture book of Mrs. Hannover's," Sahar said. "All the wolves in that book had gray eyes, like Miss Rand."

Hannover raised her eyes to the Irishman. "Does that sound like someone you know, Mr. Fahey?"

"Sounds like a lot of people I know," he replied with a noisy slurp of his curry stew.

"You raised quite a commotion for your people at Light of the World," I said to Hannover. "It takes a broadside to raise Dutch bureaucrats from their torpor."

Smiling at that, she spooned a dollop of rice onto a banana leaf and passed the bowl. "The fate of a few foreign missionaries at a remote outpost was the least of the governor's worries. He has his hands full protecting the seven thousand or so souls perched along the Musi River at Palembang, not to mention the outlying plantations."

"But our Mrs. Hannover prevailed," said Sahar, and there was no hiding the devotion in her voice.

"I made the situation at Light of the World the most of his worries."

"Aided by Providence, as you say," Fahey added, rubbing his chin.

"If you have Providence, you need aught else, gentlemen," she said quietly. "And my husband urged our enterprise."

"He guided us," said Sahar.

"He guides us in all things," the missionary said, as if this fact were widely known.

I couldn't hide my wonder. "Your husband let you make this risky journey—two women alone?"

"My husband is never far from me, Captain Vanders." Hannover produced a locket with a photogravure of an austere, sharp-featured man with melancholy eyes, thin to the point of frailty: an autumnal leaf clinging to a tree.

I don't know how long Devadatta had been standing outside the open window, but I abruptly became aware of the white turban and the flicker of his fingers. Excusing myself, I went outside. My engineer was pacing, fit to be tied.

"They've up and gone, Captain, sir."

"They?"

"Run off." He shook his fists. "These Malays are a shiftless, ignorant people! And very lazy."

"Calm down, Devadatta."

"We had about three quarters of the fuel loaded, sir. When I looked up, they were nowhere in sight."

"There must be a simple explanation. Perhaps they got hungry."

We walked behind the main house, and I noticed the cook-house was deserted, too. Only a slither of blue smoke rose from the clay pot pitched over the coals. The grounds seemed to have emptied out; even the animals were nowhere to be seen, and from the jungle came nothing but silence, not even the yapping of the excited dog. At the edge of the clearing, squatting on his haunches and pointing, was Diem's man, Kung. I squatted beside him and asked him what he had seen, but he didn't reply. His attention was on the jungle trail before us. His finger twitched like a divining rod.

"Too quiet of a sudden," said Fahey, by my side. He pulled his pistol from his belt. *My* pistol, I reminded myself with some chagrin.

Kung was on his feet. The next thing I knew, we were following him into the jungle and down the trail. About a hundred yards on was a stream that fed into the river to our right. Kung hopped over the stream. The trail led on a dozen more yards or so to a sun-dappled clearing, a break in the canopy of leaves that surrounded us. The station manager had been working this part of the forest for hardwood fuel.

This is where we found the first piece of clothing. The others had caught up with us. I held up the green cloth.

"A turban," said Devadatta. "One of my workers was wearing this."

As if to embody our unspoken fear, an unsettling roar broke the silence, startling a covey of wild pigeons. White-winged, they rose from the tangle of the clearing like fear itself.

"Tiger," said Fahey. "But he's far off."

"Oh, Lord!" Hannover covered her mouth and pointed to a tall ironwood tree at the far eastern edge of the clearing. Human or animal, we could not tell: a skinned torso had been impaled on the tree, its blood running down the bark.

A rustling in the thicket to the right caught my attention. I leaped over a fallen log and plunged into the wet confusion of leaves and vines. I followed the jungle trail, barely a pace wide, to a stream bordered by tall, lacy ferns and wild taro. I paused and knelt to listen. There was no sound but the soothing ripple of water over smooth stones. Cupping my hands, I dipped them into the cool water. I noticed how the exposed river stones formed a pattern, one that seemed oddly familiar. There were five of them, each larger than the other, like miniature stepping-stones that led out into the middle of the stream until it became lost in a tangle of sedge farther on. At this dark margin, the stream widened to a meandering river of another place and time until I discovered, with a twinge of apprehension, a glade of birch and elm and willow. Looking around, I remembered each tree, the patch of lilies of the valley growing out of the late winter's leaves, the carpet of moss along the river's edge, the twitter of sparrows overhead. They belonged to a Maryland spring of nine years before. Dogwood blossoms spun giddily in the Potomac current. There I found the five rocks, stepping-stones to deeper water. Here, where the river narrowed, she had claimed a rocky outcropping on which to perch and comb her hair. She had abandoned her shoes and stockings on the bank and jumped from rock to rock to where the water was dark and green. Petticoats and the hem of her yellow dress tucked about her knees, she sat on the boulder and ran a tortoiseshell comb down waves of long auburn hair. Even as I looked on and admired and yearned, her image faded and turned dark. When I looked down, I saw my hands outspread under the ripples of the stream, drowned and deathly white, and I was seized with panic.

"Captain Vanders, sir!"

Fahey's shout broke through my reverie. The stream was but a jungle watercourse again, overhung with ferns and the heart-shaped leaves of wild taro. A magnificent butterfly caught my eye, hovering in a beam of sunlight above a spiderweb. Its wide wings, as broad as my two hands together, were a deep royal blue and speckled with a spray of golden drops. Below, from a gossamer bridge across the stream, a fat, orange-bodied spider raised two legs like cutlasses and lunged. The butterfly knew its peril and flitted off. Foiled, the predator shook its silver net.

"Vanders, sir!"

The anxiety in his voice made me realize Fahey might think I was up to something. I weighed my chances of surprising him against the safety of the others. Reluctantly, I trudged back the way I came, making as much noise as possible.

Everyone was crowded around the ironwood tree when I emerged into the clearing. I recognized that the torso was that of a small dog, impaled on the tree trunk with a short-feathered spear.

"I searched but found nothing," I said to appease Fahey's scowl.

"His yapping days are over." The Irishman pulled at the spear, and the carcass dropped to the base of the tree.

Bridgett Hannover dropped her hands from her eyes. "It's not a child!"

"Is that what you saw, Mrs. Hannover?" Fahey laughed. "It's a mongrel as ugly as God makes them. Uglier, without its skin."

"This is a Kubu warning," Sahar said, examining the spear.

"Their villages are in the Kampar River basin. I do not know what they are doing so far south of their homeland."

"What kind of a warning?" I asked.

"It is best that we all go back to the boat," she replied, turning from the macabre sight. A pale Bridgett Hannover slipped her arm about the girl's waist, and they started back to the station. Bridgett Hannover gave me a conflicted glance, but we all realized that, whatever had happened to the station workers, we had best look to our own safety. As if to confirm our decision, another ghostly roar greeted us, but this time closer, beyond the clearing with its disturbing omen. We returned to the station grounds not exactly in full flight but moving as swiftly and silently as we could. Fahey covered our retreat.

Thirty minutes later Devadatta and I finished carrying wood into the engine room while Fahey kept watch from the top deck. There was little in the way of provisions at the station, and no one left to buy them from, but fortunately, *Lorelei* had come with a full larder of rice and flour. Fish, fruit, and wild game were plentiful along the coast. With all accounted for, we slipped the mooring lines and left the deserted station. *Lorelei* was once more under way, a plume of dark smoke billowing from her stack and the great stern-wheel churning.

We made good speed the rest of the day, Devadatta having informed me that there was enough fuel aboard to reach the next station on the Kampar River, some hundred miles up the coast. We could make that with a night and another day of steady steaming, provided the weather held and the sea remained calm. Then we would reach a crisis. The Kampar peninsula was the midpoint of our journey north to the Asahan. It was also Sumatra's closest point to Malaya, the jumping-off spot from which Fahey wanted us to veer across the strait so he could link up with his fellow outlaws in Malacca.

While our passengers napped to escape the heat, I spent the afternoon in the wheelhouse fretting over my stolen command, knowing that I must do something soon. The party was still intact and alive, the flurry of excitement at the fueling station having delayed any deadly plans Fahey may have had. Most certainly, he would act by the time we reached the Kampar. There was one thing in my favor. Fahey was a conspiracy of one, and that left me three other men to organize into a force. He had the firearms, that was true, but he couldn't remain on guard throughout the night and day following. At some point he would drop his guard, and we must be prepared to disarm him. I decided to confide in Devadatta. Although we hadn't spoken of it, I knew he suspected some kind of trouble with Fahey. I felt sure I could count on my engineer's loyalty and resourcefulness. With the felon back in irons, I could then weigh the choice of heading back and turning myself in or continuing with the mission. Perhaps not much of a choice, but completing the mission held out the hope that Charles Brooke might intercede and straighten out the mess I had gotten myself in. After all, I mused ruefully, I was the *only* captain in his damned navy.

That was not all that preoccupied my thoughts as we steamed north; I was disturbed by a deeper apprehension that had stayed with me since our jungle excursion earlier that day. The apparition I had encountered by the stream was no illusion of the night but something seen, in the words of the poet, "as I lay broad waking."

She had leaped out of my memory like Athena out of the head of Jove, but instead of spear and shield, she came armed with a history of sorrows. I had no doubt where memory had transported me—nine years before, on a warm spring day in 1866, along the sun-dappled banks of the Potomac River.

A fine setting for a sunny romance, it held a somber tale. I had sought to bury it deep, a sailor's guilty secret sealed in a lead casket and sunk in bottomless ocean. But like the miser's stolen slippers, the casket kept fatefully reappearing. I would see it washed up on a forlorn island's shores or glimpsed among the exotic goods of a floating bazaar, or inexplicably waiting with my gear as I crossed the bow to a new berth and a new ship.

I had dreamed of marrying Grace Tremaine ever since I had first seen her in her father's gig in the summer of 1863, not long after the battle of Gettysburg, a flowery bonnet tilting on her auburn tresses, a taunting look in those willful gray eyes. Winning her was a far chance, I knew, for she had more suitors than my namesake's Penelope and, though barely seventeen, possessed the attributes of beauty, grace, and wit to deserve them. She was less scrupulous than the beautiful Ithacan, though: she was more conscious of the powerful hold she had over men, and loved to lead them on a dance. That is not to say Ulysses's wife did not enjoy toying with the trifling suitors. Such play was more than amusement, though, for she defended honor, home, and hearth. Grace Tremaine's conceits were more Circe-like. If she did not revel in turning men to swine, she had no compunction about turning them into puppy dogs nipping at her heels or lambkins gamboling about her on the green.

I was among those gambolers, I confess. I did not care what I was turned into as long as it was delighting to her eyes. My suit was made all the more desperate by the fact that my only brother, Morgan, had declared his love for the same girl.

Naturally, this led to a sharper complication, not the least because it was Morgan's way to covet whatever was mine, even if I didn't have it yet. I meant to curtail him. So, flush with my appointment as first lieutenant in the United States Navy, buoyed by a commendation for my war service, and with every reason to believe a valorous naval career was before me, I took Grace Tremaine picnicking on the Potomac. I meant to propose marriage and seal the promise of our union before Morgan or anyone else could do so.

She began teasing me right away, not the least by taking off her stockings and shoes and stepping barefoot over rocks that led out to the deeper current. There she placed herself on a rocky outcropping and, hiking her skirts above her knees, let loose her long, flowing auburn hair so that it shimmered in the sunlight.

With some ceremony, she began brushing it. I'm sure she knew what effect this display would have on me; she was not ignorant of the constraints on sailors at sea, her father having been a merchant captain whose contributions to the war had been partly responsible for landing him a seat in the Maryland State Senate. She also knew the depth of my passion for her, which had been scrawled across scores of ardent shipboard letters during the last two years of the war. Being so close to her at last, I was nearly sick with anticipation and desire, but also stung by her manipulation, and when I joined her on the outcropping that overlooked the swift, dark green current of the river, I pressed my suit. She laughed gaily, thrilled by my adoration, thrilled that she could bring forth such half-articulate passion from a young man. She allowed me to take her hand, she allowed me to kiss it, but when I attempted to take her in my arms, she pushed me away and took a peevish and sarcastic tone. I mistook myself, she said; I was behaving like a boyish boor; but at length her biting words edged ever closer to a truth I would not comprehend or credit but could not ignore.

"It's Morgan, isn't it?" I cried, rising and standing over her as she continued to deliberately, methodically run the tortoiseshell brush down her hair.

"Run along and get the picnic basket," she said, laughing with full knowledge of my humiliation and jealousy. "I'm hungry, Ulysses."

There were just the two of us in this wooded river glade, far from town, together and alone, each of us leagues apart from the other, filled and empty with our separate hungers.

I was standing directly over her, looking down as she made careful strokes with the brush, the white skin of her smooth calves bright against the gray lichen-sided rock, the swirling current five feet below. I was suddenly possessed of an anger I had never felt before, a rage that made me shiver as I stood barefoot on the cold, rough rock beside the coldhearted girl. I wanted to pull her up and shake her free of her coy traps and coquetries, until the warm, loving woman I sensed at last emerged, and in this fit of shame and anger and frustration, I reached down and grasped her shoulders, my senses entangled in the earthy, lilac scent of her hair, the cool spray of the deep water as it raced below, speaking to me a furtive and Mephistophelean counsel. I closed my eyes, trying to close my mind against the inescapable thoughts that took giddy hold of me . . .

~⌒

On opening my eyes, I beheld Mephisto himself, at least in his Irish incarnation, leaning heavily against the doorway of the wheelhouse, wearing the familiar rakish smirk that confirmed the winning cards he held. We stood for a while, neither of us speaking. The sun was already beginning to dip below the mountains on our port side, giving some relief from the fabulous Sumatra heat. Finally, Rowan Fahey pulled my pistol from his belt and hefted it.

"Union sidearm, isn't it?"

"A Navy Colt. You can tell by the two men-of-war engraved on the cylinder."

Fahey examined the gun admiringly. "There's a stylish touch, isn't it! Union naval officer, was that your ambition? Why, you mustn't have been much more than a sprat when things kicked up."

"I went to sea at thirteen, and at seventeen, I found myself aboard a frigate chasing down Confederate blockade runners."

He tapped my chest with the barrel of the revolver. "It might surprise you to know that blockade running was a former specialty of mine."

"No surprise," I answered, surly enough.

"That war has been over for a decade. There's a decade I won't see again. Just as well," he added ruefully.

"Running guns kept you busy. Or was it robbing banks?"

Fahey burst out laughing. "Busting banks always seemed such a birdbrained enterprise. Most of the birds get caught."

"Then how about kidnapping, extortion, and murder? That might be a way to come out to the Orient and make a name for yourself."

"No call for perjoration, Vanders." Fahey's resentful tone suggested I had given offense, but I suspected he reveled in any steepening of his notoriety. "I never undertook a job that had the shedding of blood as its object. I admit to the romance of occasionally robbing trains."

"That's how you see yourself, isn't it—as some kind of a romantic rogue. You've got a dozen seas and the Pacific to plunder and pillage."

"Oh, a veritable Bully Hayes, I am!" he averred, quite pleased. "Now, yourself, you must have held a commission at the end of your war, after all that derring-do."

"First lieutenant."

"Then you would have been in line for a captaincy ere long, and a career toting about gold braid and ceremonial swords and undoing the young debs who threw themselves at your feet. What was your rank on that ship in the Kuching harbor, the *Siren*? First mate, wasn't it? Thereby hangs a tale."

"That's where we'll leave it, then—hanging."

"All right," Fahey agreed, "that's where we'll leave both our tales. Besides, it's the present enterprise that brings me knocking at your door."

"I suppose you want me to swing into the next clearing in the mangrove and tell our guests to swim for it."

"You're bound to think the worst of me. Actually, I've come to hand over your pistol and play the role of first mate in earnest—under certain conditions."

He flipped the revolver over and handed me the weapon. I looked at him closely, suspicion mingling with disbelief. I took hold of the handle of the gun, but he still held tightly to the barrel. "Under certain conditions," he repeated.

"All right, what do you have in mind?"

"The short of it is that I'm willing to pitch in with your little adventure and say we head up the Asahan to that mission of Mrs. Hannover's." Now I was merely astonished. He held up his hand. "Don't ask me for explanations. I'll sign on as first mate for the duration. Besides, I know something of the territory, at least as far as the Asahan."

"All right, let's hear your conditions."

He held up three fingers. "First, there will be no mention of my having been your prisoner. Second, when the business is over at the mission, you head across the strait to the place I've told you about, drop me off, and that will be the end of us. You and I will be quits, free and clear."

"And third?"

"That wog doctor and his little pal, Kung, get dumped off at the next fueling station."

"What have you got against Diem?"

Fahey turned down his lips in distaste. "Prissy little bastard, isn't he? He's got the jinx written all over him." He shook the barrel of the gun. "That's my offer, and it's not for deliberation. It's for here and now. And I'll want your word on it."

The thought crossed my mind to have at him and decide the issue then and there, but his grip on the pistol told me the contest would be gravely in doubt.

"What if I don't agree to your terms?"

He angled his big, curly head to the port side of the ship. "There's a clearing in the mangrove right over there."

"All right, then. You get two out of the three. I'll let you have your liberty; I'll get you to safe harbor after the mission. But I'll be damned if I'm going to dump my passengers in the middle of the Sumatra jungle." I gripped the handle of the gun more firmly. "Especially a prize like Diem. Stowaway or not, jinx or not, the fact that Diem turned up on this ship is nothing short of Bridgett Hannover's Providence at work. Prissy and arrogant or not, the man has a direct line to Radjah Dulah. Do you know what that means? The radjah is the one man in northern Sumatra who has the power to help us. We'll need him if we're going to get to Light of the World, and we'll need him if there's anybody to get out. Diem stays, or we've got no deal."

Fahey seemed on the point of taking back his offer, but his look softened. The pistol slipped into my hand. "I'll want your word on it," he said.

As we shook hands, I became aware of another presence standing outside the wheelhouse. Dr. Diem's pince-nez caught the crimson fires of the sun before he removed them and pulled a linen handkerchief from his breast pocket to clean them. Fahey released my hand and shouldered Diem aside as he left.

"That man doesn't like me," said Diem, squinting after the Irishman as he descended the ladder.

"Mr. Rowan Fahey has little in the way of goodwill for his fellows. He's not motivated by your brand of idealism, Dr. Diem."

"Altruism, if that is what you mean—I'd substitute the term with curiosity, of a perverse order. I like to search out the keys to our haunted rooms, the ones we are afraid to enter." He carefully folded the handkerchief and slipped it back into his pocket. "Perhaps I am a voyeur, most of all." He placed the pince-nez precisely on the bridge of his short nose, as if to examine my reaction to his little joke. "At the moment, Captain, I am in search of some peace of mind. Master Kung and I are stowaways, after all."

It was a good hour to seek peace of mind, with the sun low on the horizon. Ahead, a spray of white wind-blown blossoms bobbed in the smooth water. In the slanted beams of twilight they seemed like paper boats bearing votive candles.

"Then perhaps you can clear up the mystery as to how you stole aboard."

"Master Kung and I had been keeping close watch on *Lorelei* from the Prince William Hotel, especially since your arrival on board in the care of Beets's soldiers. We'd been stranded in Kota Baru for over a week, and I was desperate to get to Bahal, Radjah

Dulah's capital on the Asahan. When Fahey overpowered the guards, we saw our chance and slipped aboard. I thought you might be heading for Palembang. From there I might be able to hire transport up the coast. But as it is, your destination coincides with mine precisely. Money is no object—or we can make ourselves useful."

"I know of no stowaways aboard *Lorelei*. Doctor."

Diem nodded as if he'd expected that answer. "Your acceptance is extended to both of us, I take that to mean."

"Then answer a question for me. I've been puzzled by what happened back there at Jambi Station. Kung... he sensed, before any of us, that something was wrong."

Diem revealed something of a smile. "His people are Gobi people, and among them he is regarded as something of a diviner and a healer. But he is a wanderer most of all. He has known many trades; earning his way, like most men in Asia, by the sweat of his brow."

"I have not heard him complain. I have not heard any word from him, for that matter."

"Nor will you. Master Kung is a mute. He is able-bodied, and even been to sea. Besides, he is a masterful cook, even with the simplest fare."

"He has already found a friend in my engineer. I saw Kung teaching Devadatta that sign language of his earlier." I pointed out a school of porpoises off our starboard bow, admiring their grace as they lifted their sleek bodies out of the water.

"We humans are the malcontents," Diem remarked, echoing my unspoken thought. "As for the signing language, I taught Kung. The system was devised by a Frenchman, Abbé Sicard. Your man Devadatta, by the way, tells me it will be a week before we sight the mouth of the river."

"Devadatta is my engineer, Doctor, and no man's but his own."

"No offense offered, Captain."

I pulled down the navigation chart and spread it out across the drop leaf that made into a plotting board. "I count four days to the mouth of the Asahan, including fueling stops and layovers to strip and clean the boiler. The trip up the river is another tale—fifty miles of water that could end up seeming like five hundred. It's a deep river, and wide enough for maneuvering the first ten miles—at least according to sailors I talked to in Kuching. But none of them had been up the river. And we have no guide until we get to Bahal, Radjah Dulah's capital. Although we might pick up one at a trading post along the way."

"So we don't know how long it will take," Diem said with a frown. "What else worries you?"

"I worry about the weather. I worry about malaria. I worry about rebels against the Dutch. Roving bands of headhunters. The heat, the damned insects. But most of all, the weather. If we're lucky, we'll have three weeks before the monsoon sets in. After that, *Lorelei* won't be able to navigate the river, upstream or down."

Diem made a slight bow and then turned before stepping out of the wheelhouse. "Curious, about Mrs. Hannover this afternoon."

"How do mean?"

"She mistook that flayed and decapitated dog for a child."

"Should I make something of that, Doctor?"

But he had gone, and I was grateful to get back to my navigation without having to stage a coup or watch my passengers walk the plank. I was grateful, but I would have been more settled if Dr. Diem had given me an answer.

7

The east coast of Sumatra is like a great baroque cathedral organ whose pipes are made of mangrove, nipa palm, and bamboo. For six hundred miles, a dozen rivers pour into the sea and make an intricate fugue. The Jambi River bubbles along in a kind of breathless ease, the Kampar rolls along in a resonant continuo. Farther north, the black reptilian waters of the Rokan speak of bleak despair. The Asahan River, its source in Lake Tuba's magical waters, teases our ears with supple, elusive harmonies. All along this fertile and undulating coastline, the waters teem with fish, the sky aches with birds, especially along the estuaries that are the outpourings of the island's earthly music, and now and then a great rhinoceros comes crashing out of the jungle, its head erect and nostrils flared in an ecstasy of alarm.

Along those winding rivers of sound, one finds the people of Sumatra in hints and clues. Sheer walls of vegetation, for the most part, hem in the riverbanks. The clues to habitation are the openings in the walls, inlets that wander through the overgrown labyrinth until, by sheer illusion, a turn reveals a break in the gnarly, miasmal swamp and a village is revealed, standing on stilts like boys startled by their own ingenuity, and circled by a stockade. Beyond the waterways, the interior of the island is deserted except for the great beasts that roam the land, the herds of wild carabao and elephants that lumber through the forests like earthquakes, the tigers, the orangutans and a dozen other primates, and other species that have yet to be classified or even seen by living men. Like the unspinning of a stray thought, a jungle track will lead to a patch of wet rice or taro or yams, or perhaps to the next village, but beyond these familiar points, all trails dissolve into the rain forest, and the rest of the island belongs to the children of nature. Only the primitive hunting and gathering tribes venture into the vast and subtle warrens of its forests, but they are rarely seen . . .

The long, muggy heat of the afternoon had drawn to a close. I put down Alfred Wallace's notes on Sumatra. Two days out from our fueling stop on the Jambi River, we had paused to maintain the engine. Any wildlife such as Wallace described had been driven off by Devadatta's clamor as he blew the boiler and scaled it free of brine. The banging and scraping scarcely came to my ears, so absorbing did I find Wallace's account, but the din had ceased, and I became aware of someone standing beside me.

"Seems we have another uninvited guest aboard," said Fahey, crooking his finger.

We walked around to the starboard side, and Fahey motioned me to be quiet. We were standing outside the louvered window of the cabin Mrs. Hannover shared with Sahar. The conversation between the two women rose and fell with anxious words. I was about to reprimand Fahey for not minding his own business when a man's voice, frail and unintelligible, interrupted the two women.

"I've forgiven you," Hannover's voice answered in a trancelike whisper. "You know I've—"

The man replied in an accusatory tone, the words again lost.

"You've seen how I love you," Hannover implored. And then: "Get that slut out of here!" There was a crash of crockery against the cabin wall. "Get her out!"

"Mrs. Hannover. Mrs. Hannover, are you all right?" I tried the door handle, but it was locked. An abrupt silence followed by a groan and muffled cries.

"Go away!" Sahar warned us.

"I'm afraid I must ask you to open this door."

"Leave us be!"

"We'll break it down if we have to!" Fahey shouted.

The key turned in the lock, and Sahar opened the door halfway. Pieces of a water pitcher lay scattered on the floor behind her. She had thrown off her veil; her dark, lustrous hair was loose and in disarray. She glared at us, determined to protect her mistress. I felt the young woman's uncanny power, made all the more telling by the stigmatism, a barrier she kept between herself and the world.

"I'd like to speak to Mrs. Hannover," I said firmly.

"She's not well."

"Perhaps I can help." It was Dr. Diem at my elbow.

"She is in *my* care!"

"It's all right, Sahar." Hannover's voice came weakly from within. "Let them in."

Reluctantly, the Malay woman stepped aside. Mrs. Hannover lay on her cot, a compress across her forehead, the back of one hand pressed against her lips.

"We were—alarmed," I said, trying to cover my embarrassment.

"I'm fine, Captain. I felt faint." Diem sat on her cot and lifted her wrist. "It's only the heat," she protested.

"So where's your chum?" Fahey stood in the middle of the floor with a suspicious and uneasy air.

"There's no one else here," Sahar replied tartly. "You can see for yourself."

"We heard the voice of a man."

"I've been ill." Hannover looked at us in some confusion.

"She has fits," said Sahar. "They pass."

"Her pulse is three times the normal rate," said Diem. "I can provide a sedative."

"*I'll* take care of her." Sahar went over to Hannover's side and placed a protective hand on her shoulder.

"I'll be fine," said Hannover, looking up meekly at Sahar and taking her hand. "I'll just rest awhile."

"Kung has been making some soup," I said, not knowing what else to say as I backed out of the cabin. "Perhaps some broth..."

"Yes, some broth..."

❧

"I don't care what any man says," Fahey said with a belligerent shake of his head. "I heard what I heard. And so did the captain here."

"I don't know what I heard, Fahey."

"I came too late to hear," said Diem, flaking aside some of the white flesh of the fish before him with his knife. "But I would hazard a guess that Mrs. Hannover's companion is a *turahan*."

Kung emerged from the makeshift galley in the cargo hold, bearing a bowl of rice. He placed it between us, exchanged a wordless sign with Diem, bowed, and departed.

"He's a good cook," said Fahey, helping himself to another from the plate of fried snapper.

"What do you mean, Dr. Diem, a *turahan*?"

"A medium, an adept—that's the rough meaning of the word. You've noticed the stigmatism. Among the Malay, that's a sign that she has the gift."

"I took her for a witch, with that evil eye of hers," harrumphed Fahey. "Odd company for Hannover."

The yellow flame stirred in the storm lantern as if in reply. Its light fell on the wooden bowls in front of us. Gathered on the foredeck we sat on flour kegs as we ate our evening meal. The impenetrable night surrounded us, and the water lapped against the hull, driven by just enough wind to keep most of the insects down.

"I lived among the Bataks when I was a boy," said Diem. "My

father was a businessman in Canton, and he had dealings with the feudal lords, or *datus*, of northern Sumatra, in Atjeh and around Lake Toba. My father often traveled to Sumatra in the old days, for he liked to keep his hands in the pot, as he was fond of saying. He didn't trust his agents, at least not very far. It was about 1835 or so—very soon after the Dutch put down a Muslim revolt—that he formed a partnership and then a friendship with Radjah Dulah. The radjah had been a good ally during the revolt, and the Dutch rewarded him by giving him a free hand in the north. When I was fifteen, the radjah extended his hospitality to me. I lived at the radjah's court for over a year. I made friends with the radjah's son, Prince Bandarak."

I scooped some rice and fish onto a hard biscuit. "This is the same Bandarak the radjah believes is possessed."

"His only son."

Fahey wiped his hands on his trousers and reached for the coffeepot. "So what does all this have to do with the missionary's spook chaser?"

"I suppose that is where my interest in mesmerism finds its origin. Among the Batak people, the *turahan* holds a high place of honor. The radjah's favorite wife, Prince Bandarak's mother, consulted her *turahan* before she turned Christian."

"Mesmerism!" Fahey said in a malicious tone. "I've seen one of 'em at work, and a dandy show it was. He had one fellow going, standing on his head and singing lullabies, and the other one swallowing goldfish. Once it was all over, neither of them could remember any of it. Except for the goldfish eater, that is. He puked all over the stage." Fahey guffawed and winked at me.

Diem didn't allow himself to be drawn in. He removed his pince-nez and rubbed the bridge of his nose. "You may think they are mere showmen, Mr. Fahey. But Anton Mesmer was the first man to undertake a scientific cure for mental ailments since the ancient Greeks."

Fahey turned bored. "When things start turning to the ancient Greeks, I know I'll never get a straight answer." He tossed the dregs of his cup over the bow and stood up. "I'll bid good night."

Diem appeared to check himself from saying something as Fahey clomped up to the second deck.

"The *turahan,*" I reminded him.

"Perform two important functions," said Diem, polishing his lenses with a handkerchief. "They operate independently of the shamans and sorcerers, the *gurus.* They are a kind of people apart. The *turahan* mediate between our world and the spirit world. That is what Sahar is to Mrs. Hannover. Mrs. Hannover has suffered a great loss—and recently."

"Do you think that is what her behavior in the forest was about? Back at the Jambi, I mean."

Diem weighed the question before he replied. "She also spoke of her husband, if you'll recall. I do not know what the background is here, but Sahar is the link to whatever she has lost."

"I find it hard to believe that Mrs. Hannover has employed a medium."

"Why should that be so strange? When a Malay succumbs to a superstitious fear, no one bats an eye. But when a European starts seeing demons and talking to ghosts, we question his sanity."

"I see what you mean."

"Do you?" Diem asked doubtfully.

⚓

On my way back to my cabin, I climbed to the wheelhouse to inform Devadatta of the watch-standing schedule. I knew that he and Kung had taken to having their meals by the longboat. As I climbed, a sweet haunting melody suddenly took hold of me and transported me back to America, ten years before. It was a Union sailor's ballad, "Shenandoah," and I had not heard it for many years. The sound of the harmonica was a whisper above the breeze. I saw Kung's silhouette as he crooned to the night sky crowded with stars. Devadatta sat cross-legged on the deck and waved his finger to and fro. I stood in the darkness unseen, heartsick at a song that brought back memories of home and a country I had lost and to which I could not return. I had learned how to suppress such thoughts, but since the Jambi River, this had become harder to do.

"Where did he learn that?" I barely spoke the words, but my voice was loud enough that Kung broke off his song.

"Oh, Captain, did you not know that Master Kung here served on an American whaler? Truly, he knows some very Yankee songs."

"Your Chinese friend is full of surprises."

"He has seen a few things, been here and there."

That seemed to me as accurate a description of Kung, on a succinct level, as I myself had observed. Even his clothes were a patchwork of places he had been. He favored a red tartary skullcap and a blue cotton vest bordered with frayed embroidery. His pantaloons were of the loose kind worn by Chinese coolies. The belt, though, was made of thin iron plates, and its buckle was a square of carved whalebone. A curious array of tins, philters, and a small brass gong hung from it. Around his neck, Kung wore an amulet, a shark's tooth etched with a tiny outspread hand, and a pouch that I supposed contained a fetish or a magic powder. He was either supremely innocent or full of guile; every feeling was plainly written on the shifting geography of his face, with a slightly comic transparency, expressed by a curious twist or skew of his eyebrows. Add to this a wispy set of whiskers that were not quite mustaches, and here was a sage or fool, take your pick, whose very appearance proclaimed his difference and his outlook on the world. His first duty was looking after Diem, which he went about with quiet efficiency. He had taken over the galley, as Diem had suggested, producing savory and much appreciated meals. With Devadatta, he had struck up a friendship based, as I took it, on the intuition of kindred spirits. Besides, my ever curious engineer had quickly learned Kung's signing language.

"We are trading our mysteries," said Devadatta. "I am training him to become an assistant engineer. He, in turn, is teaching me about his oracle.' "

"What might this be?" I asked, sitting beside them and accepting Kung's offer of tea.

"It has to do with that bag of sticks, 'wands,' he calls them, that he carries about in that pouch. It's an old Chinese art, he claims, going back to the beginning. Everything is in constant motion, the sky, the earth, the oceans, the forests, and so on. You affirm the changes of things when you toss the sticks. They fall in a certain pattern. So you can come to the changes seeking advice."

"An oracle, is it? All right, ask Master Kung to toss the sticks for me. What's waiting for us up the Asahan? What will we find at Light of the World?"

The engineer made a series of hand gestures, and Kung nodded. Devadatta moved the candle back to his knees so Kung had room for the toss. Sweeping the surface of the deck with his palm, Kung tugged the sticks loose from the pouch and threw them down. He then picked them up from the deck and divided them into two bunches. He subdivided these into bundles of four. After he broke them into six piles, he took out a scrap of paper and the stub of a pencil from a tin on his belt and wrote down a pattern—a series of six lines, three complete, three broken. I looked at Devadatta, who began an animated conversation in signs. When they had finished, Kung lifted his hands, palms together, three times to his forehead.

"He says the oracle is called the Well. There are a set number of patterns, each one with a name."

"What does the Well signify?"

"The thing you desire," Devadatta translated Kung's signs.

Kung pointed to one set of sticks put to one side. "There's something else. It means ..." The engineer shook his head.

"Go on, then."

"Beware of getting the thing you desire."

⤙⊸

Devadatta's work on the boiler wasn't finished until late, so we anchored in place that night. I took the opportunity to return to Alfred Wallace's notes. The more I read of the biologist's 1857 journey into the Sumatra wilderness, the more it seemed like the account of a waking dream. I didn't know exactly where this blending of fact and fancy began, perhaps with his first sighting of the Golden Sura. The Sura was not his object; indeed, he didn't even know of its existence at the time. He was looking for another elusive specimen, the leaf butterfly, a spray of rainbow color in its flight but almost impossible to find once it alights, so perfectly does the camouflage pattern on its folded wings resemble a jungle leaf. Wallace had caught sight of one and went racing under the forest canopy to capture it. He became separated from his guide and realized he had gotten himself lost. After walking in circles for close to half an hour, he made the one error you cannot afford to make in the bush: he lost reason and panicked. Crying out for his guide, he ran—

A rapping on the cabin door abruptly ended my reading. My pocket watch told me it was nearly midnight. I had left Kung and Devadatta sipping tea on the top deck nearly two hours ago, and I thought everyone had turned in. When I opened the door, a flustered Mrs. Hannover apologized for the intrusion. She wore a white silk shawl over her gray dress and was ill at ease until I insisted that her presence was not an intrusion. "I am sorry to disturb you," she said, refusing my offer of a chair. "It's late, I know, and I won't detain you long. I couldn't sleep—I couldn't sleep until I explained. About earlier this evening."

"There's no need, Mrs. Hannover."

"Sahar is very protective of me." She gripped the edges of her shawl with rough, chafed hands. The plain gold wedding band seemed embedded in the flesh of her finger. "Sometimes the truth of the matter gets confused . . ." She cleared her throat, not looking at me directly. "The truth of things is that my husband, Miles, is gone from me. For over a year now. He was killed in a hunting accident outside of Palembang. Since then . . . It was at the time of my grief that Sahar appeared. She had been recommended to me by someone in our native congregation. She has been of great solace to me."

"As a *turahan*."

She looked at me with astonishment. "Then you know." She gave out a sigh as if a great burden had passed from her. "This makes things much easier. Thanks to Sahar, I have found my Miles again. Ours has been a great companionship, Captain Vanders, and one not to be thwarted by the veil that separates this world from the next. And there is a next world, as sure as I stand here before you. Sahar's gift has confirmed my faith. Though many might laugh or condemn—"

"If it's a matter of my discretion—"

"I merely wished to bring the matter to your understanding. Your consideration—shows in you. Though you may think our meeting merely fortuitous, I believe my husband guided me to the *Lorelei*. And he will help see us to our goal."

"We shall need all the help we can to get up the Asahan," I replied. "Natural or supernatural."

"In the time of our Savior," Mrs. Hannover affirmed, "the supernatural *was* natural. Beyond this, I trust in your seamanship, Captain."

"I'm glad I have your confidence."

She produced an envelope from beneath her shawl. "I have the letter from Noel Ames, the letter that has set your expedition in motion. I think it only fair that you know what it contains." She pulled out several sheets of paper. "It begins like this." She held up the first page with a neat, minuscule script. "And ends like this." The writing on the last sheet sloped across the page in a nearly illegible scrawl. "The letter is meandering, written over three days. Listen:

" 'I can't tell you, my dear Bridgett, the sense of imminence that has gripped my soul these past few days. And yet it is mingled with the feeling of the most exalted ecstasy. These feelings are so intense, I tremble.... It is as if I have become attuned to the very respiration in a leaf, the flutter of a bird alighting in some distant forest . . . I am changed, changed, and exalted in my crime. Forgive me, dear Bridgett, if you can.

" 'How could she have been among us for so long all unknown? It was all there. So simple. We have traduced her, spurned her, suppressed her. Listen to her pace outside my window in the dark. Listen to her growl. What folly! "For she shall take the bitter fruit and make it sweet, the brackish water and make it pure." How dull we have been to be led by blind prophets!'

"The rest is in this vein." She folded the papers and slipped them back into the envelope.

"Written in a delirium."

"Yes, I could attribute this to fever. Especially since his previous letters were so filled with his projects, his plans to expand his work into the outlying villages, to set up chapels and dispensaries. He begged me for more medical supplies. Noel is also a physician, a pragmatic man, a man of action not given to the visionary side of religion. The man who wrote this is not the Noel Ames I know."

"This woman he spoke of, someone among us, someone unknown. Who might this be?"

"If anyone at all . . ." She looked away. "The letter itself was a cause for alarm. But when I heard what the tribesmen had to say, I knew I must act."

"Those who brought the letter?"

"Minangkabau Horseriders—Christians. They were terrified. A horde of demons—the Mamaqs, they called them—had fallen on some of their villages near Lake Toba. Many were slaughtered. Not long after, Reverend Ames left the mission on some church business. Before he left, he entrusted them with this letter. That night their village was attacked, but they drove off the Mamaqs. The following morning they moved their families into the Barisan Mountains for safety, and the two men set out for Palembang with Ames's letter."

"This happened nearly two months ago."

"It took the messengers three weeks to travel overland to Palembang. That's over four hundred miles of rugged country, even on horseback."

"And of the others—Mrs. Ames and the American, Deborah Rand?"

"Miss Deborah Rand." She placed a slight underscore on the word "Miss," as if to isolate it. "Both of them were to accompany Noel into the north country. At least that is what he told the Horseriders."

"You've told me something about Noel's character. What can you tell me about the missionaries?"

Hannover was fanning herself with the envelope. She blew at a wisp of wet hair that had slid down her brow. "It's so close in here. Do you mind if we continue our talk on the deck?"

"No, of course."

The moon had come up, a full moon so intense that it obliterated any traces of the stars and shed beams of light, like the folds of a cloak, along the surface of the water. The frogs were out in full chorus, and from time to time we heard the odd clacking sound, like two hollow pieces of wood struck together, made by crocodiles in search of a mate.

"The Ameses and the Hannovers go back some years," she began, crossing her shawl over her breast. "Miles and Noel and Susannah and I worked among the Arunda primitives in Australia for three years before we found new assignments in the Indies. But we had met long before that—on a pilgrimage to Jerusalem.

Noel is from Boston, where our ministry has its headquarters, but Susannah is from an old Pennsylvania Quaker family. They are opposites. He is flamboyant, befriends everyone at the drop of a hat, very—physical, as I've said. Susannah is the kind of person who goes about everything patiently and efficiently. Noel jokingly refers to her as his 'silent partner.' And it's true; Susannah is a quietist, in both senses. Both Miles and I were so happy when the church synod gave their approval for Light of the World. Miles had petitioned on their behalf. The ministry was reluctant at first . . ."

"Why?"

"Because so little is known about Sumatra. The ministry likes to place its resources where it knows it will have government backing and support. In Australia, the territorial government wanted a missionary presence to help stop the white settlers from killing off the Arunda. They would hunt the tribesmen like animals. We put a stop to that. We were all proud of our work among the Arunda."

"I would have guessed you had spent time in Australia."

She found this amusing in a way that suggested she had heard it before. "From my accent, you mean. My speech is a hotchpotch and melting pot of every place I've lived. But I was born in English coal country, in Lancashire. My father immigrated to Canada when I was girl. He was after gold, but he never found it. He never realized that his true riches were in his family, in the good Scotch-Irish woman who married him and bore him seven children, the woman he treated with coldness and contempt."

"I was not trying to pry, Mrs. Hannover."

"No, I know that." She sighed. "I'm glad my father raised me to be a scoffer and an atheist."

"You—an atheist." I was surprised again by this unprepossessing woman who had led such an original life.

"Oh, yes. I imbibed the dark liquor of my father's pessimism. And I emerged out of that blindness to find Miles. We met in

Kansas before the Civil War—or 'Bloody Kansas,' as it was known—for the territory had become a battleground between slaveholders and the Free Soilers. Miles was an abolitionist and the most powerful preacher I had ever heard. His voice was an instrument of salvation—of my salvation. I went to hear him speak because I liked his politics, and then I came to like his God. For there is more than one Power, Mr. Vanders, so Miles believed. 'They contend with each other like prizefighters, and the purse is our obedience,' he would say. Miles said that he had put his money on Jehovah, but the fight was still in the early rounds.

"We were married within one month, and I don't think we were ever more than two or three years in one place after that. Those were good years." She drew herself up, as if against the luxury of a fond memory. "I thank you, Captain, for listening. I know it's late."

"The other missionary at Light of the World," I persisted. I wanted to talk. "Deborah Rand. How did she come to Light of the World?"

We strolled forward until we stood at the railing that overlooked the bow. The mangrove thickets concealed the shore in a dark, shapeless tangle off our port side. "I knew her mother's family, the Birnhams. One of them, Deborah's aunt, had joined our ministry in Hawaii. Mrs. Birnham wrote to ask if we might find a place for her niece, then twenty-two, in the East Indies. Noel Ames had written us not long before, asking if we could send someone up to Light of the World; his teacher, a Mr. Towndes, had just died of the fever. The position seemed ready-made, yet we hesitated."

"A difficult posting."

"Upland Sumatra is rough country for anyone. Susannah Ames is a hardy soul who has spent much of her life in remote places. Deborah Rand was untested and untried, even as a teacher. You won't find Light of the World on a map. My husband wrote back to Mrs. Birnham expressing our . . . concerns. Three months later a polite young woman showed up at our bungalow door in Palembang and introduced herself as Miss Deborah Rand and announced herself ready to assist Reverend Ames at his mission. My husband admired her . . . determination. He admired that trait in anyone," she hastened to add. "We were presented with a fait accompli. The short of it is she stayed with us a few weeks until Miles could arrange her passage up the coast."

"Have you had reason to regret that decision?"

I could sense her hesitation before she answered, "No, not in so many words. No—but it was Miles's decision."

"Yet you still had doubts about Deborah Rand."

"Miles's judgments were always sound, but he was given to impulsiveness. I don't think—"

The creaking of a timber on the starboard passageway silenced Bridgett Hannover's thought. Giving me a sharp look, as if to wonder whether we had been overheard, she clutched her shawl and bid me good night.

It had been a curious interview, one that hinted at a hidden tension about her husband's decision to send Deborah Rand to work with Noel Ames. Puzzling this out, I turned my attention to a sea that gleamed phosphorescent in the moonlight. The timber creaked again, accompanied by the pungent smell of East Indies tobacco.

"If that's the same Deborah Rand I knew," said Fahey as he leaned against the railing across from me, "she'd put the lift in a priest's frock, if there was ever a girl to do it."

8

Fahey flipped the butt end of his cigar into the water. A guttering storm lamp hanging from a sconce cast his dark, curly head and broad shoulders in relief. He reminded me of a bilious satyr nursing an old grudge.

"How long have you been eavesdropping?" I whispered angrily.

"It's in my interest to know what takes place on the *Lorelei,* if you please. But in this case, I merely stumbled into a conversation."

"Then you can stumble your way out of one."

"Aye-aye, sir." Fahey tossed off a mock salute and turned to descend to the main deck.

"One question, though," I said. He paused on the gangway. "Explain your remark about Deborah Rand."

"It was a long time ago."

"You knew her."

"It's not that uncommon a name." He draped his muscular arms along the railing, his eye on a great spotted moth that had discovered the deadly allure of the lamp. "The Deborah Rand I knew was from Connecticut. You see, she had promised to marry up with an Irishman newly come to the land of promise and opportunity. So he dreamed a fool's dream. He schemed to set himself up as shipping magnate. He had even purchased a scow to start his first fleet. Went way over his head in debt to do it. Only the poor deluded sap failed to factor in a few things. The worst of it was he had failed to account for custom in the Promised Land. Namely, that a poor, uppity mick just off the boat should know his place. You can't crawl out of steerage and walk into a drawing room, not even in America."

"Her family put an end to it, did they?"

"She was going to break the ties that bound her, or so she swore. On a wintry night, he waited for her at an inn by a whaling town on the coast." The moth skittered across the burning surface of the mantel and flew off. "He waited. The fire went out in the great room of the inn. It turned bitter cold when the dawn came up. And the bottle was as empty as the man."

"That explains your sudden turnabout, doesn't it? Why you've decided to travel up to Light of the World. You aim to see if this Deborah Rand is your Deborah Rand?"

He let his voice soften into regret. "You may think this farcical coming from me. But I wonder if you ever lost someone you craved."

"No." I said it too bluntly. "Nothing."

He had caught my dissembling. "Ah, and where is she now?"

"I was engaged—once. I thought I was. That was long ago."

"Mayhap that goes to explain why you're running an old stern-wheeler up some Sumatra backwater?"

I was glad for the dark while my cheeks burned. "That has nothing to do with you."

"If you're that far gone, you might think about pitching in with me when we get to Malacca. No one asks questions in that crowd, and it's even shares for all."

"I'm not that far gone, Fahey."

"That's as it may be." He shrugged and took two steps down the gangway, then turned. "Although I knew a jack-tar in Yokohama who would have danced a livelier tune."

"What the hell do you mean by that?" I called after him as he descended the ladder.

Back in my cabin, I prepared myself for bed, although I was far from sleepy. The leaves of Alfred Wallace's manuscript were still strewn across the desk, and I started to gather them up. My attention was once more drawn to the account of the Golden Sura. Wallace had been seeking a master of camouflage known as the leaf butterfly when suddenly the Golden Sura appeared on the trail, its royal wings beating in the sunlight . . .

Crying out for my guide, I ran down a path having no idea where it might lead me, perhaps deeper into the forest, where I should be run to ground by some wild beast or headhunter. I had never known such flyaway panic. Then I saw the butterfly in front of me and checked my headlong stride. It was dipping and fluttering in the middle of the trail. When I saw the stripe across its wings, like a script composed of molten gold, I knew I was in the presence of something rare and strange. The Golden Sura, Papilio aurensis, is held in great reverence by the Muslim Malays. They fall down on their knees and lift their voices to Allah whenever they encounter a member of the species, for legend says its speckled wings hold the Koran's last, ineffable thought. It did appear a messenger from another world.

The Sura poised in the air before me and then fluttered down the track. I took it into my head that if I followed it, the creature would lead me out of the forest and into safety. Keeping some yards ahead, the insect did not deviate from the trail, until — how do I describe this! — it vanished, and in its place was a young woman. She stood before me smiling, completely unadorned, more beautiful than I remembered her. I knew her — yes, smiling, beckoning to me with a toss of her long auburn hair, although I had never looked upon her nakedness when she was alive. She had been taken away from me by influenza in 1852, in the very year we were to be married.

Of course I followed her, this apparition more real to me than

*anything that had ever lived before or since. She kept before me
drawing me on, her hair undone and flowing down her back,
and she laughed, a laugh so familiar and dear to me that I drank
it down like joyful nectar. My feet seemed to leave the ground,
and unshackled by gravity, I pursued her—and lost her. At last
I stumbled into a little clearing, the sunlight numbing in its
intensity, my heart alive with wonder. And across that clearing
was my Malay guide Randurman, and he, too, had come to a
stop, his chest heaving from the exertion of running.*

*"You saw her, too," he managed to force out. "She passed this
way, didn't she?"*

"Yes," I said to him, equally breathless. "She passed this way."

*"I had never thought to see her again," he said, shaking his
head in disbelief. "It was so long ago. We were betrothed . . ."*

"But she was taken away from you."

*"Yes, kidnapped. She was bathing in the river. They came up
to her in a boat. I never saw her again. Except . . ."*

"The Golden Sura. You saw it, too."

*"Oh yes," he said excitedly. "The Golden Sura flew over my
head, and then there was my Yasmine, standing before me on the
trail."*

When I looked up again, the watch on my desk showed two A.M.
I now understood what Wallace's encounter with the Golden Sura
meant to him and why he had kept his journal a secret. Who
would believe a scientist who had seen a ghost? Only someone
who had seen a ghost.

In this bemused state, I went up to the wheelhouse to relieve
Devadatta of the watch, whistling the refrain of an old Union
ballad under my breath. And stopped. The image stole upon me
like a thief. The stream by the Jambi River. There had been a
flutter of blue wings above the spiderweb, a flicker of gold.

I had followed the five stones that led out into the Potomac, and they had led to Grace Tremaine combing her hair. She was humming a song, the same ballad I had been whistling. I stood over her, and then, her voice grown harsh and taunting, I remembered my rage, and the empty outcropping, and nothing left but the rush of insensate water below. But there was more. I felt the water over and under me, dragging me, pulling me down with invisible force until I saw her ahead of me, a lilac blossom twirling in the void, lost, lifeless, turning. I shot up to the surface desperate for air.

Yet I had never been underwater at all. I had been kneeling by the Jambi stream when I saw the blue wings of the insect hovering and heard Fahey calling my name. Could it have been Wallace's Sura I had seen, or was my mind beginning to misgive? If the Sura ... What subtle, devious power could have arranged this intersection of winged herald and Wallace's lost love—and mine?

Devadatta was standing faithfully at the wheel, peering out into the dark mystery of the river. He had set his turban aside. His head was cleanly shaven and oiled, which made his great ears stick out all the more. "I was thinking of that fellow Sancho Panza," he said. "You know, the squire of the Spanish knight Don Kixit."

"So you are familiar with the adventures of the Knight of the Woeful Countenance?" I asked, smiling at the whimsical pronunciation of the hero's name.

"Most assuredly I am. Captain Fritz left me the book of Mr. Cervantes along with that of Mr. Bulfinch. As for Sancho—he never once doubted Don Kixit, although Don Kixit was seized by a great folly. And for his loyalty, Sancho Panza was made governor of an island."

"What do you make of that, Devadatta?"

"That a fool can follow a madman and still gain from the experience."

"I catch your drift. Perhaps our expedition is tilting at windmills."

"That remains to be seen," was the engineer's diffident reply. "All my life, I've been dreaming of a grand adventure filled with danger, hairbreadth escapes, and despised villains. At the end of the adventure, I would find myself honored and respected, a man of wealth and substance."

"And perhaps with a province of your own to govern."

"That is not so foolish a wish as it may seem, Captain."

"Perhaps not."

"The real trick is in finding the right madman to follow."

With that, he was gone, leaving me to consider, in the remaining hours of darkness, what kind of madman I had become.

9

The steamboat slipped up the coast of Sumatra like a white wraith, a thin trail of wood-fired smoke in her wake, not as black as coal but enough to betray our presence. A Dutch frigate or cutter could have swept down on us in an instant, but the farther north we went, the less likely that was to happen. I kept us in constant movement, stopping only to scale the boilers or perform other maintenance. We had plenty of wood, at least enough to last us until we gained the Asahan, and we were amply provisioned with rice, flour, dried beans, biscuit, and fresh fish, caught daily by Kung. Although I was relieved by our progress, a new apprehension set in. Where the Dutch left off, the pirates took over. Malay pirates were masters of the moment, appearing out of thin air, attacking savagely and in packs like jackals. And they took no prisoners.

These were real threats, and I felt I could face them, but there was something else as well, a sense of foreboding that grew with each mile. This remote coast is banshee in its wildness, and the portents had been with us since the first day on the *Renown*, when the bloom of blood-red shrimp seemed to set all of nature into a feeding frenzy. The *Renown*'s captain had warned of a hostile land, and Wallace's journal described one of jarring illusions. There was augury, too, in my unsettling vision by the Jambi stream. Another power menaced us, but I could not give it a name. It traveled in our wake and lurked in the mangroves like a malignant vapor. At night it stalked the decks and invaded our dreams. A morbid fancy, no doubt, and yet...

These worries troubled my confidence even as I was learning the weight of command, particularly now that I had struck my odd peace with Fahey. Of our other travelers I saw little, except at meals. From time to time Bridgett and her *turahan* took the air on the passenger deck, the gray owl with her feline familiar, but mostly they kept to their cabin and their séances with Reverend Hannover. Diem kept to himself as well, although he would occasionally be seen on the promenade, weighty medical tome in hand. We seemed each to be traveling in our distances, each in his own world, monks in our cells. Perhaps this was just as well, but it did not make me less uneasy, for the friction was there just beneath the surface.

And there was a new suspicion to deal with—that one of our fellow travelers might not be what he seemed.

The suspicion grew out of an event that happened when we were two days steaming from the Asahan, off a peninsula known as the Rokan Hook. I was in the wheelhouse when Devadatta waved from below to signal that he had finished the engine overhaul that had kept us anchored off the river for much of the day. It was nearly dusk, a time when waves of mosquitoes rose from the swamp to relieve the biting midges that had dined on us all afternoon. For this reason alone, I was glad to get under way. With steam in the boiler, I called down to Fahey to weigh anchor and asked Diem to lend a hand, Master Kung being busy in the galley with the evening meal.

"Glad to be free of this torture chamber," I cried down to the engineer. He waved again as I turned the bow into the current. In a few moments *Lorelei* had found deep water, and we were back to chugging up the coast, grateful for the sea breeze. I paid little notice to the black smoke swirling up from the galley—until there was a popping explosion like the sound of a shotgun report. My first thought was that the boiler had blown a rivet, but smoke continued to billow from the cargo hold. I secured the wheel and slid down to the passenger deck. By the time I had reached the main deck, Kung had come flying out of the hold, waving his arms wildly, in a vain attempt to beat down the flames that engulfed him. A second later he dove off the foredeck and into the bright blue water of the Malacca Strait.

Almost immediately, I realized his peril. The current off the Hook is swift, deep, and northerly, which meant that our overboard was being carried quickly out of reach. He seemed to have disappeared entirely, but then he bobbed to the surface some thirty yards to starboard. He treaded water furiously as I tossed him a line, but it fell short by at least a dozen feet. He struck out against the current with painful strokes as I prepared for another throw. He had maneuvered himself in good position when the white tip of a dorsal fin broke the surface about ten yards behind him. The mako sharks in the strait have a fearsome reputation as man-eaters, and this fellow was a big one, at least twenty feet to judge by the distance between dorsal and tail. I cried out a warning to Kung, who spun around in time to meet the charge of the beast. He went under in a boil of foam, and the next thing I knew, I was in the water myself, the rope about my waist. As the current bore me to him, Kung shot to the surface with a great whooshing inhale and, spinning about, struck out for me. Soon I had an arm under both of his, while I spun about myself, trying to keep my eye on the shark. Devadatta began hauling us in, and for a few anxious moments, I felt like nothing so much as a piece of live bait for a hungry fish. Tasty bait indeed, for the mako broke surface once more, right behind Kung, its cavernous mouth ringed with vicious white stilettos, wide and ready to close on the Chinaman's legs. Suddenly, Kung was jerked free of my hold and seemed to slip right into the shark's jaws. Then both man and monster disappeared. A furious thrashing of white water followed while I looked helplessly on. After some seconds, the water stopped its agitation. The surface was calm and empty until, a few feet away, a bald head, white as porcelain, bobbed to the top, and then two arms outspread, all connected, I was pleased to see. Once again, I threw my arm around Kung. Devadatta resumed dragging us in. As for our hungry mako, he did not rise again, and I could not help but attribute Kung's escape to some queer Gobi wizardry, since I had thought him a dead man. While Fahey and our engineer hauled the nearly unconscious Kung aboard, I pulled myself over the side. Meanwhile, Diem, Bridgett, and Sahar had pulled together a bucket brigade to douse the conflagration in the hold. While Diem tended to Kung's burns, I joined the others to assess the damage. Plumes of wet, dirty smoke slithered through a charred hole in the roof. The galley partition with its little cookstove lay in a smoldering heap, the deck around it charred. Except for that and the damage to the roof, *Lorelei* appeared to have no mortal wounds. Had the fire spread aft, we would have been finished.

"Will we be forced to turn back, Captain?" Bridgett Hannover's soot-streaked face was screwed up with worry. I reassured her that we were still afloat but would need to anchor for the night so I could make a complete inspection. That meant running up the coast for another hour or so until we found a cove to hide in— and hope we weren't discovered. The smoke from the fire would have been seen for miles.

That night, long after the others had turned in, I slipped into the engine room. Signaling my engineer to keep quiet, I settled down next to him and accepted the offer of one of his hand-rolled cheroots.

We smoked in silence until I observed that it seemed Master Kung had made a remarkable recovery for a man who had suffered burns over half his body. When I last saw him, he was sitting on the deck in Diem's cabin, playing a fast and furious card game of Japanese *hanafuda,* his face lit up with silent pleasure.

The engineer replied with a rolling smoke ring, "Master Kung's powers are inscrutable."

"I'll give him credit for a charmed life," I said. "Here's a fellow who can shrug off combustion and a shark attack and all within an hour. I wish I had such a constitution."

"Yet Kung considers his powers to be nothing at all. He says that compared to other practitioners, he's just a toddler. Still, the disappearance of the shark was most impressive, do you not think?"

"As mysterious as the fire. Kung claims that galley stove ignited for no reason."

Devadatta was quiet for a moment, his eyes intent on the glowing tip of the cigar he held. "It is as I feared."

"What do you mean by that?"

"Perhaps we do have an evil *asura* among us."

"So you have suspicions, too."

"Not Kung, I think," the Indian hastened to add.

"And why not Kung? Perhaps he fears for Diem's safety if we make our destination."

"Not Master Kung," Devadatta repeated, weighing his words.

"Better have out with it," I said.

"Taking command," he began. "Truly of all the occupations, it is the most perilous. The last skipper of *Lorelei,* for example, went mad, poor fellow." The engineer looked past my puzzlement, drawing deeply on his cigar. "Captain Fritz brought us down from Bombay to Kota Baru almost a year ago. He used to stick out a chest round as a stump, thump it, and say, with a big red face, something like: *'Ja, Ich bin ein Hohenzollern.'*" Devadatta blew out his cheeks and thumped his own scrawny breast. "Like that."

"He was Austrian. Extravagant blowhards. The lot of them."

Devadatta rolled his eyes upward. "The Alps. He talked about the Alps. Truly, I wondered what a mountain man like that was doing skippering out of Bombay."

"They have a navy of sorts, the Austrians. In the Adriatic."

"This Captain Fritz. He oiled his whiskers with patchouli." Devadatta wiggled his fingers under his pointed chin. "Like a coxcomb. He was fond of plum brandy and gin, much too fond, I think; it made him try to inspire his crew with the tip of his boot. He had a heavy boot, did Captain Fritz." The Indian grimaced. "But his rough manner did him little good. I think he took that old story about *Lorelei* to heart. The one I told him on a night when he was in his cups."

"What story was that?"

"That there was some kind of a Mischief aboard this ship. I heard it from the previous engineer of *Lorelei*. He told me this Mischief had been there from the first and made life aboard difficult, and for evil-tempered officers, most certainly. It seems they did not last long on our ship. Naturally, I felt duty-bound to inform Captain Fritz about this legend." Devadatta held up his hand as if taking an oath. "Mind you, I did not call the captain evil-tempered in so many words, sir; all I said was that this Mischief could be troublesome."

"How troublesome?"

"Oh, things would go missing here and there, like a cargo manifest or a compass. When you most needed them. They would turn up again, although not in their right places. It was very distressing, you see. And there were the accidents—boiler shutdowns, very surprising leaks. Not long after I told the captain about this Mischief, he huffed and puffed about ordering us to scour the ship and make sure it wasn't aboard. He wanted everything carried out of the ship, every piece of gear, furniture, charts, everything carried out and placed on the quay—we were in Madagascar at the time. Then the Fritz—as we called him—made an inspection. We found nothing, but I don't think he was convinced."

"Why is that?"

Devadatta shrugged in complete innocence. "I don't know, but somehow this idea of the Mischief had gotten stuck in his head. It became something very real to him, a creeping shadow. Fritz thought it hated him, but he didn't know what he had done to make it so. He said it was like a—like the one in Mr. Bulfinch who punishes those who are insolent to the gods—"

"Nemesis."

"Yes, like the Nemesis." The engineer's face brightened. "One night Fritz even stumbled up and down the decks firing his pistol. He challenged this shadow to a duel and bellowed out loud how the Mischief wasn't going to get the best of him. But it did."

"How was that?"

"About the third day out of Madagascar. One morning the captain wouldn't come out of his cabin. He said he wanted someone on guard at his cabin door round the clock. He wanted his meals brought to him and left outside. That was the only time he opened the door. He took in the plate, he put out the plate. This went on for some days. Sometimes we could hear him talking to himself. Then one night I was standing watch, and the door creaked open. He told me to come in. He was in his nightshirt; he was a fright, a dirty, unshaven man, terrible to look upon, and mean, as if the inner man had become the outer, but perhaps there was little difference. The Fritz told me this shadow had gotten into his cabin. I looked everywhere. But there was no one. He cursed and raved and kicked me out. That was the last I saw of Captain Fritz. The next morning we sailed into Kota Baru, and Commandant Beets strutted aboard, you know, the way he walks, like a field marshal. When he knocked on the captain's door and nobody answered, we broke in. The cabin was turned upside down. And on his desk was the name written out on a sheet of paper. 'M-i-s-c-h-i-e-f.' Just so. And something else I will tell you, the name was not in the Fritz's hand."

"Come now, Devadatta," I chided him. "A man can't vanish into thin air."

"Commandant Beets said so, too! He immediately thought Fritz might be a spy, so he sent out search parties. But they never found him. Then, as I told you when you first came aboard, Beets thought I was a spy, too. So I was confined to *Lorelei*. He let the deckhands go, and they found berths on some passing ship."

"And the *Lorelei* stayed moored to the quay."

The engineer threw up his hands. "Oh, how she sat! It seems she had been bought to haul tin downriver from the mines. But there was an inquiry, and they couldn't do anything with her until it was over. Most assuredly, I think the inquiry got forgotten. Anyway, the mines went broke long before she arrived."

"So you think our *Lorelei* is under a hoodoo?"

"A hoodoo, Captain?"

"An evil spell of some kind."

"I merely offer a little history, sir. You are nothing like Captain Fritz," he assured me with a toothy smile. "There hasn't been any Mischief on board since Captain Fritz left—until now. But I think this business of the galley fire is a different kind of trouble. Besides, if we find human causes for mysterious occurrences, there are other suspects."

"Certainly not the women." I tossed the cheroot over the side. "You mean that damned Fahey."

The Indian cast down his eyes. "I think Fahey is what he is, like it or not."

"You can speak plainly."

"I mean we will not let him be stealing your command again."

I looked at the Indian with some surprise. "So you knew about that."

"The first night I knew. He was behaving most extravagantly like a felon. I was waiting for you to give the order for us to seize him. But it seems you talked him out of it, Captain."

"He talked me out of it, strange to say."

"Yes, Captain, that is strange to say." Devadatta produced a pair of scissors and clipped off the dead end of his cheroot. He stuck the butt in a cigar box full of stubs. "I shall keep a watch on Mr. Fahey."

"You do that, Engineer." I stood up. "It's nearly dawn. How do we stand for open water?"

"Champing at the bit," said the Indian, patting the engine casing affectionately.

"Then let's give *Lorelei* the reins."

I paused at the engine-room door, my hand on the latch. I wanted to tell Devadatta how uncannily his tale of "Mischief" coincided with my own sense that we were traveling under a shadow. But to admit that would be to give credence to the madness of Captain Fritz, and thereby admit to the possibility of my own. Besides, my clever engineer had done well to remind me about seeking natural causes for supernatural events. Outside of sheer accident, a human agent of misfortune was the only explanation for the fire. But there was no likely saboteur. We all had our reasons for wanting the mission to succeed.

I took the ladder with steady tread to the passenger deck. The cabins were silent. I entered the wheelhouse, lit a hurricane lamp, hung it from a peg, and pulled out the charts. The way out of the cove presented no problem, even in the dark, but there was a narrow channel running between the shore and a small rocky island that might cause trouble. The charts were of no help. I decided to swing to the starboard side of the island to be safe. As I rolled up the map, I heard an unearthly cry from the shore.

"Ulysses!"

The cry chilled me to the bone, for I had prayed never to hear it again. Not in this world. The thought stole swift upon me; now that I had seen her once more, she might never let me go. I stepped outside, my arm trembling as I held the lamp aloft, peering into the deep and desolate wall the jungle presents at night.

"Ulysses . . ."

There was a distant rumble of thunder and, from somewhere within the forest, the raucous cry of a hornbill. Perhaps that was all I had heard. A hornbill given to shrill, eerie sounds, or the mingled snarl of a tiger and the shriek of its prey. A spatter of rain had fallen, leaving a curtain of mist curling on the water. All was still. Shrugging off my unease, I called down to Devadatta to weigh anchor. A few moments later, sparks poured out of *Lorelei*'s stack, and the stern-wheel turned with a reassuring shudder and rush of water. We headed into the lifting light.

10

Fahey swung up to the top deck and, leaning into the wheel-house, pointed to a dark hollow ahead of us, a break in the mangrove wall. I pulled out a battered spyglass from its niche in the wheelhouse and trained it at the line of jungle across the shimmering morning haze.

"That's it, all right," he said, mopping his brow with a bandanna. "The mouth of the Asahan."

I let out whoop of relief. We had been drifting at the edge of the mudflats for an interminable morning while the low tide held us at bay. At last the tide had turned and was drawing us toward a low-lying sandbar that had obscured the mouth of the river. Glad as I was to have found our elusive stream, our position left us uncomfortably exposed. The sooner we were away from the coast and chugging up the river, the better.

As we drifted in with the tide, the denizens of the river mouth eyed us warily. Blue-shelled crabs lurked among the steepled roots of the mangrove, but the wide expanse of flats belonged to a huge colony of mudskippers. Half fish, half lizard, these grotesque amphibians had adapted to life in water and on land. Hundreds of them lay at the edge of the water breathing laboriously through gills that served as lungs when they were onshore. Their bulging eyes made them look like the mutations of an alchemist's arcane experiments, aspiring homunculi that had reverted to reptiles and were on a long, slow slide back into the sea. The pale blue herons stalking the flats ignored them as if they were beneath contempt, or poisonous, or both.

There was no sign of a village or any other human habitation, only the tangled maze of the swamp and the birdlike shriek of gibbons at play in the distant jungle.

With the pungent smells of rotting vegetation and sea life that came off the mudflats, there rose another, sweet and rancid. I traced the source of the odor to black slicks of oil that crept across the surface of the water, moving as if under their own power, amorphous shapes whose viscous tentacles skirled about to the dictates of current and tide.

"Those oil blooms slide down from the north," said Diem, joining me in the wheelhouse. "Near Atjeh, there are pools where it has seeped out of the earth. The tribes make regular visits to scoop up the stuff for their lamps."

"I wonder how large the deposits are."

Diem did not offer an answer but sat down beside me as I worked to free a kink from the steering cable. Although I wasn't in the mood for talk, I humored him. It seemed he needed the company. I had seen little of him since our stop on the Jambi some days ago. He had taken to eating alone in his cabin, perhaps because he sensed the others, Bridgett and Fahey in particular, didn't relish his company. We talked casually about the weather and the difficulties we might face upriver, and before long I got him talking about his work in Paris.

"My father was against it—my going to Paris. He wanted me to take over the trading business."

"Is your father still alive?"

"No, he passed on some years ago, somewhat reconciled. My younger brother, Trong, now runs the firm. Prosperously, I'm glad to say." He knelt beside me and peered into the steering compartment, now freed of its housing. "Perhaps I can be of assistance."

"You can start by handing me that wrench. This steering cable keeps slipping."

"I arrived in Paris in 1865," he continued. "And stayed a decade."

"That's a long time to be away from home," I said wistfully.

"Annam? I don't miss it." Diem made a disavowing wave of his delicate hand. "I found my home in psychology, as the new science of mind was coming to be called. My internship was at the Hôpital de la Charité under a physician, Pierre Briquet, who was becoming notorious for his original ideas about hysteria. He had a clinic there to diagnose and treat the malady."

"A woman's malady, isn't it?" I recalled how more than one doctor had attributed my mother's frequent fainting fits to hysteria. I noticed they had always increased in number and severity with the return of my father from his voyages. And little wonder. When he was onshore, he monopolized her every moment, hovered over her, talked to her incessantly, cajoling her, advising her, admonishing her. When he was not around, we boys were greedy for her time. Perhaps we all adored her too much. Perhaps we sensed that we would lose her. Her fits were her means of escape. At last she freed herself from him and us entirely.

"The world knows hysteria as a female affliction," Diem explained, "and indeed the ancient Greeks thought it so, for the name itself denotes a sickness of the womb. But men, too, are susceptible, although not in as great a number. The symptoms are largely the same. Briquet saw a link between the puzzling physical and emotional symptoms of hysterics, like paralysis or blindness, for which there was no physical cause, and the torments of the mind."

For a long time after my mother went away, I would find myself standing by our front door, thinking she might be out there, waiting in silence. She never was. "Perhaps women are unhappier than men," I said at last.

"Certainly Dr. Briquet thought them more susceptible to loss and sorrow, to troubles in the family, and prey to violent emotions."

I slipped the steering cable from the pulley and began examining it for frays. "I wonder about that. A man can feel loss and sorrow, too. And as keenly."

"Naturally, men feel loss." Diem removed from his pocket a gilt snuffbox with a mirrored facing and clicked open the lid. Inside was a gold heart-shaped locket with a ruby set in the middle. "The root of hysteria is seated in our emotions," he continued. "Those with rich emotional lives are less prone to hysteria, although Dr. Briquet thought there was a link with inheritance. I see it another way. There are two paths to hysteria. Deprive someone of affection, care, reassurance. Or humiliate him—strip away his self-respect. Find the root and you find the cure."

"As opposed to casting out devils, is that it?"

"The real devils are ignorance and fear."

"Why not stay in France? Why bring your practice to an obscure river in a ghost-haunted land?"

"What better place to track down devils?" The glibness of his reply suggested something else.

"Or to escape them?"

"Oh, there are some devils in Paris." He laughed knowingly. "If you are not French . . ."

"And one door in particular?" I asked. He started as if I had guessed a secret. I continued, "It is not so hard to picture a lonely man seeking solace. Especially in Paris."

"You mean a sailor's idea of love," he replied with a tinge of contempt.

I could see I had touched a nerve and drew back. "I meant no insult, Doctor."

"I can see I was wrong about you, Captain." He closed the lid of the snuffbox as if to shield a memory. When he looked at me again, it was with a new interest, or wariness.

"In what way?"

"It can scarcely matter now." The gilt box disappeared into his pocket. "I owe Radjah Dulah for a past kindness. His son and I were once fast friends. In a way, I'm going home. You may find it hard to believe, but Prince Bandarak and I roved these forests and mountains like the red Indians in your country, barefoot, in breechclouts, and with bows in our hands."

I looked over at this dandified bantam with the starched collar and the silk cravat and smiled with him. "I admit I'm having a hard time picturing that." I stood up to test the tension on the wheel. Satisfied, I put away my tools. Diem's eyes were on the waves spilling over the sandbar.

"One day that tide will roll out to sea and not return," he observed. "A German physicist, Clausius, thought that all things in the universe ultimately run down and reach a frozen state. When the sun finally burns out, our system returns to ice. Entropy, he called it."

"A melancholy prospect."

"Yet inevitable. As the candle burns down, the system begins the long, slow process of reversion. You can see the same entropic processes at work in living organisms. At thirty, the human being is at physical apogee. Then decline, degeneration, decay. At seventy, the same specimen has shriveled into a shell, an attenuated version of a newborn, pathetic and infantile."

I pointed to the mudskippers on the shore, hopping out of the mud and wriggling into the rising tide. "Those little fellows seem to have reached a happy balance; they are at home on land or in water. Come what may, I think they'll find the means to adjust."

"That's all very well if one aspires to live in the mud."

"In this world of Clausius, why aspire to be anything at all?"

"There you have it, Captain." Diem's fine-boned features, normally as aloof as a carved idol's, took on an unaccustomed fire. "To embrace the entropic notion is to embrace futility. In the East we have embraced that notion for generations. That is why we have become mired in place, while you in the West learn and tinker like undisciplined, precocious children. Meanwhile, the rest of us cope with barbarism and anarchy. This is what brings me back here. This is what I struggle against. Because it is will and intellect that turn the entropic tide back on itself, that renew energy within the system and make life triumphant. That is why I practice Western medicine, and that is why I have come to cure the sickness of the Bataks by healing their prince." He rose suddenly. "Now I'll let you get on with your repairs."

Diem made a slight bow as he left the wheelhouse, as if to acknowledge that we shared some secret thought. But what was it? He had said only part of what he had wanted to say, or this theory of entropy was a metaphor for a more personal loss, and the rest lay hidden behind a door he feared to open.

By the time Diem left the wheelhouse, Fahey, Devadatta, and Kung had poled us into position to float over the submerged sandbar and into the mouth of the Asahan. Little used, the entrance had become choked over time with silt and debris, so we had difficulty maneuvering the steamboat into position. But we slipped into the Asahan at last, the overarching mangrove and nibong palms eclipsing the fierce sunlight and casting us into the gloom of a watery catacomb. The Asahan is a black-water river that provides no clue as to what lurks in its depths. When the sounding line showed enough play, Devadatta fired up the boiler, and the great wheel began to churn with a shudder. I had Fahey keep a keen eye out for submerged logs and hidden shoals. Mangrove limbs scratched across the top deck and slid against the wheelhouse windows like the talons of some teasing beast, obstructing my line of sight. We crawled along like this for nearly a half mile, with frequent stops to sound the river and but a few yards to maneuver port and starboard. It was the perfect setting for an ambush, so Diem and Master Kung kept rifles at the ready. I feared that if the river hemmed us in any more, we should have to pole our way back down, but after we had navigated a serpentine bend, the Asahan suddenly opened her dark heart.

Some fifty yards ahead were two tiny islets on either side of the stream, forming a portal, with two tall She-Oaks growing out of them. Their tangled limbs were wreathed in a profusion of gray-green shoots, giving the trees the appearance of hunchbacked and hoary-headed crones resentful of our intrusion. Beyond this uninviting gate, the river widened dramatically, with spears of sunlight plunging into its ebony surface. Fahey was on the foredeck with a pole. As he signaled to proceed, the She-Oaks shook with mournful, keening sounds. I saw a score of grim, bleached faces scowling among the branches, like heralds from Tartarus. Sahar dropped to her knees on the foredeck at the sight and sound, covering her ears. Devadatta was suddenly in the wheelhouse shaking as if with a fever. Fahey stood on the bow like one charmed as the pole slipped through his fingers and into the stream. This troubled lamentation pressed on us from all sides as we passed beneath the trees. Fearing myself at some terrifying brink, I pulled out my revolver, leaned through the window, took aim, and fired. A death mask shattered into myriad pieces, breaking the spell. The gunshot echoed in the close swamp, and scores of wild white pigeons rose out of the She-Oaks like the last pale thoughts of the newly dead. The wails died away, the ghostly choir faded, and we slipped between the islets with only the clatter of old bones as a trailing percussion. Above us on either side, a score of human skulls glared down from the oak limbs, choristers when the wind blew through their eyeless sockets and fleshless mouths. Such were the joyless sirens that greeted our arrival on the Asahan.

It was only natural that our little group gravitated that night to the foredeck for courage and companionship and a welcome crab stew prepared by Master Kung. We had anchored in midriver, grateful for the coolness brought by the night but apprehensive of its effects on our imaginations. The talk turned to the ominous skull-decked trees.

"This is the work of the Mamaqs," Sahar told us solemnly, hugging her knees as if to protect herself from the memory.

"Why do people fear them so?" Bridgett asked.

"They are spirits—of a kind. They are humans—of a kind. When the world becomes old and sick," Sahar intoned, "they rise out of the earth and renew it with fire. And they are led by their Sakti."

"What is this Sakti?"

"We Malays have another name for her," Sahar continued. "She is Bhairawas—the Terrible One. Should her glance fall on you, you are blasted where you stand. She can turn men into crocodiles, or stones, or ghouls who feed upon dead things."

"She leads the Mamaqs?" I asked.

"She leads them now. And she brings the cleansing fire."

"What does that mean? Are they supernatural beings?"

"They bring death and ruin. And a new world is born."

"Purged by fire," Bridgett said darkly, looking at me across the glow of the lantern. I suspected her thoughts were on Noel Ames's last letter.

"A sort of Malay end of time," Diem observed. "The Bataks have this legend, too. All the Sumatra tribes believe in it."

"Well, *I* for one have had enough talk of demons and devils," said Fahey, slapping his thighs and getting up. "You sound like a clutch of bog Irish gathered around a peat fire to scare each other half to death." Then he noticed Master Kung sliding a mouth organ across his lips. "Come now, you crazy dwarf mute, you wouldn't know a sailor's hornpipe, would you?"

The Chinaman sounded a scale; Fahey began clapping his hands and stamping his foot, and Kung commenced to spill out as fine a version of a whaler's tune as I'd ever heard. Fahey had us push back our seats, and in a trice he was whirling about the foredeck in a right pretty Bristol sailor's jig. Soon we were all clapping along to the music, although Bridgett pushed him away playfully when he offered her his hand. I remembered the gist of the dance and, throwing off my jacket, jumped up to join him for a few fierce minutes before I begged off laughing and nearly out of breath. At length Fahey himself dropped to the deck in a heap, and we all felt lifted out of our fear and doldrums for the moment. Shortly after, the two women made their good nights. When the light in their cabin went on, Fahey leaned over and pulled a clear bottle out from under the empty flour keg that served as his seat. He held it to the light and popped the cork, passing the bottle under my nose.

"That's gin," I suggested.

"Or instant death, seeing as Sweelinck made it," Fahey said with a wink, and took a long pull. "He was brotherly enough to share his stash after we ran from Beets's jail. And a more fiery blend of Dutch courage you'd be hard pressed to find."

We were all open to a touch of Dutch courage that night— except for the teetotaling Kung—even if the stuff had been brewed in Sweelinck's laundry tub and might be put to better use as a solvent. But it went down quickly. Too quickly, I thought as I reached for the bottle a second time.

The night was rare for its coolness, and sprays of raindrops played across the face of the water, hinting at a squall in the Malacca Strait. The liquor had oiled our affability, to use a phrase my father was fond of; we traded stories and jokes, and Diem recalled some of his adventures from the court of Radjah Dulah.

"What sort of man is the radjah?" I asked.

"Before the radjah, the Bataks were a divided people," Diem replied, reflecting. "They were in a permanent state of civil war. Forty years ago he united them against an invasion from Atjeh in the north. He has been on the throne ever since, and he has proved a farsighted leader."

"The Dutch speak of him as a man to reckon with," I said, recalling the conversation I overheard in the Prince William Hotel.

"From the Dutch, Radjah Dulah learned the value of a well-trained and disciplined army. He has also prepared his only son, Bandarak, to play a role in a changing world. So he has had him trained in statecraft and provided him with foreign tutors. And there is something else—what we might call the 'Alexander Factor.'"

"And what might that be?" I asked, taking another pull of the wretched, soothing stuff in Fahey's bottle.

"The radjah claims he is a direct descendant of Alexander the Great."

Fahey burst out laughing. "This is good. I like this one."

"The point is the Bataks believe it, Mr. Fahey," Diem went on patiently, but nettled by the other's scorn. "The Bataks believe the radjah has caught Alexander's spirit in some strange way. Some of the old warriors claim they have seen him all in gold, leading them into battle."

"All in gold, you say?" Fahey exclaimed derisively. "I'd like to see that!"

"The radjah's claim to Alexander's power was a clever move," Diem continued. "This made it easier for his mother to gain control of the Women's Council and give the throne to her son."

"What do the women have to do with it?" Fahey asked thickly. His mouth was twisted in wry amusement.

"The line of succession among the Bataks is matrilineal. The queen and the electors, the female elders, hold the supreme political power."

"Women name the king?"

"They do."

"It's unnatural," said Fahey.

"But why Alexander?" I asked.

"The Indians brought over the notion, when they conquered Sumatra in the ninth century, that their rule was derived from that of the great Macedonian king."

"Our Hindu kings claimed the inheritance," Devadatta hastened to explain. "Then our Mogul kings did the same. So the storyteller in our village would say. He knew many thrilling adventures of the great king we call Iskandar."

"Here's a shitload of fancy," Fahey muttered at Diem. "Do you take me for a fool?"

"I can't improve upon nature, Mr. Fahey," Diem said curtly, starting to rise. "I'll bid you all a good night."

Fahey laid hold of Diem's arm. "You need taking down a peg," he said menacingly.

Diem lifted Fahey's hand from his sleeve. "You're drunk, Mr. Fahey."

"You're a chink whoremaster to say I'm drunk."

I stepped between them. "All right, Fahey, you've had a snootful. Go to your quarters to sleep it off."

"Don't get in the way." Fahey shoved me back and turned on Diem. "I've had enough of his high-and-mightiness here. You put a book in a slope's hand and suddenly he thinks he's more than a monkey. I've had my full of him." Fahey made as if to back away from the confrontation but, too late, I saw the feint. He turned with a roundhouse aimed for Diem's head.

He never connected. The next thing any of us knew, Master Kung had stepped in the path of the blow, and Fahey was lying flat on his back. The Irishman's look of supreme amazement coincided with a rumble of approaching thunder. He scrambled to his feet and this time went straight for Kung with a knife. I didn't even see Kung move, but Fahey went hurtling back as if he had been poleaxed. He stumbled over our plates and, losing his balance, collapsed with a clatter.

The squall was upon us with a fierce spatter of rain followed by a thunderous explosion so close it drove me to my feet, hands over my ears. Bridgett Hannover stood beside me with a pistol smoking in her hand. I looked around and was relieved to find that she hadn't shot anyone. But her spate of fury was not over. She flew at Fahey and yanked the knife from him, then threw it over the side.

"This is what damnable liquor does to men!" she shouted at us. She picked up the bottle and hurled it over the side as well. The entire night sky lit up with a discharge of lightning that seemed to emanate from the infuriated woman on *Lorelei*'s bow.

"*You* are captain of this vessel," she hissed at me, her hair sodden with rain and her eyes fierce. "Then tend to business!" She pointed beyond us to the dark shadow of the forest. "I won't waste my breath on speaking temperance to blind men, but I will tell you that the drinking is over for the night. Get us up the Asahan before you put a demon in your belly, Captain Vanders. Tend to business!"

Gathering her righteousness about her like a cloak, she climbed the ladder to her cabin. "I'll break any bottle I see aboard this boat, gentlemen," she shouted from the deck above. She waved the pistol. "And I'll shoot any man who puts a bottle to his lips." The night sky lit up behind her as if to confirm the new commandments.

We looked around at one another sheepishly, then one by one, slunk off to our cabins, leaving Fahey to snore in the rain.

Fahey's run-in with Diem and Kung had shattered any hope I held for camaraderie aboard our vessel. This incident was followed by a mishap in the morning that made me realize once again how fragile our expedition was. A submerged tree trunk had ripped into our stern-wheel and snapped one of the blades. I placed the blame squarely on Kung, who had been posted to the bow as lookout. For the first time since the galley fire, suspicion flickered in my mind, especially since we had no spares to replace the damage. However, Kung seemed contrite enough and angrier with himself than I could be. So I made an inspection and decided that we could probably limp along until we arrived at Spoorwegen's Landing, a trading post about five miles upriver. Not for the first time, I fumed at the choice I had made, or that Charles Brooke had talked me into. I was a rope-and-canvas sailor to my core; I had never been easy with the advent of steam and the clumsy iron-bellied hybrids that came with it, half ship, half manufactory. Yet I had to admit that the pulse of *Lorelei*'s engine and the steady vibration of her stern-wheel brought a sense of power that billowing canvas did not. There were times when I stood in the wheelhouse feeling her power rising up my arms to my shoulders, proud of her seaworthiness and pleased with her limber keel. At such times I felt that a steamboat captain was none too bad a thing to be. Then a connecting rod would freeze, the boiler would blow a leak, a blade would snap.

Perhaps there was a hoodoo on the steamship after all, despite my engineer's denials. Perhaps the Mischief was in subtle league with the invisible and legendary Mamaqs to damn our enterprise. I heard no "supple, elusive harmonies" on the Asahan, as Alfred Wallace had poetically phrased it. Wallace had not actually seen the river, so he could not know that, at first appearance, the fabled stream was less fabulous than a brooding presence.

Still, the prospect of steaming into Spoorwegen's Landing gave some lift to my troubled spirit. The owner had built a sawmill along the river, and that meant a remedy for our stern-wheel, as well as a respite from our journey. I looked forward to news and advice from an old Sumatra hand.

The founder of the trading post, Bernhard Spoorwegen, had become an East Indies legend. A Belgian by birth, he had shipped out on a Dutch merchant vessel in the 1840s and, so the story went, quickly sized up the potential for trade among the northern Sumatra tribes, the Muslim merchants in Atjeh, and the Dutch in Palembang. The Dutch saw the advantage to having a European outpost on the Asahan, especially one with a sawmill. With the bitter fighting between the Dutch and the Muslim rebels dying down, Spoorwegen set up a post on the river and soon won the friendship of all parties, for he was an ingratiating, tolerant sort of man who dealt fairly with everyone. It was also said the Dutch saw another advantage in Spoorwegen's venture, namely that he would keep the authorities informed of Muslim or Batak unrest and incursions into the area by other Europeans. In brief, Spoor-wegen was rumored to be an agent for the Dutch East India Company.

We steamed up the Asahan with Devadatta taking soundings so we didn't end up marooned on a mud bank. With the line paying out five marks or more, we found the river of ample depth. Soon the stern-wheeler was paddling along with plenty of room beneath the keel and a good quarter mile to maneuver port and starboard. Toward noon there was a clearing in the swamp that opened to a vista of cultivated gardens, stands of pepper and papaya. A neat circle of wooden buildings crowned a small rise looking over the plantation. With their wood-shingle roofs and tidy design, the buildings—including a bungalow behind the trading post proper—reminded me of an incongruous clutch of New Jersey shore cottages set down in the middle of a steamy Jurassic landscape. A bright red-and-white sign proclaimed the Spoorwegen name. I was pleased to see a barn-sized outbuilding surrounded with piles of cut timber and cords of fuel.

The sight of the trading post brought everyone on deck, but as Devadatta cut the engine and we drifted to the sturdy dock, the voices of our passengers died down. Wild doves cooed eerily from the treetops as we pulled closer to shore, but there was no sound of human activity, and no one came out to meet us.

I thought it prudent to advise Mrs. Hannover and Sahar to remain on board until the place was reconnoitered, and I told the missionary to keep her pistol handy. Devadatta remained on board, too, in case we needed to cast off in a hurry. The rest of us trooped onto the dock and down the stone path to the main building and post store. The size of a small barn, it was laid out like a stateside general store with barrels of biscuits in one corner and barrels of nails in another, shelves of neatly arranged bundles of fabric, a line of bonnets mounted on pegs, tins and bottles of preserved food and condiments, the floor covered with fresh sawdust. There were even panes of glass in the windows. The place smelled of harness oil, pitch, molasses, and overripe bananas, blackened bunches of which hung from the rafters, surrounded by swarms of fruit flies and tiny wasps. That struck me as odd. Everything else was in such order.

When no one answered our calls, we fanned out to cover different areas of the post. I took a stairway at the back of the store that led to the living quarters. Stepping into a sitting room, I felt as if I had been transported from a remote outpost in Sumatra to the home of a prosperous European family—stuffed chairs covered with deep purple velvet, a carved love seat in one corner, and in another, a daybed of striped chintz. There was a daguerreotype in a polished silver frame. A young girl dressed in a pinafore looked out on the world with a blank stare as she rested a tentative hand on the shoulder of a plump, bored woman with drooping curls. The dining room was taken up with a sideboard filled with delft china and a carved oak table with seating for ten. That was when I saw the first bright red drops spattered across the polished surface of the table. I touched one of the drops and, rubbing it between forefinger and thumb, knew in an instant what it was.

The drops formed a trail that led down a dim corridor to the back of the house. The first room I encountered was a neatly appointed guest room, with an unpolished teak dresser and a single bed covered with a lacy counterpane. Beyond this, the drops became sticky pools, and I had to steady myself by grabbing the door frame as I nearly slid into the next bedroom. An elegant four-poster stood in the middle. The morning sunlight poured through tall windows and fell on a simple wooden cross tilting on the white wall above the bed. Arcs of blood spattered the wall, like the tails of comets that had spun out of control. Below, the bedclothes had been flung back as if someone had awoken from a nightmare. As if to confirm its reality, a woman's severed hand, wearing a gold wedding band, lay on a pillow like a ghoulish offering.

I backed out of the grisly chamber and followed the blood to the room at the end of the corridor. It was a child's room, with toys, dolls, a hobbyhorse, and picture books, but these had all been flung about as if by someone in a mad frenzy. The floorboards were slippery in this room, too, the bed similarly disheveled and stained with gore.

I stumbled back down the corridor and stood in the semidarkness trying to comprehend what had happened. I was no stranger to the sights or smells of death, but the sense of dread, of desolation, was greater in this house then I had ever experienced on any blood-soaked battleground. It was made more chilling by the fact that there were no bodies, merely the traces of what appeared to be murderous fury.

A mechanical chime interrupted my gloomy forebodings. Pulling out my revolver, I followed the sound back to the dining room. An ornate ormolu clock hung on a wall niche above the sideboard. On the eleventh note, it fell silent. I went to a window that overlooked the outbuildings and warehouses of Spoorwegen's station. Directly below was an enclosed courtyard. Sitting in the sun, a huge, broad-shouldered man smoked a clay pipe. He was wearing a flat-brimmed hat with a bowl-shaped crown, of a style my father used to call Moravian. A brown bottle was on the table before him.

A back stairway, I discovered, led to the courtyard. As I walked up, the man nodded a distracted greeting. "Mr. Spoorwegen?"

He replied by beckoning me with a heavy hand. I took a seat with him at the table. Below a coarse and sun-burnished face, a spade-shaped beard of deep yellow, streaked with red, spread across his chest. His eyes were ringed with wrinkles and dark shadows that gave him an owlish appearance, watchful and unnerving. With a whittling knife, he gouged at a block of balsa wood. The backs of his hairy hands were matted with grime.

"What has happened here?" The words did not sound as if they were mine.

"How far do you plan to travel upriver?" he asked in thickly accented English.

"To Bahal. Then on to Light of the World."

He grunted with amusement. "That light has gone out, *menheer*. Moses is in Egypt. Joseph is in a deep hole in the earth. *She* is in charge of the light up there now."

"Who is in charge, exactly? Do you mean the mission?"

He admonished me with a squint. "Where else would I mean?" He tapped a forefinger on the table, as if counting. "You will need charts. You will need victuals. You will need fuel. Bernhard Spoorwegen can supply all these things." He tapped his chest. "We'll set you up with an account. 'Take what you need. Pay when you can.' That's my motto."

"Charts, yes." I felt cornered by the trader's obliviousness. "There was blood—for God's sake, man!"

"Ach, that's what you seek—a guide up the river. Costs more, of course."

"No charts, no guides. Where is your family? Are you the only one here?"

He opened his mouth to laugh, then leaned over to confide in me. "There are no charts for the Asahan, Captain." He put a finger to his lips. "Shhh . . . Never give her your name. Speak softly. The four winds are her ears."

I asked him what this had to do with Light of the World, and he said he had visited the place once. When had he last been there? He was not sure. I asked him about the Ameses and Deborah Rand, did he know if they were still alive?

"Ask the Mamaqs," he replied abruptly, then gave me a smile as if we shared a secret. "We see the way things tend."

I could no longer contain my frustration. "This tells me nothing, sir. What in blazes has happened here?"

"Oh, aye, aye," he answered with irritation. "Nothing. There was nothing left to do, you see." Then his eyes welled with tears. "I must do what I can or the contagion will spread. For this I will be blamed." He raised his hand to stroke his beard, and I saw in a glance what had bothered me. The red streaks in his beard were dried clots of blood that had dribbled down his shirtfront.

Then the grief in his eyes turned murderous. I saw the glint of sunlight on metal just as he raised the shotgun over the table. I knocked the weapon aside. My sudden movement and the explosion sent me toppling with the table. I was quickly back on my feet, but Spoorwegen had already run out of the courtyard with speed surprising in so big a man. His floppy hat lay on the sunlit paving stones.

A piercing scream from the direction of the sawmill diverted my attention. A white wooden gate led out of the courtyard, and I followed a worn path to the building. Bridgett Hannover was leaning against the side of the shed. Sahar was rubbing her neck with one hand and holding a handkerchief beneath her chin with the other.

Diem emerged from the shed as I came up, shaking his head. When my eyes had adjusted to the shade, I saw mother and daughter lying together on a pile of golden sawdust, their hands touching, their feet bare. The woman was missing her left hand. Their clothing matched that of the daguerreotypes I had seen in Spoorwegen's parlor, but that was all there was to identify them. What was left of their faces had been gnawed at, the flesh gouged and torn away from the bone. It was as if some wild animal had been at them, or someone with the intent of obliterating their identities. I covered their heads with a burlap sack.

A rifle report from the other side of the mill sent me running in that direction. A moment later there was a shotgun blast from the jungle. I started along a trail and nearly collided with two Malays, their eyes white with terror. They fell down at my feet, beseeching me for help and pointing frantically up the jungle track. I looked at these frightened men and thought I was seeing double. Indeed I was. The Malays were identical twins. The Tuan Spoorwegen was dead, that much I could make out of their story; they had seen the body. The Tuan Spoorwegen was dead and they were free.

"Yes, he's dead all right," said Rowan Fahey, stepping out of the thick jungle. He held a rifle and Spoorwegen's shotgun. "Blew his own head off, poor bastard."

><

"They say," Sahar began, nodding at the two Malays squatting at her feet. "They say they were workers at the sawmill."

Ours was a sober circle that night on the foredeck, as befitted those who had trooped back from a grim burial ceremony. Illuminated by a hurricane lantern and sitting primly on a keg of nails, Sahar translated the story of the Malay twins, the brothers Nasiruddin, as they named themselves. They spoke all at once, in a hushed jumble, casting fearful glances as if some invisible agent might overhear them.

Against my engineer's advice, I had decided to bring the men aboard. I knew Devadatta's estimation of Malays was clouded by prejudice. There was an overriding consideration—the men claimed to know the Asahan, and they were willing to guide us to Radjah Dulah's seat at Bahal.

"The Tuan Spoorwegen was a good man," Sahar continued. "Until he returned from a trip upriver a month ago. He traded goods with the inland tribes from a river barge. When he returned, he was on foot. He was very quiet at first, distracted. He did not seem to know anyone. Of the two Malay men with him, he did not say. His wife said he had come down with a fever, but Spoorwegen was no longer Spoorwegen. Spoorwegen became a Mamaq man."

"The Mamaqs again," Fahey said with a grimace.

I turned to the two Malays squatting before us. "How did Spoorwegen behave after he became a Mamaq man?"

"The Sakti of the Mamaqs turned Tuan Spoorwegen's soul," the one closest to me said, the words tumbling out, his voice rising. "The trader had looked upon her face and fell sick. He became suspicious of everyone. He spoke to things that were not there. He scared the workers, telling them they were all filled with disease and would die. Some went away after that. Then he brought out the guns. He started shooting one morning and everyone ran off."

"Why did these men stay?" I asked Sahar.

"They had nowhere to run, Captain. So they hid in the jungle for two days. Besides, they were devoted to Mrs. Spoorwegen and her daughter."

"Not devoted enough."

"They had no way of knowing what Spoorwegen did. There were no screams or cries. Perhaps he murdered them in the night. Besides, they were terribly afraid."

"The blood in that house," I said, remembering.

"The Lord protects us!" Bridgett said in a hushed voice.

The enormity of what we had experienced sank in upon us. There was fear, and the fear threatened to widen into despair. As if she sensed this, Bridgett Hannover rose and stood looking out over the dark water, where bats swooped in search of luminous fireflies. She clutched her worn leather-bound Bible. She lifted her voice in an old hymn, one that I dimly remembered from my childhood—a haunting melody inspired by a line in the Twenty-fourth Psalm: "Who is this King of glory? The Lord of hosts, He is the King of glory."

In the strangeness of that faraway place, and after speaking of the day's terrible events, that voice, clear, strong, and sweet, was like a beacon against the darkness in all its forms. All of us were rapt while she sang, transported to that inner space where faith and hope and trust are renewed and fears are stilled. When she had finished singing, she bravely went around the circle and embraced us all. Quietly, without a word, we embraced one another, and our fractured company was for a moment healed. Even Fahey and Diem shook hands, and Devadatta and the Malays hugged one another, and we broke up at last, some to sleep and some to duty.

≻⊜

The end to Bernhard Spoorwegen's labors came about midnight, hours after we had laid him in his grave. Fahey, Devadatta, and I had finished bolting a replacement blade to the stern-wheel when my engineer began coughing and pointed to the shore.

A shroud of smoke darker than the night itself rose over the sawmill, accompanied by the acrid smell of burning tar and timber.

It enveloped the structure and suddenly ignited in an explosion like a dry tree touched off by lightning. The flames raced from outbuilding to outbuilding until Spoorwegen's home and store at last were engulfed. I gave the order to cast off, and while the Malays slipped the mooring ropes, Fahey stood with his rifle ready. The passengers came out on the second deck as we slid out into the smooth black water of the Asahan. The great conflagration lit the way for us. Giving the wheel to Devadatta, I went aft to scour the fiery landscape. Shadowy figures moved among the burning buildings, but I could make out no details. It was not long before we navigated a bend in the river and the inferno fell behind us, its glow pulsing and flickering at treetop level, a malevolent reminder of the horror we had left behind.

"What is out there, Captain?" Bridgett Hannover was standing at the entrance of the wheelhouse with her arm around Sahar.

"Perhaps you should ask your *turahan*. She speaks with the spirits." I did not intend sarcasm, though I knew immediately it would be taken that way. But Bridgett seemed too distracted to reply. "Spoorwegen spoke of a woman," I added solemnly. "He feared her power."

Sahar pulled free of Bridgett and went forward to the very edge of the top deck. She seemed to study the darkness that had returned to envelop us. She raised her arms high in the air, but when she spoke, it was only to add to the riddle.

"She is there. Waiting."

"Who?" I cried out, angry at this mystification. "Who is waiting?"

"At Light of the World!" she replied excitedly. "At Light of the World . . . where she has always been." Her voice sank to a whisper in the vast Sumatra silence. "Where we shall die."

Bridgett's steady arm caught her friend before Sahar collapsed to the deck.

There wasn't much sleep to be had that night, but when at last I drifted into troubled slumber, it was only to be roused by angry voices. The hazy golden light of dawn was already glimmering on the river when I threw open my cabin door. On the main deck below, Devadatta was shaking a crowbar at the two Malay brothers cowering at the edge of the bow. One of them looked ready to dive headfirst into the water. I could make no sense of my engineer's string of Hindi invective, but when I called him to his task, he cried out one word: "Sabotage!" It was clear what culprits he had in mind.

"What is all this about, Devadatta?"

"I had drifted off in the engine room when I saw these two trying to slip inside. One of them had a wrench in his hand, intent on trouble—I'm sure of it. I reached for my crowbar, but when I woke up..." His lip curled as he pointed at the Malays. "They had slipped away."

"They came to you in a dream, is that it?"

The brothers broke into a stream of furious Malay. I could pick out only a word or two. Some danger... the engineer attacked them...

"They were trying to warn your engineer." Sahar leaned out from the railing above and pointed upstream. "About *that*."

Barely visible in the early-morning mist was the outline of a tree-covered islet. We had been fortunate to anchor where we did. Had we steamed farther upriver in the night, we surely would have run aground.

As it was, the island presented us with another dilemma. The long, serpentine strip of land split the Asahan into two streams, leaving us with an unexpected choice. Both forks appeared wide enough to be navigable.

As if anticipating my thoughts, Sahar pointed to the stream on the left. "The twins say that way will get us to the compound of Radjah Dulah."

"Where does the other fork lead, Sahar? Ask them."

The brothers shook their heads vehemently at Sahar's question. "They say the right fork is a dangerous backwater," she explained. "They say your boat will come to grief."

I looked from the scowling countenance of my engineer to the injured looks of the Malay twins. Obviously, they all felt their honor was at stake. "We will take the left fork," I decided. "Now let's get under way."

"With your permission, Captain," Devadatta protested. "I would not give a dried fig for what these untouchables have to say."

"Mr. Devadatta, I need you to tend to the engine and get some steam in that boiler. As for the Malays, they know this river, and we do not. And we have no evidence, outside of your dreaming imagination, that they mean foul play."

Devadatta resigned himself to my humor. Seeing as some face saving was called for, I told the engineer to put one of the twins to work stoking the boiler, where he could keep an eye on him. The other I placed on the bow with the sounding line in hand.

Fahey stepped out of the galley with his fist wrapped around a stuffed pancake and a grin of monumental pleasure. "Fried eggs and bacon. Courtesy of Spoorwegen." Saluting us all, he stuffed the concoction into his mouth whole.

We steamed ahead for the next three hours but at decreasing speed. The river, while deep enough, had narrowed in width. We now had about a forty-yard clearance on each side, and I was uneasy with the diminished maneuvering room. We could always back-paddle if the way ahead was obstructed, but retracing our path was time-consuming and riddled with risk. The *Lorelei* pushed on steadily, a thin grayish trail of smoke and cinder streaming from her stack. I felt oddly elated with a boyish sense of adventure and danger—and grateful for a ship that had proved much more of a champion than her title might allow. It does not take long for affection or disaffection to set between a sailor and his boat, and even more so between a captain and his command, for although sailing is a profession, it is also a calling. This surrender to a higher power colors a sailor's work. I suppose that explains why there is such a body of lore and superstition surrounding the vocation, whether it be in the sky's omens, the crisscross of currents, the conjunction of certain seabirds at certain latitudes, or the signifying play of porpoises or sharks in a ship's wake. It was partly this lore, and a family tradition, that brought me down to the sea.

Brought *both* of us down to the sea—for there was never an interest of mine that didn't bring my brother, Morgan, tagging along, just as he had after my birth, a few minutes later. He was never further behind, it seemed. I had not seen him since that last hurried embrace in the door of a Baltimore jail ten years before. Reports over the years had him sailoring in the Pacific, too, but we had never come face-to-face. Just as well. Those reports had placed him in bad company.

Morgan liked to think his darker nature was our mother's fault because she had spurned him as a baby. He could not drink her milk and was given to a wet nurse. Looking back on it, I had to wonder if the venom that seeped into his blood and vitals didn't find its source in that early rejection. I can find no other explanation. Although our mother was always cool to the both of us— she had never wanted children, particularly not rambunctious male twins—she was never cruel or unkind. As for relations between Morgan and me, there had always been a good-natured rivalry, as there is between boys in any family, but the contest turned bitter in our thirteenth year.

Our father had plans for his sons and in 1858 set them into motion. His ideas fit in perfectly with my own inclinations, as I'd had ships and the sea in my head from as long as I would remember. For Morgan, though, our father had his heart set on a medical career. There were tumultuous scenes; Morgan had it in his head that he, too, would be a sailor. The outcome of this conflict was that my sullen and embittered twin was sent off to boarding school to prepare for medicine, and I was taken aboard my father's sloop, the *Osprey,* as a cabin boy.

My father had developed a habit of "listening" to his ship, and that was early learned. He had developed a special ear, had that seasoned old man, and more than once his intuitive knowledge of the ship saved our lives. With a deck swaying beneath his feet, he was the living opposite of the gruff old sea dog—a soft-spoken, dreamy-natured autocrat who commanded and earned the admiration of his men by virtue of his seamanship. When he set his seabag down on the Jersey shore, he was out of tune. Restless, easily riled, not knowing what to do with himself, he swaggered too much and drank too much and listened to no one. He made our mother's life wretched with his outbreaks of unreasoning jealousy. The twenty years' difference in their ages was partly to blame. There was no evading the fact that my father's possessiveness drove her to desperate measures.

She was naturally high-spirited and had developed habits of independence during my father's long absences. A comely brunette with mischievous eyes, she liked men, and men admired her. One evening she didn't come back from a visit to relatives in Camden County. My father went after her and discovered the relatives in a state of confusion. No, they hadn't seen her. Was she coming to pay a visit, then? This was the first and greatest of a series of sorrows and losses that battered this good man and, at last, drove him under. As for my mother, she vanished after my brother and I turned fourteen. I never saw her again.

⌒≈

While my mind turned over these old coins, I "listened" to *Lorelei* as my father would have done—the thrumming of the steamboat's engine and the creak of her timbers as the Asahan rushed under her keel. The dense walls of nipa and nibong palms gave way to a shadowy demesne of entangled casuarinas and mangrove trees gripped by root and vine. There was movement along the banks, which at first I took for a herd of rare Sumatra short-tailed deer, stepping in and out of the sunspots. Then I noticed that the Malay twin on our bow was missing, and the sounding line was paying out from its coil on the deck.

There was about thirty yards of water on either side of the ship. I rang the ship's bell with furious alarm just as the first dugout canoe slipped from one of the inlets. At first it seemed derelict. Then its occupants rose up and, with unnerving war whoops, delivered a volley of arrows and musket shot. Shouting in terror, Devadatta ran out of the engine room. Master Kung beat a fierce call to arms on his cymbal. The Mamaqs were, as we had been forewarned, terrible to behold.

Their faces were hidden beneath beehive helmets made of wattle painted with symbols and around their wrists and ankles were bracelets of coiled thorn. Stained black as pitch, with jagged white thunderbolts snaking down their chests and legs, they shrieked their hideous war cries to the awful drone of bullroarers. These fearsome warriors seemed to have emerged from the primeval ooze of the earth itself to drive their enemies to despair. Shaking spears and bundles of arrows, they came at us in frenzied droves as if seeking pain and death.

Fahey got off the first shot on our side, and one of the warriors toppled out of his canoe. I took heart at this, for it proved our specters were mortal, at least. Heedless of casualties, the lead dugout, a half dozen others in its wake, made straight for *Lorelei*. Seeing as the path ahead and our portside were blocked by canoes, there seemed nothing to do but fight it out in the middle of the river. We were in a desperate situation, that was clear. I locked the wheel and, stepping outside, aimed my pistol at a Mamaq about to hurl his spear. I had barely a second to see the movement out of the corner of my eye. The edge of the hatchet glanced on my shoulder as I twisted to get out of the way. One of the Nasiruddin twins slammed against the side of the wheelhouse. The force of his collision gave me the opportunity to grapple with him and try to wrest the hatchet free. We were locked in a precarious circling dance on the open deck, where a false step could send us tumbling into the river. My opponent found an opening in my guard. The swing would have disemboweled me, but the hatchet never completed its arc. Instead, it flew out of my attacker's hand. As the twin grabbed his stomach, I pushed him away. He stumbled over the side and plunged into the river.

Devadatta lowered his rifle. I had no time to thank him. The lead canoes had slipped alongside, and the first warriors leaped onto the deck. We both let go a volley that stopped them. Fahey continued to fire from the main deck. I also heard pistol fire from the passenger deck and knew that Bridgett Hannover had pitched in to the defense.

With canoes encircling us, we would soon be boarded and overwhelmed. Our best defense was from the passenger deck, where we could fire with at least partial cover, especially since it appeared our attackers would win no awards for marksmanship. I hastened down the ladder in time to see Bridgett discharge her revolver into the face of a Mamaq ascending from the main deck. He fell back on two comrades, which opened up a field of fire for the rest of us. Two empty canoes drifted past while a third went around picking up the capsized. Rising out of the water, sleek as an eel, the other Nasiruddin twin pulled himself aboard this dugout and shook his fist at us. Meanwhile, the warriors in the flotilla directly ahead stood up to loose their arrows and spears.

The missiles never reached their targets. Instead, a fusillade of arrows fell on the Mamaqs. In a moment the attackers had become defenders. A group of strange war canoes broke into view in front of us, their high prows carved in the shape of grinning crocodiles. Sweeping around a bend, they fell on the main force of Mamaqs. Now under assault from the rear, the Mamaqs were thrown into confusion. They might have been able to regroup and repel their attackers, but their surprise turned into panic. As swiftly as they had launched their attack, the Mamaqs drove their canoes back to shore.

The author of their terror was the captain of the crocodile boats, a tall, armored apparition who stood fearlessly on the bow of the lead canoe. Over his head he waved a short sword of the type used by Rome's legions in Caesar's time. He was all over burnished gold, from the tip of his red-plumed helmet to the sculptured breastplate, down to the greaves buckled on his shins. He exhorted his warriors with a war cry that surmounted the din of battle.

"Iskandar! Iskandar!" his warriors cried. As the Mamaqs broke away, leaving their wounded comrades to the fury of their attackers, Fahey took aim to bring down the last Mamaq who had leaped on deck. With a groan, the man fell back into a river littered with dead. I took a quick roll call to see that we were all accounted for.

Within a few moments, the crocodile boats cleared the Mamaq dugouts from the river. These warriors each wore the tanned hide of a crocodile, with the beast's great gaping maw situated on their heads as a helmet. The rest of the skin fell over the shoulders like a cape. Buckled at the waist, it was ingenious camouflage and armor. The warriors, their eyes made huge by green and yellow war paint, now turned their glares on us. One of their captains jabbed his barbed spear at me. I cocked the hammer of my Colt. For a moment it looked as if we might have to defend ourselves from our rescuers. Dr. Diem came up and pushed down the barrel of my pistol.

"You'll have no need of that." He addressed the warriors in the canoes in a strange, sibilant tongue. They bowed their heads in reply. "They are Bataks from Bahal. These are the Crocodile Boys—the elite troops of Radjah Dulah."

"The fellow in the golden armor?" asked Fahey, looking around. "Where did he get to?"

Bridgett Hannover opened the chamber of her revolver and clinked the spent casings into her hand. "Iskandar—isn't that what they called him?"

"All over Asia," Diem reminded us, "that name means only one thing; Alexander the Great."

Fahey whistled under his breath. "Well, I'll be damned and roasted in hell."

"I'll take that as an apology," Diem answered with a smug little smile.

13

Dr. Diem and Kung made the rounds, tending to wounds. Devadatta had been cut on the cheek by a spear, and a musket ball had bounced off one of Fahey's ribs, no harm to the blarney. More than ever I was grateful for the presence of my stowaway from Kota Baru, not the least for the fine embroidery he performed on my shoulder where the Malay twin's hatchet had laid open the flesh. Diem conducted the operation on the top deck as evening settled in and bats swooped silently among the trees on the riverbanks. Kung set up a makeshift operating table with a basin of steaming water at hand. When Bridgett Hannover joined us, I took the opportunity to compliment her on her marksmanship.

Her freckled face still lit with excitement, she took the recognition in stride. "Outside of preaching, hunting was my husband's great passion. He gave me this revolver, and he taught me to use it. It's not the first occasion I've had to be thankful for his training."

"And grateful we are for that. What about Sahar?"

She offered a wry smile. "I think it's time I pulled her out from under the cot in our cabin."

"I concur with Captain Vanders," Diem said as he pulled in the last stitch to close my wound. "You should be complimented on your handling of a gun. You didn't blink an eye."

I detected no tone of sarcasm in Diem's words, but Hannover

arched an eyebrow. "Did you expect me to lose my head like Sahar?"

"I'm sure I implied nothing like that, Mrs. Hannover."

"Then what did you imply, Dr. Diem?"

"That you are a good shot, nothing more."

"It's not what a woman is good at, is it? Not in Tongkin, I think, where the women hobble about on bound feet."

Diem paused in his work on my shoulder. "Oh, and how are women bound in England?"

If Bridgett appreciated the irony, she did not show it. "God gave me a good eye and a steady hand. Those will do me right no matter where I am."

"I for one am grateful to that big fellow over there," I said, nodding in the direction of the tall Batak warrior giving orders from the bow to the canoe escort gliding in front of us. Vanda and his Crocodile Boys had helped us to turn the steamboat around. We were now back at the fork of the river and poised to ascend the right channel, the direction Devadatta had urged before we were betrayed by the Malay twins. I had already made amends with my engineer and thanked him for saving my life. To assure him of my continued confidence, I presented him with a cedarwood humidor containing five of the finest Dutch cigars made. He was greatly pleased.

"And our benefactor?" Bridgett asked. "Our mysterious Iskandar?"

Diem tied the final stitch and nodded to Kung. "Vanda has nothing to say about that. If our man in the golden armor is flesh and bone and not an avatar, I suspect he is with the advance party that went to announce our presence to Radjah Dulah."

Kung poured liquid from a vial into a basin of boiled water he had brought up for the physician. He held the basin while Diem washed his hands.

"There's worse," said the physician. "There's smallpox where we're headed—in Bahal, the radjah's capital."

That night the Crocodile Boys caught and roasted a wild boar. To this we added several pounds of milled white rice, a gift that pleased the Bataks; it was a commodity highly prized and usually served only at the royal court. At my request, Vanda assigned three of his men to keep guard on board *Lorelei,* one to each deck. Both Bridgett and Sahar were in a stir after the ambush and I thought the guards would help them sleep more easily. With my wound throbbing, I retired to my cabin early. After completing my journal entry, my eyes fell on the unopened books that Irene Burdett-Couts had left with me the morning I set sail—so long ago, it seemed!—from the Kuching harbor. One was an intriguing old curiosity, a kind of rutter written in Portuguese, for navigating the Malay Archipelago. It was filled with naval charts, delightful to study but now out of date by about two hundred years. The Asahan did not even appear on the vague outline of a map showing Sumatra's east coast. As I was perusing the rutter, I heard a muffled sound outside my door and saw the latch began to lift. I pulled the Colt from its holster and cocked the hammer, for I was as on edge as the others. The menacing shadow that fell across my cabin floor, however, turned out to be a savage from the Celtic tribe. Rowan Fahey put a finger to his lips.

Closing the door with a scarce audible creak, he looked about the close confines of my cabin as if sniffing out a spy. His suspicion fell on my pistol. "Put that thing away. Do you think I have come to do you harm? The opposite, you'll find."

"What's this all about, Fahey?" I kept the pistol where it was, for he was too close, and I did not like his stealthy entrance. The hunting knife at his belt made me no less easy.

"I think it's time you know the drift of things," he said at last. "I'm the rajah's man." He paused to gauge my reaction, which was, naturally, confounded. "The White Rajah of Sarawak has sent me along to guarantee the success of your enterprise." He gauged my reaction again, surprise now run to chagrin. "No, it's not that he distrusts you entirely. It's just that Brooke and I have had some dealings over the years, especially in matters that require not only a strong arm but, let's say, shadowy finesse."

"Why go through this elaborate ruse—bringing you to Kota Baru in chains? Why make off with the *Lorelei* in the dead of night?"

"For two very good reasons," whispered the Irishman as he took a seat on my bunk. "First off, the rajah wanted to show the Dutch that he could deliver the goods—namely yours truly in chains. Secondly, he put an awesome responsibility in your hands, Ulysses, and he needed to test your mettle."

"And you are his insurance, is that it?"

"The rajah wants this expedition to succeed in the worst way. If it does, he ends up pleasing everyone—the English, the Americans, the mission folk. The Dutch are not pleased, of course, but they'll come around. The last thing they want is dead missionaries on their doorstep. Such gratitude is powerful medicine in our rajah's hands. Plus, he gets a steamboat out of the deal."

"So the two of you cooked up the plan of pirating *Lorelei* to spring you from the trap?"

"Commandant Beets was most accommodating, wasn't he? He played right into our hands." Fahey broke into that choirboy grin, a mask for deviltry. "But I see you don't believe me." He slipped his hand inside his broadcloth shirt and pulled out a note-sized parchment. With a self-important flourish, he pointed to the red wax seal. "The rajah's signet, you'll mark."

I broke the seal to find a message set forth in a brisk, familiar hand:

> *Captain Vanders:*
> *When Rowan Fahey delivers this note to your hands, you will know he is earnestly in the rajah's employ and has been attached to your command to ensure its success. Bring him*

into your confidence, for I know he will prove his worth.

To aid in your endeavor, you will find thirty Enfield carbines and ammunition stored beneath the cargo deck. You will also find a culverin, powder, and shot.

Godspeed in your mission. We anxiously await your return.

I remain, faithfully,
Irene Burdett-Couts
For HH Charles Brooke, Rajah of Sarawak

I squinted at the script once more. "It's genuine—or so it appears."

"It would take me a full year and not to produce such flourishes. Besides, you can verify the truth of things when we get the chance to inspect the weapons. We can't do that now—not with those Batak savages aboard."

I leaned back in my chair and studied Fahey's countenance with a new, if grudging, appreciation. "So it seems we're conspirators indeed, but on a whole different level. That still doesn't quit me of piracy."

Fahey rose and stretched his arms. "I wouldn't lose any more sleep over it. The rajah will fix the thing for you. He's good at that." The Irishman opened the door a crack and looked both ways.

"Then this business about you and Deborah Rand—that was a ruse, too, wasn't it? You never knew a Deborah Rand."

"Mayhap I did. That's nothing to you!" A glower fell over his countenance as if he had been reminded of something he'd as soon forget. "Sometimes there's an extra ace up somebody else's sleeve. If there's a divinity, Vanders, he deals a black hand—especially to Irishmen."

～◉

I went over Irene's letter several times before I took to my bunk, wondering if she did "anxiously await" my return. I could find no

flaw in Fahey's explanation. Yet I couldn't shake myself free of
doubt. Rowan Fahey was what he seemed and wasn't, and damned
good at whoever he chose to be. Yet there were the guns. It was
more than small comfort knowing there were arms aboard *Lorelei*.
Our engagement with the Mamaqs had proved there would be
more battles to come. It seemed the Mamaqs and their bloodthirsty
Sakti were well advised of our arrival on the Asahan.

><=

Sometime in the early morning, I was awakened by a shout that
seemed to come from the main deck. I swung off my bunk, alert,
but there was no further sound. I again pulled my Colt from its
holster and stole barefoot along the deserted passenger deck. By
the time I reached the forward rail, there was already a commotion
on the foredeck, torches, a lantern, moving figures, sharp words.

"What is it, Captain?" Bridgett Hannover was by my side and
fastening her shift.

"Trouble, Bridgett."

By now I could make out Devadatta in his white turban and
canvas trousers, bending over a prostrate body and surrounded by
two of the Batak guards posted to guard the ship. Torches flitted
across the water. The Batak encampment onshore had been
aroused.

I went below to join my engineer, just in time to greet Vanda
leaping aboard from an adjoining canoe. Both of us looked down
on the man sprawled faceup on the deck—the third Batak guard.
Devadatta rose from the body as Dr. Diem pushed his way through
and knelt beside the man. He applied two fingers against the side
of the guard's neck and pulled out his watch. A moment later he
looked up, shaking his head. I knelt beside him. There wasn't a
mark on the dead guard, no blood, no sign of a struggle. Only his
features gave a clue as to what had happened. His lips were twisted
in a savage grimace, as if he had been leering at the very specter
that had struck him down.

Vanda questioned Diem in the Batak tongue. Though taciturn by nature, the tall warrior was having a difficult time controlling his agitation and the rumbling menaces of his men. He gestured at Diem with a broad fist that was missing the last two fingers.

Diem hurriedly translated. "Vanda wants to know how he can explain this to his men. The Mamaqs are now far from this place. This can't be blamed on them."

The sounds of a struggle came from the cargo hold. Immediately, several scowling Bataks pushed Fahey and Kung forward. "What the hell do you call this?" the Irishman spluttered. Then his eyes fell on the corpse. He gave me a sharp glance, as if warning me to keep silent, and looked away.

Vanda sent a line of spearmen to take up stations along the sides of the ship. "He says he has no choice," Diem explained. "Until we reach Bahal, we're all under guard."

"Surely he doesn't think we had anything to do with this?" Bridgett cried out from the deck above.

"He's calling it a murder," Diem replied. "The radjah will decide the matter. Until then we're all under suspicion."

Fahey shook himself free of the men who held him. "That gets him and any of his own off the hook, doesn't it?"

"Oh, no. Vanda is responsible. He could pay for the loss of this man with his own life."

"And what of us . . ." Devadatta's voice trailed off as if he knew the answer.

Diem's silence confirmed it.

14

"It is as I feared," Bridgett Hannover confided as I steered toward the landing at Bahal the following morning. "Miles told me the night we left Spoorwegen's Landing that we would be held in thrall. He said I must be brave, braver than I had ever been."

I wasn't about to listen to the missionary's account of her latest séance with her dead husband. My ship had been impounded, a score of armed Batak warriors lined our decks, and we were all under the suspicion of murder, a surreal condition made real by the body laid out on the foredeck and swathed in a winding sheet. Still, we would have need of the missionary's courage and experience in the days ahead.

"We shall find a way out of this," I said at last, as if to banish my own doubt.

"Miles is apprehensive, of course."

"Of course," I said, placing my hand on her shoulder. I could not help but feel sympathy for her, so keenly did she feel her husband's loss.

Radjah Dulah's capital had appeared out of the wall of the swamp like a mirage, a teeming compound of high-peaked houses surrounded by a teak palisade and pressed on three sides by the thick confusion of the rain forest. I was disappointed. The gables of the radjah's palace, another walled enclosure at the center of the sprawling village, did not glitter with gold. As for the imposing palisade, it sagged in places. There were no flags or pennants flying, but plumes of gray smoke cast a pall over the community. I had entertained some notion of a lost and fabled realm out of the pages of a romance, but this was merely a tawdry, ramshackle village, with mangy dogs and lean pigs foraging under the houses, set down in the backwater of a jungle river that scarcely anyone knew or even cared about. There was a feeling of oppression, reminding us that Bahal labored under the curse of a smallpox epidemic. As chorus to the tragedy, a small group of women dressed in pale batiks ventured out to the landing, saw the corpse so visible on our deck, and let forth a dispirited wail.

Vanda's war canoe transported the six of us to the landing. Only Devadatta was elated, pointing excitedly at the carved gates that loomed over us as we stepped onshore. Made of panels of planed teak, they were covered with intricate reliefs. The carvings were Indian in style and design. He told me they recalled the splendors of the Vijaya kingdom that had ruled southern India before the Muslim conquest and had been so curiously transplanted to the soil of Sumatra. War elephants swayed in procession, their howdahs bristling with spears; the bodies of defeated warriors littered a battlefield, and defeated kings bowed before the victor's regal chariot. A priest held a garland over the head of one victorious king. Other scenes showed the building of great stone temples, and religious processions held to honor the trinity of Hindu gods, as Devadatta had explained them to me—Brahma, the creator of worlds; Vishnu, the giver of life and knowledge; and Shiva, the dancing god at the center of the universe who rises above all the opposites and makes them one.

The inheritors of this grand tradition stood on either side of the muddy main thoroughfare, a people whose open faces and dark, wavy hair proclaimed traces of their Indian ancestry. They took our measure in sullen, inhospitable silence, their grim countenances smeared with ash. From several houses came the muffled cries of lamentation. An acrid odor hung in the air, the smell of the bitter herbs that mask contagion.

The bleak silence was broken by a tumultuous cadence of kettledrums. Brass horns blared, chimes tinkled, and cymbals clashed as a procession of colored parasols, adorned with glass and mirrors, advanced from the other end of the thoroughfare. Amid this swaying panoply was Radjah Dulah, borne aloft on a sedan chair by six plumed warriors and scowling as if he suffered from dyspepsia. Over his head waved a giant crimson parasol fringed with gold tassels. He wore a tall headdress festooned with hornbill feathers, a cape sewn from the bright feathers of smaller birds of a kind I had seen worn by chieftains in Hawaii, and a pectoral necklace made of gold and silver beads. Except for the scowl, he looked as stoical and enigmatic as any Augustus stamped on a Roman coin.

When our two processions met in the main square, the strident music stopped. For a giddy moment our fates seemed to sway between the extremes of hostility and hospitality. The balance was decided when an immense woman of many chins, swaddled in several layers of bright orange cloth, elbowed her way through the throng to stand before the radjah. She examined us through tiny eye-slits until her gaze came to rest on Vanda, at the head of our escort.

She spoke to him in a deep, peevish baritone as Diem whispered in my ear. "She is asking him if we are the travelers his war party rescued from the Mamaqs."

Vanda dropped to one knee and bowed his head. "They are, Lady Seowan. They have traveled up the river in a vessel that has a heart of steam."

The radjah nodded almost imperceptibly to the big woman. "These men are Dutchmen?" she asked.

"I do not think they are Dutchmen, Lady," Vanda replied. "But they have brought calamity with them, I fear. We have lost a soldier—Serai Sejong was slain last night."

The woman called Seowan glowered at this bringer of bad news. "He did not die of battle wounds?"

"No, Lady," Vanda replied. "I bring the foreigners under guard so they may answer to the radjah in this matter."

The radjah spoke then, or rather made a curious whirring sound with his tongue. He held out his hands. They were taken by two of his guards, while two other men held out their hands for the radjah's feet. Thus supported above the ground like a sacred bird, he inspected his visitors. Gradually, the creases in his face tightened in disapproval. He made a sign by crossing one hand over the other.

"Do you think they are *efrits?*" the big woman asked, using the Batak word for shape-shifters.

"If Radjah Dulah will allow," I said, stepping forward, "I am in command of the expedition. We travel to the radjah's court under the orders of Rajah Brooke of Sarawak, whose letter of introduction I bear. I can explain everything."

The radjah looked down at the letter bearing Brooke's red wax seal and said nothing.

Lady Seowan also was not impressed. Her lower lip curled in contempt. "Perhaps you can explain why your rajah sends assassins."

"My rajah holds your lord in highest esteem—" I started to explain.

"You deny the charge?" gasped the big woman in exaggerated injury. "When you were caught red-handed!"

At this moment Diem made a deep bow and saluted. "If the radjah will permit, perhaps he will recognize his son of many years ago, Phan Dom Diem, he who was given the Batak name of Si Nilam. As requested, I have come to bring what humble healing powers I have to the court of my lord, Radjah Dulah."

It seemed the radjah might trade his scowl for a smile. Then he rapped the head of his lead bearer with a fly whisk, and his men carried him around Diem in a complete circle. Another rap of the fly whisk brought them to a stop. The radjah shifted a sly gaze to the big woman.

"Radjah Dulah says that this man who calls himself by the name of Si Nilam is lying through his teeth. It is clear that he is an impostor and that the whole rat pack of you have come to stir up mischief."

The announcement was the cue for the radjah's guard to lower their spears and herd all of us into a circular hut fenced with upright staves and covered with pandanus thatch. When the wooden bars swung shut on us, the drums took up their throbbing rhythm again, and the horns blared, and we watched the whole procession recede behind another set of carved doors that led to the royal compound. The good citizens of Bahal then took up murmuring and, after that, handfuls of animal dung. These offerings they threw at us for a good half hour, until we were all spattered with excrement, our backs turned to our assailants as we huddled together in the stifling heat without water and without a clue as to our fate.

"You've brought us to a pretty pass," Fahey snarled at Diem. "Am I covered with rose petals? No, I'm covered with shite! And here you are a sneaking, impostering son of a bitch. Vanders, I told you we'd rue the day we didn't heave him over the side. Him and his rogue dwarf here!"

"I *am* who I claim to be," Diem said, beleaguered. "I don't know what the radjah's game is. He *knows* who I am."

"I think he wants my ship," I said dispiritedly. "He's after the *Lorelei*."

Fahey lowered his head as if he meant to assimilate this new insight. "Any river radjah would want the *Lorelei,* that's a fact," he grunted. "With a steamship, you could control the whole length of the Asahan."

"Perhaps he is after our heads," Devadatta offered mournfully. "Before his men eat us."

"The Bataks are not cannibals," Diem said consolingly. "Anymore."

Devadatta was not convinced. "Perhaps they mean to revive the custom."

"Little matter if you're without a head," griped Fahey.

Our speculations drifted off into miserable grumbles and then into moody silence as the height of the morning wore on and we stank and sweated in our cage. About noon there was a commotion at the royal compound. The gates flew open and a line of white-plumed warriors, the radjah's personal guard, quick-marched to our hut. Their captain, a curved kris in his hand, barked an order, and we emerged out of the suffocating heat into the blinding sun.

He herded our bedraggled company into the middle of the royal compound. At the end of the courtyard was a shell-shaped outdoor audience chamber draped in purple and gold. At the center of the stage was the radjah's throne, covered with a crimson cloth and set with pearls and precious stones. The spindly old man sat cross-legged on it and, from time to time, inclined his head to one of the two women at his side. The woman on his left was the corpulent emissary who had spoken for the radjah earlier. The other was a wizened crone decked in volumes of royal yellow cloth. She sucked noisily at her toothless gums and stared remorselessly at us like a judge who weighed dead men's souls. The whole compound was cordoned off by a square of Crocodile Boys.

Humiliated in our soiled clothes, certain we were about to meet an ignominious death, our only hope and comfort was a psalm recited by Bridgett until her voice was drowned by the pitiless rumble of native tympanis and the war cries that went up from the throats of the guards. Behind us, we heard the sound of heavy, clanking steps, steps that moved swiftly and ominously across the crushed coral covering the radjah's compound. Not one of us dared to look around. The cries of the guards ascended into a high-pitched ululation of praise.

The mighty Iskandar strode into view, the sunlight dancing across his golden armor and radiating his power. He held a heavy sword with a sinister curve to its blade. His identity was hidden beneath his helmet: the same man, or specter, who had led the Crocodile Boys against the Mamaqs, though now seen in the soulless role of an executioner. The warriors' cries subsided and the drums fell silent as the grim and gilded reaper paced before us, pausing there, pausing there, to gaze into a trembling countenance. The only sound beside the tread of his boots was Bridgett's mumbled exhortation that we should fear no evil.

"Indeed, you shall have nothing to fear," said Iskandar in perfect English. *"Provided"*—he stopped directly in front of the missionary. Her voice trailed off into a thin whisper. "Provided you confess your murders, your crimes, and your sins in toto."

We all stood in complete silence, not sure what we had heard but praying as ardently for Bridgett as she had prayed for us. Iskandar heaved a deep sigh. "No, I suppose you won't." A moment later he turned and pointed the deadly sword at Master Kung and thundered in an anguished voice: "But things have made it so that I must be heaven's scourge and minister!"

The guards behind the Chinaman drove him to his knees. Iskandar swung the sword high over his head.

Diem suddenly stepped forward and fearlessly confronted the executioner. "This man is innocent of any crime. He merely offers his life for ours."

"And you!" said Iskandar, turning his attention to the physician. "Are *you* prepared to take his place?"

Diem was thrown roughly to the ground beside Kung. In a final act of defiance, he glared up at the man who was about to end his life. Iskandar raised his sword again—and slowly lowered it. His hand went out to Diem and lifted him up. "Fear not, good Horatio," said the executioner, lifting off his helmet. "Do I not know a friend? What word do you bring from Wittenberg?"

"Prince Bandarak?" asked Diem in one astonished breath.

"The same. Now, what word from Wittenberg?"

"Words?"

"Good," said the other, clapping him on the back. "More than one. We must talk." Here was the prince we had heard so much about. His complexion was nearly fair, a light cinnamon, and he carried himself with a regal if studied mien, a parody of nobility. Teeth filed to sharp points confirmed the self-mockery in his smile. Adding to this barbaric touch, a blue vein fell across his forehead like a lightning bolt, and his nose, though finely molded, was broken in one place. His dark eyes flickered with uncertainties and portents like a general whose sleep, on the eve of a battle, has been racked with bad dreams.

"Prince Bandarak welcomes you, ladies and gentlemen, to the court of my father," the prince announced with a sweeping gesture. "And because this day we have found our old friend, we proclaim a general amnesty, commute all sentences, and throw open the jails."

Passing his sword to a subaltern, he placed his hands on Diem's shoulders and smiled as affably as filed teeth might allow at the shaken physician. "Truly you are my brother Si Nilam who lived with us so many years ago—as my father now recalls." The prince made a dismissive gesture to those seated in the royal dais. "This is Bahal, where we have an inner rot. But it's Wittenberg I long to hear of. I would embrace you forthwith but that you stink to high heaven and are in desperate need of a bath. A bath, nourishing food, and comfortable quarters will be provided to all of you directly. And then, my brother Si Nilam," he added solemnly, "then we will talk."

"I welcome," Diem started in a very thin voice. "I welcome the opportunity to speak with my brother Bandarak once more."

"The funeral meats but coldly furnish the marriage table," Bandarak whispered with a broad wink. Then, raising his voice: "Good, good, see that you do." With that the prince put his helmet under his arm and marched out of the compound whistling "London Bridge Is Falling Down."

15

Someone has stolen my son's brains. Who has done this to him? My gurus give me blank faces, empty hands." The lord of the Bataks lifted his stringy arms in supplication, speaking in a high falsetto like a remorseful old bandit in a Chinese opera. Behind him was a great painted tapa cloth that told the story of his reign, the temples built, the feasts given, the wars waged. Standing in his feathered cape before his crimson-draped throne in the great open shell of his audience hall, the radjah was a tired, bedraggled actor lost on his own stage.

The worst of it was the radjah was beginning to lose faith in the role, as Diem had explained to us over a breakfast of fresh fruit and coconut nectar. He knew he was only a figurehead. Real power resided in the person of the toothless old woman who sat at the radjah's right: Iruweh, the queen mother. However, her power was being challenged by the woman on his left, Seowan of the many chins, the radjah's new favorite. An ambitious and cunning woman, the favorite had crowded out all her rivals. Her hatred for Prince Bandarak, the radjah's only son, was well known. The power of these two women was backed by the high council now sitting across from Diem, Bridgett Hannover, and me in a semicircle behind the radjah's throne. The key figure in the mix, Diem had told us, was Ingit, the war chief, a self-important fellow with a ragged scar down one cheek who sat next directly behind Seowan, a mark of the con-cubine's favor. This confused political picture did not bode well for enlisting the radjah's help in rescuing the missionaries.

"I do not know what my son will do next," lamented the rad-jah. "He is a lackluster. He is a reprobate. He and his Crocodile Boys! Imagine a son who plots against his own father!"

"Most unnatural in a son." Seowan scowled. Her cheeks were rouged with a cosmetic the color of ripe cantaloupe.

"When did this affliction come upon him, my father?" asked Diem.

"A year ago, following his mother's death. He mourned in the extreme. He fell into a deep sadness from which he did not come out. Then I knew he was cursed. None of my gurus could do a thing with him. He called them a bunch of quacks. He began speaking in riddles and insulting everyone. Even me, his own fa-ther! At last I sought the help of your Reverend Ames." Radjah Dulah wagged a finger at Bridgett Hannover as he limped across the stage of his throne room, trailing his feathered mantle on the floor. "The reverend prayed over him. His wife prayed over him. Miss Rand prayed over him. He only became worse!"

"They cannot be blamed, Your Highness," said Bridgett stoutly. "Your son must be ready to receive the Lord's grace for prayer to work its miracle."

"Christian chatter." Seowan did not conceal her contempt. "That did not save them from the Mamaqs, either."

"Then you know what has happened to our people!" The words leaped from Bridgett's throat. "Mrs. Ames. Susannah Ames. What do you know of her? And Miss Rand."

The radjah and Seowan exchanged glances.

"We know nothing for sure," Seowan said carefully. "A month ago your mission was overrun by the Mamaqs. Since then—"

"Didn't you try to find out?"

"This Sakti of the Mamaqs has probably thrown them in a deep, dark hole," mused the radjah. "The only thing I have heard from the Mamaq Sakti is her demand for tribute. When we refused, she began her campaign of terror and revenge, burning our villages and taking slaves."

"These the Sakti turns into more Mamaqs to do her bidding," said Seowan.

"By sorcery!" sputtered Iruweh, the old queen mother. "She has come as we always knew she must come. At the end of the Ten Thousand Years. When the world is reborn in fire and blood."

"The Sakti," queried Diem. "She is the queen of the Mamaqs?"

"She is a wizard who commands giants," Ingit solemnly averred.

"When the Mamaqs came down from the great lake at Toba and seized this place you call Light of the World," said the radjah, "we tried to take it back."

"Lord Ingit valiantly led our forces," Seowan added sadly. "Even his great courage could not prevail."

"The Mamaq giants rose up over the walls of the mission," Ingit offered in his own defense, although he could not conceal his awe. "Twenty feet or more. They called down curses on our heads in brazen tongues. There was nothing I could do. My men broke and ran."

"Where was the great Iskandar, Your Highness?" I asked. "Just his appearance on the river two days ago sent the Mamaqs running in terror."

"On the day of our attack, Prince Bandarak could not be found."

"Oh, he was later found rolling around in a buffalo wallow and singing like a girl bathing in the river." Seowan had trouble hiding her contempt.

"The fit had come upon him." The radjah threw up his hands again. "He was useless to us that day. So it is he drifts from himself, in and out of his lunacy. But now you are here, Si Nilam, my son." He nodded affectionately to Dr. Diem. "Bandarak says you are his brother, and I have admonished those who falsely advised me that you were an imposter." The radjah cast a stern look at his head wizard, a feathered eminence who stared stonily ahead, nursing the injury to his reputation. "Now I have faith you will find the cure for my son's affliction. And for this disease that ravages us all."

"The radjah has faith," Seowan said diffidently, "that you will succeed where Christian prayers and our own gurus have failed."

"And how long has the epidemic been among you, my father?"

"Another affliction put upon us by the Mamaqs," moaned the radjah. "Not only has my son lost his wits, we are now cursed with this pox. After we launched the attack on the mission, my people began to sicken and die."

Diem was eager to disassociate the power of the Mamaqs with the appearance of the epidemic. He reminded the radjah of another outbreak of the dread disease. "I remember such an epidemic when I lived with you here, years ago."

"Not like this," said Ingit. "Hardly a house has been spared. Half of my warriors have been taken off by this pestilence."

"It will kill us all!" cried Seowan. Lest any doubt her terror, she threw her robe over her head and wailed.

"Not if you allow me to treat the village." Diem held up a glass vial containing a clear liquid. "There is a treatment for this sickness now. I can inoculate your people."

"Beware, my husband!" Seowan threw off her shawl. "How do we know we can trust this Si Nilam? Perhaps he plans to drug us and steal our powers."

"It is only a scratch on the arm." Diem pulled off his suit coat and rolled up his sleeve. "Like this."

"What do you propose?" The radjah bobbed his head from side to side, inspecting the vaccination on Diem's bicep. He looked tempted to touch the scar, then seemed to think better of it.

"Allow me to go from house to house. Master Kung and I will inoculate all those who have yet to contract the disease, beginning with the children." Diem put the vial back in his pocket. "We will do what we can for the others."

"But you will not fail me?" the radjah asked of Diem, wringing his hands.

"I will try, my father. As far as science will allow."

"If you do fail, my father will chop you into little messes." The heir to the Batak throne stood before us. "Chop, chop, chop."

What a transformation from the invincible Iskandar! The prince's long hair was matted with tufts of grass and leaves. He stood before us wearing only a greasy loincloth, his body caked with mud and dirt as if he had been crawling about in a mangrove swamp. A viper writhed in his hand, the snake's fangs curved like scimitars and dripping venom.

"I will pose you a riddle," he said, jumping onto the radjah's stage and presenting the snake to the royal court. "How is it that the head of a serpent"—he turned his head sharply to look on his father—"can have no thoughts of its own?" With the hissing viper, he made a playful jab at Seowan, who rose to her feet in a ponderous bloom of terror.

"You have no answer, my mother?" He rolled his eyes as if he had made a blunder. "My mind misgives, I took you for my mother, so forgive me that. My mother lives in darkness, too, but not by choice. Then, then, then, let me pose you another. How is it that a woman can couple with a man and give birth"—he strode over to the council, all of whom were on their feet—"to the same man who coupled with her?

"*No*, Father!" he cried out, running back to the radjah's throne. "If you lift your voice in song, her light will drown you. If you smother her light, her voice will cover you with the stinking earth."

The radjah rose from his throne, covering his ears, and left. Seowan followed, her blunt nose lifted in the air. One by one, the council members disappeared behind the great woven chronicle that covered the length of the stage.

"Look at them scurry!" Bandarak jumped on the throne and shouted after them. "Rats behind the arras!"

16

I think you must draw the conclusion that the missionaries are dead," Diem said solemnly, studying our faces as we sat in a grim group on the deck of *Lorelei*. "Besides, you cannot make it farther up the Asahan without a strong military force. Where will you find it? The people are terrified of the Mamaqs and exhausted by disease. True, Master Kung and I have been able to make some inroads against the smallpox . . ."

It was a modest admission by our physician, for during the three days we had moored in the pestilence-ridden capital, he had worked a minor miracle—and by means of an ingenious stratagem. Knowing the Batak sorcerers were hostile to him, he had the radjah call them together in their lord's presence. Diem then set about flattering them. Theirs was an ancient and hallowed art, he told them, and furthermore—to their astonishment—he confessed that his Western medicine was useless without their aid. He could not quarantine the sick without the gurus going into each stricken household and ensuring that the house soul, the *perubatan,* was removed to a safe place. Since the sick must be uprooted and the houses burned, the fetish, kept in a carved box, must be preserved until its family was restored to health. Furthermore, only the gurus knew the location of these fetishes. The medicine men debated the proposal heatedly, and one faction walked out in a pique, but most of them realized their prestige was on the line and signed on to Diem's plan. Besides, they had a canny angle of their own, for if Diem succeeded, they would share the glory; if Diem failed, they could point their fingers at the foreign quack and scoundrel.

At this point it looked like Diem's plan was working. Although, when I looked over to the smoke rising from the funeral pyres outside the palisade, I knew the contest was far from over. And I knew we must escape this oppression one way or the other. But our ship's council, held away from the ears of our Batak hosts, was fractious, as I knew it would be.

"Given the circumstances," Diem continued, "I think you must consider returning back down the river and seeking the aid of the Dutch."

"I won't hear of it!" Bridgett replied, and she looked around at all of us, her blue eyes flashing, her square chin jutting forward. "We haven't come this far to turn around. I'm not going to abandon the Ameses."

Fahey shook his head at her obstinacy. "Listen, Bridgett, the chance any of them is alive is slim. If they are, the Mamaqs have them. And if the Mamaqs have them, we probably don't want to see what's left of them."

"The situation at Bahal is like Javanese puppetry," Diem said. "We are only looking at shadows flitting across the screen. Radjah Dulah is failing, and grief over the death of his mother seems to have driven the heir mad."

"Seems to? The prince wouldn't be the first person grief has unraveled," said Bridgett.

"An eloquent grief," I qualified. "And delivered in English, too."

"Grief may have been the trigger." Diem held out his cup as Kung poured tea from a kettle. "His father had such high hopes for Bandarak. All dashed. But I agree with Captain Vanders, there's more than grief to the prince's madness."

Our Indian engineer had been sitting thoughtfully in our midst, his pointed chin resting in his hands. Now he broke his silence. "The people believe that Seowan had something to do with the death of Bandarak's mother."

"Aye, there's bound to be murder in the mix," said Fahey. "You've already got giants, bloodthirsty Mamaqs, assorted demons, and a female Sakti who lords it over the lot of them." He listed them on his fingers. "Throw in a cyclops or two, and all we'll need is a Homer to write the epic."

"With Bandarak to write the next chapter," I said.

"How do you mean?" asked the Irishman, squinting at me.

"The prince wants a secret meeting with us tonight at the armory."

"At the armory?" Fahey asked. "What's all this about?"

"Our fortunes ride on it," I said mysteriously. And left it at that.

⤙⤚

"That's the building," said Devadatta, with a finger to his lips. The armory was set among some horsehair trees to one side of the longhouse where Bandarak and his Crocodile Boys slept. A heavy rain shower provided Devadatta with the opportunity to scamper across the clearing. Fahey followed under the next cloud. It took a full five minutes, an interminable amount of time when one is in fear of being discovered, for the next cloud to veil the light from a three-quarter moon. Barefoot, I followed the others and had reached the near border of the grove when I stubbed my toe against a root and pitched forward.

"Damn!"

Fahey's hand was over my mouth as he lifted me out of the sandy mud. "You'll have all of us in a stewpot, Vanders," he hissed. We held our breaths for the outcry. None came.

Devadatta was the first one inside. I followed. At the back of the hut, a small wooden votary shrine emitted a thin, gauzy ray of light. In the center, improbably mounted on a dressmaker's mannequin, was the golden armor of the greatest warrior ever known. On his knees, Devadatta looked up at the panoply with a sense of wonder and adoration. It was a marvel of the ancient armorer's craft, the breastplate hammered with what appeared to be highlights from the Macedonian's conquests across the Asian continent, the battle of Issus where Black Clitus had saved his life, the burning of Persepolis, and on the right pectoral, the Greek phalanx engaged with the trumpeting elephants of the Indian general Porus on the Ganges, Alexander's farthest shore. A shoulder belt of white leather was draped over the harness, the jeweled hilt of the general's sword glittering in the half-light. Beneath the cuirass was a fringed girdle made of pointed leather strips studded with gold medallions. The helmet, with the familiar plume of crimson horsehair we had first seen in the war canoes, topped the display. Fahey pulled it off and, holding it above him, as if it were a crown and he Napoleon, slowly lowered it to his head.

"That's not for you," gasped Devadatta, nearly leaping up to snatch it away from the Irishman.

"You're right," Fahey replied, lifting the headgear beyond the Indian's grasp. "It would seem the ancient Greeks had small craniums. Little wonder, since they weren't raised on poteen." He shook the helmet. Something rattled inside. "Wait," he whispered. "What have we here?" Kneeling before the votive shrine, he directed the light of the oil lamp inside the helmet. He pulled out a cloth label.

" 'The property of Freddie Ireland,' " he read doubtfully. " 'The Emerald Isle Repertory, Rush Street, Dublin.' " He made a low chuckle: "So this is what happened to the prince of the music halls! Disappeared at sea five years ago on his way to a tour of Her Majesty's outposts in India." He rapped the helmet with his knuckles. "It's gold all right, gold paint washed over a tin pot."

"Make way, gentlemen, for I am a little too much in the sun." Bandarak's whisper came from the doorway of the hut. Peering behind into the darkness, the prince quickly hopped inside. "We must be sure not to disturb my Crocodiles," he said, putting a finger to his lips. "If they find you here, they may not understand and would carve you up before I could do a thing." He held out his hand for the helmet. "Behold Iskandar's hat." He sighed as he raised the gilt helmet. "I found this in an old leather trunk after a great wave had carried it up the river. I found the armor, and the soul of Iskandar was passed on to me. Now I am the soul of Iskandar."

I had come to the meeting with the hope that Bandarak, or at least the soul of Iskandar, might be reasoned with. If not, then we were all up for the stew pot, as Fahey put it, and it didn't much matter what I said. "We are honored you have agreed to meet us here, Prince."

"You have asked an audience with Iskandar and myself, and we are here." Bandarak lowered the helmet over his head and sat cross-legged before us. He was every inch the prince now that the mud had been cleaned off. His hair had been plaited and tipped with wooden beads, and he wore an embroidered vest with a pair of dark *sarung,* or Malay trousers. "What word have you brought, Vanders, son of Brooke? How stands the wind for Poland?"

"Poland," I hemmed, my mind racing. "Poland has turned a deaf ear toward us, my Lord. Even now he plots with the Mamaqs against you."

"He does?"

I put a finger to my lips. "Then we must steal a march on him."

"March we must. But where?"

"Even now the Mamaqs look down from their mountain stronghold at Light of the World and laugh at Iskandar and his Crocodile Boys."

The prince's long-jawed face turned incredulous. "They do?"

"For some months they have mocked you."

Bandarak did not seem convinced. "No one jests at the great Iskandar."

"Precisely my point, Prince. They must be uprooted from their stronghold and destroyed."

Bandarak shook a finger at me. "I think you might be trying to fool me," he said as he would to a child. "They have giants up there."

"Why should the mighty Iskandar, who has conquered all the known world, be troubled by a few giants?"

"There is truth in what you say." The prince put his hand to his cheek and spoke as if delivering an aside in a play. "I am only mad north by northwest." He winked at me. "I know a hawk from a handsaw."

Devadatta looked over at me in some perplexity. "Prince Bandarak is a masterful Prince Hamlet," I explained.

Bandarak slapped his thigh. "This is capital. You've guessed my secret!" He paused to gain control of himself while the humor filled his eyes with tears. "Reverend Ames was my friend, you know. When he learned I knew English, he gave me instruction in the Bible, which I did not like. We also read the plays of Shakespeare, which I did—Cymbeline, the folly of Romeo O Romeo, and the story of Prince Hamlet, which made me cry. When my mother died last year, I knew that someone at court had murdered her, but I could not prove it. Not my father, I think, but one among his toadies. So, I adopted a pose, gentlemen. I put on the Prince of Denmark's mad robes in the hope that some damning word or action might be revealed in my presence, for secrets are safe with the benighted." He crossed his arms and lifted his head theatrically. "Thus you have seen me. And thus I will continue to be until the murderer is uncovered. Now, as for the problem at the Light of the World—"

"You know about the missionaries."

"I have wanted to help them." He added plaintively, "But this business about the giants is real."

"You believe this story?" asked Fahey.

"The point is, *they* believe it," he said, indicating the community with a sweep of his arm. "Our war chief, Ingit, tried to attack the mission and failed. Now no one will go near the accursed place. Not even my Crocodiles will go."

"We may not need them, Prince Bandarak. Just the sight of Iskandar will turn the tide. That and the cannon we carry."

The prince was all attention. "You have a cannon?"

"Aye, a cannon, Your Majesty," Fahey enthused. "Stuffed with thunder to make a Mamaq run."

"A bow-chaser, it's called," I added. "And new carbines for brave men."

"New carbines, do you say?" The prince put a finger to his lips, considering. "Perhaps I might find some brave men for new carbines."

"The *Lorelei* will lead us upriver," I said.

"And you will go up to Light of the World?" Bandarak asked with some misgiving.

"My engineer and I, of course. Mrs. Hannover and her *turahan* will come, too. And Mr. Fahey here, our first mate."

"Good!" announced Bandarak, clapping his hands. "I'll sleep on it for a month and give you my decision."

"We will need to go tomorrow, Prince. Or not at all."

The lightning vein troubled Bandarak's brow. "Tomorrow? Is that not rash?"

"A quick decisive stroke, my prince. With such a triumph, you can unite all the Toba Bataks behind you. Then you can deal with your enemies here in the capital."

"I have longed for that, to unmask them. And unmask myself." The prince broke into a warm, winning smile that not even his filed teeth could mar. He gave me a comradely slap on the shoulder. "This is what I have been waiting for."

"We shall prove a brave and potent band, my prince," I said, as if I might even believe it.

"Now," said Bandarak, pulling Freddie Ireland's gilded sword from its scabbard, "the Mamaq Sakti shall feel the weight of Iskandar's steel."

"And the boom of his cannon," Devadatta reminded him.

"Boom," echoed the prince, with a whooshing sound. "Can you not hear it roar?"

⤚◌⤙

I would at last be satisfied about the weapons aboard *Lorelei*. And none too soon, now that we were about to embark on the last and most uncertain part of our journey up the Asahan. We took a canoe over to the ship that night. By lantern light, we lifted several of the boards from the cargo-hold deck. Fahey reached in and pulled out a new Enfield carbine with carrying strap, We pulled out thirty of them, just as Irene Burdett-Couts had promised in her note. We also wrestled out a six-pounder, a dozen round shot, six grape-shot canisters, black powder, and ammunition for the carbines.

"Well, Vanders, this changes the odds somewhat," Fahey said at last, mopping his brow and arms with the red bandanna he had untied from his neck. "Bless the bleedin' Rajah Brooke."

"How did you come into the rajah's pay, anyway? John Bull is his paymaster, as you know. But you're not a man for scruples, are you?"

His humor took an ironic turn. "Scruples be damned when it comes to putting some dancing room between my neck and a Dutch noose. But this is a limited operation—see that you get up the river, and see that you get back. If I hadn't taken charge of the *Lorelei*, you'd still be cooling your heels. Besides, when his Minister Between the Sheets, Miss Irene Burdett-Couts . . ." His mouth twisted in a leer. "When she makes an offer, a man listens. She has more ears at work for her than any *datu* or sultan in the Malay Archipelago. Aye, and knives to do her bidding."

"You should mind your filthy tongue where a lady is concerned."

"A lady, is it?" he scoffed. "You're a bigger fool than I took you for."

"You don't trust her?"

"No more than I trust you." He saw he had caught me off guard. "It was while we were standing over the graves of those poor Spoorwegens that my memory gave me a knock."

"What are you talking about?"

"I'm talking about Yokohama, Japan, some three years back."

"Go on."

"You had a breezy berth back there in Kuching before we set sail on the mad rescue party. First mate on the *Siren,* wasn't it? Why give that up?"

"What of it?"

"And here I mistook you for a seagoing Yankee lawyer!" He chuckled at the thought of it. "But I never mistake a face."

"So you said when we first met in the Kuching jail. What's that have to do with Yokohama?"

"As I say, it was when we were standing over the graves of those poor, damned Spoorwegens that the text of the conversation came back to me. There was Bridgett Hannover reading from Saint Paul, and there I was kneading a lump of earth in my fist to throw on the coffins we'd banged together. And there was you looking into the hole as pale as the corpses. I was thinking on the saints, nothing good, mind you, when the name and the face came together. The man in Yokohama went by the name of Simon Paul, but damn me if that was the real one. That fellow and you had a lot in common, I'd say."

Fahey dug into his hip pocket and pulled out a pint bottle. He held it next to the light and swirled the contents. "I'd say there's enough in this for each to have a pull. Last of the Spoorwegen rum. Good, too."

I tipped the brown bottle and let the liquid course down my throat. It was silvery to the tongue and made the heart glow. Fine Curacao rum, no doubt about it.

"I didn't make the connection at first because this Simon Paul fellow had a whaler's fringe about his chin, but I remember the discussion clearly, for the fellow had a plan of robbery he was trying to enlist me in. He said he knew of this Nipponese daimyo who hung out in the knocking shops the Japanners had set up for the foreign sailors. Seems this lord liked to slum with the foreign gaijin. Carried lots of gold on him. He drank his way from house to house, sometimes alone, sometimes with one samurai retainer. It would be easy to waylay him while he slept it off in one of the tarthouses."

"So you went in with him."

"I declined the offer." He wiped his lips with the back of his hand before he went on. "I told him somebody was likely to get killed, and it wouldn't be the daimyo. That was the end of it. Three years ago, it was—in the spring of 1872."

"And you never saw him again?"

"Not until you yourself walked into the White Rajah's jail."

He offered the bottle again, but I shook my head. "To square the record, in the spring of 1872 I was beached on Norfolk Island. My brigantine had suffered some bad weather—"

"There you are!" He grinned, clapping his palm to his forehead. "My mind misgives. You couldn't have been two places at once, now, could you? This world is filled with illusions and cheating resemblances." He lifted the bottle and let the last of the liquor slide down his throat. "Still, it's uncanny," he added, and his eyes held the gleam of conviction. "And when you became my keeper back in Kuching, I had to ask myself, 'I wonder if Rajah Brooke knows what kind of jaybird he has on the payroll.'"

"I told you, I'm not that man."

"Strange events aboard *Lorelei*," he persisted. "The fire in the galley, the snapped blade, and that dead Batak who brought us close to losing our heads. Someone doesn't want us to reach our destination."

"Do you really think I'd sabotage my own command?"

He paused to consider this, his eyes not leaving me. "Who else, then? Bridgett and her Malay are set on getting up to the mission. Diem and that dwarf of his had their own business in Bahal. Who else does it leave? Besides, there's a Dutch lilt to that name of yours."

"So that makes me a Dutch spy, is that it?"

"A man can be what he's not by simply being what he is. It's happened often enough."

"Let me ask you something, then, about this look-alike of mine in Yokohama. You said he had a whaler's beard. Did you notice anything else about him?"

"Except the resemblance, nah—there was nothing."

"No mark on him?"

Fahey tapped his head and smiled. "Come to think of it, he had a tattoo. On the right wrist, I think. Yes, on the right."

"Two men wrestling and behind them some stars—the Gemini."

"Perhaps that was the theme . . . Damn fine tattoo it was. Tinted most delicately, pink and blue, like the Chinese tattoo masters do."

I held out my wrists. Fahey lifted the lantern and whistled under his breath. "All right, mayhap you're not the man," he said doubtfully. And then he squinted again. "But you know of him!"

"I know of him. But that's nothing to do with sabotage on the *Lorelei*. And by process of elimination, you've left only one candidate."

Fahey laughed again, but with an underlying wariness. "Hah! You'd try to turn the tables on me, is that it?" He left the hold and stepped out on the foredeck. The air was humid and thick with the miasmal smells that follow a spurt of rain in the tropics. Still, moving outside dispelled the tension between us. I set the lantern on a keg as we looked out over the dark water. "You might be right," he said at last. "Except that I want to get up to the mission as much as any of us. I want to finish this thing and be on my way. But first I must be free."

"Free of what?"

"You know as well as I."

"Free of her," I said, remembering. "You want to be free of the girl who dashed your hopes. The girl who never showed up that winter's night at a seaport inn."

"I'll be free only when I find out for sure." There was temper in his dark eyes. "I wouldn't hurt her, if that's what you're thinking."

"I was thinking you're not the only one who wants to be free."

"You know her?" Fahey's eyebrow rose like a spike.

"No, I don't mean Deborah Rand. I've felt another presence ever since Jambi Station, an echo of someone else, of someone I may have known. She's there, too, where your Deborah Rand is, at Light of the World."

"Mayhap we're going the way of Spoorwegen," Fahey said glumly. "After a while, this place begins to bore into your skull."

"Whatever it is, Fahey, I'm damn well queasy about it. I'm drawn to it—and repelled at the same time."

I found myself talking about Wallace's mysterious journal, his encounter with his lost betrothed in the jungle, of Captain Fritz and the Mischief, of the things I'd seen and heard, or not seen and heard, and realizing how damned ridiculous I must sound.

Only Fahey wasn't laughing.

W e turned a bend the next morning, and the garish parasols of Bahal vanished behind a curtain of misty rain, the blaring trumpets and pounding tympanis of our farewell hushed by the brooding audience of the forest. Our last link with the known world, familiar even in its exoticism, had been severed. We were steaming north, the brave *Lorelei* bearing the war scars of our encounter with the Mamaqs, casting a spume of black smoke like a challenge. Twenty war canoes with crocodile-snouted prows led the way, the rowers silently driving their spear-shaped paddles into the jet water, dark as a squid's signature.

We had embarked on the last leg of our journey, our bow turned north toward Light of the World and the vast, mysterious headwater of Lake Toba. This great crater lake, formed in the mouth of an extinct volcano, was the source for the Asahan and a half-dozen other rivers that coursed down the high ridges of the Barisan Mountains to the northwestern and eastern shores of Sumatra. It was also the source of the legends collecting around that fabled and energetic race described by Captain Claridge, the *Rajo Alam*. The Lords of the Wind, I recalled, had first settled Sumatra and raised mighty stone cities. Their ancient capital thrived on an island in Lake Toba called Samosir. Prince Bandarak had described it to me as a forbidding place avoided by the Bataks and the other tribes.

The power of the lake's water had carved Pamuntang Gorge, whose steep, rugged walls, towering some seventy feet above us, we reached by noon. Ten miles of twisting and increasingly turbulent water lay between us and the mission.

During an advance foray by the lead canoes, I left the wheelhouse to see to our rescue force. Since Diem and Master Kung had stayed behind to deal with the epidemic, our original group had been reduced to four, but we had Bandarak, who traveled with us on *Lorelei,* and his force of a hundred Crocodile Boys.

A thick spray was already breaking on rocks ahead of us when I went below. The turbulent water might conceal any of a dozen hazards that could doom our expedition. Bridgett Hannover was leaning on the forward rail of the second deck and staring intently at the swells ahead. One look was enough to tell me her fear.

I said to her, "We'll have white water, all right, but the question is whether there's enough room and depth to maneuver around the rocks. A stern-wheeler has never been up this far, so we have no way of knowing. The Bataks can help nose us around some of the trouble with pull ropes."

"What about the Mamaqs?"

I pointed to the ridges above. "There are two scouting parties, one on each side of the gorge. They'll signal us if there is trouble ahead." I asked after Sahar.

"She's sick in our cabin again." Bridgett's eyes had lost their piercing authority, her features gone gray and sallow. "She's terrified, if you want the truth of it. I tried to get her to stay in Bahal, but poor girl, she won't leave my side."

"You look none the better yourself, Bridgett."

"I've been through worse than this," she said, straightening up self-consciously. "I know she's still alive."

"She?"

"The Ameses," she said, and some color stained her cheeks. "And Miss Rand. They must be alive."

When I peeked in the engine room, my engineer was squatting over the engine casing with oil can in hand. He wore a fresh garland of exotic blooms about his neck and one looped about his turban, gifts from female admirers in the village, where he had cut quite a figure. He had even been rowed out to the ship at sunup by a bevy of Batak beauties who showered him with laughter and hibiscus blooms until he clambered aboard, flustered that I had been looking on from the top deck with no small amusement. I decided to make him squirm a bit more.

"Why, Devadatta—I'll think you'll have to turn your thoughts to marriage when we come back down the river."

"It's not that!" Devadatta's protest was almost convincing. "Being Indian, sir, I'm thought of as long-lost family among these Bataks. Since I am in charge of the heart of the ship with a heart of steam, I have unfortunately become more esteemed than I intended—at least heretofore."

"I'm sure of it."

"Besides, the big splash was all for Prince Bandarak," he added, adroitly shifting the subject.

The prince had surprised us all by putting on quite a show for his father. He had marched his Crocodile Boys into the royal compound in full regalia, tympanis booming. He had shown his father the Enfield rifles and sworn his intention to drive the Mamaqs from the Asahan and restore the radjah's lost honor. As the Crocodiles shouted his name, the court swung to his favor. The old rajah wavered, for he wished to protect his son. Then Seowan came to Bandarak's defense and exhorted the radjah to allow his son to lead the expedition. Surprised and swayed by his concubine's insistence, the radjah reluctantly agreed, but it must have been apparent to more than a few at court that Seowan had everything to gain if some misfortune befell the prince.

Leaving Devadatta to lavish his usual care on *Lorelei*'s jealous heart, I found Fahey in the cargo hold. He had an array of carpenter's tools out on the deck and was at work constructing a carriage for the swivel cannon that Irene Burdett-Couts had romantically, though inaccurately, described as a culverin; that type of long-nosed artillery had been obsolete for over a century. Our six-pound bow-chaser had been cast more recently than that but was still an antique, a muzzle loader dating from the Napoleonic wars. It was a serviceable piece, though, and might tip the scales in our favor.

"Now, if I can only find enough wood from this scrap," Fahey said, tossing aside a length of timber. "She's got to have an elevated carriage if she's going to be any use to us. Even with elevation, we'll have to get in close enough to make an impression."

"I'd make it two hundred yards."

Fahey appraised a block of planed wood. "Aye, three hundred yards at the outside. The bark might prove more potent than the bite. Assuming the Mamaqs have never known cannon fire."

I found the prince standing by the stern-wheel and staring at *Lorelei's* wake. His mood had shifted dramatically in the few hours since he had come aboard. Replacing yesterday's bravado was a brooding anxiety. No doubt the reality of the enterprise had at last settled upon him, the certainty that we would encounter Mamaq giants and the uncertainty as to what other terrors that may lie ahead. I wondered how many others at the court wished the prince would find a hero's death. It would be a convenient way for his enemies to rid themselves of the heir, as well as a troublesome madman whose ravings hinted at dark crimes and retribution.

"There is providence in the fall of an eagle, Vanders Son of Brooke," he recited without turning around. "If it be not now, it will be, and if it is now, then it falls upon a king as well as the beggar in the storm. I weep for the poor lost prince of Denmark, though he will not weep for me."

"How is that, my prince?"

"It's a bloody business!" he muttered. "Once you've unsheathed a blade, then it must pierce something, brain, belly, or a tender heart. Still, someone needs to drive out the giants, so why shouldn't it be me? Yet I have seen the warrant." He turned with a strange light burning in his eyes. He opened his palm as if to show me a paper. "It bears her signature, mark you. But written in my blood."

"What warrant is this?"

He rubbed his brow as if he had lost the thought. "Right now it signifies nothing. It is merely a command. But wait, my good friend, when we get to Albion—"

"You mean Light of the World, sir."

"No, I mean Albion, sir. Now go about your sheets and jibs."

I left him gazing into the swirling waters, but what they signified to him I could only guess. It seemed to me that the obscure banter and Hamletisms were merely his practice, his way of honing the pretense he had created for himself. My worry was that the role he had conjured out of an old tragedy might engulf the actor. If the prince faltered, then even our slim chance at rescuing the Ameses and Deborah Rand would be dashed.

The first challenge to our progress came the following morning. We had navigated upriver without mishap. There had been a prickly stretch of white water about seven miles above Bahal, but the Crocodiles proved adept with the pull ropes, and *Lorelie*'s shallow draft eased over and around the worst patches. At length the white water gave way to a gliding current and then to a large basin that had been hollowed out of the rock wall on our port side. Here the water was deep, black, and still, a perfect anchorage with a small pebbled landing at the base of the cliff face. Leading down to this cove, a rough inclined staircase had been chiseled into the rock wall. We took the staircase carrying our gear, the cannon, and Fahey's gun carriage. The steps went up a hundred feet, a dizzying climb; all the while, our attention was fixed on the cliff above, an ideal spot for an ambush.

Our scouting parties had been sent out to prevent this kind of surprise, but though we made it to the top of the gorge safely, there was no sign of them. Bandarak dispatched a search party to find them. We waited an anxious thirty minutes until a single shot broke the silence. There was some debate between Bandarak and Vanda as to what this shot signified since the search party had been ordered to fall back and report if they encountered any trouble. When none of the searchers showed, Bandarak gave the order to advance, and we moved cautiously through the high bush, our force of Crocodile Boys fanning out on either side. Bridgett, Fahey, Bandarak, his bodyguard, and I made the core of the force, since we had all been outfitted with the Enfields cached in the *Lorelei*. Devadatta waited on *Lorelei* with Sahar and a half-dozen warriors, ready to weigh anchor in a hurry.

The bush thinned out after a half mile or so and opened to a broad savanna. This was the homeland of the Minangkabau, a tribe of doughty horse breeders and traders known simply as the Horseriders. The savanna's gently rolling hills formed the sides of a great valley, at the head of which was the mission called Light of the World.

A former Dutch fortress, its granite walls sheathed in crumbling stucco, the mission rose with ponderous determination thirty feet above the plain. It had been garrisoned for almost a century, but somewhere along the line, we were told in Bahal, the resolve had faltered. The cannon that once threatened the valley from its corner bastions had been removed thirty years before by its last dispirited garrison. When Reverend Noel Ames had chanced upon the abandoned outpost in his missionary travels, he decided to claim the building and give it a name that burned with evangelical zeal. The light from that flame, it appeared, had flickered low, for the only hint that the fortress had been given over to the Lord's work was the remnant of a stone cross above the main gate, gouged, chipped, its right arm missing. In this forlorn corner of the world, as remote from civilized Europe as could be imagined, the singular monument struck me as a towering paradox, at once dedicated to the God of War and the Prince of Peace, the exclamation point to a vain decree proclaiming progress, order, and a hopeful faith. Now the fortress mission was in the possession of warriors of a savage race. Though they were out of sight, they seemed to have left their deadly imprint on the ghastly geography that surrounded their new domain.

The savanna that greeted us was not green and verdant. It was scorched and wilted, as if a great wildfire had roared through the hills. Here and there, the husks of solitary trees stood like blackened gallows, surrounded by vegetation turned yellow, diseased, and sickly. This was the scene of desolation that stretched for a mile on either side, extending to the walls of the mission fortress that dominated the valley.

A messenger from the rescue party came racing down the charred track to report to Prince Bandarak. Almost immediately, the prince sent his troops at a quick march up the road. We were not long behind. The scene that confronted us at the first Horserider village confirmed the ferocity of our foe. The village had been sacked and burned some weeks before, to judge by the blackened timbers of the houses and the pale yellow shoots already snaking through the ruins. Of the former inhabitants, there was no trace. In the village commons, we found five of the Batak scouts. They had been pulled up by their necks on tall poles, to which they had also been tethered by their feet and ankles. Naked, the flesh torn off their faces to expose bloody skulls, their torsos hung some ten feet above, jaws gaping as if to suck in the thick, oppressive air. Their murderers had vanished.

Immediately, there was fierce discussion among the captains and their men, already unnerved by the prospect of going into battle against giants. The horrific sight that confronted us had added another layer to their terror. Several of the warriors were shaking their heads, and one of them took off his crocodile armor and flung it to the ground.

I wondered how Bandarak would handle the situation. If the expedition became unraveled here, we would have to pull up stakes and head back down the river. If there was ever a moment to test Bandarak's mettle or his madness, this was it.

Jumping on a stone rice trough, he confronted his men by first pulling off his ceremonial bird-feather cape, symbol of his royal rank. Underneath he wore a woven vest, which he removed, and then his pantaloons and breechcloth. Standing naked before his men, he addressed them as one warrior to another. Pointing to the scars on his body, of which there were many, he tore a leaf from the real Iskandar's book and recounted the battles in which he had received his wounds. He exhorted his men to remember those battles, and that he had suffered as do ordinary soldiers. He then went a bit further than Alexander. Demanding a curved kris from a captain, he held out one arm, the dagger poised above. He said that if his men proved cowards and would not honor him and their slain comrades, then he could no longer bear the shame and would take his own life before them. To prove he meant business, he slid the blade of the kris down his inner arm. Blood flowed down his wrist and dripped from his fingers. His men stood transfixed. He switched the kris to his bloody hand and held out his other arm. As he lowered the dagger, one of his captains grabbed the prince's hand and implored him not to hurt himself further. The Crocodile Boys fell as one to their knees and moaned and keened and cried. One of them shouted to the prince not to shame and humiliate them further. They would follow him to the ends of the earth. They would charge into the very mouths of giants to bring glory to their brave prince and avenge their slain comrades.

Here was a flash of Bandarak the war chief, and my spirits lifted at the sight. Bending on one knee before the prince, I offered my handkerchief, emblazoned in gold thread with the arms of Rajah Brooke. Bandarak looked down at me with a quizzical smile and barely nodded. One of his captains snatched the cloth and used it to bind his prince's wound.

With this immediate crisis behind us, our company descended the sere, autumnal slopes of the valley, our passage uncontested.

Eerily absent were the customary cries of jungle animals and birds. The farther we advanced into the valley, the more we could feel the presence of a powerful but invisible force. It was as if the air had taken on the opaque distortions and density of water, which made trudging through it a slow and uneasy progress. I felt both light-headed and lead-footed, and this disorientation excited my sense of foreboding. I could see the same disquiet reflected in all the faces of our company.

After an hour, we ended up on the crest of a hillock, part of a ridge that faced the grim, seemingly deserted walls of the mission. Our six-pounder had a clear line of fire from this position, an advantage that was heightened by an elevation that seemed nearly parallel with the top of the mission walls. However, it did not give us view as to what might lay inside.

Bandarak called for a war council. Some of the chieftains argued for immediate action, others for an early-morning assault. Fahey weighed in as artillery officer and suggested that we test the defenses with a few rounds from the six-pounder to see if bombardment stirred up any response. We couldn't be sure that the Mamaqs had even decided to make a stand at the mission. I concurred with this strategy, and Prince Bandarak agreed, to a point. He decided on a short bombardment to be followed by a general assault. Already his men were preparing scaling ladders from lengths of giant bamboo we had carried with us from Bahal.

The prince's decision ended further argument. He set about deploying his men in a wide arc behind the ridge. Fahey's gun carriage was serviceable enough, and he had solved the problem of elevation by stacking wooden wedges of different thickness in a notch below the barrel. Along with powder, there was the round shot and grapeshot to deliver. The Irishman began with round shot while I reckoned our coordinates with the aid of an old spyglass. Bridgett primed the weapon with gunpowder and rammed home the shot.

The bow-chaser made an impressive boom, but the first shot

plowed into the earth well short of the mission. A second shot bounced off the wall. It was only with the third round that we gauged the height to lob into the mission enclosure. There was no reply from our enemies, however, not so much as a yell of defiance, so Bandarak gave the order for his men to advance. They went up the valley in three disciplined squares, carrying their ladders, with a skirmish line of carabineers before them. The Bataks had learned a thing or two from Dutch infantry tactics.

By now the sun was in descent, casting long shadows behind a line of hills to our left. The Crocodile Boys, reptilian armor trailing down their backs, were over halfway to the mission when the giants introduced themselves.

One moment the front ramparts of the mission were bare; the next they were occupied by figures that rose shoulders, neck, and head some ten feet above the top of the walls, bobbing back and forth, waving spears and swords and accompanied by a terrible din of drums and war whoops. Turning the spyglass on them, I studied these giants with amazement and consternation. Their heads were immense, with long faces and ears, some with chin whiskers, others wearing helmets, their lips twisted with fury at this assault upon their realm. As an added element of terror, their eyes caught the fiery light of sunset and blazed forth with fierce malevolence. More disconcerting yet was the effect these specters had upon the ranks of attackers. When they saw and heard what they were up against, the Crocodile Boys came to a jarring halt, turned on their heels, and ran, many of them dropping their weapons and ladders in their haste. At the same moment, the wooden gates of the mission swung open, and a storm of Mamaqs, like implacable golems summoned from the steaming innards of the earth, fell on their retreating enemies.

Just when it looked as if our assault on Light of the World had turned into a rout, two extraordinary things happened. Fahey fired the six-pounder, this time stuffed with grapeshot. These small balls of lead were packed with a load of powder and designed to detonate over the target, sending hundreds of projectiles into the enemy's ranks. That was exactly what they did, exploding over the giants on the ramparts and setting them on fire. As the flames leaped up their glowering countenances, the invincible Iskandar at last made his appearance on the battlefield, galloping behind his men on a charger. I swung the spyglass in this direction and saw that the war horse was a half-starved nag that had apparently wandered into Bandarak's camp.

The effect, however, was electric. At the sight of this adversary bodied forth in golden armor, with a crimson plume and cape streaming behind—and mounted on a charger!—the Mamaq pursuers halted in a confused mass in the middle of the battlefield. They milled about, then at once were standing in an illumination nearly as bright as noon. One of their captains pointed to the ramparts behind them, and the warriors released an exclamation of horror. Their monstrous overlords had been transformed into great spears of flame that immolated their own dream of slaughter on the battlefield.

Bridgett and Fahey had, by this time, loaded the cannon with a new load of grapeshot, lowered the elevation, and blasted the deadly package into the midst of the stunned Mamaqs. The Crocodile Boys had regrouped after their leader swept through their broken ranks, his sword pointing the way to victory. Taking heart, they quickly turned around, picking up their weapons as they ran and, bellowing their war cries, fell on the disordered mass of their enemies.

This was all too much for the Mamaqs. Confronted by the invincible Iskandar, riddled with grapeshot, their very gods having gone up in flames, they broke and ran, some heading back into the mission but most fleeing upland, making for a line of hills due north where the savanna gave way to the darkness and safety of the forest.

I became caught up in the passion of the moment and, lacking cutlass or rapier, presented my spyglass and raced down the hill.

Hallooing and whooping and waving the brass telescope over my head like the club of Heracles, I must have appeared a ridiculous sight, but no more absurd than Prince Bandarak himself. Flailing his arms above his bony charger, hurling great oaths and imprecations, he sat in the middle of the field going nowhere, for his mount had proved obstinate and dug in its hooves. Meanwhile, his Crocodiles raced into the fort. Coming up behind the prince's stubborn charger, I gave him a thwack on his hindquarters with the spyglass. Perhaps thanks to this incentive, or perhaps because the nag scented forage and water in the mission, he suddenly bolted forward, the prince holding on to his mane for dear life. Consequently, the prince and I were among the last to enter the conquered fortress, though our artillery officers, Bridgett and Fahey, were not far behind.

Inside, the Mamaq giants, those terrible overlords, lay in a smoking heap at the base of the ramparts. With the discharge of tension our victory occasioned, I burst out laughing at the sight of these rag dolls, for that was nearly what they were—giant wooden puppets, artfully carved and painted. Tall bamboo poles attached to their arms allowed them to be raised and lowered. An ingenious piece of Mamaq conjuring!

Smoke from the smoldering marionettes and a shed that had caught fire drifted across what had once been a parade ground for Dutch soldiers. All around us, the Crocodiles shrilled their victory whoops. Bridgett looked about at the confusion until her attention fixed on a curtained window within the colonnade that surrounded the parade ground. "Susannah!" she cried out. "Noel!" She headed for the apartment with the curtains. Whether or not she had seen the missionaries, I could not tell.

The uproar of continued fighting came from the north end of the parade ground. Fahey and I followed it. A determined band of enemy warriors had clustered about a semicircle of grisly war banners, bleached skulls affixed to tall poles and fringed with dyed human hair. They had chosen their ground before the mission chapel, to judge by the partially burned cross hung at a crazy angle over the entrance, and they fought with a desperation that did not yield an inch of ground unless a body filled it. Yet their fierce energy could not save them, and one by one, they fell to the spears and daggers of the Crocodiles. In a few moments, there was nothing left but a heap of dead and twitching dying, the latter to feel the final fury and bloodlust of the revenging Bataks. Even Bandarak had succumbed to the dark urge for carnage, and there was nothing for Fahey and me to do but pass into the chapel, our rifles at the ready.

The heat, the dust, the cries of the victors, and the shrieks of the dying receded as we entered the cooler confines of the long room with an altar at its end, from which oil lamps gave off a subdued glow. There was no feeling of sanctuary in this place, only a sickening odor of rot and decay. As our eyes adjusted to the gloom, we saw that waste and refuse lay scattered about the room amid the broken shards of the prayer boxes and pews. The altar cloth was still intact, but as we advanced, we saw that it was steeped with bloodstains. Set between the lamps was a silver cross, defiled with what appeared to be pieces of dried and shriveled flesh, whether beast or human I could not tell. Before the cross was a statuette, glistening sleek and black. Fahey and I looked at each other in wonder. It was a grossly distorted image of a pregnant woman, her face twisted in pain.

Our wondering thoughts were cut short by a scuttling in the darkness beyond the altar. Fahey raised his rifle. A flicker of movement and a stifled cry like that of a terrified animal. I could make out a shape crouched against the far wall, inching away. I scooped up one of the oil lamps from the altar and advanced, holding the light above my head. The shadows leaped back to reveal a Mamaq woman. Now that the light had exposed her, she jumped to her feet and, baring her teeth like a cornered beast, waved a curved dagger to warn us off. Even in the dim light, there could be no doubt she was a young woman, for she was naked except for a brief loincloth and the luminous coating of black and white war paint peculiar to the Mamaqs. Her hair shone with the same silvery paint, pulled in stiff points to resemble serpents. The paint also covered the face of this Medusa, which made the whites of her eyes stand out with a kind of hypnotic intensity, as if she might indeed turn men to stone. Back against the wall, she jabbed the dagger at us and hissed through lips that had been dyed blood red.

We stood there in uneasy immobility, Fahey fingering the bolt of his Enfield, me frozen in place with the lamp over my head, the Mamaq female with knife at the ready, her shoulders lowered and ready to pounce, when the voice of Bridgett Hannover rang out behind us cold and clear.

"Deborah Rand!" she cried. "*Here* your evil ends."

The report of her rifle sent the Mamaq reeling against the wall as the room was thrown into darkness.

Absolute silence followed the report of Bridgett Hannover's rifle. Startled by the gunshot, I had dropped the oil lamp, and we were plunged into darkness. I could hear Fahey fumbling about, then the sharp scratch of a match. The light fell on the crumpled figure of the woman in Mamaq paint, shivering and clutching at her shoulder. Bridgett tore a piece of her petticoat to stanch the wound. Fahey found an old blanket, and together we wrapped the groaning woman in it. Bridgett opened an interior door, and we carried our prisoner to a large adjoining room filled with two neat lines of cots. We placed Deborah Rand on one of them while Bridgett went into a room at the far end of the dispensary. Returning with bandages and antiseptic, the missionary sat down on the cot and rolled up her sleeves. Fahey stayed Bridgett's hand from treating the patient.

"I'll be the one to look after her," he said with a scowl. He looked over at me worriedly. "She damn near killed the girl, Vanders."

"Then *I'll* be the one to mend her," Bridgett replied. "Let go of my arm, Mr. Fahey. You have better things to do right now than play the Irish hooligan. The best help you can be is to stand guard at the door and keep the rampaging Bataks from coming in here. If they find her, *they'll* kill her."

Up to this point, our patient had been unconscious, but suddenly, her eyes shot open—furious gray eyes full of pain—and she began to struggle. As we tried to hold her down, she tried to bite Bridgett's arm and kick herself free. The spasm was brief, however, and she sank back into unconsciousness.

"We'll have to restrain her," said Bridgett. She handed me a tongue depressor and a roll of gauze bandage. "Slip the wood between her teeth and bind her mouth." When she saw me hesitate, she stuck the depressor between the woman's teeth. "We can't have her trying to bite us while we're fixing her, Captain. And we can't have her bringing the Bataks in here. Now bind her mouth and then bind her ankles."

With that done, the missionary directed me to bring in boiling water from the next room, where she had already started a kettle on a cast-iron stove. Bridgett's medical efficiency didn't exactly surprise me, but I had to remind myself that this woman had lived in remote parts of the world, ministering to the bodies as well as the spirits of her exotic converts.

She cleaned the wound with gauze and antiseptic. When she looked at me again, it was with a nod of relief. "The bullet has gone through." She pointed to the back of the dispensary. "The staircase leads to the upstairs apartments. I don't know the condition of the rooms, but we'll need to find her a snug place to convalesce, and one with a strong door."

The staircase opened on a corridor that covered the length of the west wall of the building. There were one- and two-room apartments on either side, originally designed as officers' quarters. The rooms had been ransacked, the few pieces of furniture smashed and burned, refuse on the floor, and on the walls were lurid charcoal drawings—Mamaq warriors attacking a village, rearing horses, and strange towers with human figures bound to them. The animals and the figures were pierced with spears and arrows.

Each of the rooms had been similarly pillaged, except the last.

It was a small, tidy bedroom with a grilled window looking toward the distant Barisan Mountains. There was a cot with a colorful patchwork quilt of American make. A wardrobe stood in one corner opposite a simple, worn dressing table. Placed neatly on top was a tortoiseshell hand mirror and matching hairbrush. A silver hair ornament sat beside the brush. The door was made of sturdy ironwood planks, braced with iron bolsters. There was a small barred window in the door, with a wooden shutter that could be opened from the outside. It was likely that the room had once been an army jail.

When I returned to the dispensary, Bridgett had finished her doctoring. She had also cleaned most of the paint off Deborah Rand's face. The look of pain had been smoothed out. A gaunt face, slightly protruding eyes, a straight pinched nose, and long ears, the kind of features my mother would have described as "fair Scots." Yet this fair one had undergone a transformation. Nothing here of the eager young American as Bridgett had described her. Some age-old shadow had descended on her, partly explained by her spiked and pigmented hair and her tanned face, but there was in her aspect a kind of civet wildness one might associate with a catlike predator. She seemed like she would be more in her element in a lair near a watering hole than exchanging pleasantries over tea. There was decisiveness here, too, and power, and I couldn't help but admire what I saw, and feel drawn to her, even as I was repelled by the thought of what this transformation might mean.

Such were my thoughts when I stood over her. I half wished she would not rouse from her sleep, for I feared what might spring back to life. If Bridgett thought as I, she did not show it. She had been busily scrubbing the rest of the patient; three basins of water were black with pigment, and Bridgett had thrown a sheet over her. When the missionary was ready, Fahey and I carried Deborah Rand to the little bedroom on the second floor, Bridgett following. Leaving Fahey to assist, I went outside to try and find Prince Bandarak.

The war whoops of victory had given way to a grim silence about the parade ground. The dead had been removed. The war standards of the Mamaqs had been broken and lay in a heap. The burning shed had been reduced to a smoldering ruin, but great black clouds of smoke were rising from outside the north wall of the fortress. The air was thick with a sweet and sickening odor; I had smelled that stench before. I climbed a flight of stone steps that led to a bastion at the northwest corner of the mission. There was an old Dutch cemetery below, bounded by a rusting wrought-iron fence. Next to it, the Crocodiles had dug a wide pit to cremate their dead. As the flames roared high, the warriors completed a pyramid of Mamaq heads at the base of the pit, a sacrificial offering and salute to their slain comrades. As for the enemy bodies, I could see some Crocodiles dragging torsos and limbs to a place within the forest. Some of the soldiers were hacking at the mutilated bodies in their frenzy and grief.

"Witness this army, Vanders," said a melancholy voice at my side. "Witness this army of such mass and charge, soon to be corpses. But I'm not so delicate a prince, do you think, nor so puffed up with divine ambition?"

Prince Bandarak reeked of carnage, a musk of blood and sweat, and his armor was spattered with gore. Blood had splashed across his cheeks in the fighting and drenched his hands and arms. Yet his mood did not stem from remorse so much as having failed to complete the ghoulish business.

"I will go after the Mamaqs," he added. "And finish them." He said this with such grim finality that there seemed no point in disputing the decision.

"Is this wise, my prince?" I pointed to the Crocodiles below, making a low chant at the funeral pyre. "Your men are exhausted. Besides, the Mamaqs have been soundly beaten."

"If I do not chase them down," he said, "they will gather again."

"Then let's call up reinforcements from Bahal."

"Numbers oppress us." He was as haggard as a man with weights tied to him. "Powers are another thing, for the dead mock us, Captain, if we stand still. I hear them chanting from the ashes of their villages. 'Who will avenge us,' they cry, 'if not Bandarak? Who will avenge us, if not you?' And those who dwelt in this place. Reverend Ames was a friend of mine. But you found something, didn't you?"

"Yes," I said cautiously.

"She is a changed thing."

"What do you mean?" I was sure none of the Bataks had seen our wounded captive.

The chant of the warriors, punctuated with shrill cries of vengeance, rose in pitch as the pyre roared into the twilit sky.

"What happens when nature is forced back on itself?" Bandarak asked aloud, more to himself than to me. "It grows an old head." He tapped my arm in the manner of one offering a sage riddle. "Cut off the head, and you beget another. But where is the head of heads? The Mamaqs boil out of the earth like maggots out of a rotting corpse. Hear them shriek!" He pushed his hands over his ears as if he were trying to shut out the sound: "I shall shut them up!"

There is a terrifying vacancy in the eyes of the mad, terrifying because it tears at the corners of our own sense of security, at our notions that there is a fixing agent to the chaos of the material world. Bandarak had seen behind the sham and, like a body falling through infinite space, had become one with the grander disorder. What I feared had come to pass.

Within the hour, he had gathered up his forces. Once more astride the bony white nag, he led his Crocodiles north, wearing the theatrical armor of Freddie Ireland, holding his head high. I watched the army move across the blighted valley, their voices raised in a dirge, until the last soldier vanished into the forest and their song was no more. I wondered if we would ever see them again.

When I returned to the dispensary, I could hear Bridgett moving about in the adjoining room. Waning sunlight fell through the yellow curtains. This window had caught the missionary's attention when we first entered the mission. She stood over a desk, flipping through a record book.

"These are Noel's papers," she said, glancing up at me. "The last entry in this record is July thirteenth, nearly four months ago. According to the entry, he was to travel on the following day to dedicate a new chapel and dispensary in the village of Tuan Medang, and then to have a picnic at Lake Toba Falls. The word 'falls' is underlined and followed by an exclamation point. The thirteenth is also the date of Noel's letter."

"The entry is made with a steady hand like all the others. The letter shows a man in a volatile state of mind," I commented.

"That's right. I don't think Noel ever returned from that trip to Toba Falls. No other document—none here, at least—bears a later date." She closed the volume. "Susannah would have accompanied him to the dedication."

"And Deborah Rand?"

She placed a hand over her face, fighting back tears. I walked over to the doorway, looked out into the empty dispensary, and closed the door.

"I know you are exhausted, Bridgett."

"I know what you are going to say!" she replied petulantly. "The answer is, I don't know."

"What evil has Miss Rand done?"

"I can't answer you."

"Was it because we found her in the war paint of the Mamaqs? Was that it? Why did you shoot her?"

"I don't know, I tell you." She collapsed to the desk, her shoulders shaking with sobs.

I knelt and put my arm around her. "Forgive me."

"Too much has happened here." She tried to draw herself out of her turmoil. "I don't know what has happened here." I searched for my handkerchief and remembered that I had given it to Bandarak earlier. We had just fought a battle. We had just defeated the Mamaqs. It seemed long ago, part of another day, and yet my fatigue told me otherwise. Bridgett wiped the tears away with the heel of her hand. "Too much has happened here," she repeated, catching her breath. "The Ameses are not in the mission. You've seen the chapel, the living quarters."

"In ruins. Except for Ames's office, the dispensary, and the one bedroom upstairs. The one where we carried Miss Rand."

"That is her room, anyway."

"Why would that room, of all the apartments, remain untouched? Perhaps the Mamaqs kept her captive there." Bridgett's shrug told me she had no answer and did not care. I looked around the room, its shelves and cabinets neatly stocked with medicines and surgical tools, a physician's table in one corner. There were pieces of a shattered picture frame on the floor, however, and this I examined. Behind the shards of glass, a weary Christ wearing a golden crown wreathed with thorns, a jeweled cape over a homespun robe, and holding a mystical lantern whose beams infused the surrounding darkness. He was knocking on a cottage door long overgrown with weeds, the house of Adam, I suspected. The image reminded me of Diogenes searching for an honest man.

Bridgett rose stiffly and opened a medicine cabinet. "I was about to prepare her a laudanum sedative. It will ease the pain and let her sleep." She began to ready the potion. "I will tend to her, help her, make her well. Whatever has happened to her, I know that good care and the power of faith can restore her. But I will need Sahar to help. You were going back to the *Lorelei* in the morning, Captain?"

"At first light. Fahey and I can take turns standing watch tonight."

"And the Bataks?"

"They have gone off with the prince to chase the Mamaqs to their lairs."

She poured water from a pitcher into the tincture she had prepared. "This leaves us without protection."

"I don't think the mission is much on the prince's mind. He is obsessed with the Mamaqs."

"The Mamaqs," she wondered. "Just who are the Mamaqs?"

As if in answer, there came a long, despairing howl from the upstairs apartment. Bridgett nearly dropped the pitcher. We looked at each other in consternation mingled with fear. I flung open the door, and we began running across the dispensary to the stairs.

When we reached the upstairs apartment, Fahey was peering into the room through the peep in the door.

"What has happened here, Mr. Fahey?" cried Bridgett.

"One moment she was lying peacefully." Fahey's mouth worked in confusion. "The next she was up and howling like a banshee. Look at her there, cowering in the corner." We followed his gaze. Deborah Rand had thrown off her sheet and, naked, hissed at us from where she had crouched down beside the wardrobe. The wound in her shoulder had opened again, and a stream of blood was seeping down one breast. I stared at her with fascination. I had never thought to see a civilized woman degraded into so exotic and pitiable a creature. It was as if a window had been opened onto our dark ancestry, what we were before we seized fire to drive off the terrors of the night. Her gray eyes were filled with pain and distrust, and I remembered how Sahar had once described Deborah Rand as having the eyes of a wolf.

"I'll see to her," said Bridgett. "Open the door!" Reluctantly, Fahey obeyed, opening the door just enough for Bridgett to slip through.

"We'll hold her, Bridgett," I said.

"No, let me try to calm her. Mr. Fahey, you remain at the door if I should require assistance." She turned back to me. "Captain, bring the Bible from Reverend Ames's office."

When she was in the room, she began speaking softly; I couldn't catch the words. Deborah Rand remained crouched in her corner, her eyes roving the room as if gauging an escape. Bridgett knelt and crept closer. She spoke again, her voice steady and reassuring. It sounded like she was reciting a prayer or a psalm. The young woman seemed to lose some of her tension. Her eyelids began to waver. She reached out, and Bridgett caught her arm and then slipped her own around her. "I'll need fresh bandages and hot water, Mr. Fahey," she ordered. "Captain, the Bible. Be brisk about it!"

I don't like it. I don't like any of it." Fahey broke off his complaint when Bridgett came to the door and took the hot water and the Bible. Then she shooed us out, locking the door. I caught a glimpse of Deborah Rand lying on the bed, a fresh dressing over her wound.

"How else would you have it?" I asked him. "You're a hero. You've rescued the fair damsel from the heathens."

"We don't know what we've rescued, Vanders." He pulled a half-smoked cheroot from his shirt pocket and lit it with a flint. "Take a look at her. She's gone heathen herself. Why, she's scarcely human."

"We don't know what Deborah has been through."

"They've turned her," he grumbled. "It's like the settlers kidnapped by red Indians in your country. I've read the tales. They turn renegade themselves."

"Whatever she's become, she's in need of our help. Or doesn't that matter to you?"

The fatigue showed in the slump of the Irishman's shoulders and in his distraction. "That—creature in there. I never set eyes on her before."

"There's still the business of the other missionaries to sort out."

Fahey's laugh was hollow. "They're cold Mamaq stew. We'll never find 'em. Naught but their marrowless bones, at any rate."

"We don't know that."

"I know that."

I stepped in front of him. "We don't move from here until I've given the word."

"Belay that," he said menacingly. "I can borrow back that command of yours whenever I see fit." He glowered at me, and his hand slipped to the knife at his belt.

"Keep down your voices out there," Bridgett admonished from the door.

"We're in enough of a fix without being at each other's throats," I whispered. "We may have to mount a defense of the fort as it is."

"What do you mean by that?"

"I mean Prince Bandarak has set off with his soldiers to chase the Mamaqs. We can't move through hostile territory without him."

"God *damn* that loony savage!" Fahey spat, throwing down his smoke.

"Gentlemen!" Bridgett's reprimand rang out from behind the door.

⤜◯

By the time I stepped outside again, night had fallen. I was surprised to see a low campfire in the middle of the parade ground. Huddled about the fire were six or seven tribesmen, shorn of their reptilian battle gear and intent upon turning a carcass on a spit. The sight made me draw up, as if I had discovered a dark, savage ritual, a feeling that was not unnatural given the terrible carnage I had witnessed that day.

I was relieved to see the familiar figure of Vanda step out of the shadows. In a patois of Dutch and Malay, he made me understand that one of his men had bagged a deer in the forest and

that he would bring us food shortly. His men would also see that
we had a supply of water from a stream to the west of Dutch
cemetery.

"Bandarak's order is for us to stay here. There are twelve of
us, Si Vanders, including three who are with the *Lorelei*. They will
guard the boat and carry messages to Bahal. Already I have sent
one back to announce the prince's great victory."

I commented that he was the only one with a rifle.

Vanda looked pensive. "The prince took the rest of the riflemen
with him."

"The prince will be victorious," I reassured him.

"Yes." There was no emotion in his curt reply.

Although I was anxious to get back to my ship, exhaustion won
out, and I bedded down for the night in the dispensary. Despite
the aches in my body, my eyes would not close. I rehearsed the
drama of the day. All action swept toward the perplexing climax,
the last desperate stand of the Mamaqs before the desecrated
chapel, and then the discovery of Deborah Rand.

What had happened to her?

I knew nothing of Deborah Rand, except for the brief history
Bridgett Hannover had told me. So I had no gauge for understanding the events at Light of the World in the year since any
European had last seen the missionaries. The last letter from Reverend Ames revealed something about his state of mind but told
us nothing about his wife and Deborah. Nor did his letter have
anything to say about the Mamaqs.

Obviously, she had been captured. I did not want to think on
any number of horrors she might have experienced. As for her
wild appearance, she may have been daubed in the Mamaq colors
against her will in some savage rite, or she may have adapted the
guise as a defense against her captors. Yet she did not embrace us
as her saviors, either. She had been ready to do battle when we
found her. As if *we* belonged to a hostile tribe.

However, her descent into the primitive—if that was what it

was—must have been caught up with the fate of her missing colleagues. Had they been taken unawares by the Mamaqs, subjected to torture, and slaughtered? Had Deborah Rand witnessed this? Stories of Europeans driven mad by the sight of barbaric rituals, including mutilation and cannibalism, were known in this part of the world.

Both Bridgett Hannover and Rowan Fahey held pieces to the puzzle that was Deborah Rand, and both of them were holding something back. Despite Fahey's denial, I suspected this Deborah Rand was the girl he had known in Connecticut, the girl who had jilted him years before. Yet he had denied her. Even if he feared what she had become, his denial left unanswered questions. As for Bridgett, her evasions only served to heighten my suspicions. What had happened between the women that Bridgett would try to take Rand's life? What evil was she trying to end?

The swirl of questions eventually became tangled with the skein of a fitful dream as I tossed on my dispensary cot. I was running down a dense jungle path in full flight from some invisible pursuer. At last, winded, a pain stabbing in my side, knowing I could run no farther, I turned to face my adversary. I discovered neither monster nor demon but the very object of Alfred Wallace's desire, the rare butterfly known as the Golden Sura, rippling its deep blue wings chased with golden drops, just like the one I glimpsed at the Jambi Station stream that triggered such painful memories of Grace Tremaine. My heart pounding with expectation, I followed the creature as it swept overhead—and was gone. I stood in this desolate place, lost and surrounded by the eerie, unaccountable sounds of the jungle at night, and realized I was not alone. She waited farther down the path. Long hair spilled across her breasts, outlined the curve of her hips, and fell to her thighs. Wordlessly, she held out her arms. I sensed at once who she was, knew the meaning of that embrace, and was seized with fear and panic. As I backed away, she became something else again, something inhuman; her back arched, and she dropped to the ground in the nimble and menacing stance of a jungle cat, her hands spread out before her. Her face tilted up with a snarl as if she were sniffing the scent of her prey, her disheveled hair resolved itself into a tiger's glistening coat, and her feet and hands became great paws whose claws leaned hard into the earth, ready to leap. Finding my legs again, I bolted back down the path . . . to find myself back in my cot in the mission dispensary. I took a deep breath.

It was then I heard the tapping, the tap of her claws as she padded along the colonnade. To my terror, I saw that the door was open and a shaft of moonlight was glimmering at the portal. I tried to rise but could not; my limbs were frozen in place. The light fell on the tiger's immense head, ringed with stripes not of orange and black but of black and phosphorous silver, the colors of the Mamaqs. Swiftly, inevitably, the beast made her approach, sped down the center of the dispensary, thick beams of light falling through her eye sockets, her jaws open with teeth bared like sabers. The beast broke into a lope, then into a run, and when she reached the foot of my cot, she leaped straight for me. She spread her paws, the beams of light bearing down as they became gray eyes laughing at me from a rock on a river, gray eyes suddenly dark with terror as her hands went to her throat and she tumbled into the stream, a girl struggling to free herself, and once more that hideous howl echoed down the corridor of the mission, filling all space.

"Ulysses . . ."

I sat bolt upright, my hands gripping the sides of the cot, my face flushed and drenched with sweat.

"It's nearly daylight. You cried out in your sleep."

Bridgett Hannover was standing over me. She shook my shoulders again softly. "I didn't mean to startle you." Her eyes were blue and earnest. I looked about for the tiger, but there was only Bridgett Hannover. Her hand was on my shoulder. I placed my hand over hers, and our fingers held for a moment. Then she slid her hand away and stood before me, a prim, plain woman as resolute as her smock of missionary gray. "It's nearly daylight, Captain, and I need you to fetch Sahar as soon as possible."

"Miss Rand . . ."

"She's resting now, after a difficult night."

"I heard . . ."

"What did you hear, Captain?"

"Nothing." A shaft of pearl-gray morning light was falling through the open doorway of the dispensary.

"There's water for you to wash up in the next room. I found a tin of biscuits in the office. And there's venison the Bataks brought. But there's nothing else, no coffee or tea. No flour or other things. We will need provisions from the ship."

"Yes, of course."

"Miss Rand is resting comfortably, Captain, I assure you. I am praying over her. I am praying over her as I have for no one else in my life."

⤚⊸

Vanda and I and two other Bataks set off across valley within the hour. Retracing our path through the blighted land was another travail. I noticed that an aggressive vine with waxy, spade-shaped leaves had taken hold in the undergrowth, crowding out the other vegetation. Deprived of sunlight, everything else was brown and dying. It was as if the very processes of life had become arrested and started to decline. Vanda told me that even the earth had been poisoned by the Mamaqs, and I was almost inclined to believe him, except to note that we were at the end of the dry season. Thick clouds were beginning to gather over the mountains to the north and the west. Vanda, ever a man of few words, shrugged off any natural explanation.

Perhaps this was the end of the Great Cycle, as the Malays and the tribal peoples believed. Perhaps nature had turned against itself, as the prince had expressed it. Perhaps the appearance of a savage Deborah Rand was somehow a piece with the other aberrations and upheavals we had witnessed, an outbreak of madness not unlike the epidemic of smallpox that had swept over Bahal. Alfred Wallace had warned me in his secret journal of the shifting nature of this ground, but prophets bring no peace. Rather, I was left with the uneasy feeling that we were all, like the children of Pelops, being driven by an irresistible force toward some shattering discovery. And if fate was in control, then what was to become of my command?

It was while I was lost in these ruminations that Vanda bid me stop and listen. We had crossed over three quarters of the valley, and the hammer of the sun had begun to beat down upon us. I watched the faces of the two other Bataks as they listened to it, at first a soughing sound, as if a breeze were sheering very close to the ground, although there wasn't a breath of wind. It was a low, conspiratorial whispering, a churning of the undergrowth, a mad and careening scurry, a myriad of babbling voices set to a rising pitch. At the far western end of the valley, swaths of vegetation collapsed as if invisible scythes were at work, sweeping all before them. Our two Crocodiles took to their heels for the edge of the forest. Vanda looked around, licking his lips in consternation, and then practically pulled me off my feet. The next thing I knew, we were both running as if our lives depended on it, running before the unseen and irresistible invasion. At one point I passed even the fleet Vanda in my terror. As we made it to the forest perimeter, they swept through, a tumultuous squealing army, thousands upon thousands of brown rats caught up in a frenzy of mass movement, sweeping everything before them like a biblical plague. We stopped and must have marveled at the squirming onslaught for a full five minutes. Then, as quickly as the panic had set in, it subsided, the horde followed up by a few uncertain stragglers soon disappearing within the tangles of waxy yellow leaves. Vanda looked over at me as if to admonish an unbeliever.

An hour later, we were once more on the solid deck of the *Lorelei* and within the cool confines of Pamuntang Gorge. While the Bataks reported the omen we had just witnessed—for how else could they interpret it?—to their comrades, Devadatta and I sat and enjoyed a cup of rich Sumatra coffee, as sweet as one could stand it, for my engineer could never have enough sugar. I recounted our adventure of the previous day. He told me he had spent the afternoon in a fret, listening to the gunfire and explosions, until one of the Crocodiles had arrived to proclaim the prince's victory.

While I recounted the events that had made us masters of Light of the World, Sahar joined us on the foredeck, her dark blue *kain sarong* hemmed with gold embroidery, her head modestly covered with a long veil of black silk that set her apart as an adept. She offered a fleeting, unaccustomed smile. Except for the unnerving marble-white eye, she might have been esteemed a great beauty. However, the normal contentment of home and family had been closed to her, for the profession of *turahan,* Bridgett had once told me, was like that of a Roman vestal. She must remain chaste or run the risk of losing her occult powers.

Devadatta excused himself to attend to the engine. It was the first time Sahar and I had sat alone since the boat bearing the *turahan* and Bridgett Hannover had collided with *Lorelei* in the Sumatra Strait.

Our conversation naturally turned to Bridgett. She was anxious to have Sahar's help in caring for the wounded. I left it at that. Then I wondered how Sahar had first met the missionary.

"Mrs. Hannover's grief was great after the death of her husband. Her life, too, was in danger, for she had lost the will to live. A mutual friend, a Christian Malay woman, brought me to her."

"And were you so sure you could communicate with her departed husband?"

"I am merely the bridge between this and other worlds, Captain. There are times when the spirit will not cross the bridge. But I was successful with Mr. Miles."

"He died in a hunting accident, Bridgett told me."

"Yes, but I do not know much about that."

I could see the subject made her uneasy, so I asked how she had discovered her peculiar talents. She had visions when she was a child, she told me. Sometimes she could see events before they happened, but she could not see very far ahead, and the visions could be confused by voices. The voices were from those who had already passed over, her great-grandmother, for one. Her parents recognized the signs of the *turahan* and took her to a guru, who, having satisfied himself that her talents were genuine, referred her to a mentor. I was surprised to learn that there were schools for occult study among the Malays, and that was why the Malay *turahan* were much esteemed. In times past, they had served as advisers to royal houses throughout the Orient and even in the imperial courts of Japan and China. However, the schools no longer flourished. First the Portuese came, then the Dutch, and the Malays became a lost people. Sahar spoke not with bitterness but with wistfulness, as if she belonged to a race of spirits whose days were numbered in a merely human world.

Then she was very still. She accepted my hand as she rose. Her touch was as cold as arctic ice. She marked my reaction and said, "I have been dying for a long time. Only Mrs. Hannover has kept me alive. For I must keep her alive."

"You still fear for her?"

"We never should have come here. Don't you know what this place is?" Her voice sank with disappointment. "And we would not be here—except that her will is too strong. And yours."

"Mine?"

"Strong enough to overcome fire and death and misfortune."

Chagrin and accusation in her tone. And then I understood, recalling my earlier suspicions of sabotage. "It was you," I whispered. "The fire in the galley, the Batak who died on board . . ."

"What does that matter now?" She drew herself up as if bracing for a struggle. "I am ready to go now," she said. "My mistress should not be alone with the one you took in the mission."

"What harm can she do? Besides, Fahey is there."

"You saw them in their hordes as you crossed the valley. They are hers."

"The rats?" I asked, wondering how Sahar knew. "They were in a panic. Thirst, no doubt."

"Yes, they thirst. *She* thirsts." The *turahan*'s gaze held me. "Why do you fear the tiger?" she asked. "The one that haunts your dreams."

I wanted to laugh off her uncanny knowledge but could not.

"You fear because the tiger does not know what she is. Sometimes she is a predatory beast. Sometimes she is a desirable woman beside a stream. Only her touch is cold, as cold as my touch was to you just now."

"What else can you tell me?"

"Only what I am told, Captain." Her glance searched mine, but she shook her head at last. "Bring me to Mrs. Hannover. Bring me to her straightaway."

$\sim\!\!\!\!\sim$

Some minutes later, Vanda and his men guided Sahar up the stone staircase to the top of the gorge. Devadatta and I watched them until they had vanished over the edge.

"What will you do now?" asked the engineer. I knew he was hoping I'd give the order to return downstream.

A pox on dreams and omens and oracles!

My work was unfinished.

There would be no return to Bahal until there was some proof as to the fate of the Ameses. Deborah Rand was the only one left who could tell us what had happened to the missionaries and what storms had overwhelmed Light of the World. Bridgett Hannover's prayers might be fervent, but we couldn't wait on miracles to bring the young woman around. As Deborah held the key to our dilemma, so the thought struck me, Dr. Diem might possess the key to Deborah Rand. The opportunity to practice his skills in mesmerism, or psychology, as he called it, might be an enticement he could not resist. I wrote to him directly, describing the situation at Light of the World, the condition of Deborah Rand, and imploring him to leave Master Kung in charge of healing at Bahal and come upriver to help us. That afternoon two of our Batak messengers took a canoe downstream.

Renewed by this decision and refreshed by a peaceful night's sleep on *Lorelei,* I set out the following morning for the mission.

B y mesmerism!" cried Bridgett. "I won't hear of it."

"You've prayed over her and sung over her and denounced the devil over her for the last two days," Fahey insisted, thumping his fist on the desk. "And where did that get you? She snarls like a caged cat. And she bites." He held up a bandaged wrist. "Mayhap our high and mighty slope doctor is naught but a snake charmer. We've given the Scriptures a turn, now let him try his mumbo jumbo."

"The high and mighty slope doctor appreciates your confidence, Mr. Fahey." Diem stood in the doorway of Noel Ames's mission office, polishing the lenses of his pince-nez with a linen handkerchief. "As for mesmerism, Mrs. Hannover, that's not my practice. I've been observing our patient. Who caused her to be bound to her cot?"

"I did," said Hannover. "She became violent early this morning. Before you arrived. When the fit is over, we release her."

"Mr. Fahey and I have already done so. Restraining her in this way only deepens her terror. I've seen these symptoms before. They are typical of a kind of hysteria known as reversion, but I need to know more about Miss Rand to effect a cure."

"Can you do something for her?" I asked Diem.

"I can do something, but I need Mrs. Hannover's help. She knows her better than any here."

I could see that Diem meant to entice Bridgett into his camp. But I could also see that Bridgett Hannover had chosen her ground and wasn't about to abandon it, an impression that was reinforced by the presence of the veiled Sahar standing beside her like a brooding fate over a battlefield. Bridgett's dedication to Deborah Rand had been singular and tireless, she had nursed her tenderly and had probably saved her life, but our patient remained in a savage state, communicating in growls and gestures and barbaric sounds that I supposed were Mamaq words. She refused to allow Bridgett to bathe her or to dress her hair, although she had consented to wearing a baggy old frock that she tore at in her frequent fits. These were abrupt shifts of mood that would send her into caterwauling tantrums or sulks in a corner. When Bridgett sang to her, she would fall into a drowsy, listless state, but the least disturbance—the sound of a footfall in the corridor, the forlorn cry of a bird outside the window— would rouse her into a cunning wariness. Our patient would sometimes stand on her cot for hours at a time, staring out the window, her fists gripped tightly about the ironwork grille, her forehead pressed against the bars. At these times she would make a low unintelligible murmuring, as if entreating some unseen power to her aid. And she seized every opportunity to make a run for it. Fahey told me of the violent episodes that had erupted over the two days I was aboard *Lorelei*, awaiting the arrival of Diem. More than once Fahey and Bridgett had been compelled to bind her to the cot.

Bridgett was not conceding, and I couldn't help but feel that her obsession to bring Deborah Rand back from the dark place she had strayed was partly driven by her own remorse. It was understandable that she would view Diem as a rival, not as a fellow healer, although I recalled the dislike that had been there all along. Why, I did not know, although I knew it wasn't rooted in Fahey's brand of bigotry.

"I just need more time," said Bridgett desperately. "She followed the tune to a hymn I sang to her last night. She mumbled some of the words. I know she recognized it."

"And then knocked you over when she tried to escape," replied Fahey.

"Time is running out for us, Bridgett," I said. "We've got both the Mamaqs and the onset of the monsoon to worry about. And Bandarak's decision to chase after the Mamaqs has left us defenseless."

"Three days without word from him," Fahey reminded us.

"Miss Rand was their captive," Devadatta observed. "Perhaps they will try to get her back."

"I say we give Diem a chance," Fahey repeated. "We can't leave her in this state, like an animal."

"She is one of them!" Sahar said impatiently. "The Mamaqs have turned her with sorcery."

"And wouldn't you know but a black tabby crossed my path this very morning," Fahey sneered. "Now we're all damned and doomed and served up hot to the devil."

"The devil claims his own, Mr. Fahey," Bridgett replied. "Righteous thinking is needed now. And the power of prayer."

The Irishman threw her a dark glance. "It's clear thinking that tells me all your hosannas and hallyloos have got us nowhere. The girl is no better off than when we pulled her out of that heathenized chapel three days ago. After she had been *shot*," he added pointedly.

Silence fell upon us. I knew Bridgett Hannover and her *turahan* would resist Diem's interference, but Fahey was an unexpected ally. He had never been friendly to the Annamese physician, but I suspected some obstinate link to the faith of his fathers made him mistrust a collaboration of heathen infidel and Protestant Antichrist even more. During the past two days, he had placed himself in a chair outside Rand's room, a self-appointed guard and guardian of our captive.

Sahar lifted her veil. Her baleful glance moved around the room in mute reproof of our blindness. "None of you—not even you, Mrs. Hannover—knows the danger we are in at this moment. Look at this."

From beneath her shawl, she held out a worn black leather book and unlocked the clasp. She placed the open book on the desk.

"Where did you get this?" Bridgett flipped through the pages. "It's a diary."

"*Her* diary," Sahar confirmed. "I found it in her room, hidden in the wardrobe. Do you want to know what happened here? Do you want to know what happened to the Ameses? I tell you, these same things will happen again. None of us will escape unless—" The *turahan* stiffened her back as if to give greater weight to her words. "I have a duty to you, Mrs. Hannover. As we came up the coast, I felt this thing closing in on us. At Jambi Station, I felt it. No power can withstand it, not even the power of the Lord Jesus, for He never knew the shape or form of this thing."

Bridgett slapped the book with her palm as if to drive out a devil. "The Lord Jesus withstood the power of Satan in the desert, He spurned his temptations. You know this. You are a Christian woman now."

"I am a *Malay* woman, Mrs. Hannover. We have known this evil from the beginning, we recognize it when it comes, and we know when its power has been lifted. We are under its power now. Read and you will see. What can be done? After you read, you will know what must be done." Sahar closed her veil and withdrew.

"They're like the Irish," said Fahey to break the silence. "You'll never get the superstition out of these people. Never in a thousand years."

I took the cloth-bound journal from Bridgett Hannover and flipped through the pages. The first entry began on September 9, 1874, apparently the day Deborah Rand had arrived at Light of the World. The entries ran through to this April, in a neat, meticulous hand, up to a few weeks ago, when they ended abruptly.

There was a blank page and then just three words, scrawled in large crooked letters, without a date. The lettering was not in black ink but in a dull, rust-colored red. It read simply:

KILL THEM ALL.

Diem and Fahey were peering over my shoulder. At length, Fahey reached over and closed the cover as if to seal up the words themselves.

"We can make too much of this." There was a quaver in Bridgett's voice.

"Well, we know she's been in a disturbed state of mind," said Fahey. "We didn't need this diary to tell us that."

"And it is this state of disturbance that we need to address," said Diem.

"I'll— We can speak more of this," Bridgett said distractedly, "at a later time."

Diem knew his opportunity. "The more delay, the less likely the chance I can reach her."

A cry from upstairs startled our deliberations. It was Deborah, a shriek more of delight than of terror. It was followed by a high-pitched squeal of pain. We left the dispensary and scrambled up the stairs. Fahey broke into a run when he reached the second-floor corridor. I was right behind him as he flung open the door to Deborah's room.

Deborah Rand stood in the middle of the floor. The dim light obscured what she held in her hands. And then it moved, its long, hairless tail jerking spasmodically in fright. One of the army that had infested the valley, the rat lifted its sharp snout, bared its teeth, and squealed again at its tormentor. The look on Deborah Rand's face was chilling. Her eyes were fixated on her prey, totally absorbed with the feel of its fear and the power she had over it. She held the frantic animal out to us as if she might make an offering, then lowered her head over the creature as if she might nuzzle it. The rat tensed and quivered, then shuddered violently and was still. When Deborah lifted her head again, the severed head of the beast was between her teeth and its blood dripping down her chin. It seemed a kind of ecstasy had come over her. She became wary then, crouched, and slid into a corner, holding her prize close to her as if we would snatch it away. With a warning snarl, she returned to her grisly meal.

Devadatta and I trudged back to *Lorelei* that night, reaching the steamer as darkness set in. The journey across the Valley of Desolation, as we had come to call it, was as unsettling as the rest of the day had been: ruined villages, a blighted landscape that even the wondrous varicolored birds of Sumatra had abandoned. Only here and there, the low black swoop and raucous call of a carrion eater and the scuttle of the omnipresent rats in the underbrush.

As I looked back across the heat-struck hills, the mission looked more than ever like a monument to thwarted ambition and folly. The blackened remnants of one of the Mamaq giants still dangled from a corner bastion at a crazy angle, a scarecrow that had lost its rags in a storm. As if to complete the allegory, a rumpled blanket of purple clouds hung over the distant peaks to the north, reminding me that the monsoon was but days away. Sumatra is such a huge island that there are two monsoons, one for the south, one for the north. Diem had lived through the northern season and told me that it came on of a sudden and fiercely, quickly flooding the rivers and turning road and jungle track into muddy morasses.

That fact, and the precarious nature of our predicament, dictated that I plan for contingencies. The frustrating truth was that planning was all I could do for the time being. I could not move *Lorelei* downstream until we found the Ameses or were assured of their fate. After I made a tour of the ship to see that was all in order, particularly if we had to make a quick breakaway, I settled down on the steering deck to weigh matters. The delicious coolness of the *Lorelei*'s nook in this bend in the river blended with that of the night, a welcome relief from a heat so oppressive and humid that one worked up a sweat by standing still in the shade.

Devadatta joined me topside for a meal of fresh river perch and rice, followed by steaming cups of tea. I enlivened my cup with a jolt of rum. On the foredeck below, our guard of Crocodile Boys had assembled for a game of draughts.

The events we had witnessed at the mission were on our minds.

"The Malay woman may be right," said Devadatta. "What if Miss Rand is possessed of a demon?"

"Surely you are not that superstitious, Devadatta."

"I see that she is not herself. And if she is beside herself, then who inhabits her?" He rubbed his arms to calm a shiver. "We have come to an evil place."

"I am hoping Mrs. Hannover will allow Dr. Diem to find out what it is that inhabits Deborah Rand."

"With all respect, Captain, I think Dr. Diem is like one who goes around at night without a lantern and knocks on doors. He does not see a door until he walks into it, and he does not know what lies behind the door until it is opened."

"Dr. Diem has spent many years studying the science of the mind."

"The mind is invisible, is it not? How can science study what can't be seen? Tell me that, Captain."

"Didn't you tell me yourself about that cousin of yours who believed your steam engine was inhabited by a *rakshasa* and feared that you had dabbled in the black arts to master it?"

"The engine operates on physical principles. I can run water through my fingers. I can hold my hand over a flame and feel its warmth. And I can see how a flame can transform water into steam. I can see how steam pressure can turn gears and how these gears can turn a great wheel through the water."

"And when you told your cousin this, what did he say?"

"He said he would pray for my *atman*." The engineer chortled.

"But this is something else again. My cousin was blinded by his superstition."

"Then you must admit to the need for an open mind, if one is to see truly. We can apply that same principle to Dr. Diem's science of the mind."

"I think Dr. Diem will open a door and find a demon behind it. Once that door is open . . . Besides, there is a look in Miss Rand's eye. I would be most careful if I were you."

"She is afraid. Naturally, she would defend herself."

Devadatta finished his tea, put down the cup, and sighed. "I do not speak of her fear. There is something else. There is a hunger in her. And I do not mean for rats, sir, although it does seem as if she has acquired a taste for them, too."

"Are you trying to be humorous?"

The candle between us cast long shadows on the engineer's drawn face. Sitting cross-legged on the deck, he reminded me of a sage yogi contemplating the great scheme of life. "You are the sole captain of the Regal Sarawak Navy, and that is a great thing, but I think that in obtusity, you are a little like Don Kixit. By that I mean you are, in a certain way, an innocent man. The captain, I hope, will forgive my plain speaking."

"What has this to do with Deborah Rand?"

"Because I have seen something else in the eyes of Deborah Rand. In Hindu legend, there is a *devi* who waits for men to come and bathe in her river, and then she drags them in."

"Like the *Lorelei*."

"Oh yes, I do know the story behind the name of our ship. It was Captain Fritz who told me. The *Lorelei* lives on a rock in the river Rhine. And she sings sailors to their doom. Like the Sirens in Mr. Bulfinch's book."

"Their song nearly drove Ulysses mad."

"But unlike you, Captain, the Ulysses in the story was protected from doing his men harm. They lashed him to the mast while they plugged up their own ears with wax."

"Deborah Rand is no siren, Devadatta. She has been through a terrible ordeal, and it has disordered her reason."

"As desire disorders reason."

"She did not *wish* to become what she is. She did not choose this fate."

"With respect, Captain, she did. And we do."

I stretched out on the deck. The narrow strip of night sky that lay above the sheer walls of the gorge was flooded with a river of stars. I felt as if I could reach out and touch them. "You know, Sahar believes we should kill her. Is that what you are suggesting?"

"We are too late, Captain." The engineer sighed, stretching out beside me. "She is lost to us. Leave her to the Mamaqs."

"And the missionaries?"

"They are dead. I feel that in my bones. Even if we find them, we will not want to find them."

I knew Devadatta's dread. My sinister dream in the dispensary two nights before lingered like a fever. He was right. Deborah Rand *was* possessed—by terror, a terror that could infect us all.

"There is duty," said Devadatta, as if reading my thoughts. "There is also a more potent law—that of self-preservation, Captain."

We spoke no more that night, but turned our attention to the heavens, listening to the playful tumble of water as it rushed over rills downstream.

21

About Deborah Rand," a pale and weary Bridgett Hannover began the following morning. "I will tell you what I can."

The missionary had invited Diem and me to her apartment in the mission. These quarters were down the hall from Deborah's and large enough for her and Sahar to have spaces separated by a bamboo curtain. The walls had a fresh coat of whitewash, and the floor had been swept and scoured. Bridgett had brought up two of the dispensary cots for herself and her companion. A small table, chairs, and washstand completed the spartan arrangements. Exhaustion seemed to have drained even the blue from Bridgett's eyes.

"She slept last night—at least some of the night. For the most part, she sits up on her cot huddled against the wall. From time to time, she whimpers, as if with cold or fear. Then I sing to her, and she rests for a while."

Sahar poured tea. Bridgett held her cup gingerly, peering into the steaming liquid as if she might read some helpful message in the leaves.

"You mentioned that you knew the family," Diem offered.

"I've told Captain Vanders some of this background, so I hope he will bear with me. It begins with Amelia Birnham, Deborah's aunt. She has worked with one of our missions in Hawaii for many years. It was she who suggested to me, by letter, that her niece come to work at Light of the World. Noel Ames did need help, since his teacher, a Mr. Lanier, had succumbed to fever. My husband, however, discouraged Mrs. Birnham, given the remoteness and the difficulty of the post and Deborah's inexperience. We had never met her, of course. This was some eighteen months ago.

"Three months later, a young woman knocked on our door in Palembang, introduced herself as Deborah Rand, and told us she was ready to assume her teaching duties at Light of the World. We were astonished. Miles admired her spirit and decided to take a chance on her. She stayed with us about two months until arrangements could be made to transport her up-country."

"How did she behave when she stayed with you?" asked Diem.

"Behave . . ." Some color came back into Bridgett's cheeks.

"I mean your impression of her character and personality."

"A young woman brought up with advantages, but not stand-offish in any way. Dedicated in her faith. I give her credit for trying to fit into our unorthodox household. She was helpful, perhaps overeager to please, and very keen on getting up-country as soon as possible."

"How did she try to fit in?"

"Miles and I have always insisted on having native converts live with us. We train them to become lay preachers. Many Europeans have difficulty with that."

"And Miss Rand had no difficulty."

"None at all. She regarded it as an excellent opportunity to immerse herself in Malay. She is very interested in languages. Highly desirable for someone in our line of work."

"Still, you had reservations about her abilities."

"Miles did not." She shook her head, then looked at Diem with a trace of suspicion. "I did not learn the rest until after she had left for Light of the World. By then my Miles was dead."

Diem spoke gently. "Your husband . . ."

"Died in a hunting accident. A month after Deborah left. As

Captain Vanders already knows." She placed her tea, unsipped, on the table. "As for the rest, I have not spoken of this before. I received another letter from Deborah's aunt. Deborah, it seemed, had decided not to wait for confirmation. She had simply booked passage from Hawaii to the Indies without notice or explanation. Mrs. Birnham had written to express her own misgivings about Deborah's fitness for the post. Initially, she thought the change would be good for Deborah. She needed a challenge. There had been some difficulty with a young man, apparently, and Deborah had been very depressed. I don't know the whole story. Mrs. Birnham was too discreet to provide the details. Reading between the lines, however . . . the family had her incarcerated for a period. Before she came to live with her aunt."

Diem had been listening, head bowed, his arms wrapped around his sides. He lifted his head at this news. "By incarcerated—you mean she had been placed in an asylum."

"That was my understanding."

Diem began to pace the room with methodical steps. "When you first met her . . . 'helpful,' 'dedicated,' were the adjectives you used. Do any others come to mind?"

"Zealous. Yes, that comes to mind. In the matter of faith. I suppose there are many who might apply that term to me, or any missionary, for that matter. I like to think of myself as a reflective person, even in those matters I hold most dear. Deborah, however, has a powerful light inside of her. One almost has to step back from the heat of it or be singed. She set about her teaching here with exuberance. Perhaps too much. The children at the mission school were in awe of her—even, it turned out, a bit frightened of her. Reverend Ames wrote me about this. He found her zeal refreshing, if troubling. So he put her to work assisting him as he traveled through the villages. It was Deborah's idea to establish satellite missions all over northern Sumatra, with Light of the World as the hub. Then Light of the World went silent, except for that last, impenetrable letter from Noel Ames."

"I will need to see that letter, if you please." Diem removed his pince-nez again to massage the bridge of his nose. "Did you ever hear from Mrs. Ames about the situation at the mission?"

"Susannah was not much for writing. She left that to Noel. She would pen notes from time to time. Some little story about the children. She lavished attention on the children who came to the school, having none of her own."

"And you, Mrs. Hannover, you never had children of your own?"

"No," she said abruptly, and paled. "What does this have to do . . ."

"I did not mean to pry."

I broke the silence that followed. "What is it you propose to do with Deborah, Dr. Diem?"

He turned to Bridgett. "I plan to treat her with your assistance, Bridgett. I will need to bring you into the healing process. You are, after all, our only link to her past."

Bridgett rose from her chair to face Diem. She struggled but could not conceal her inner turmoil. "What is this healing process of yours?"

Diem slipped the enameled snuffbox from his waistcoat and turned it over in his hand. The mirror in the lid flickered feebly in the dim light of the windowless room. "I want it to be clear that I do not practice mesmerism as it popularly understood. I have nothing to do with stage tricks or sideshow antics. I have learned some of the techniques of neurohypnotism. The name was coined by an English physician, Dr. James Braid, to distinguish his method of artificially induced sleep from mesmerism. They are not the same process, although they share similar aims."

"Do you plan to induce this artificial sleep in Deborah Rand?" I asked.

"I need to examine her before I can make that determination."

"What aim do you have in mind?" asked Bridgett. "To turn this poor girl from a savage into an automaton?"

Diem bristled at the remark. "I know this is the popular conception about hypnotism. Charlatans have debased what Anton Mesmer knew was a powerful tool for healing. I can't take responsibility for that."

Bridgett considered. "You said I can be with her."

"She will be in your care, if you wish, provided you follow my instructions. I would prefer your help, in fact, since she recognizes you. The therapy sessions, however, are restricted to the patient and myself."

"And what if your treatment fails? Where does that leave Deborah?"

"I won't deny there is some risk, particularly of relapse."

"She could remain in this state indefinitely?" I asked.

"Bridgett is in charge of miracles, Captain. I can only observe and treat the hysterical symptoms. For the time being, since we'll be working together, I am hoping she will provide me with an introduction to our patient."

Bridgett led us down the corridor to Deborah's room, where Fahey was still sitting on a stool, resolutely on guard. Deborah was standing on her cot, staring out the barred window. When the key turned in the door, she turned and dropped swiftly to the floor. She was dressed in the loose torn frock, her arms and feet bare and smudged with dirt, her hair still white and matted with Mamaq paint. She was a bizarre creature, gawky, pitiable, threatening all at once. With a skittish glance and one arm moving spasmodically, she studied us, gauging whether we meant her harm. I gave a start when her glance lingered on me, held me. She studied me as a tiger studies, knowing. Yet I could not look away, despite my unease.

Diem stepped into the room and diverted her attention. She crouched and emitted a low growl of warning. She looked as if she might be prepared to spring at this unfamiliar intruder, and I think if she had, the genteel and slightly built Diem would have had the worst of it. The physician began speaking under his breath in a soothing timbre, lifting the snuffbox from his pocket by a chain, holding it to a ray of sunlight falling through the open window. Deborah's attention immediately turned to this glittering object. The mirror became a prism that reflected all the colors of the spectrum as it turned.

Diem continued to direct her attention to the prism, speaking softly all the while. Several minutes passed in this manner, Diem murmuring, the mirror shimmering, gaining Deborah Rand's rapt attention. Her body slowly relaxed, as if she had been relieved of some enormous weight. At his nod, she uncoiled from her position on the floor and stood.

I could catch only parts of Diem's speech, but I did hear the words "water" and "wash."

Deborah Rand's eyes closed, and Diem took her hand and bade her sit on the cot. Then he turned to Bridgett. "You can fetch water for her bath now. She'll let you bathe her and wash her hair, after which she will sleep." Bridgett stood absolutely immobile. "Come along."

Bridgett visibly gathered her remaining strength and flew out the door and down the corridor, crying for Sahar to bring water and towels.

Fahey held the door open for Diem in nearly respectful wonder. The physician slipped the snuffbox back into his waistcoat and clapped his hand on my shoulder.

"Round one, Vanders," he said with a peremptory smile. "She's receptive to the method. Many are not. While she sleeps, I'll pore over that diary of hers and Ames's letter, too. We'll see what more we can uncover about Miss Deborah Rand."

22

That night Devadatta found a slow leak below the waterline, serious enough to cause a list to starboard. There was no human agent to blame this time; it was clear *Lorelei* had taken a hit when we were navigating a patch of white water coming up-river. There was careful work to do, especially as the bilge had to be pumped, so we labored around the clock to shore up the damage. When the job was completed, Devadatta and I clapped each other on the back and decided to be prudent about watchstanding, just in case. We agreed to two-section watches during the night, relieving each other every four hours. One of us would always be aboard from then on.

When I returned to the mission two days later, I could see that our patient had been worked on, too. Diem had called on Bridgett, Sahar, Fahey, and me to gather outside Deborah's room. With a touch of theater, he swung open the door and, bowing, allowed us to gaze on his handiwork. I could scare credit my eyes with the transformation.

I think it was the first time I had seen her standing at full height. Gone was the ragged frock, replaced by a country-blue dress with laces at the bodice. Her face had been cleaned of its Mamaq war paint, her color now as vibrant as a girl's. Her hair had been washed free of the silvery clay and her dark, wavy hair now fell below her shoulders in a braid. She resembled a highland Kate or Maureen, for there was a hardiness in her bearing, and rolling, heather-tinted hills in her movements, like the daughter of some Pictish lord who had been raised to ride and battle outlanders at the far edges of the clan's dominion.

I did not at first notice that this Briar Rose moved in artificial sleep to Diem's commands. The physician bade her walk around the room and she did so with the confidence of a woman who had been schooled in social graces. When she took her seat on a chair beside her cot, she was a fine lady presiding over a salon. Folding her hands on her lap, she held her head with an aristocratic mien. For his part, Diem was delighted with Deborah Rand, proud that this newborn woman was, in a sense, his creation. But hours before, Deborah Rand had scuttled about on all fours, baring her teeth, scarcely human. Somehow, she had recovered her civilized self. The change did not seem possible.

"I could run a needle through her finger in this state," Diem explained. "And through suggestion, she would feel no pain, and no blood would flow through the pinprick. These are the kinds of tricks the stage mesmerists practice, making their sleepers perform like jackanapes."

"And they have no memory of their antics, do they?" asked Fahey. "Afterward, I mean."

"The sleeper remembers or forgets depending on the suggestion implanted by the healer." Diem returned his attention to his patient. "Deborah?"

"Yes, Dr. Diem." The voice was scarcely audible, a whisper snatched away in a storm.

"We've made a good first start this morning. Now I want you to return to your bed and sleep through until the morning, when I'll wake you. When you awake, you will have only this memory— you are safe, you are cared for. You are not to fear anything. Do you understand?"

She replied with a barely perceptible nod. Bridgett and Sahar took her by the hands and led her to the cot. Diem bowed for all of us to proceed him as we walked out into the corridor. "Sleep must work its magic with the autosuggestion. If things follow this course, I can begin working in earnest tomorrow."

Diem appeared relaxed, even affable, although the rings under his dark eyes marked the strain of the challenge before him. His cravat was loose and his shirtsleeves rolled up. I was reminded of how fastidious he was normally, remote and even melancholy in nature.

"Deborah went through a crisis last night, Vanders. That was our *good* fortune." He nodded, obviously pleased. "After bathing her, Bridgett had given her a hairbrush and mirror. She studied the objects and then, unaccountably, began silently to cry. She retreated to a corner, the tears rolling down her face, and there she stayed, holding the brush, transfixed by her image in the mirror."

"I went over to her," Bridgett added. "I put my arms around her, and we cried and rocked back and forth. And then she spoke to me, two words. 'Help me,' she said. Like a lost and frightened child. I called for Dr. Diem."

"I have an opening, that's the important thing. Those homely implements, the brush and mirror, triggered some memory." Diem pressed his fingertips together and brought them to his lips, peering at us over his glasses. "The danger is in oversimplification, for we are dealing with a very complex mental state. The phenomenon is not unknown—I've mentioned it to you before: reversion. There are cases of this condition that have been known and studied for almost half a century.

"I worked on several such cases in Paris. Perhaps the most striking instance is that of a young woman, not much older than Deborah, who had run off from her farm in the Loire Valley one summer and vanished. Some months after her disappearance, there were a number of bizarre attacks on sheep. Part of the flesh had been gnawed away, but in each case, the throat was torn out. People blamed the attacks on wolves until a shepherd brought a report about a savage living in the woods. A hunting party found nothing but lost one of its mastiffs—discovered later with its throat gouged. Not surprisingly, the simple villagers became convinced they were besieged by a werewolf. The attacks continued inter-mittently over two years. There would be a rash of them, and then nothing for several months. Until one morning, when Jeanne Dor-nay—that was the name of the missing woman—walked into the village, knocked on a door, and asked for a glass of cider. Her hair was long and matted, and she was naked except for the filth that covered her. She remembered nothing of what had happened to her in the past two years."

"Jeanne Dornay was the attacker, wasn't she?"

With a nod, Diem confirmed the answer, then went on. "She ended up in Dr. Briquet's clinic in the Hôpital de la Charité in Paris. We were experimenting with neurohypnotism as a treatment for hysterical cases. Jeanne Dornay was one of our subjects.

"Her case illustrates the problems involved. Hypnotism can be used to treat derangement but only for a limited period. With Jeanne, we were able to bring her out of her atavistic state, but she would always fall back. She would be fine for weeks at a time, and then one morning, we would find her crawling on all fours.

"One of our colleagues hit upon the idea of probing Jeanne's past while she was in the hypnotic state. She responded to this kind of 'talking therapy.' It seems that right before Jeanne's dis-appearance, she had had a terrible row with her father over an opportunity for her to study voice in Paris. Jeanne was famous in the Loire for the beauty of her singing in the church choir. She had her heart set on the scholarship. Her father had always been a severe man, brutal and puritanical and unforgiving. When she insisted on going to Paris—perhaps the first overt act of indepen-dence in her life—he beat her savagely and nearly killed her."

"And didn't I hear when I was a boy about the Midwife Maeve," exclaimed Fahey. "She strangled young sprats right out of the womb, so they wouldn't grow up and become like the son who stole her silver candlesticks and left her a pauper."

Diem took out his snuffbox and studied its facets in the light. "When Jeanne, under hypnosis, recounted this story of conflict with her father, she remembered what she had done. From that day forward, she returned to normalcy."

"You propose to use this talking therapy with Deborah Rand?"

"That I do. The door is open a crack, yes, but we do not know where it will lead. I can tell you this: Miss Rand has experienced a profound psychological shock—what one of our German colleagues has termed a neurological trauma—but we don't know where the shock is lodged. It most likely originates with her capture by the Mamaqs. However, it may stem from an earlier wound. As we know, she has a troubled mental history. If it is far older— some event in her childhood, for instance—I may not be able to reach her for a long time. Perhaps not at all."

"We know the wound," Bridgett said tonelessly. "I've gone over in my mind a thousand times why I shot her. I simply blacked out. That horrible painted face and eyes filled with hate—"

"No, I don't think that is our trauma, Bridgett," Diem said comfortingly. He paused for a breath, as if he might explore Bridgett's motive, but then shook his head. "No."

"And what of her diary?" I asked. "Didn't that tell you anything?"

"The diary is . . ." Diem searched for the word. "*Transparent.* For the most part, a mundane record of events, her activities with the Ameses, the schoolchildren, and so on. It is hard to find a person behind the words. And that is curious for a record of such an intimate nature. She tells us nothing of her past. No mention of relatives or friends. No revelation of an emotional life. It is as if she can write about only what is directly in front of her, and then only in passing, as if they were events of no consequence. At first—" Diem interrupted himself and nodded in the direction of the sleeping Deborah Rand. "When she arrived at the mission in

September of last year," he continued in a lower voice, "she took up her teaching duties. She was unsuccessful and unhappy in this role. She was despondent for a time, but her enthusiasm picked up when Ames began to bring her with him on his tours of the tribal villages. Apparently, this gave her the inspiration for village clinics. About this time, in January, relations turned cool between Deborah and Susannah Ames. There was some dispute—no details are provided—over Deborah's authority in mission activities. The last entry—before those terrible words were written, I surmise, in her own blood—has to do with an upcoming trip to a village near Lake Toba, some miles northeast of here. She and the Ameses were to journey by horseback together. She was excited about the trip because this village, Tuan Medang, will be the site for the first dispensary."

"Noel Ames's last entry in the office record book confirms this," said Bridgett. "After that, silence."

"It is reasonable to suppose they met with the Mamaqs during this journey," said Diem. "That will take time to sort out."

"We don't have the luxury of time," I reminded him. "We have a week, two at most, before the monsoon sets in. The Asahan will become a torrent. I don't dare bring *Lorelei* downriver under those conditions."

"We could be locked in these highlands for three months," Fahey added.

"I can't be definite about the length of the therapy," Diem replied. "If we touch the right chords, we will know what we need to know in a few days. But more often the treatment can extend over weeks, months. And I wouldn't want to move her until we know for certain the fate of the Ameses."

"I can't wait out the monsoon," I repeated.

"Finding the Ameses is our object." Bridgett was adamant. "No matter how long that takes."

"Certainly, whatever we can accomplish before the monsoon," I reassured her. "But when the clouds begin to thicken over Lake

Toba, we will have to bring Miss Rand and *Lorelei* down to Bahal. After that, I must bring the ship to Rajah Brooke in Kuching."

"You can move your steamship wherever and whenever you want, Mr. Vanders," Bridgett said doggedly, "but Miss Rand is my responsibility. I won't go back, and nor will she, until I know what has happened here."

Dr. Diem pulled out his pocket watch and snapped open the gold cover. "Perhaps we can continue this discussion over lunch. I understand that Sahar is preparing the afternoon meal."

><del></del>

Dr. Diem had his way, with Bridgett Hannover as a firm and unexpected ally. He could work his therapy at least until the weather turned.

For the rest of the day, the crushing heat kept us to our rooms. We stirred again with the onset of twilight. Bridgett and Sahar went back to their labors in cleaning—perhaps "purifying" would be a better word—the defiled chapel, a project in which they were assisted by the remaining Bataks. Vanda was glad to give his men something to do. The silence from Prince Bandarak and his cohort had them on edge. The land was cursed here, they said, the Mamaqs had poisoned the very air. There was a danger that our guards would simply pack up their canoes and leave for Bahal.

From the parapet of the old fort, I scanned the northern horizon with the spyglass. From time to time, I saw flashes of light from that direction, which I took for summer lightning. The dry hills and empty villages were streaked with the wheat-colored rays of sunlight that slanted across the slopes.

"Your thoughts are on our mad princeling, I'll wager." Fahey leaned on his elbows to peer down to the bottom of the wall. "I'm thinking the madder Mamaqs have given him more bloody contest than he was expecting—or they gave him the slip."

"In either case, they'll be back."

"You think they'll come back for her, is that it?"

"The thought crossed my mind. I don't know what Deborah Rand meant to those tribesmen, but I can't forget how desperately they fought and died before the chapel. It was as if they were trying to prevent her capture."

"For sure she's a comely white woman. That's a prize. Why else do men go to war, if not to take women?"

"Perhaps." I shifted my glass to the east. "It's the diary I have on my mind," I went on, folding the glass. "The missionaries were about to make a trip to a village northeast of here."

"What of it?" Fahey pulled out a pouch of tobacco and poured a line of flakes across a square of paper. "Say, you're not think-ing—"

"It's just a few miles from here."

"Good luck to you. Me, I'm not in the mood for getting flayed by tender Mamaq knives. Besides, I'm squeamish about leaving Deborah Rand to the tender mercies of Hannover and her Malay witch." The deep furrow dipped down the length of Fahey's brow. "I don't buy Hannover's talk about 'blacking out.' I'm sure she would have blown her brains out, but that the poor light made her miss the mark."

"Whatever may have gone on between the two of them in the past, Hannover knows Deborah is the only one who can tell us what happened to the missionaries."

"I still don't trust them," rumbled the Irishman.

"Or your shipmates, I'd wager."

"Not a manjack alive—or woman, either."

"Then why all the deep concern for Deborah Rand? She's not the girl you knew, after all."

"That's so."

"Then it wouldn't be any concern of yours to know that the girl was tossed into an asylum by her family five years ago. It was to keep her from running off with a fellow. Perhaps it was to prevent her from keeping an appointment at a seaside Connecticut inn."

"You're talking nonsense," he answered with a scowl. "Let's drop this thing."

"Bridgett Hannover knows a thing or two about Deborah's past."

A look of craft crept into his dark eyes. "It's one thing for you to hoist my jib when you can't keep your eyes off her yourself."

"You're daft, Fahey."

"Daft, is it? Somebody's mesmerized all right, but it's not Deborah Rand. She'll have her claws in all of us before long." The Irishman drew a deep puff of smoke and flicked the cigarette over the side. "You look after your own, and I'll look after mine. The sooner this business is cleared up, the sooner we're back down the river, and the sooner I'm carousing with the scum of the earth in Malacca."

23

The next morning Diem set about recovering Deborah Rand, and I set out across the valley with Vanda, both of us armed with Enfields. Anxious about guarding the mission while his leader might be in danger, Vanda hoped a foray might bring news of Bandarak.

The prince had driven the Mamaqs across this same terrain a few days before. The fleeing tribesmen had dropped some of their weapons among the tall yellow weeds. Vanda picked up one of their hideous helmets and held it to his ear as if it might reveal the whereabouts of his lost prince. When it refused to give up its secrets, he tossed it into the underbrush. As soon as we entered the forest, the trail branched into five directions. At the crossroads, we discovered Rowan Fahey waiting on a log, carbine beside him, whittling down a piece of balsa.

"If you're going to make merry with your life, then I'm coming along to protect my investment," he offered by way of explanation, swinging a knapsack on his shoulder. "I can't get downriver without a sailor to navigate."

Vanda thought the village of Tuan Medang to be about three miles off if we took the northernmost trail. Our path paralleled a tumbling brook partially obscured by thick undergrowth and ferns. Rain had fallen in the early morning, so we were soaked through before we had gone very far. As the sun rose, so did the insects in their stinging hordes. A cloud of tiny wasps swarmed about our heads, while leeches and millipedes lay in wait among the glossy green leaves of creepers and vines. The forest, always a presence to be reckoned with, exuded a surly vigilance as if it resented our intrusion. The gibbons screeched down at us from their lofty perches in the forest canopy. The thickets crackled with the movement of unseen animals or, for all we knew, Mamaqs waiting in ambush. Once I caught a glimpse of the massive tusked head of a wild elephant, his trunk reaching for some leafy treat overhead. Catching our scent, he backed noisily out of sight.

Sometime about noon, Vanda, who had been scouting ahead, signaled to us to take cover. We could discern the outlines of a bamboo stockade around the bend. To find any human habitation in this nearly impenetrable wilderness was always startling, but the utter silence, not even broken by the raucous cry of a hornbill, was unnerving. There were no shouts and cries of children, nor the musical cadence of women pounding rice, no acrid odor of baking sago. No smoke drifted from a friendly cook-fire as we entered the village compound. Only a barbaric cockerel with spindly, featherless legs challenged our arrival, but it quickly shied away and slipped beneath a house. Unlike the blackened villages of the Horseriders in the valley, this forest community was untouched, every structure standing and intact, but it had become a ghost town. It was as if the entire population, some hundreds I supposed, had dropped everything to dance away to the tune of an irresistible Pied Piper.

Fahey pointed to a rise at the far end of the village. At its top was a small building with a white cross nailed to the gable. This was most likely the mission outpost Deborah Rand and Noel Ames had set out to establish. Fahey nodded to indicate that he would investigate this building while Vanda and I scouted in opposite directions. My path took me to the chief's house, easily identified by the ornately carved panel over the lintel. Inside, shelves of stoneware pots and crockery lined one wall in domestic order. They were surmounted by a row of wooden pegs, carved into the fantastic shapes of mythical beasts from which depended bottles filled with liquids of varying hues. There was a raised dais in the center of the floor, marked off by four carved columns of teak. Behind the chief's quarters was a men's longhouse, perhaps a hundred feet in length. Along its eaves, wreathed with fresh foliage, hung a variety of animal and human skulls. It was the custom among certain Sumatra tribes, Alfred Wallace had once told me, to keep their ancestors and clan totems on display in this fashion. It was a convenient if gruesome way of tracing the family tree. This building, too, betrayed no sign of disorder, the sleeping mats rolled up along the walls, bows and spears stacked neatly in one corner.

I emerged through the rear entrance of the lodge. Here a trail led to another gate in the stockade, which stood open, like the main gate. I struck down the narrow, well-worn trail. Almost immediately, I came to a stop. Overhead, blue wings quivered on a pink hibiscus blossom. The splash of gold across these cobalt wings told me I was once more in the presence of Wallace's legendary butterfly. Its beauty held me spellbound, for I had but a fleeting glimpse of the specimen on my first encounter at Jambi Station. Its appearance made me profoundly uneasy, for I knew where it meant to lead me.

Lifting itself from its roseate throne, it grandly flew ahead. I couldn't help but follow it. The path widened, and the leaves parted until I was standing on the bank of a broad, rippling stream. The Golden Sura floated over the water and vanished into the shadows of the forest on the far shore, as serene as an emissary from another world. I stood on the bank of the stream and looked around with a feeling of dread. But there was no one. I was completely alone. At last, remembering my thirst, I knelt down and, cupping my hands, let the cool, healing water cascade down my forehead. When I opened my eyes, she was sitting on a rock, perhaps a dozen yards to my right, brushing her hair. She hummed a familiar air popular ten years before...

With a catch in my heart, I knew where the Sura had led me. Once again I was standing on the bank of the Potomac on a green spring day at the end of a long war.

She wore a yellow crinoline dress decorated with a thin border of lace at the neckline that outlined her bare shoulders, white as pearl in the sunlight. There were the same five rocks that led into the swift current. She sat on an outcropping that hung over the dark water, her petticoats tucked around her knees, wielding her brush with bold, swift strokes, shaking long auburn tresses that fell to the small of her back. I was young, but I had come to understand the fragility of living beings, and she sat before me, the very pulse and vibrancy of life itself. She had it within her power to make me the happiest man in the world that day. But when the moment came, she had cast me into bleak despair. I had stumbled over my proposal, blurting out what I had so carefully rehearsed, hoping she wouldn't think me an utter fool. She listened intently, her eyes smiling, but not without a hint of mockery. And then she wondered aloud why it had taken me so long. She had hoped I would ask, but I knew immediately I had spoken too soon. She had hoped I would ask so she might consider the matter, now that it was out in the open. She couldn't give me an answer now, she hastened to add, but she would give me an answer soon. It was not what I had wanted to hear. I wanted her to declare her love for me. I wanted an avowal that would bind us forever. But it was always the same between us—we always said something approximate. Her polite evasion confirmed how everything between us was so tangential, always short of the mark. "It's Morgan, isn't it?" I accused her. "You love my brother. Isn't that the truth?" She took my hand and shook it as if I was being an impatient, obstinate boy, and in truth, I was scarcely older than one. I kissed her hand fervently and tried to take her in my arms, sick with both humiliation and desire. She ruffled my hair and pushed me away and said how hungry she was. I stood over her, and I knew I must go and get the picnic basket in the buggy, that I must go now, before ... but I could not stop myself from looking back, tears stinging the corners of my eyes, aching for her, furious with her, in love with her.

><-⊙

A gunshot drove a covey of wild pigeons into the air. Wrenched back to time and place, I raced up the trail to the compound. The shot had come from the direction where I had last seen Fahey, on a rise at the edge of the village. I shot the bolt of the rifle as I ran, zigzagging among the maze of houses where every turn might bring an ambush. Vanda was standing outside the little mission at the top of the hill, his nose in the air as if he were trying to scent the presence of trouble. I ran right past him and into the mission church with its white cross.

Fahey stood in the gloom, making no sound or movement. There were no seats in this prayer house, only an altar, which held Fahey's fascination. I sensed a sharp odor, as of coal tar or turpentine. An oil lamp flicked on the altar. Its blue light fell on a blackened skull. Unlike the skulls hanging in the longhouse, this one was intact, the skin drawn tight over the cranium, as if it had been tanned. The eyelids fell over empty sockets, but the skin was so well preserved that the tiny veins on the lids were visible; its lips twisted in some final gruesome question. It was impossible to say how old this relic might be and to whom it might have belonged. Perhaps this grisly fetish explained, to those who could read its significance, the fate of the villagers of Tuan Medang.

I went outside, unable to breathe in that close and terrifying place. Vanda had not moved, seemingly lost in contemplation. From our point on the rise, the entire village was open to view. Nothing stirred. No sign of activity in the surrounding hills.

"We're bringing this Mamaq trophy with us." Fahey emerged from the prayer house bearing a woven basket. "Perhaps someone can tell us who it was or what it means. Perhaps our man Vanda knows."

The Crocodile captain took the basket from Fahey and pulled the head out by its stiffened hair. Turning it from side to side, he spat ceremoniously on each eyelid and thrust the head back in the basket.

"Now, what was that all about?" Fahey wondered aloud.

Vanda offered no explanation. He was already trudging back down the hill, but he had to check his stride abruptly.

Someone stood in our path, leaning heavily on a staff. He held out a large, crudely carved cross that hung from a strip of rawhide about his withered neck.

"I am Christian?" he cried out in English, as if he wasn't sure. "Christian?"

≻⊂⊙

The old man we took back with us was called Nias, and he had come to live in the village of Tuan Medang two years before. His dark skin, diminutive height, and wiry hair identified him as belonging to one of the Negrito tribes that inhabited the interior. The original inhabitants of Sumatra, they had been pushed back farther and farther into the jungle over the centuries. The people of Tuan Medang, Nias explained, had come out of the remote forest to settle within a few miles of the mission. They felt Reverend Ames would be able to protect them from the Mamaqs. In this hope, they had been disappointed.

Two months ago, Nias had been kidnapped and enslaved by the Mamaqs.

"With the three missionaries," he added.

There was uneasy silence in the mission dispensary until Bridgett Hannover spoke. "Three of them?"

"The Reverend Mr. Ames. The Reverend Mrs. Ames. The Reverend Miss Rand." Nias counted off the names on fingers as creased as old leather. Perhaps in his seventies, he spoke with animation, fidgeting constantly, squeezing a polished stone in one hand, toying with his beads, scratching himself. He wore a hair band of woven seeds, and his earlobes had been pierced with a dozen tiny ivory spikes. His only clothing was an elaborate fringed breechclout and a tapestry of ritual tattoos that extended, in running commentary, across his chest, arms, and thighs. He did not like the idea of sitting on a dispensary cot, so he squatted on the floor as he spoke to us, puffing on a rolled tobacco leaf. "They wanted to ride north, to see the falls below Lake Toba."

"Who wanted to go there?" Hannover asked anxiously.

"Why, they all did, but I suppose it was mostly the wish of Reverend Ames and Miss Rand. This was after they dedicated the new church at Tuan Medang. So the chief sent me to guide them. When we arrived at the falls—maybe an hour's journey from the village—the Mamaqs fell upon us. They took us in boats across the lake to the island of Samosir, where they have a lair. They have all gone crazy, those Mamaqs."

"They did not trouble you before?"

"Oh no! We always got along just fine, we villagers and the Mamaqs. There was never any trouble between us. In fact, they paid my chief tribute twice a year. They are a very simple people, the Mamaqs. But something stirred them up."

"What stirred them up, exactly?"

Nias scratched his head. "I could tell you more if I spoke their language. I got only bits and pieces while they held me—while they held us." He lowered his head to his hand. "I am sorry for the missionaries. Their souls are with God now. The Glory agrees with them, I'm sure."

"Then you know what happened to them," said Diem.

"The Mamaqs killed them. Well, they tortured the Reverend Ames. On the cross. Like our Savior. He was a brave man."

"They crucified him?"

"On a tower of wood—he was stretched across it. They cut off strips of his flesh." He looked up at us with wide eyes.

The groan escaped Bridgett in a whisper as she bit back tears. "The women—Mrs. Ames, Miss Rand?"

"After the Mamaqs had their pleasure with the Reverend Ames, the reverend ladies were taken off somewhere. I did not see them again. My guess is that the Mamaqs killed them, too."

"I don't understand," Bridgett persisted. "You say the Mamaqs took you to Samosir. But all the tribes consider the place accursed."

"Because the ghosts of the Old Ones confound the senses of anyone who trespasses there." Nias clutched his crucifix. "But I am Christian, and except for my cross, I would have been driven crazy, too. Like the Mamaqs. They came to Samosir because something drove them there. Something they feared even more than the Old Ones. They live far to the north of that place, near the river Panei. One thing they said—that their gods had failed them. A kindly old Mamaq widow who gave me food told me their gods had been eaten by new gods and their sacred lands lapped by tongues of fire. There was black blood across the land, or so she said."

Fahey leaned forward. "Black blood? What did she mean by that?"

Nias shrugged and regarded the drooping tobacco leaf. "Who can understand the Mamaqs?"

"But you never saw the missionary women again?"

"After they killed the Reverend Mr. Ames, they took the women away, as I said. Me they kept in a pen with many captives, Horseriders, mostly. As if we were pigs! About a week later, there was a huge feast. The old woman told me that the Mamaqs had been given a queen by their gurus. The queen would find new homelands for them. Then their warriors came and took away twenty of us who had been captured. All through the night, I listened to their screams. I wept for their suffering. After the feast, the warriors prepared themselves for battle. They took their queen and headed south."

"Did you see this queen?" asked Bridgett.

"From a distance, I saw her. They carried her down the main street of the camp on a tall chair, like the carriage of the Batak king. She held a spear in one hand and a sword in the other. And she was painted for battle. Black and silver. And her hair glowed like a star. The old woman told me these had been the war colors of the Mamaqs since they had lost their homelands: silver for flames, black for the blood of their angry land."

Nias concluded his story by telling us how he had escaped some days ago, after the Mamaqs had suffered a terrible defeat in battle. Some stragglers came to Samosir, and there was panic. There were orders to kill the remaining prisoners, but in the confusion, the kindly old widow—Nias told us with a grin that she had gone sweet on him!—set him free. He stole a canoe and returned to his village, only to find it deserted. There he had met up with our party.

"One last question," Diem announced. "Tell me, Nias, did the women witness the torture of Reverend Ames?"

"We all saw that," the old man replied. "First they built the tower in the center of the encampment, and then they strapped him on it. That's where they cut him up. He was crucified there, like our Lord. That makes him an angel already, doesn't it? Then they led the white women off." The old man shook his head. "I do not know why the Mamaqs have gone crazy."

Bridgett stood up and smoothed the front of her gray dress with nervous hands. "You did not see the two women again, after the Mamaqs led them away?"

"Never again," Nias replied, dropping the stub of the tobacco leaf on the floor.

"Then there is hope that Susannah may yet be alive." Bridgett Hannover's glance roved from face to face as if she might spy some reciprocal spark of hope. "Perhaps even Reverend Ames has survived his ordeal."

"Oh, the dear Reverend Ames is an immortal!" Nias said with conviction.

"What do you mean?" asked Bridgett.

Nias reached out for the woven basket at Fahey's feet and pulled it over. "That old Mamaq woman who was sweet on me brought me a gift the night of my escape. I carried it to Tuan Medang. The Reverend Ames raised that house of worship, and I thought he would be comfortable there."

"What are you saying?" asked Bridgett, like someone calling in the darkness.

Nias lifted the tanned head out of the basket and waved his hand over it as if to release some magical power. "I thought if I placed him on the altar," he went on, "he might bring the people back to our village. Behold the Reverend Ames! The Glory agrees with him, does it not?"

⤙⊙

That night on the deck of the *Lorelei,* Fahey and I learned from Devadatta that the river had provided us with some clue as to the fate of Bandarak's warriors.

"The body came sliding down the rill." The engineer pointed to the miniature fall that tumbled above us. "I snagged it with a gaff and pulled it aboard. One of the Bataks identified it as his cousin, or what was left of him. He had been among those who went with Bandarak in pursuit of the Mamaqs. When Vanda showed up, they put the body in one of the canoes and went back to Bahal."

"They've all left, haven't they?" I realized that without the presence of the Bataks, we were truly isolated. And beset with a stark, logistical problem in addition to the enigmas that bedeviled us.

Fahey's thinking was echoing mine. "How will we get the ship downstream? Did Vanda say when they would return?"

"He spoke nothing about coming back," the engineer replied

glumly. "He just said that it was time for him to report to Radjah Dulah. He is fearful about what will happen to his people if Bandarak does not return. He fears that Seowan will use this as an excuse to oust Radjah Dulah and put her lover on the throne. There's no one to stop them now."

"Her lover?" Both Fahey and I expressed the same surprise.

"The war chief, Ingit, that is to say," the engineer hastened to confirm.

"There's a brave fellow," said Fahey, chuckling and slapping his thigh. "I would have thought there was a little too much of her for anyone to love."

"Truly, you are well spoken on that point, Mr. Fahey," Devadatta replied, his eyes shining with amusement. "She and Ingit have been plotting. And things will not go well for us if they seize power. So Vanda has told me. Both of them do not like the idea of Christian missionaries so close to Batak territory. If something unfortunate should happen to us up here, they would not be displeased. Indeed, Vanda thinks they might even try to seize *Lorelei* and make Batak power supreme, from the Asahan all the way north to Atjeh."

"Enemies on either side of us," said Fahey.

"At least we know the heft of Batak power," I added.

"Aye," Fahey replied, leaning over the deck and washing the coffee out of his cup, now that I had uncorked the rum. "There's too much of what we don't know for my liking. They've all disappeared—the Mamaqs, the Crocodiles, the damned preachers. The only one left to tell the tale is that old man from a deserted village."

"And Deborah Rand."

"And Deborah Rand," Fahey confirmed. "Somehow she made her escape from the painted bastards."

"By painting herself with their colors."

"But they caught up with her at the mission," Fahey said.

"The Mamaqs who made a pitched fight on the parade ground—they were protecting Deborah Rand."

Fahey swished the rum about in his cup and drained it in a gulp. "Imagine yourself in her place, witnessing the horrors she saw. Who wouldn't be driven out of her wits? She was a victim of horrors."

I was not too surprised that Fahey had softened his judgment of her. She had been a captive, true enough, but I was beginning to wonder if she wasn't in some way a collaborator. I could scarcely credit the idea myself. Yet it opened into a much deeper and more difficult question: who was Deborah Rand?

I listened to the night sounds of the river as if they might provide an answer. But I had no interpreter for the thrumming chorus of frogs or the tumble of water over the rill. I recalled how Diem had seemed pleased with what Nias had told us that afternoon. "Diem thinks the torture of Ames might have unhinged her. He told me as much before we left the mission."

"He is looking for one of those traumas, as he calls them, isn't he?" grumbled Fahey.

"I don't think Bridgett Hannover was convinced of that."

Devadatta slapped his arm and vigorously rubbed the insect bite. "What if Miss Deborah Rand is not what she pretends to be?"

"What do you mean, Devadatta?" I asked.

"In my village, back in Travancore, there was a girl who was about to be married to a man she despised. It was her parents' choice, you see. So she feigned madness, hoping he would reject her."

"Did it work?"

"Oh yes, the suitor spurned her. But she was condemned to live out her game for the rest of her life. If she admitted she was sane after all, she would be stoned. So she slept with the cows in the fields, and everyone said she had become a child of Rama. Perhaps she did go mad, after all."

Fahey didn't hide his contempt. "Would a woman be play acting when she bit into the carcass of a rat? I don't think so. Not a white woman, at least."

"Truly, I wish Master Kung was with us," said Devadatta, sighing. "His yarrow-stick oracle would throw light on this matter."

"His master is another kind of diviner." Fahey laughed. "They are a brace of tricksters, the both of them." With that, he pulled the bottle of rum closer and refilled his cup. "I think when I retire, Vanders, it will be to the life of a gentleman farmer."

"I have a hard time picturing that."

"Why so? One way or another, we end up pitching manure. Or paying someone to do it for us. That's half the struggle of agriculture, isn't it now—preparing the soil?"

I filled my own cup. "I suppose."

"But today marks the first day I've ever planted a human head."

I laughed. "Old Nias says he's going to water it every day. He thinks some kind of sacred lily is going to grow out of it."

"When that happens, I'll fall to my knees and swear Luther's creed."

"You're halfway there already, Fahey. It seems you've forsworn popery."

"Popery, yes, but I'll never give up the Mother Mary."

This struck Devadatta as humorous. "Then that makes you naught but a pagan, Mr. Fahey."

"And why is that, you kingpin engine wallah?"

"Because the Mother of God is the great mother of us all. And the mother of us all—well, everyone recognizes that." He lifted his hands. "We are in her body."

"Even the Mamaqs have their goddess," I reminded him. "Or what was that idol we found in the mission church?"

"Yes, a Medusa if ever I saw one," said Fahey.

"Like our own Hindu goddess of Kali—she needs fresh blood to keep alive." Devadatta slapped his arm again. "Like these mosquitoes must have *my* blood to keep alive."

"There's no comparison to the Queen of Heaven!" Fahey said heatedly. "She spreads her cloak around all the poor damned suffering bastards of the earth."

"As does Parvati," Devadatta said, "who is but Kali's true inverse and other side. They are one and the same goddess."

This banter about the powers of deities went on for some while, Fahey growing prolix with the application of the liquor. I went topside to be alone with my thoughts. Yet I feared to be alone with them, knowing they would creep back to the apparition I had seen that morning. Try as I might to compel the genie to slither back into its lamp, it was all too late.

She had asked me to get the picnic basket. It was a brisk ten-minute hike back up the wooded trail to the buggy. *Had I gone back as she asked? Or had I bowed to that wounded monster, the proud lover humbled and made small and flush with rage?*

I couldn't remember. At some point I was running along the grassy riverbank. I called for her, calls that turned frantic, a pace that became a mad scramble. I dove into the dark water. She was in an eddy farther on, arms outspread as if finally ready to embrace me, on her lips an incongruous smile as if she had been pleasantly surprised. When I brought Grace Tremaine back to town, her body beside me in the buggy, I could not tell them how I had pulled her out of the stream and held her to me, rocking back and forth and whispering her name as if by incantation I might summon her back from where she had gone. I had ceased to speak at all, not even to offer a consoling word to the father who stormed into the doctor's office and demanded that the blanket be lifted so he could see his child, impossible to be dead. Nor could I summon a word in my defense when he said to me, all too loudly in that crowded room, "You have taken her from me, sir, and I shall see you hang."

That night, out of a troubled sleep, my eyes opened. I felt the presence of someone else in my cabin. I could barely discern the outline of a woman, her face in shadow.

"You ran from Baltimore. You bolted from prison. As spineless cowards do." Her laugh was an unearthly tone, spiteful and cold. "Grant you, it took some nerve to break parole, ship out, and break your father's heart." I swung my legs over the bunk knocking over the bottle of rum with a clatter. My head was still swimming.

"You ran and you never stopped running. But there's nothing for it, is there? For any of you." She sighed. "You, Fahey, Diem must chase phantoms or be chased by them. Oh, and hoary old Wallace, too. What do you think the Golden Sura is all about? A soul? Something in search of a soul? Or the witness to a man who has lost his?"

"Go!" I groaned, shaking my head. "Leave me be."

The cabin door swung open with a bang. A gust of wind rippled her hair and the hem of her dress. "Who really died that day, Ulysses? What did you really see? Her skirts had billowed out across the flood and dragged her under. Poor girl. Tell me who she was. Speak her name, Ulysses . . ." She lifted her hand out of shadow, and a moonbeam fell on the ghastly thing in her hand. It was a severed head, but I did not see the features until she raised it higher. My own eyes stared back at me, lips moving to speak the name I could not bear to hear again.

I picked up the bottle of rum and threw it at my tormentor. It shattered against the bulkhead. The doorway was empty. I could hear light footsteps running down the passageway. I paused at the desk, pulled my Colt from its holster. I followed her to the next cabin and flung it open.

"Show yourself!" I cried. There was laughter, mocking, sensual laughter, but this time from the other side of the deck. I lumbered aft, the blades of the stern-wheel rising up in the moonlight like some instrument of torture. Down the starboard side, I followed her. Heedlessly, I ran down the passageway and kicked in the door to the next cabin.

"Where are you, damn you?" There was no answer, but suddenly, the cabin was illuminated with candlelight.

"What is it, Captain?" Devadatta stood at the door bareheaded and in a white loincloth, the candle bobbing in his hand, his eyes wide with fear and alarm.

I turned on him. "Where did she go?"

The candle shook some more. "You would not shoot me, sir!"

"She was here. She ran into this cabin!"

"Who, sir? I saw no one."

Perhaps it was the tremor in Devadatta's voice that brought me back. I looked around at the bare walls, the empty cot, the table with basin and pitcher, a wooden peg hanging above. There was nothing else. I lowered the revolver.

"All right," I said, passing my hand over my face. "All right."

The engineer regarded me doubtfully.

"I'm not pursuing things that aren't there," I said, trying to reassure him—and myself. I looked around again. "All right, I—must have been dreaming. A rum-soaked dream. It wasn't a ghost."

"I'm glad of that, Captain. The Fritz's Mischief is the last spook I'd ever want to see again. Not—not that I ever saw the thing—in person."

"Yes, you told me."

"It drove him to a furious distraction, that Mischief did."

"Yes . . ."

"Why, he lost his senses and ran off into the jungle."

"That's enough!" I said roughly. My tongue was as thick as flannel. "Beside, I think we both know who was behind the Mischief that drove the Fritz mad. Not that he didn't deserve it—as men do when they rule with the tips of their boots."

"Forgive my fright, sir." My engineer's worried countenance

had given way to an inscrutable smile. "It's just that I would hate to lose a good captain. And I would be very much saddened to lose so fine an officer as the sole captain of the Regal Sarawak Navy. Truly, that would be an occasion of the utmost tragedy."

"I'll see that doesn't happen," I replied softly, touched by his confidence and chagrined that I had lost my temper. "Now, turn in. It's time for my watch."

24

Yes, outwardly, she behaves normally. An astonishing turnabout, some might say. Outwardly..." Diem removed his pince-nez and squinted into the obscure light of Reverend Ames's office, which he had made his own. "I can't give permission to move her downstream. Miss Rand is— Well, I'll explain all this to the group shortly."

The change in Diem was profound. He was haggard but animated at the same time with a feverish energy. He had discarded his cravat; his shirtfront was undone and stained with sweat. He had traded his leather boots for worn straw sandals, a prudent change but one that contributed to the disheveled impression. I wondered if he had slept much at all in the past three days. I had kept to the *Lorelei*, while Devadatta and I fished to provision the mission. Diem had made it clear he wished no interruption while he secluded himself with Deborah Rand. Meanwhile, the Bataks had not returned. We were isolated and exposed, and the uncertainty of our situation had come to weigh on me.

"I can't have her moved," he repeated. He snapped open his pocket watch and, without further word, strode into the dispensary, where Bridgett, Fahey, and Sahar joined us. He asked us to be seated on the cots, as if we were students in a schoolroom. We shifted uncomfortably as he buttoned his collar, a lecturer's after-thought that his appearance made slightly ridiculous.

He felt that he owed us some explanation, especially since the change in Deborah Rand's condition had been so dramatic. From a state of near-atavism and savagery, Deborah Rand had been "resurrected." She who had been lost to us had been "restored to the human fold." These were the religious expressions he used, sounding uncannily like Bridgett. There was much to marvel at in this "second baptism," yet much to perplex us. I wondered if Diem wasn't in some sense testing our capacity for belief in his new religion.

"I can bring Miss Rand only so far." He waved his pince-nez as if pointing at a chart. "That is to say, there is a barrier that I have not learned how to cross, or that we have not been able to cross together. She is Deborah Rand, but at this point, in name only."

"She remembers nothing?" Bridgett Hannover's question was nearly an accusation. "In all these sessions of yours, she has said nothing about being captured by the Mamaqs, about Susannah and Noel?"

"She does remember certain things," Diem replied, "but her memory is selective. You can understand why she doesn't want to go to that place. And if she does go to that place, I don't think she will be the person to take us there. Not Deborah Rand." He paused as if to assure himself of our mystification. "Someone else has emerged during our long hours in neurohypnosis. She calls herself—Black Mary."

Diem paused to gauge our reactions. "I know this sounds pre-posterous to you. Before I began Deborah's therapy, I explained the process of neurohypnotism to you. Perhaps I should have begun by explaining what we know of mental derangement.

"In Paris we worked with many patients whose derangements were classified under the broad term of 'hysteria.' It is a blanket term for mental ailments, many of which we simply do not understand. Still, there are two groups of hysterics. One shows physical symptoms of the underlying disorder: for example, a patient who cannot walk yet whose condition is not medical or physiological in basis. The other group act out their troubles in the obscure regions of the mind or psyche. They produce a play to tell the story of their suffering. It is a drama so compelling and often so terrifying that its author must create roles, other personalities or divisions of the self, to give it full expression—and to protect the central personality itself, lest it disintegrate. Deborah Rand's reversion is symptomatic of this last group."

Rowan Fahey shook his head in confusion. "What has this to do with Black Mary, as you call her?"

"To put it simply, the savage has been written out of Deborah's drama, at least for now, and Black Mary has taken her place," Diem replied. "The emergence of these secondary personalities is always mysterious."

"So you don't know who this Black Mary is, or why she has appeared?" I asked.

"I can tell you only that I have seen Black Mary, Captain Vanders. I have spoken with her. She knows Deborah very well. She knows what has been done to Deborah and what Deborah has done."

Bridgett Hannover spoke barely above a whisper. "And what has Deborah done?"

"What I have learned so far confirms what the old man Nias has told us. Miss Rand and the Ameses were captured by the Mamaqs near Lake Toba Falls. Deborah did witness the torture and murder of Noel Ames. It was her admission, under hypnosis, to witnessing this event, and her guilt at being unable to stop it, that enabled us to reach the point where we are. She has faced these things. She recognizes the identity of Deborah Rand—but she cannot recall the life of Deborah Rand.

"Black Mary hoards those memories. She emerges by belittling and mocking Deborah. She is scornful and defiant. Whatever she knows, she dares the listener to know, but the listener must ask to cross that threshold. I have not allowed this other persona to take me further. I am afraid that if I allow her to take over, she may kill Deborah Rand in the process. She wants to protect Deborah, but she hates her, too."

Fahey stood up and grinned at Diem as one might humor a fool. "Then let's take a look and a listen to this Black Mary of yours."

"Black Mary is as real a person as Deborah Rand, Mr. Fahey," Diem answered evenly. "But I'm not about to summon her for your or anyone else's entertainment. I cannot summon her, anyway. Not yet. She chooses her own ground.

"One last thing." Diem produced the notebook we all recognized as Deborah Rand's diary. "I found this in Miss Rand's room this morning, on her dressing table. How it traveled from my office to Miss Rand's room, I do not know. I expressly told all of you that Miss Rand was not to be exposed to anything connected with her past. I told you such exposure might produce a crisis that could be of serious harm to our patient. Perhaps I didn't make the point clearly enough." Diem's eyes roved from Fahey to Hannover to me and at last settled, briefly, on Sahar, who had been sitting quietly throughout Diem's report. She met his gaze forthrightly, even defiantly.

Diem turned on his heel to return to his office. He paused in the doorway, though, and made me aware that he wanted me to come with him.

><ⓒ

He began almost apologetically. "I believe I can tell you something, Captain. I cannot tell this to the others." He bid me take the seat beside his desk. "Do you remember some time ago, when we first entered the Asahan, we spoke of an idea—entropy."

"Yes, the gradual loss of energy in a system. I think that's how you put it."

"In an open system, that is. A world in a closed system like a vacuum would not experience this dissipation in the model devised by Clausius. But our world is not a vacuum, is it? In a world of natural processes, energy must at length run down. Whole species and the worlds they inhabit must run out, and their leaves and bones become dust and silt. Even our own sun must burn down. And all the suns. A grand theme, at once poetic and tragic. But what has this to do with Deborah Rand?" He leaned forward, a movement that showed the strain of his ordeal. "Look about you at this land of Sumatra, Captain, and what do you see? Turmoil and upheaval, from Dutch Palembang in the south to Muslim Atjeh in the north. Pestilence, decay, and rot, both without and within. It is a blighted landscape fallen under a curse. It was not like this when I stayed among the Bataks years ago. Prince Bandarak and I played and hunted in pristine valleys and forests, and there were no ominous shadows.

"Perhaps we are at the end of a cycle, as the native peoples say. If so, then another is being born. When this happens formidable powers are unleashed, and certain of us, the more sensitive and attuned, become their instrument and expression. They are harbingers of what is to come. What if I were to tell you that Deborah Rand may be such a one?"

I struggled with the idea, stunned to hear him say it. It was as if his confidence in reason, so often expressed, had given way to a troubling and self-consuming doubt. "You think that Deborah Rand—her reversion, her creation of another personality—is an expression of this?"

Diem rose from his desk and went to a window overlooking the dry, empty parade ground. "What if she has taken within her what is palpably in the air? Why she has done this, I do not know. How she has done this, I do not know." He ran a hand through hair that had taken on a patina of gray. "I am not a mystic, Captain. I have aimed to be a man of science. Men of science like to think that mystery must at last give way to reason and nature yield up her secrets. But there are certain tangles within the warp and woof of the human fabric that science cannot untie, as much as I despair in that admission. The more despairing because I come from a world so bound in tradition, so bereft of curiosity about the physical world, that it has imprisoned itself in an enigma, like an ancient idol crumbling in the jungle."

Diem returned his gaze from the window. "But with Deborah Rand, I wish I had the mystic's eye. Where I can see only a tangle, the mystic can see the carefully elaborated knot. Just what does that knot signify, Captain?

"I knew a girl in Paris," he continued, not waiting for an answer. "She was from Provence, an orphan, about twenty when I met her. Her relatives had brought her to Briquet's clinic. It seems she had fallen down a well, but after her uncle rescued her, she was deaf and dumb. Briquet assigned her case to me, my first." He pressed his fingertips together to form a bridge. "We made tremendous strides together. Under hypnosis, she drew pictures for me. Her fall down a well was not accidental; it was an attempt at suicide. The deafness, the loss of language, were symptoms of a trauma she had experienced when her uncle, her father's brother . . . She could not live with the shame any longer. The uncle had been the one to save her. You see the conflict. At last she spoke to me."

"What did she say?"

"She told me that she was in love with me. Naturally, I reacted. She was very beautiful. I was her new savior, I had resurrected her, and she worshiped me. But then I perceived my error. And I withdrew from her. I told her she was the victim of a childish infatuation. At that time I had only a textbook knowledge of the rapport. I had not experienced it."

"The rapport?"

"Mesmer experienced it. All of us engaged in this work are aware of it. The healer forms a bond of a most intimate nature with the sufferer, one founded on trust. This relationship, even the identities of the two, is in the most crucial balance. A tip of the scales, and they are both consumed. But I was not consumed in this instance. The girl disappeared from the hospital one night. Three days later her body was discovered floating in the Seine." Folding one hand over the other, he lowered his head. "She had gone back to the well."

"Surely you can't blame yourself for her suicide."

"I will not lose Miss Rand." He looked up, anguish in his eyes. "I will keep her confined to her room. She will be free of both contagion and temptation. I will not lose her."

"We all have faith in you, Diem. That's why I need to know when I can put all of us on the *Lorelei* and return to Bahal. Surely you realize how precarious our situation—"

"She is mine!" Diem replied heatedly, his face flushed with frustration and perhaps with regret for the confession. "Do you think I could ever let her go? Do you think I would let her run away again?" He waved his fingers before his eyes as if to chase away a phantasm. "Remember, I know this jungle, too. I grew up here with my friend, a model prince in every way. We hunted here, in the old days. Believe me, I have taken every precaution."

I wondered if, in that moment, he saw in himself what I had seen. Whatever it was, he pulled back from it as one pulls back from the precipice. Resolution returned as he stood up. He held out his hand. "Let's speak on this matter tomorrow."

❧

The interview with Diem had left me more unsettled than ever. I wanted desperately to turn *Lorelei* around and sail back down the gorge, to be quit of this breathless, heat-struck, and blighted valley forever.

I decided I would speak to her before leaving the mission; I would see the one who was holding us back and judge for myself. The chair before her door was empty. I suspected the attentive guard, Fahey, had gone to the kitchen, for it was nearly noon. As

I walked down the corridor, I could see her hands grasping at the bars on the door.

When I stood across from her, I realized this was the first time I had ever been alone with Deborah Rand.

"I know who you are," she whispered, moving close enough to the bars that I was aware of the lavender scent of her hair. This fell in disordered ringlets, although a yellow bow still clung to one curl. It was the first time I had been so close to those compelling gray eyes, at once inviting friendship, trust, even conspiracy, but with a hint of disbelief in their shadows, the wariness of a wild, trapped animal. "You are the captain of the *Lorelei*. Rowan Fahey has told me all about you. But he is a liar." She looked anxiously from side to side. "He isn't here, is he?"

"No. And why do you call him a liar?"

"Because he says he loves me, but I never met the man before."

"You're sure?"

"Yes!" She gripped the bars more tightly, lowering her head. "Forgive my sharpness, Captain. I know I never met him. He said I was going to come away with him, leave my parents ... How could I?" When she raised her eyes, her look was almost violent in its disbelief. "I don't even know who they are!"

"No, you wouldn't remember."

"He says he waited all through one night. It was in a seaport in America. We were going away together, but when I did not show up, he took the ship alone."

"When was this?"

"A long time ago, he told me. Five years ago. Why would he make up such a thing?"

"Does Dr. Diem know about this?"

Again she paused to look from side to side, a hint of the cunning Mamaq we had found in the chapel. "No, of course not. Mr. Fahey just told me these things. I never would have done what he says."

"I'm sure you—would not."

She reached through the bars and grasped my hand. "Then why would he make up such a lie?"

"Perhaps he has confused you with someone else."

She frowned, almost a pout. "I must have that effect on people."

"I don't understand."

"Dr. Diem has confided in me that I remind him of someone, too. Someone he once loved—and lost."

Self-consciously, I slid my hand from beneath hers. She reached for my fingers as they slipped away. "He told you this?" I asked.

"Yes, several times. He tells me I should forget all about it. But when I wake up, I do remember what he says. Other things . . . are not so clear." She moved back from the door, stepping into shadow. "I will tell you I am afraid, Captain Vanders. Dr. Diem— I know he is trying . . . to help me . . . but I know he means to keep me a prisoner here."

"You've been through—an ordeal."

She practically leaped back to the door. "I am not crazy, Captain! That's what they all want you to believe. But I know they are all crazy and you are sane. I'm telling you, Dr. Diem means to keep me a prisoner here. I want to be free of this dreadful place. I want to leave!"

"Dr. Diem—"

"Dr. Diem! Dr. Diem!" She immediately lowered her voice but could not control the frantic look in her eyes. "He drives me, *drives* me. He thinks I have done horrible things. But I have done nothing. I've told him everything. There's no reason why I should be kept here." Her eyes looked up at me, now girlishly coy. "Except that he wants more."

"What do you mean?"

"More than I can give—to him."

There was a light footfall, someone coming up the stairs. She grabbed the bars more tightly, standing on tiptoe, and whispered, "I want to go back home. I want to be free of all this madness and of people who think I am mad. I know I can trust you. You know who I am, Ulysses." She lifted a forefinger to stroke my cheek. "You, of all people, know who I am."

There was a rattling of dishes and silverware at the top of the landing.

"It's that old man," she hissed. "He is one of Diem's henchmen. And that dark woman, the Malay woman, she means to kill me. She and Hannover. I implore you!"

Nias turned the corner bearing a tray.

"I beg of you, Captain. Take me on your boat and bring me down the river. I will be no trouble to you. But I must leave this place before—"

Fahey appeared at the other end of the corridor, nearly out of breath. "You had better come down to the main gate, Ulysses— we may be in for trouble."

⋗⊚

The Minangkabau Horseriders who reined their ponies outside the mission walls told us they had been hiding in the mountains of the Barisan range to the west. They had suffered an ordeal, to judge by the gaunt appearance of both men and mounts. There were about twenty of them, a sheen of yellow dust covering their baggy black pantaloons and leather vests. Each of them wore a black silk headband inscribed with white symbols. Most carried spears and bows, but a few had muskets. Fahey and I went out to meet them accompanied by Nias, who knew their dialect. He introduced me as the captain of a wondrous steamship that had traveled up the Asahan and defeated the Mamaqs. Their chief, Muntok, his eyes hidden beneath granite brows, nodded gravely. So I was the soldier who had brought the Mamaqs to their knees.

This confirmed the rumors circulating among the mountain tribes that the Mamaqs had been routed in two battles, and their terrible queen with them, so the Horseriders had returned to the mission to see if it was safe to bring their families back home. They were pleased that the Mamaq citadel had fallen, and clearly in awe of us, for we had defeated the Mamaq giants with fifty cannon and the magic of the Christ. Was it not true that our wizard Jesus had appeared in the sky with a gold battle standard and lightning crackling from his fingers? When they learned the fate of the Reverend Ames, they were saddened and clucked their tongues. Though worshipers of other gods, they had heard he was a saintly man. The Mamaqs had brought suffering on everyone.

Their report of a second defeat was puzzling and heartening at the same time. However, they could tell us nothing more than the stories that had been passed along, that the Mamaqs had been slaughtered almost to a man somewhere north of Lake Toba, near the tribe's ancestral lands. Of Prince Bandarak and his Crocodile Boys, they knew nothing. Nor did they know anything of Nias's people, who had so mysteriously disappeared from Tuan Medang.

They asked for permission to camp outside the walls; their own valley was another day's ride to the south. We offered them a meal of fresh fish and rice, since we had brought up ample provisions from *Lorelei*. For this, they were grateful. The drought had made foraging difficult, and the wild game was scarce even in the mountains. Mostly, they had subsisted on dried meat and a small store of sago flour. Since they had brought along a string of extra ponies, they offered us four of the beasts in exchange for our protection and two sacks of rice.

We did not tell them how thin that protection actually was.

25

Deborah Rand, or something of Deborah Rand, had been a hidden presence ever since we met Bridgett Hannover and her *turahan* in the Sumatra Strait. Each stop along Sumatra's wild coast, each mile we had traveled up the black-water reaches of the Asahan, had deepened our connection with the young missionary at Light of the World. For each of us, Deborah Rand had become more than her individual history; she had become a mirror of our inner turmoil.

Diem saw her as the phoenix of a collapsing age, even as she had become confused in his mind with a girl he had once loved and driven to suicide. Like a dragon guarding a subterranean treasure, Rowan Fahey stood outside her door, although what he guarded was a moment of possibility that had vanished long before. To Sahar, she was an emanation of a cycle in time and an evil force who meant us harm. To Bridgett Hannover, there was another fateful link, a tie charged with some obscure hatred and remorse.

Had I become another moth drawn to the flame? Deborah Rand's impassioned plea for rescue had left me unsettled, anxious for her safety yet doubtful of her motives. Her elusive nature, her baffling slide in and out of personalities, challenged my understanding, though there was no denying a secret recognition between us, as if we had been drawn together at this point in time for some obscure but vital purpose. Or had I misread her intentions and her meanings as well as mine? I was beginning to wonder if I hadn't succumbed, as Wallace had, to illusions and tormenting images. Were Deborah Rand's persecutors real or imagined? Were mine? Nevertheless, our separate fears had converged in a very real and dangerous place, one that had closed in on us, from both without and within.

The lines were beginning to drift for all of us. I knew the danger, but I was unable to act with decision. Meanwhile, we prepared *Lorelei* for the journey downstream. Devadatta and I spent a full day cleaning the engine and checking the steam lines. We worked steadily, methodically, but my thoughts were not on iron shafts and fire tubes but on the anxious prisoner in the castle above the Valley of Desolation.

The next morning Devadatta pointed to the mountains above the gorge. The thick clouds had begun to move off the peaks of the Barisan range like a dark, marauding host. As if to announce hostilities, a cloudburst drove a chill rain down the gorge. I practically danced in the downpour, for the weather, as it often does in a sailor's life, had forced a decision. The northern monsoon season had arrived. We would bring *Lorelei* and Deborah Rand downstream the following morning. I resolved to set off then and there and inform everyone at the mission. Light of the World would have to be abandoned. Bridgett was likely to balk, but I was resolved to bring her on board even if she had to be bound and carried. Fahey was the question mark—he might act on his obsession and try to spirit away Deborah Rand. He might even try to seize control of the ship again. Against this possibility, I told Devadatta to arm himself.

I had kept a mount tethered at the top of the gorge. As I saddled up, I saw a rider moving swiftly across the valley. To my surprise, it was old Nias. I had not thought he was such an adept horseman. He had not ridden out for pleasure, though, as I could tell by the look on his weathered face.

"The Horseriders have taken the mission!" he cried. "They are demanding that the Mamaq Sakti be handed over. They are in an ugly mood. I think they mean to kill her, Lord."

"Who do they mean to kill, Nias?"

"Why, the Reverend Miss Rand. They say she is behind all of their troubles."

We rode back across the valley in a driving rain. Horserider guards were posted on the parapet of the mission. Two of them stopped us as we rode into the parade ground. There was a confused hubbub, with the voice of Bridgett Hannover rising stridently above the others.

"You have no proof she is the Sakti," Hannover was saying to the Horserider chief as we hurried over to the portico, spears at our backs. Sahar gave a terse translation. "Here is Captain Vanders. Explain to Chief Muntok that he must be mistaken about our Deborah Rand."

The chief, however, was adamant. One of his men had been seen her. There was no doubt she was the Mamaq sorceress who had driven them from their lands.

Bridgett explained that she had decided to ignore Diem's orders and take Deborah for a walk outside the mission walls. This brought them to the Horserider encampment. One of the warriors pointed out Deborah Rand and raised an alarm. Soon a hostile group had gathered around the two women. Deborah panicked and struck at one of the men.

The sorceress had turned her evil eye on them, the chief insisted, and, by this magic, had caused a gaping wound in the arm of one of his men, as if the arm had been singed by fire. The evil queen of the Mamaqs had taken over the body of the Rand woman. She was an accursed thing, and she must be handed over to them for justice.

"Surely the chief knows that some of his men must be liars," Bridgett replied hotly. "I was there. We were surrounded by your men. One of them threatened us with a knife. When Miss Rand tried to push him away, the man ran off. There was no magic."

The chief's face and torso might have been hewn out of mountain rock—square jaw, broad shoulders, yet with short, bowed legs, as if nature had intended him to cling to the back of a horse. He nodded to one of the men standing in the group with him. The man had a cloth wrapped around his left forearm. He removed it and held it out to us. It was a fresh wound, a long slit in which the blood was still congealing. The skin around the wound looked as if it had been burned away.

"We know this woman," said Muntok. "The man who identified her was a prisoner of the Mamaqs. He saw their queen with his own eyes. He saw them prepare her for a raid on one of our villages by painting her white skin with their colors. She led the attack on our village. She gave the orders that killed my people. She wore the black and white war paint of the Mamaq Sakti, and when she returned from the raid, her hands were red with blood. Our blood."

"How could that be?" asked Hannover. "Miss Rand is a woman of God. She herself was a prisoner of the Mamaqs. She saw the horrors committed by them. She is a victim of the Mamaq terror, not the Sakti behind it."

By the set of the chief's jaw, I could see that he wasn't buying this line of reasoning. The Rand woman had been identified as the Sakti of the dreaded Mamaqs, and they had proof of her occult powers—she had done injury to one of his men. Justice would have to be meted out.

Muntok's insistence on justice gave me an idea. Hannover's defense of Deborah Rand had made the missionary suspect in the eyes of the chief. She, too, might have fallen under Rand's spell. On the other hand, I had not been involved in the dispute, so perhaps I could wield my prestige as vanquisher of Mamaqs and captain of a steamship. By good fortune, I was wearing my uniform, since I had decided to roll out my official self to round up my fellow travelers and bring them to the *Lorelei*.

Throughout the commotion, Dr. Diem had been standing in the shade of the portico, his face ashen, his features betraying no emotion but gauging the situation carefully.

I addressed him sternly. "Where is the woman accused of being the Sakti of the Mamaq?" I was hoping he might play along with the role I was trying to create.

"She is," Diem began hesitantly, "confined in her room."

"So she cannot get loose to work mischief against the Horseriders?"

"She is locked up," said Diem more precisely, now that he had divined I was up to something. "She is always guarded. Mr. Fahey is standing guard right now."

"This is a matter of the gravest consequence, Chief Muntok," I said as officiously as I could, and I pulled out a document from my tunic. I opened it and pointed to the gold seal affixed with red wax at the bottom. "This is the authority from my government in Sarawak to deal with all legal and diplomatic matters in Dutch territory that concern English and American citizens."

Muntok shook his head, obviously impressed with the gold seal but not so sure about the jurisdiction I was trying to claim.

"The Horseriders are allies of the Dutch?" I asked.

"The Dutch know we are their good friends, ever since the revolt of Tongku Tambose so many years ago."

Encouraged by this admission, I adapted my sternest demeanor. "The document says I am authorized to settle all disputes regarding the English and American citizens at this mission. You have seen the Dutch courts, have you not?"

Muntok nodded solemnly. "I have been to the great Dutch seat of justice in Palembang. There our former chief resolved a land dispute with the radjah."

"Then I exercise my judicial power to settle this matter. Miss

Rand is an American citizen. I will try Miss Deborah Rand and determine whether or not she is guilty of any charge you wish to bring against her."

Bridgett Hannover stepped forward, a wary look in her eye. "What is it you have in mind, Vanders?"

The chieftain of the Horseriders stepped back and conferred with two older men in his group. "We make the charge of witchcraft against this woman. She is the Sakti of the Mamaqs."

"Then we must hold a court of inquiry, Chief Muntok. You have witnesses against Miss Rand, is that not right?"

"We have."

I turned to Hannover. "And on your side, Mrs. Hannover?"

Hannover appeared to waver, but I was hoping she would see I had found a way down from the confrontational heights. She did. "We do have witnesses, Captain Vanders. Dr. Diem will testify as to Miss Rand's mental condition. And—" Her blue eyes shone with inspiration. "And Nias will testify for us. He was taken prisoner with Miss Rand and the Ameses. He, too, saw the Sakti while he was a prisoner. We will call Nias."

"With your agreement," I said to the chief, "I offer to give fair judgment in this matter."

The chief looked down again at the document with the gold seal. "Tell me what shall be the outcome of your decision then, Captain, if she is found innocent or guilty."

"If she is innocent, then she remains in the care of Mrs. Hannover, her employer, and Dr. Diem, her physician, as before."

"And if she is found guilty?" asked Bridgett.

"Then I will bring her down to Palembang and hand her over to the Dutch authorities. They can sentence her for any transgression she has made against a loyal Dutch ally."

Muntok again conferred with his advisers. One of their gurus, a shriveled old fellow with one tooth jutting from his lower law, vigorously shook a staff dressed with colored horsehair. "We agree to present this matter to your court, Captain," said Muntok solemnly, "but not to Dutch justice. The evil has been done to us. If she is found guilty, we insist on administering punishment."

"They will kill her," Diem whispered at my side.

"The evil has been done to all the tribes," I answered. "The Bataks have suffered, too."

The chief looked at me unwaveringly from beneath those craggy brows. I knew there was no further room for compromise. I was well aware of the two dozen muskets and spears that backed up his claim to retribution.

"Accepted," I said. "If she is found guilty, I will turn her over to your custody. On one condition—that you do not administer punishment until a Dutch representative from Palembang is present as a witness."

Muntok nodded his agreement.

Diem was behind me. "They still mean to kill her."

"I'm still the magistrate," I whispered.

"When do we hold this court of yours?"

"Now," I said. "The weather has decided that matter for us."

26

Within that very hour, I smacked a wooden mallet on a rickety table and announced the beginning of the inquiry. By any civilized measure of Western jurisprudence, this haphazard court teetered on the edge of absurdity. To my left, Chief Muntok, his advisers, and the Horserider witnesses shifted uncomfortably on creaking wooden chairs. As for the tribal rank and file, I had allowed their presence in the dispensary but insisted that they stack their weapons outside the main door. In black pantaloons and headbands, they squatted at the back of the room, passing around fuming tobacco sticks and munching on betel nut wrapped in pepper leaves. Bridgett Hannover sat across from them, to my right. Since Nias possessed the requisite languages, he was interpreter but would also be called on to testify. A stool was placed between my bench and the row of chairs as a witness box.

I explained to the court that our arrangements were along the style of an American courtroom but the roles and procedures were those of the Dutch. The chief asked a few questions about procedure. While we were engaged in this discussion, Fahey and Diem escorted Deborah Rand into the room, and the hubbub ceased.

Attired in a simple gray dress with a high collar, her hair demurely caught up with a net at the back, this tall, angular woman cut the proper figure for a missionary. Rowan Fahey looked around at the assembly with a scowl, as if to challenge anyone who would say otherwise. Apprehensive for his patient but knowing he must go along with the event, Diem fussed and fidgeted as Deborah took a seat beside Bridgett. His attentiveness struck me as more than clinical; it was distracted, even intimate. Deborah Rand appeared confident but kept her eyes modestly downcast, an apt pose for one who wished to create the impression that she was unjustly accused but obedient to the law. Only once did she briefly look up, and that was at me. There was a flash of anger in that look, and a plea.

With everyone in place, I called the inquiry to order. After reviewing court procedures, I asked Chief Muntok to set forth the accusations.

"One minute, Captain." Bridgett's voice rang out. She walked up to my table with a deliberate tread and put down her worn Bible. "I do not know if any of the tribesmen here are Christian, but it is right that each Christian give true testimony by His Word."

I explained Bridgett's point of procedure to Chief Muntok. He avowed that none of his clan was Christian but that they answered to him for the truth, and he personally answered to their god Rau, who did not forgive liars. I accepted this condition and then asked him to provide the first testimony.

Muntok rose to the task and made an impressive accounting for his people. He described the events of that morning, the identification of the Sakti, her use of demon magic. He went on to detail the sufferings of his people during the brief reign of the Mamaqs, the tortures and the killings, the enslavement of women and children. Of equal grief to these horsemen, their prize steeds had been slaughtered, as the Mamaqs feared the unfamiliar beasts were devils. When their bloodlust and thirst for cruelty were satisfied, the Mamaqs put the Horserider villages to the torch.

Bolon, the tribesman who had first accused Deborah Rand, then took the witness stand. He was a spindly fellow with a nervous twitch in his cheek and a raw canker on one side of his nose. He recounted how he and four comrades had been snared by the Mamaqs while they were leading a string of wild ponies back to the village. They had been taken blindfolded to a secret Mamaq war camp. The Mamaqs chose one of them to be tortured. They tied their victim to a strange wooden tower and then flayed him alive. That night a larger party of warriors arrived with the Sakti, who was borne aloft on a gold litter. They held a feast, and the Sakti was carried to the pens where the captives were held. To his astonishment, this queen was a white woman.

"Had you seen this white woman before?" I asked.

"No. Not before. But I see her now. She is sitting there." He pointed without hesitation at Deborah Rand, quickly averting his eyes. "This woman gave the order that another of my comrades be taken out and tortured." There was a dark rumble of agreement from the tribesmen in the back of the room.

"How do you know this is the woman? It was dark, as you say."

"In the light of the torches they carried. I saw her clearly."

"How light was it when you saw her?" I looked around at the dimly lit dispensary. "As light as it is now?"

"About the same," said Bolon, blinking. "Perhaps darker."

"All right, then," I said, pointing to the back of the room. "Was this woman about as far away as the last man at the back of the room?"

Bolon stood up, squinted, and nodded in the affirmative.

"Tell me the name of that man smoking tobacco leaf at the end of the room."

"There are several men smoking tobacco leaf."

"I mean the man at the very back."

"Oh, that one." Bolon squinted again, holding a forefinger to stretch his eyelid. "Oh, that one!" he repeated more confidently. "That is my friend Gokal."

I called to the man with the red headband to stand up. "Is your name Gokal?"

"No, Magistrate," said the man. "However, it is an excellent name."

The laughter that followed helped dispel some of the tension. I dismissed Bolon. Immediately, I turned to the tribesmen who had witnessed Deborah Rand's demon magic that morning. The man whose arm had been split open and singed was called on again to show his wound.

"How did you come to have this wound?" I asked.

"The two white women were walking through our camp. When Bolon cried out that he had seen the Mamaq Sakti, I came running up. That white woman over there"—he pointed at Deborah—"gave me the evil eye and then pointed at me. The next thing I knew, there was a flash of light, and my arm was on fire."

"Did you have any wound on that arm before?"

The man shook his head.

"I call our physician to examine the wound of this man."

Diem explained to the court that he was a medical doctor and the personal physician of Radjah Dulah, and that he had examined the wound of the man who claimed to be the victim of the Sakti's magic. The wound had been made by a knife or a spear point, Diem said, and the gray skin was gangrene setting in. It was an old wound, he added matter-of-factly, perhaps a week old but newly reopened.

I asked the wounded man what harm the accused woman had caused him if his injury was in fact a week old. He finally admitted that she had made a threatening gesture at him.

"Perhaps because she was surrounded by a throng of angry men?"

The fellow looked around helplessly. "Perhaps."

I dismissed him and asked the other Horserider witnesses to step forward and offer testimony on what had happened that morning. There was a hasty conference among the tribal elders. The witnesses wished to be excused from testifying, as they were no longer in agreement about what had happened.

I had hoped the pendulum would take a swing in this direction, but I hadn't reckoned on it happening so quickly. I turned to Rowan Fahey to report on how we had discovered Deborah Rand. He described how we had found her cowering in a corner, a terrified victim of Mamaq brutality, like the Horseriders themselves.

She had been held by the Mamaqs for weeks, Diem then volunteered, seeing an opening. She had probably been tortured, and if she had been taken around with their army, it was as a trophy of their power, to show their contempt for the Christians and the Dutch. Her captors had degraded her to the level of a beast, subdued her human spirit, and stolen her memory. Diem was at his best, gauging his explanation to the understanding of the tribesmen he was trying to convince. I could see that Muntok and his group of advisers listened with great care.

The time had come to bring old Nias to the witness stand. He looked around the dispensary as if searching for an exit, then limped reluctantly across the room. In a scarcely audible voice, he wanted to know if he was required to swear on the Bible.

Seeing as he was a Christian, I explained, it was necessary for him to swear just as Mr. Fahey and Dr. Diem had done before him.

"Is it necessary that I tell the Horseriders the same thing as I tell the rest of you?" he whispered.

"Of course, Nias, the truth is the truth. Now put your hand on the Bible and swear you will tell the complete truth."

The old man touched the Good Book and pulled his hand away as if he had touched living flame. "The complete truth," he mumbled. "I swear it." And repeated the words to the tribesmen in their tongue.

I prodded Nias through a retelling of his story, his role as guide for the Ameses and Deborah Rand to the falls below Lake Toba after they had dedicated the new prayer house at his village of Tuan Medang.

"A pleasant occasion," he said. "The Reverend Ames and Miss Rand were laughing very much together as we rode. It was going to be a jolly picnic."

"That is when the Mamaqs ambushed you and took you prisoner?"

"Yes—that is, after Mrs. Ames disappeared."

"Disappeared? What do you mean by that?"

"I mean she didn't come back after she went to visit the waterfall."

My eyebrows must have risen to my hairline. "You said nothing about this before. Previously, you told us Mrs. Ames was taken prisoner by the Mamaqs, along with the rest of your party."

"You did not have me place my hand on the Holy Book before."

"Then you lied when you told us the story the first time?"

The old man paused, working a string of worry beads through his fingers. "I was asked to say nothing of this," he said, barely above a whisper.

"Who asked you to say nothing of this? Speak up!"

"First, Reverend Mr. Ames." Nias turned in his seat to point at the accused. "Then . . . the Reverend Miss Rand told me never to speak to anyone of what had happened at the falls."

"When did she say this?"

"That evening when you last visited her—when I brought her the dinner tray. She said she would kill me with magic if I told the truth."

He feared even to look at me. I told him to translate exactly what he had just said. I had prepared myself for the growl of discontent that went through the Horserider ranks. One of the old wizards nodded forcefully as if to say "I told you so."

"Continue, Nias."

"When we reached the Toba Falls that afternoon, Reverend Ames asked me to scout ahead, along the rim of the falls, for the best place to picnic, to see the roaring water. I did as they said.

When I had reached nearly the opposite side of the falls, I saw a horse plunge over the side. I could not believe my eyes. I ran back. But when I returned some minutes later, Mrs. Ames was gone from the place. Reverend Ames and Miss Rand were very upset. Mrs. Ames's horse had bolted and met with a terrible accident, they told me. And Reverend Ames said I should be quiet about this until he released me from my word. People might misunderstand, he said. But I was confused. Then the Mamaqs fell upon us."

"So you do not know what happened to Mrs. Ames?"

"I did not see what happened."

"So Mrs. Ames was not with you when you went to Samosir Island with the Mamaqs?"

"There were just the three of us—Reverend Ames, Miss Rand, and myself."

"What happened while you were imprisoned on Samosir?"

"It is as I have told you. Except in the matter of one thing." Nias looked over to me as if seeking strength to continue. I nodded to him. "I saw the face of the Mamaq Sakti."

It was all I could do to quell the exclamations from all sides of the room.

"This was after the murder of Reverend Ames," Nias went on. "I will never forget that night. There was the long procession after the Sakti had been proclaimed. The soldiers came by carrying her on the chair, and there were such bloodcurdling noises made by the women. The priests whirled around in trances, for they had drunk much *tuba* that night. Hell had opened its gates and let the devils out. I thought it might be my last night to live. That is when the Sakti came by, held aloft by her soldiers. She passed so close to me, I could have almost reached out and touched her. She turned when she passed by and looked at me directly. Perhaps her power had sought me out. I shall never forget that. She was painted all over in the white and black stripes of the Sakti. But even with the paint, I recognized her. And then I knew it was this woman here." He pointed at Deborah Rand. "How this came about, I do not know."

There was silence in the dispensary until the murmur of the Horseriders' voices rose to an excited pitch. I called out for order, but there was one voice raised above all the others.

"Wait!" cried Deborah Rand. She sprang from her chair to confront the court. "I will not be accused of these things!"

Again I called out for silence.

She turned to me, her eyes seeking mine for help. "I have the right to know what happened. I have the right to find out the truth."

"How can you?" I asked. "You say you have no recollection of these events."

"I have no recollection of these events. I have no recollection of threatening old Nias, either. But I want to know!" She turned to Diem but spoke for all to hear. "There is one way for me to recall what happened." She stepped forward to address all in the room, even as the physician tried to hold her back. "I implore Dr. Diem to put me under hypnosis. I want him to do this now."

"This is folly," Diem protested. "There is no guarantee that I can even lead you to the truth under hypnosis. You would place yourself in jeopardy. I can't allow it."

"You yourself have told me that a crisis can trigger lost memories. We have such a moment now."

Chief Muntok waited impatiently for Nias to translate and signaled that he wanted to speak. "This woman stands accused of being the Sakti. Even a separate eyewitness has identified her. Turn her over to us for justice."

"The defendant does have the right to be heard!" I answered smartly, banging the mallet on the desk to curb the din.

"I won't be a party to this charade," said Diem.

"You *must* honor my request, Doctor," Deborah pleaded. "However the truth comes out, I have that right."

Bridgett Hannover rose from her chair. "And we all have the

right to know what happened to Susannah Ames. Her testimony can end this thing for us. A person cannot lie under neurohypnosis. You have told us so, Dr. Diem."

"It is my right," said Deborah Rand, all of her energy focused on Diem. "It is my right."

27

Deborah Rand took the witness seat. Back straight, hands folded in her lap, she stared stonily ahead into the empty space before her. In this willful attitude, one could well imagine the leader of a savage tribe.

Diem paced in silent deliberation and then walked over to Deborah and whispered in her ear. Her reply was simply to shake her head with a conviction that said all his arguments were for naught; she was resolved to undergo the ordeal. Diem then turned his attention to the court, having regained his composure.

"I will place Miss Rand in a sleep," the doctor announced. We all looked on with grim fascination. Rowan Fahey's regard was mixed with an apprehension so profound it had drained all of the ruddiness from his cheeks. Bridgett Hannover's attention moved from Deborah to Diem watchfully, as if she suspected them of some trick. Sahar seemed to have trouble breathing; she had parted her veil and dabbed at her brow with a handkerchief, one hand over her breast.

"I will place her in a sleep," Diem repeated, his eyes on Muntok and his advisers. "In this state, she may be able to tell us what happened at the time of her capture and afterward. The Mamaqs have stolen parts of her memory, as I have told you, and we may not be able to cross that barrier. If we cannot, then she must not be blamed."

Diem looked directly at Muntok as he said these last words.

The chief nodded. Diem took the gilded snuffbox from his waist-coat and held it before Deborah Rand. He spoke to her softly, coaxingly, as he tipped the mirror back and forth. In a few moments, her eyelids fluttered. She sat as still as an effigy, her long neck inclined slightly to the right. Diem then gave us to understand we were to maintain strict silence.

"Deborah, I want you to go back to the day when you were last with Reverend Ames and Susannah Ames. Do you remember that afternoon? In the village of Tuan Medang."

"We went to the village to dedicate the new dispensary."

"What happened after the dedication?"

"We traveled by horseback, the three of us—no, the four of us, for we had a guide. We went to see the falls south of Lake Toba."

"Do you remember the guide, Deborah?"

"Yes, he was an old man named Nias. He had been baptized and was very keen to do the Lord's work."

"You rode to the falls. What happened when you got there?"

"We were going to have a picnic lunch at the falls. We were going to..." She fell silent. Her eyes appeared to be moving beneath their lids. Diem repeated the question. "Nias had walked off to find us a good spot for viewing the falls."

"You were alone with Reverend and Mrs. Ames?"

"Yes. We were on the rim of the falls on horseback."

"What happened then?"

"There was...a commotion behind us. *They* came out of the forest. Susannah was screaming and striking her horse across the haunches with her riding crop. She was trying to get away from them."

"Who were they?"

"They were fiends. Men smeared with clay and paint all over them. They wore helmets made of the same gray clay and wattle. They went for the horses first, with their arrows and spears. The horses were screaming. Susannah's horse reared up and ran off. I looked around for Susannah, but she was gone. Then..."

"What do you see now?"

"Oh my God . . . They have hoisted him on the tower."

"Who is that?"

"Noel. And he sees me looking on and cries out. 'Be brave!' he cries out to me. 'Be brave.' They crucify him. They are tearing off strips of his skin; they are burning him with torches. He is screaming and crying out for death, and I am screaming with him." Deborah Rand held herself and rocked back and forth in the chair, her mouth open as if she might repeat those screams, but her mute expression of horror gave way to laughter. The laughter was pitched low, a nearly masculine timbre. The young woman ceased to rock and straightened her back. Reaching behind, she pulled off the net that held her hair and shook her head until her dark tresses were loose and free. She stroked her cheeks and, leaning back, crossed one leg over the other, exposing her knees. The Horseriders muttered at a gesture they saw as both provocative and offensive.

"Now you've gone and scared the silly little bitch!" She laughed, slapping her knee. This arch and sneering woman was no longer recognizable as Deborah Rand. It was as if we had witnessed a deformation of her soul.

Immediately, Diem was on his guard. "Who is this?"

"You've heard of me, Dr. Diem. We've met before."

There was a stirring among the Horseriders as Nias tried to explain what was happening. The old medicine man half rose out of his seat, rattling his horsehair fetish as if to ward off evil.

"What has happened to Deborah?" asked Diem.

"Deborah Rand can no longer answer your questions, so I've taken over for her. She does not have the stomach for it, does our Debbie."

"You are Mary."

"Aye, you know me now, my friend. Mary the black and comely. Black and comely are my sins."

Lowering his head, Diem paced before the witness chair. Making an abrupt turn, he confronted her. "All right, then, tell us what happened, if you know the truth. If we can trust you to tell the truth."

"Debbie is the little liar!" the woman cried out as if she had been prepared for his challenge. "Black Mary knows the truth. She's not afraid to speak it, Dr. Diem! On the contrary, you have been the one backing away from me. You've grown too fond of Debbie, I think."

"Tell us what happened the day at the falls. Tell me now what Deborah was afraid to say."

"Such a tawdry little tale," she said, as if introducing a beguiling piece of gossip. "Deborah and Noel went at it like mongrels in heat. It was weeks before his insipid Susannah caught on. Noel had completely lost his head over poor little Debbie. She, in turn, felt she was under a curse. It was happening again. She always ended up throwing herself at someone else's beau. Or husband. Deborah yearns for forbidden fruit. She's a slut. And, unfortunately, she is a stupid one. I'm the one who has to do the dirty work.

"The plan," she said, leaning toward Diem but still speaking loud enough for all of us to hear. "The plan was to kill the other little bitch."

"You mean Susannah Ames?"

"No, another monkey in heat, you ass!" She laughed out loud, a raucous crow of triumph that filled the large room, then trailed away. "But it didn't come off. Not as things were planned."

"Whose plan?"

"It was Noel's idea. He had become obsessed with Debbie, like— you." Her forefinger pointed at Diem. Her eyes were open now, and she did not speak like one in a trance. She turned in her seat and let the finger move as if a needle on a compass. It stopped to point at Rowan Fahey. "And you." The accusing finger veered to me. "This one, too." She laughed again, coarse and congratulatory.

"So you and Noel—" Diem tried to continue.

"*Deborah* and Noel! They took Susannah to the falls with the intention of doing her in. They planned on an accident—she loses her step along the rim of the falls. Treacherous ground, you know. Come to think of it, that's what happened. An accident. Just not the one they planned. The Mamaqs saw to that. Susannah's horse bolted—horse and rider plunged into the cascade. A convenient break for the would-be homicides. Almost free . . . But the Mamaqs had other plans."

"You were taken to Samosir Island."

"Oh, we were taken there. And when they had done with Noel Hannover, they started in on Deborah. But could she take it? Not *her*! So it was time for me to make my appearance."

She rose and addressed the court as if the hypnotic spell had worn off and she was suddenly aware of an audience. "They kept us in a hut. When it came time for them to take me to the tower, Deborah failed, *but I did not*. I had stolen a knife. The chief priest came into the hut, and I stood up to him. I pulled out the blade and plunged it into his heart. When the priest fell, I prepared to die. But nothing happened to me. The Mamaq chieftains and priests in that hut fell to their knees. I had fulfilled a Mamaq prophecy. They proclaimed me their Sakti. I became what they wanted me to be. To save the both of us: Deborah, who had gotten us into this mess, and *myself*. Besides, as I learned, the Mamaq cause was just."

"How can you call those monsters just?" Bridgett Hannover cried out. She turned to me. "This court is finished. She has admitted everything. We know now who she is and what she has done."

"And you would have me killed!" Black Mary shouted back. "For your own revenge. Because that sad drunkard husband of yours couldn't keep his hands off our little Debbie."

"*You* are the lying bitch!" The shadow of loathing that passed over Bridgett Hannover's countenance was startling.

Black Mary pressed the point. "Then why did you try to shoot Deborah Rand when you first came across her in the mission?"

"I am not on trial here," Bridgett returned hotly.

"No, but the truth is," said Black Mary. "The truth is, your husband recoiled from his own sin. He sent Deborah Rand up to Light of the World, as remote and distant a post as could be found. We shan't quibble over guilt, for there was enough to go around. Your Miles found a solution in his hunting rifle."

"He didn't kill just himself that day," Bridgett said softly.

"No, he killed the life that was inside of you, too. You wrote to our Deborah about it. She was ultimately responsible for two deaths, your husband's and that of the child you were carrying, the child you miscarried. You wrote to her in anger and in vengeance, and this set in motion another chain of events. Weak, foolish little Debbie sought solace in the arms of Noel Ames—yet another upright, married, and God-fearing man."

Black Mary turned her scorn to Diem, to Fahey, to me. "No. You cannot blame Deborah Rand for what you would make of her. Each one of you desire her, each one of you would take her if you had the chance. I stand in the way—and now you must contend with me.

"But *you*," she said, fixing on Hannover. "You came to this mission with but one thought: to kill her. Ames wrote to you— oh yes, I know, for your Malay woman has whispered that and a hundred other deadly things in my ear since you captured me. Noel Ames wrote to you, and you figured out what had happened between him and our Debbie. And you decided to put an end to the sins of Deborah Rand."

At that moment there was a buffeting of wind as hard as a fist, and a shutter was flung against the open window. A peal of thunder rolled across the Valley of Desolation as the rain began to pound with fury on the tin roof of the colonnade, the first hard rain of the monsoon.

Deborah Rand raised her voice to compete with the clamor. "When you failed at the outset, you put this contemptible creature to work." She pointed at Sahar, who looked back at her with a feverish gaze. "You gave her the order to poison me. I was not fooled. And this morning, just before this trial, your creature brought me a bowl of fruit. I knew what this meant and told my friend." She nodded to Fahey. "He went back to the kitchen and switched bowls.

"Sahar, you ate the fruit intended for me. Behold the result." With a toss of her head, she raised her arm and pointed at the *turahan*, who was bent nearly double and clawing at her stomach in agony. Her eyes fixed on Deborah Rand, she stumbled forward and, with a strangled cry, vomited a stream of blood that covered her chin and breast and spattered on the floor.

The tribesmen, who had comprehended only a part of what had passed in the last moments, saw the scornful gesture of the Mamaq sorceress and the sudden violence of Sahar's reaction. When the *turahan* fell to the floor writhing in pain, both eyes white and upturned, the tribesmen panicked. Even Montuk forsook his dignity and broke for the door but paused before he passed into the storm. Grabbing a throwing spear from one of his men, he hurled the weapon at Deborah Rand. Rowan Fahey leaped and knocked her out of the way. The spear hurtled past, and I dove to the floor, upending my table. The cries of the infuriated tribesmen were taken up into the vortex of the shrieking wind.

Pulling out my revolver, I peered over the table edge. Only Nias had not moved from his seat. Staring into vacantness like one charmed, he held up his wooden crucifix with both hands. The dispensary doorway was empty. Rain lashed the parade ground, and lightning shivered the sky to the roll and crackle of thunderclaps. A curtain of darkness had closed on the room. I could barely make out Hannover and Diem on their knees before Sahar, curled on the floor. I called out in this darkness for Rowan Fahey. I called out for the woman he had saved. There was no answer. The Irishman and Deborah Rand were gone.

28

Gunfire, confused cries, and rolls of thunder covered my scramble out of the dispensary. A back entrance to the pantry bordered the north wall of the fort. One of Montuk's men, armed with a spear, stood guard outside, his mountain pony tethered nearby. I jumped him, brought my pistol down on the side of his head, and claimed his steed. A muddied track led into the forest, and that was the path I wagered they had taken, Rowan Fahey and his jilting lover, Deborah Rand. I did not know if she went with him of her own accord or if she was his prisoner, but I feared the worst, not knowing which was worse, as I urged on my nervous mount.

My fear was confirmed when I heard the crack of a rifle ahead, followed by a lightning ball that bounced and sizzled from tree to tree like a phosphor shell. Spooked at the sight, my pony screamed and bolted. By the time I was able to rein him in, I had lost my way. Far above me, the forest trees shook and moaned in the wind. There, in that stormy path, I lost heart and cursed the folly that had driven me to pursue them.

Suddenly, I was not alone. A spectral horse and rider barred my way. My skittish animal reared up, and it was all I could do to stay in the saddle. Deborah Rand was silhouetted by a shimmer of pearl light thrown off by lightning, but she and her mount were completely still, undisturbed by the roil of the elements all about us.

I was not surprised to find her. Something was unfinished between us. She had drawn me to Light of the World and, at last, this solitary place for a purpose that perhaps neither of us fully understood. But in one thing I was resolved—to bring her back down the river with me. Our mounts stood facing each other, whinnying softly, as the rain spiraled down through the forest canopy.

"I know why you are here," she said, as if reading my thoughts. "Come with me first. There is something I want you to see."

Without waiting for a reply, she turned her horse around, and I followed.

It was twilight by the time we reached the rim of Lake Toba Falls. Swollen and enraged by the onset of the first monsoon storm, the waters were dark with soil and debris, and entire trees, their limbs dragging behind, were hurled over the cataract like victims of sacrifice. Animals, too, had been caught in the current—the dead and bloated corpse of a boar bobbed beside a white-eared doe, still alive, struggling to keep her head above the water. Both fell and were lost in the roaring mist and tumble that dissolved into the chasm two hundred feet below. We halted our horses at the edge of this abyss. Deborah Rand looked down into the murky chaos, and I wondered if this was the spot where Susannah Ames plunged to her death. Deborah turned her mare back to the riverbank. In time, the fury of the storm dwindled, so it was in a steady, windless drizzle that we continued along the slippery trail. About a mile on, the river broadened, and the southern tip of the forested island known as Samosir hove into view some hundred yards from the shore. My companion slid off her mount and, searching the brush, pulled off branches to reveal a dugout canoe painted with Mamaq symbols.

"Do you mean to return to Samosir?" I asked as I tethered our horses under the spreading branches of a flame tree.

She was quick to gauge my thought. "You will find no Mamaqs there. They have gone away." We pushed the canoe into the stream. She got in and held up a paddle. "Come with me," she called, as if she were homeward-bound. "The current is swift here, so put your back into it, Captain!"

Even with strenuous paddling, the current swept us south of the island, where I was able to snag a limb of an uprooted camphor tree that had fallen into the lake. We dragged the canoe onshore and sat on the beach to recover our wind. South of us, the water churned thick and white as it funneled to the falls.

"You are worried about your ship," she said.

"You can see for yourself."

"You have time. A mile down from the falls, the gorge narrows. It's like a dam—it fills with flotsam."

"I won't go down the river until you come with me."

She rose silently and headed into the forest. A trail led inland about a quarter of a mile and opened on a deserted village in a small valley, surrounded by thickly wooded hills. A semicircle of stone houses defined the town center, with ruder bamboo structures ringing them. Many of these had been toppled by the storm. The stone houses were made of hewn blocks of granite, very old, neatly dressed, and fitted expertly without mortar of any kind. The roofs were lumber, roughly hewn, overlaid with woven fronds. Pottery and tools lay strewn about as if the inhabitants had left hurriedly. I knew then I was standing in the middle of what had been the Mamaq stronghold. As if to confirm my suspicion, the charred remains of a wooden tower, resembling the frame of a Plains Indian tepee, creaked in the wind, encircled by painted rocks. On such a frame, I mused, had Reverend Ames been flayed alive.

And now the former queen of the Mamaqs, tall and lithe and with a determined stride, led me to a house at the western edge of the encampment. Lifting a bull-hide door, I followed her into the murky interior, half wondering if I'd find a band of savage assassins ready to cut my throat. When none appeared, I set about making a fire from the stock of dry wood in the house, my teeth chattering. When Deborah returned, she produced two green breadfruit from behind her back as if they were the fruit of the gods.

"What about Fahey?" I asked.

"He's none the worse," she said as she split the breadfruit with a wooden cleaver. "A little knock on the head. I left him not far past the five trails that fork at the north end of the valley."

"He meant to harm you?"

"It doesn't matter. I am free of him. I knew I would meet you on the trail. I knew you would follow."

"Muntok and his men were not far behind me, I think."

"They won't come here. Only the Mamaqs are not afraid of disturbing the Rajo Alam. The Old Ones, the tribesmen called them."

"What is so special about the Mamaqs?"

"They were not afraid of anything—until now. Besides, they thought the spirits of the ancient builders would confer some of their powers. That is why they took over this long-abandoned village. The stonecutters of the Old Ones lived here. There is a quarry farther on."

"The stonecutters only? Is there more to this settlement?"

"Much more. The island has always been a sacred place, filled with wonders and terrors." She shivered as her eyes roved about the walls, and I knew she was referring to her ordeal as a captive. "That's over now, Ulysses."

It was the first time she had spoken my name. I watched as she prepared the breadfruit, burying the cut halves at the edges of the fire and raking the crimson coals over them. The light fell on her hair, deepening the dark hues, still beaded with rain and swept back into a rough braid. She looked over the fire at me with a secretive smile, as if we were sharing a forbidden adventure, the crackling flames discovering the soft silver of her eyes and the burnished hue of her cheeks. She was in harmony with this remote and wild place, with the calamitous rain and wind that sighed through the creaking trees like a ghost. Her spirit had nothing to do with the prim missionary gray she wore. I could see her daubed with charcoal and lime and circling, spear in hand, a village sleeping peacefully in the night, the Sakti of a savage tribe.

"The Mamaqs nearly had us fooled," I said. "The Bataks were terrified of their uncanny powers. Then we saw their giants burst into flame on the mission walls."

"The giants were my idea."

"Your idea?"

"You've seen the puppet shows in every Malay town and village. If you believe in ogres, then huge puppets can be ogres."

"But why? Why help the Mamaqs?"

"I was—and am—their queen," she answered, as if this fact might be known to the world. "Although the word 'Sakti' means more than that to the Mamaqs. Dozens of them died defending me at the mission. You saw that for yourself."

"Is this Black Mary speaking? Or Deborah Rand?"

She laughed out loud. "Does it matter? But, if you prefer, Deborah Rand. Mary has served her purpose. And you needn't look at me like someone falling off a cliff."

I gathered my wits as I stared into the leaping yellow flames. "She was not real, was she? None of this was real."

She laughed softly now. "Hunger is real, Ulysses Vanders. Thirst is real." She rummaged in the back of the hut and pulled out two lengths of red cotton cloth. "You're shivering—take your clothes off." She began to unbutton her dress. "We'll wrap ourselves in these. And here." She handed me a round ceramic bottle with a delicate stem. I held it to the light. As I turned it in my hand, I could follow a little boat's journey down a misty river, poled by a solitary fisherman. The riverbank was thick with bamboo, and huge heart-shaped leaves, and hidden within the leaves— eyes. I pointed this out to Deborah.

"Not eyes," she said, amused. "Look again."

Not eyes but butterflies flitting among the leaves along the riverbank. Such was the artisan's humor. This imaginary scene seemed alive with tiny watchers.

On the other side of the fire, Deborah slipped out of her dress, petticoat, and underclothes, thinking nothing of her nakedness, or perhaps realizing that I had gazed upon her before, and not caring if I gazed again. Gaze I did, and with far different emotions than when I first saw her wielding a knife in the ruined chapel. After arranging the clothes on a makeshift wooden stand before the fire, she wrapped the red cotton cloth about her, fastening it with a knot above her breasts. She helped me pull off my boots, then my sodden clothes. I wound the rough cotton cloth around me like a Maori wrap, my shoulders bare but warmed by the fire.

She found two gourd cups. I pulled up the stopper with my rigging knife and smelled the liquor. A mixture of cinnamon and cloves and the musky-sweet smell of palm wine. It mingled with the applelike odor of baking breadfruit.

"To warm our hearts," she said, clinking her cup on mine. The liquor warmed and consoled, rich as a rum suffused with exotic spices. "I found it in one of the island temples. An offering to the gods of the Rajo Alam. Who knows how old?"

Huddled together before the fire, we enjoyed a simple, nourishing meal, fresh spring water and the nutlike pieces of breadfruit. And then we lay down together, our arms around each other, and talked. As if we had been doing this for years. Without qualm or scruple. It was as though a wand had been waved over us, creating this space, this bower, this respite from the storm. There was this other Deborah Rand, soft to the touch, womanly, inviting, beside me.

" *'She took me to her elfin grot,'* " I began, trying to remember the lines by Keats.

" *'And there she wept and sigh'd full sore.'* But this is not the stuff of romance, Ulysses. The stuff of fairy tales, perhaps, and dark as a fairy tale. How hard it is to explain—there is a momentum that works inside of us and outside of us at the same time, until we arrive at some unsuspected place. We *know* this place! We meet there an unsuspected self. And we recognize her, too. This is what happened to me with the Mamaqs. I became their queen partly because I defied them; my anger had driven me to a pitch where I didn't care what they did to me. They had tortured and slaughtered my lover before my eyes. Yes, I suppose I did go mad."

"Then it was true about you and Ames."

"Oh yes, true that we were lovers. But not true that we set out to murder Susannah that afternoon. I think that worm was beginning to gnaw at Noel, though. He knew Susannah suspected. And he felt trapped, doomed, unless some action was taken. That was why I wanted to make a clean breast of things, clear the air, tell Susannah. I didn't want some other crime on my hands. It was terrible enough about Miles Hannover, a weak, foolish man, but cunning when it came to hiding his 'hunting expeditions.' Bridgett was suspicious of every woman, any woman, and she had cause to be. I don't know how she found out about us; perhaps Miles confessed in the end, before he shot himself. With Noel Ames, that was different . . . I saw what our affair was doing to him; he became infatuated, obsessed, then unstrung. I had made a mess of things, strayed from my plan. Straying—it's a fault of mine, *the* fault of mine. Then the Mamaqs ambushed us, and that resolved everything. Susannah's death was not on my hands, at least. Her fall was an accident."

She leaned on one elbow above me, her rain-fragrant hair falling about my face, as she traced circles on my chest with a lazy finger.

"As for the Mamaqs, there was a place in their legend for a female Sakti who could overthrow the power of the head priest. I had but one object—to keep alive. The Mamaqs were desperate to find a symbol, make of that what you will. And yes, I embraced their cause, but to save lives, not take them."

"Yet lives were lost."

"Lives would have been lost in any event. I did not say I controlled the Mamaqs. Who can control a force of nature?"

"So you, too, believe in the Great Cycle."

"I believe in freedom."

"To murder and pillage?" I sat up in irritation, troubled by her glibness. "Is that the freedom you advocate?"

She sat up, too, her hands grasping her knees. "*You* were not thrown into a dark room and manacled. *You* were not thrown into a hole with the mad and the forgotten. They buried me alive. I swore I would never let that happen again."

"You mean what your family did to you. Five years ago. There was a young man—"

Her look softened. "There was a young man—"

"Rowan Fahey."

"Was it Rowan Fahey?" she asked with a bitter smile. "The Irishman thinks his hypnotism is as potent as Phan Dom Diem's! But in the end, I saw through both Mesmers."

"At the mission, during the inquiry, you thought one of us was out to kill you."

"And one of you nearly succeeded." She touched a finger to my lips and put her arms around my neck. Untying the knot between her breasts, she let the red fabric fall. "Sometimes you can hear the ancient voices at Samosir," she whispered. "Listen with me . . ."

＞⊂∋

I awoke from deep, dreamless slumber to the sound of a distant, melancholy wail coming from the hills above our hut. The *tapa* coverlet by my side was empty. Deborah was gone and, I quickly discovered, so was my Navy Colt. I rose at once, still in my Maori wrap, and, lifting the bull-hide door, stepped into the cool night air. The rain had tapered off to intermittent showers, and the monsoon moon, that mistress of enigmas, hung above the forest canopy, full and candid but partially hidden by scarves of scudding clouds. When I called for Deborah, there was no reply, but the wind from the hills brought the same cry that had wakened me, clearer now and achingly familiar.

"Ulysses!"

A shiver of fear ran through me at that disembodied cry. I knew that voice and its hauntings; it had been with me waking and dreaming all through our journey. It had beguiled me from the jungle as we cruised up the Sumatra coast; that same insinuating voice had mocked me in my cabin just nights before.

I didn't know what awaited me on the hilltop, but there was no turning back. If I didn't confront her now, she would pursue me and drive me mad, so I plunged heedlessly into the jungle and began to climb. The path was narrow and crooked, thick with sharp thorns, wet leaves that clung to my skin, ground vines that caught and tugged as if trying to bring me to my knees.

"Ulysses . . ."

I rushed on until, my heart and temples throbbing, I stood within a stand of teak whose shaggy trunks rose like columns into the vault of the forest far above. Here the air was sickly sweet and heady with the odors of old vegetation and woody decay. The ground cover thinned, and bulging roots, like dragon coils, snaked across the ground to snare boulders and crack them in their grasp. Wreathed in ancient silence, the venerable grove felt as hallowed as the nave of a Gothic cathedral, but one that had long since been plundered by vandals. As if to confirm my impression, two rounded pillars, white as bone, stood at the crest of the hill like ghostly mourners praying at a tomb.

There between the upright stones stood the apparition I had at last come to face. This time she did not fade and vanish into the misty air but waited my approach. Her outspread arms told me she had come to affirm the truth that bound us and, at last, claim me for her own. As fresh and alive as she had been that last morning on the Potomac, her beautiful auburn hair spilled over her shoulders and to her hips in curls and spirals. She wore nothing else; her embraces were now for me alone, and for me alone all her secrets.

"Come to me, Ulysses, come . . ."

There was only one emotion impelling me as I stumbled forward, drawing closer to the summit of the hill, one desire; to be united with her forever. There was no other cause or consequence but her and no other meaning. She was meaning itself in her every feature, in the devouring passion of her look, in the yearning expressed by her outstretched arms to bring me to her, drawing me ever closer. I cannot say what caused me at that moment to look up at the obelisks that framed her, but my attention was seized by the strange design chiseled into each stone, and for a fateful instant, I paused—this design was well known to me by now, this butterfly with outstretched wings. The tracery across its wings was unmistakable, an enigmatic script that warned of illusion and disillusion and the folly of human desire.

As I paused, seemingly between my world of sorrows and a world of limitless delight, with all that I ached for nearly in my grasp, another voice came from behind, sharp and clear.

"Ulysses!"

I could not tear myself away from Grace Tremaine. But neither did I fall into her embrace. I trembled on the balance until, almost imperceptibly, I saw a bleak loneliness creep into my beloved's face. In place of longing, I saw an infinite sadness, for both of us knew. She was there not for herself but as an emissary for some hidden power whose desire was far more complete than mine. Even in that recognition, I saw a final piece of the drama that had been enacted between us nine years before, one that had eluded and tormented me ever since.

I was once more immersed in the dark green flood of the Potomac, carried some yards downstream from the rocky outcropping where she had been brushing her hair, circling as I treaded water, calling out for her ever more frantically, until at last I found her in an eddy farther down, her hair spread out across the water, the yellow dress billowing about her as if she rested on a yellow lily, and her arms outspread. I swept her into my arms and, in that instant, knew she had been lost to me. The cold, stiff body told me so, but her eyes, though sightless, held one last parting gaze. That gaze led back up the river, to the outcropping, and there, on top of a rock, was the picnic basket I had gone to the buggy for. I *had* gone back. I had overcome the rage that had possessed me as I stood over her. Despite her rejection and ridicule, despite my resentment and shame, I had walked away. The terrible fate that had overwhelmed her had happened in those minutes while I was gone.

Grace Tremaine stood before me between the white stone pillars, her arms still held out, but she had become forlorn; our longings had always been separate, and already her image was beginning to turn opaque and insubstantial. But even in that moment of recognition of who we were and what had once passed between us—or because of it—I stepped forward and reached out, as I might yet claim her and bring her back—

"Ulysses!"

I turned to see Deborah Rand madly scrambling up the hill.

"Stop, Ulysses." She was out of breath, her hand against her side, nearly doubled over with the exertion of her climb. I looked back at Grace Tremaine. If I didn't reach out now, I would lose her utterly. Torn with fear of losing Grace, confusion over Deborah's sudden appearance, I hesitated.

"Ulysses, you must stop." Arms outstretched and trembling, Deborah pointed my revolver right at me. "Do not move," she managed in another gasp. "I *will* shoot, if you make me."

Heedless, driven by one blinding desire, I thrust out my hand for Grace Tremaine. In that instant, the report of the pistol shattered any union between the living and the dead, between earthly desire and its impossible object, between infinite silence and the mere clamor of the world. It resounded within the cathedral of teak, its echo returned by the surrounding hills. The space between the stone pillars was empty. The voice was stilled, the sound of the gun was stilled, and only the thrumming of returning rain and the screech of a startled ape disturbed the night.

Smoke slithered out of the pistol barrel. "I'm sorry, Ulysses," she said at last. "There was no other way to stop you."

"Stop me?" I had never felt such emptiness. "You have taken from me all that I wanted. You have killed me." Filled with my loss, I dropped to my knees and leaned against the muddy ground. But the ground gave way and I nearly lurched into—nothingness. I felt Deborah's arm locked in mine, pulling me back. She knelt beside me and, with the brilliant reappearance of the moon, pointed down. By its light, I could see the chasm spiraling below, a black vortex, its depths unknown.

"You had a fitful night," she explained softly, kneading my shoulder with her hand, "and you spoke as you slept—I could not make out the words. I drifted off myself at last, but when I awoke, I found your place empty."

"I heard a cry," I remembered, "but it seemed you had been the one to leave."

"You awoke in the midst of a dream but didn't waken from it. I feared I would not find you in time. But your trail was easy to follow, as wide as a wounded bull's." She tried a little smile. "I know this terrain. Sudden clefts and fissures open right beneath one's feet. By day it is treacherous ground, by night deadly."

"You saw nothing else?"

"When I reached the stand of teak, I saw that you had climbed nearly to the top of the rise. The Old Ones built these stone monuments. For them it was a place of sacrifice. You nearly became one yourself."

"And no one else?" I knew what I had seen but struggled with the fact that the apparition, so real to me, was unreal to anyone else.

"Only a man in frenzy, a man possessed. By what, I do not

know." Gently, she tugged me away from the precipice. I stood and drew her close to me. "But it's over now," she whispered. "It's gone—this thing you were chasing."

"Gone." The word was as empty and hollow in my mouth as this place had become.

She drew herself up as if she had recalled an important task, and placed the revolver in my hand. "Let's go back to camp so you can change into your clothes and boots. We have but little time."

❧

From the deserted village, Deborah led me along a well-worn path. We passed from the huddle of stone huts that had been the Mamaq encampment, threading among giant boulders that led to a narrow defile widening like a fan. The wind whistled down the defile, but there was no rain, and the moon lit our way. On that drift of wind I first heard their steady tread, a low roll of thunder across the ground. I heard their delirious trumpeting, distant and carried through the still night.

Above us, the walls of a miniature canyon rose in contours that changed magically from colored layers to carved figures moving in a vast procession, mighty warrior kings dressed in crowns and armor, soldiers locked in combat, the tumultuous landscape of war. These scenes gave way to the refinements of court and religious life, lines of lightly clad servants carrying augury bowls to the sacrifice of a wild bull crowned with flowers, and emissaries from other tribes bringing tribute to the king seated on a massive throne. The figures were all in bold relief, as monumental as the friezes of ancient Egypt but with the voluptuousness, the appetite, and the individuality of Hindu temple carving. All of the figures were smiling, even those caught up in the death throes of battle, as if neither death nor life held any terrors for the Old Ones of Samosir. These living friezes came together as we reached the end of the canyon; hundreds of figures pressed together, their arms uplifted to the subject of their worship, an elephant-headed god, like the Hindu Ganesh, dancing with gleeful abandon himself, his arms raised to embrace the life-giving rays of the sun.

Where the panoply of praise ended, the canyon walls opened to a paved thoroughfare lined with stupas and stone obelisks some twenty feet high. The square obelisks were topped with chiseled heads—men, women, and children—but unlike the carved elegies of Pasembah described by Captain Claridge. These faces saw neither woe nor want; they were all absorbed in some serene meditation, their eyelids closed to the world of the senses, their smooth lips registering their delight in ineffable smiles. How strange to see these transcendent beings as the calls of great beasts echoed down the canyon, a conjunction of the mad pulse of life with the equal desire to escape it. Yet the yearning to be free of desire is a desire, too, and I wondered if the Old Ones had at last faced this paradox by the time they carved the final despairing monuments seen by the captain of the *Renown*.

I joined Deborah Rand at the end of the avenue. She took my hand as we looked on a circular court. At each cardinal point stood a temple hewn, it seemed, out of the living rock. I could not detect seams in the stones or any other sign of masonry. Most wondrous of all were the gray trumpeters filing out of the surrounding jungle, making the ground tremble. There must have been forty or more elephants—the calves holding on to their mothers' tails with their trunks so slowly, grandly, rhythmically swaying, these mighty mammoths circled the courtyard.

They saluted and caressed one another with their trunks in a courtly, familiar manner, wheeling about until, at length, they came to a stop, their bodies swaying in place, the massive drums of their feet keeping a beat to some majestic music only they could hear. Suddenly, one of the bulls broke into the center of the group and rose on his hind legs. He rose once more and then again. The third time, a female broke from the herd and joined him. Both of

them rose and joined their front feet together like a couple dancing. They entwined their trunks as they fell back to earth, graceful
despite their size, as if they were making bows and curtsies. Two
other bulls and cows joined them, and then two more, until within
the rhythmic center of these enraptured animals a dozen couples
rose up, rising and touching in playful choreography.

Deborah Rand squeezed my hand, and we ran down the paved
avenue until we were outside this circle of courtship. With the
slightest of curtsies, she held open her arms. I bowed and slipped
one arm about her waist, and we spun around the circumference
of this conclave of elephants, joining them in their stately waltz,
whirling around them in giddy laughter, completely at ease with
them, as they were with us. Round and round we spun in the
moonlight, joined by a flight of nocturnal butterflies with white
wings that flitted over our heads until they seemed to vanish into
the shimmering disk of the moon itself. We whirled about to the
trumpeting of the elephants. We whirled about and down the years
until I saw Grace Tremaine again. She was at the top of the staircase in her father's house. She wore black velvet and pearls, somber
and elegant, as if emerging from mourning, and her smile, I
thought, was all for me.

We spun until we were breathless, then, hand in hand, Deborah
Rand and I ran up the hundred steps that led to the top of the
northernmost temple. Some fifty feet above, in the temple sanctuary, we watched the elephants finish their ritual and file out of
the courtyard, more silently now, here and there a trumpet of
farewell, the tread of their feet still shaking the ground as they
melted into the forest. The earth at last came still. There was only
here and there a white butterfly flitting in the moonlight and the
old medallion of the moon perched high above the tree line.

"I have lived to see the elephants dance at Samosir," she said
at last, regaining her breath. "It is not merely a legend. Old Nias
told me he knew a guru who saw the elephants dance when he

was a boy. He and a companion had stolen over to the forbidden island to see if it was true. In spite of the curse that would fall on them."

She was someone else again, a vibrant, lively woman whose breast heaved with the exhilaration of the waltz and the breathless attention of young men.

"And the punishment that befell that guru?"

"Why, he became a guru! But not after he went mad for a dozen years in the forest, eating roots and berries. Though I'm not so sure that was such a bad thing."

"And our punishment?"

She held my hand between hers. "Has already happened, Ulysses. To be what we are not. And worse! To be what we are not for such a little while."

"Grace and I danced together once," I said, the memory coming back with a pang. "It was at a naval ball in Washington. To celebrate the end of the war. She was wearing a black velvet gown and pearls as white and stately as a swan's." For a moment I thought that if I held Deborah Rand in my arms once more . . . My hand slipped from hers, for I could not.

"I can't bring her back for you, Ulysses. No one can. Some spirits will not relinquish hold of the earth out of their own fear. Others cannot go because we will not let them. If you had taken but one more step at the top of the hill, you would not be alive."

"I have been among the dead for a long time. Grace Tremaine would be alive if it were not for me."

"What happened to her?"

"I see her floating down the river," I said, reliving those terrible moments for what I hoped would be the last time. "Her skirts are spread out on the rippling surface of the water, but they are heavy and dragging her down. When I pull her to me, she is already lost. You see, I had gone back to the gig for our picnic basket. I hadn't left her alone more than twenty minutes."

"It wasn't an accident."

"No, I'm sure of that. She was an excellent swimmer."

"You did nothing to harm her."

"I loved her."

"Yet you were jealous of her."

"She made sure I was."

"She infuriated you."

"Yes, but not angry enough to hurt her." I walked to the northern wall of the temple and stared blindly into the night. "Although a murderer's thought seized me as I stood over her that last time. I thought how easy it would be close my hands about that lovely, hateful throat."

"But you did not, Ulysses. You know you did not." She stood before me, and the earnest conviction in her eyes bore into me. "Yet you ran away as if you had, as you ran away from yourself, and you have kept running ever since."

"No, I did not kill Grace Tremaine. I know that now. But I was accused of her murder."

"If not you . . ."

"I don't know." I gripped the wall before me as if I might lift it and reveal the truth. "But I cannot imagine her taking her own life—yet I have no other explanation . . ."

"How did you escape?"

"My brother, Morgan, bribed a guard."

We stood together quietly. The moon had once more slipped behind the clouds, to be replaced by an eerie glow, like that of dark, windblown torches, in the northern hills. "And all these years . . ."

"Ten years."

"You've shifted from one obscure place to another."

"From one backwater billet to another, but never working my way too high, never drawing attention to myself. When Rajah Brooke offered me the *Lorelei*—another backwater, but this was a captaincy! An odd, ramshackle sort of captaincy, but nevertheless a command."

"Her death robbed you of your future. Surely she wouldn't have wished for that."

"I blamed myself. We were never happy together."

Our arms closed around each other. She held herself tightly against me, her heart beating fiercely as if she would infuse my blood with her own. Then, with a start, she pulled away. She held me at arm's length. As one might brace a fellow traveler for a long trek though hostile country.

As if to confirm this, the strange glow to the north had become a fierce guttering flame that seemed to be eating at the horizon. "The forest is burning. Lightning must have set it off," I said.

"Not lightning," she whispered. "Nature does not set off such infernal fires. Now let us go. Where you see those flames, there our journey ends."

29

We left the island of Samosir before dawn, found our mounts, and resumed our journey, following Lake Toba's shoreline until we reached the foothills at its northern slope. Beneath a night sky occluded by storm clouds, Deborah leaned low over her wiry mountain pony and relentlessly urged the animal on. Our intimacy of the night before seemed unreal, or rather part of some existence we had left among the ancient monuments and the charmed elephants of Samosir. What remained was anticipation. And apprehension. Perhaps the mystery of this once fervent missionary turned tribal sorceress would at last be explained. Such was my hope, for the contradictions loomed too large. And there was the turmoil of my own emotions to deal with—tugged toward her yet uncertain of her, and over all, a fine fascination that excited a glimpse into some hidden design of human nature—or deep illusion.

Our climb took us along a ridge of hills strewn with thickening skirls of low-lying mist until it seemed we had taken wing, drifting far above the merely phenomenal world. Flares of reddish light, like volcanic beacons, kept us on an ever-rising northward course. The forest gradually gave way to little clearings where patches of morning fog coiled around thick scrub and tree stumps. The cuttings were recent. I could see where the logs had been dragged up the hill with chains. Suddenly, my mount reared, and it was all I could do to keep him from bolting. I saw an arm raised, a spear; I drew my revolver. Before I could fire, Deborah grabbed hold of my hand.

An armored warrior straddled our path, the gold of his plumed helmet and breastplate glinting in the half-light, the leather of his harness creaking in the wind. He held spear and sword at the ready. But I had no fear of this legend. With a joyful bound, I leaped from my mount and scrambled up the slope to greet him. The warrior remained silent and still. Slipping in the mud, I reached out for a hand. He dropped his sword, his helmet toppled, the breastplate slipped, and the scarecrow soldier swayed and dropped with a clatter. There was no moonstruck prince lodged among these sad and lifeless props of Freddie Ireland. The ground was strewn with the litter of war. Batak spears and dirks and shattered Mamaq arrows—the military gear of both armies was scattered about like a spoiled child's playthings, but of the men who had carried these weapons, there was no trace. Bandarak and his men had perished here, for a fresh battlefield holds its deathly claimants, and I could sense, with dread and sorrow, the confused moiling of these troubled spirits as they stumbled about the ground of their undoing. What calamity had overtaken them? The scene bespoke utter defeat. It seemed there was no one left to claim a victory. And he had pitied Hamlet of Denmark, this lone, tormented Batak prince! Saddest of all, there was no companion to tell the prince's tale.

Deborah Rand raised her hand in caution. "The armor was put up as a warning," she whispered. We pulled our horses out of the clearing and hid them from sight among a stand of tall mountain evergreens. We made the rest of the ascent on foot.

As we neared the summit, the air became thick, laden with a sulfurous odor, and my breathing became labored. I pointed out movement to our right. Both of us dropped behind a tree as three soldiers, wearing plumed bush hats and carbines slung over their backs, their mounts stepping gingerly along a narrow trail, were silhouetted against the scarlet sky. After the soldiers had passed, we scrambled to the top and stood under the arbor of a banyan, bare of leaves, whose aerial roots spread out in chancels and apses like a ruined cathedral.

The leafless cathedral overlooked a valley held in thrall. Wooden towers, braced and buttressed, rose out of the earth like a horde of skeletal insects, many of them topped with voracious tongues of orange flame hissing in the air. Their exhalations were the breath of bitterness itself. The stench tore at the lungs, as if some unspeakable corpse had been shoveled out of the soil. Beneath the derricks, the earth was slick and black with the treasure they pumped barrel by barrel. Rain spattered on the leaves overhead. But this was no natural rain. I looked down at my hands. They were speckled with black oil.

"This used to be Mamaq ancestral land, Ulysses."

"How long have the Dutch been here?"

"About a year and a half ago, the drilling teams began their work. At first the Mamaqs welcomed them, but when they saw what was happening to their land, how these men drew out the black blood that made everything sicken and die, they resisted. The work of millennia was overturned in a few days of fighting. They were driven out. Their social order collapsed, their gods had deserted them, and that is why they moved to Samosir. Then the raids and killings began. The Mamaqs had been cast adrift, and they spread their anarchy and chaos down the length of the Asahan."

She became reflective, as if she was trying to puzzle out her role in this catastrophe. "I became their Sakti in order to save my own skin, Ulysses. Then, too, I wanted to take revenge on the monsters who had killed Noel Ames. As I came to know them as individuals, and as a people who had been terribly wronged, I hoped to prevent them for their excesses and help them right this wrong. Perhaps I did save some lives, but their despair and rage were beyond the influence of any single power. Rage like that must run its course. And so it has, in blood and fire. The Mamaqs are broken, and what is left of the tribe has sought refuge in the Barisan. The battlefield tells the tale. The good Dutch Christians down there slaughtered the tribesmen as they ran from Prince Bandarak. And then they turned their guns on the Bataks. The bodies, most likely, were tossed into a common grave. One that the forest will quickly seal. When it comes to terror, the Mamaqs have had good teachers."

"Yes, I saw some of their work at Tuan Medang," I said. "They can make whole villages disappear."

"The Dutch do not want anyone to know what is happening here. They have stumbled upon the richest petroleum fields in the world. Imagine what that means! Kerosene for all the lamps of Asia. How much is that worth, do you think? So they have ringed the valley with demons. More fiendish yet, the Mamaqs became their unwitting agents."

"So the towers they erected, like the one on which Noel Ames was crucified—"

"Towers of sacrifice, Ulysses. Towers to appease the dark gods of the earth who claimed their land."

I gazed at the unreal scene with unsettled emotions, imagining what a Mamaq might see. One word came to my lips: "Retribution."

Standing on this forlorn ridge, her sharply angular body illumined by the intense crimson light and orange flames, Deborah Rand might have been a sibyl bearing a dark prophecy. She spread her arms over the spectral scene as if casting a spell.

" 'Ghost Eaters,' that's what the Mamaqs call these oil towers. The Ghost Eaters sent spikes into the souls of their ancestors. The ancestors wept black blood. The old gods died, and to replace them, the people went back to a myth older than them all, that of a goddess who grimaces in the act of giving birth to some new and terrible deity. Her image is soaked in the black blood that spilled out of their land."

"Like the effigy we found in the mission chapel."

"The female Sakti is like the midwife attending the birth of this new god."

"You could have told us this before."

"Yes, I could have told you that morning you found me in the chapel." She found some humor in this. "After I was taken captive, I prayed for such a rescue every waking moment. I devised elaborate plans for escape. Until I realized a terrible truth."

"About yourself?"

"No—about those who would 'free' me. I would be a thing despised. I would be an outcast to my own race and hated by the tribes who had suffered at the hands of the Mamaqs. When you broke into the chapel, I had every reason to fear for my life."

"Bridgett Hannover proved you right."

Deborah lowered her head and gripped her shoulder as if she could again feel the pain of Bridgett's bullet. When she raised her head, her look was hard and narrow, her voice rasping and bitter. "More than her to fear! There was that Irish buffoon Fahey. There was Diem, like all true believers, so easily duped. There was you, Ulysses Vanders. The captain in command, the majesty of the law. What pretense! What asses all of you are!"

"But why should any of us wish you harm?"

"Come now!" She laughed under her breath. "My death would be a convenience—once the truth about Noel and Susannah Ames was known. Then little Debbie would be expendable."

"I came up the Asahan with one purpose; to save you and the others at Light of the World."

"Did you now?" she inquired mockingly. "Ah, but when you saw Debbie, you sought something else. It's what all men seek."

"I sought nothing." Then I was faced with the truth. "Yes, I desired you."

She tossed back her head in accusation. "You were all itching to get beneath Debbie's skirts right enough, if you want to call that love. But one of you was driven by more than lust. One of you wanted us dead. But which one of Debbie's suitors was going to murder us? Fitting end for Debbie, isn't it?" She gave a low chuckle. "But not for me! Let that whore pay her dues, but not at my expense. Besides, I've paid them already." She pulled off the canvas bag she had slung over her shoulder and held it out to me. "Take it. Take it and . . . *kill them all!*"

Inside the pouch was a book tightly wrapped in oilskin. I did not need to open it. "Your diary."

"Yes, my diary." She threw her hands up to her face as if she had been blinded. She swayed, and I put my arms around her. She leaned against me, clinging to me as if her life depended on it. "Those terrible words were written in my blood." She broke free and held herself to stop from shaking, for the fit went right through her like a fever twinge. She clenched her fists, bowed her head, and the tremors stopped. "I discovered the entry in my diary after I had returned to the mission with the Mamaqs. That is how I discovered the identity of the other one. The one who revels in blood and pain. This other one who torments us . . ."

"Diem can heal these torments, Deborah."

"If only he could . . . But she is far too clever for that. Listen to me, Ulysses. I had convinced the Mamaq chiefs that they could command the river from Light of the World. From this position of strength, they could strike a deal with the other tribes, bargain land for peace. But *she* convinced the chiefs otherwise. They didn't need much persuading. They had their enemies on the run. They were intoxicated with their own power. Now *they* could make victims. The entire tribe was caught up in a remorseless bloodlust. But that's spent itself now."

"Then come back with me to the *Lorelei*."

"I'm not going back. How can I?"

I could barely trace the smile on her lips, one of regret and wistful longing. She was right. There could be no going back for Deborah Rand. Just as it had seemed there was no going back for me. And there hadn't been. For either of us. In that moment, though, I realized what I had done in my long, silent, and solitary drift from one obscure sea-lane to the next. I had confused backward and forward. I had made the past and the future the same condition. There was the flaw. And it could be turned around. I had set the metamorphosis in motion by taking the wheel of the *Lorelei*. I head reached the end of a stage, poised to become something else.

Deborah Rand was already far ahead of me, but her recognition had traveled to a different place. Within the shadow of the tree, she slipped out of her gray dress. Free of this old skin, she thrust the garment into a hollow of the banyan. About her hips, she wrapped the red cloth she had worn the night before. Kneeling down, she scooped up handfuls of the dark mud at her feet, mud oozing with the oil that had damned the valley below and its people. She streaked the stuff on her forehead and face, smeared it down her neck and arms, covering her breasts until her telltale white skin vanished beneath the skin of the earth. Before my eyes, she worked her transformation until nothing visible remained of Deborah Rand. She stood before me in the predawn darkness, a Batak spear in hand, ready for her return.

"Do you think they wait for you?" I could barely utter the words.

"I am their Sakti, after all."

"There must be something else . . ." My voice trailed off awkwardly. There was nothing else but the wrenching act of breaking this queer spell and letting ourselves go free. I would have delayed that moment for a hundred suns.

"One thing you can do for me." She pointed to the canvas pouch. "You are going back to Kuching. You spoke of a woman there who has the ear of the rajah—Irene Burdett-Couts. Take my diary to her. Explain the matter to her. She'll see that it reaches the right hands."

I felt the deep, irrevocable pang of being severed from someone—not from someone I loved, but someone I might have loved, given the right movement of the tide. "We will meet again," I offered.

"Oh, we will meet again, Ulysses, I promise you. When all of this is finished. Now close your eyes, my dear sailor man, as I kiss you. For I have one last thing to say . . ."

I felt the merest brush of her lips, like a whisper. When I opened my eyes, I was alone on the ridge. Below me were the insatiable Ghost Eaters, roaring with flame, churning the earth, rattling their chains. But Deborah Rand had gone.

"Where is she?" The brush crackled below me. "I know you're up there, Vanders." A rasping voice.

"Fahey?"

The gray figure stepping out of the early-morning mist and panting for breath was not Rowan Fahey. Dr. Phan Dom Diem had bound his forehead with a black headband. Over his soiled shirt, he wore an embroidered Horserider vest. "She was here, wasn't she?" Diem asked impatiently. He pointed a curved Batak kris at my breast. "She was here."

He followed my glance down the ridge. "You shouldn't have taken her away from me," he said with more sadness than resentment. "She is under my care . . . I can cure her. She isn't some fairy princess for you to carry off!" The physician's pince-nez no longer straddled his nose; his clothes were soaked and spattered with mud and leaves. He wore a knapsack slung over one shoulder and a carbine over the other. With a distracted air, his eyes roved over the fuming oil fields below, like a mountain hermit who had stumbled onto the folly of the world.

"I must find her, Vanders. You, of all of them, should know why."

"I think I can understand that you are in love with her, too."

"Damn you and damn Fahey, too!" His mouth tightened in a spasm that was at once a denial and an admission. "Deborah Rand is not for loving. She's not for your brand of loving."

"And what brand of loving would you bring her?"

He looked at me coldly. "She is caught in the flux and flow of her conflicting selves. They will contend, and the stronger will win out. Then she will be lost to us."

"And what if she already is?"

He was silent for a moment and then laughed the thought away. It was a self-deprecating humor, one I had never thought to hear from Diem. "Then I shall be lost with her, I suppose. What matter, as long as I find her?"

He had already moved off, following the muddy track along the rim of the hill until he vanished into the forest farther down. For the first time, I saw the boy who had haunted these mountains and forests with his friend Bandarak, lost in great hunts and mock battles. They had nothing to lose, as far as I could see, this mesmerist and his Mamaq queen. They had a vast, tiger-haunted island to pursue their possibilities. I pulled up my collar as a squall of monsoon rain swept over the ridge. Giving one last look at the infernal valley that had set in motion so many upheavals and calamities, I turned back down the ridge. It was time to bring *Lorelei* downstream.

Night gave way to morning, although I could scarcely mark
the difference. Glowering clouds, restless with electrical fits
and starts, had sealed off the sun, and we who were left stumbling
below had to make our way as best we could. My path lay along
the jungle trail Deborah Rand and I had taken, past memory-
haunted, mist-enshrouded Samosir, past the thunderous volume of
Lake Toba Falls, and down the forest track that led to Light of
the World. I expected at any moment to encounter Horserider
search parties, but I reached the Valley of Desolation without setting eyes on any of Chief Muntok's men. Perhaps they had retreated to their mountain strongholds, troubled by the portents
they had witnessed, and their terror of Deborah Rand.

Only one solitary traveler did I meet, trudging through the tall,
wet grass, grizzled head down, mumbling to himself. When he
saw me, old Nias lifted his walking staff partly in greeting, partly
in defense. I might have been the newly risen Lazarus, to judge
by his wonderment. He was, as ever, a mixed ceremony of old
pagan tattoos and amulets topped off by the wooden cross dangling
from his scrawny neck.

"I live to see you again, Lord!" he cried out.

"Where are you going, Old One?" I asked, bringing my mount
to a halt.

"Tuan Medang—to see if my people have returned. There is nothing more for me here."

"What of those at the mission?"

"The Malay *turahan* is dead, Lord," he said, spitting to his side. "She screamed and mammered all night long. We buried her this morning. Beneath a cross. But I don't think that will do her much good."

"And why is that?"

"You can't fool the Devil, Lord."

"Who helped you bury her?"

"The Reverend Mrs. Hannover." He shook his head and spat again. "She is not herself since that *turahan* died."

"And the Horseriders?"

"They rode back into the hills yesterday before dark, glad to be free of this place. I will be glad to be free of it, too."

"So there is just Mrs. Hannover at the mission?"

"She is there, but I cannot say she is alone."

"Mr. Fahey has returned?"

"Mr. Fahey I have not seen since yesterday, when he ran off with that crazy Mamaq Sakti. I feared those two might have killed you," he said.

"I am here, as you can see."

"Then travel in peace." He shifted a woven bag from one shoulder to the other. "For myself, I must go on. Besides, the Reverend Ames—may the Glory be with him forever!—needs replanting."

"What do you mean?"

Nias tapped the shoulder bag. "I could not leave him there. Who would look after him?" With a farewell salute, he resumed his journey.

"May the Glory be with you, too!" I called after him.

⤚◦

The wooden gate of the mission stood wide open, the hard-packed parade ground covered with a half inch of muddy water. I dismounted and went first into the chapel. The candles on the altar had guttered out. There were puddles on the floor where yesterday's storm had swept in the rain. I walked about in the gloom until I found the door that led to the dispensary. Before I passed on, I bent down and touched the gouge in the cement where Bridgett's rifle bullet had lodged after wounding Deborah Rand.

When I opened the door, I saw a shadowy flitter to my right, at the stairwell. Instinctively, I crouched down. None too soon. The carbine cracked, and splinters from the door landed all about me.

"Bridgett! It's Ulysses."

A forlorn cry drifted down the stairwell. It was not Bridgett's voice. It was like the eerie, disembodied voice of a child, calling because it had become lost. Carefully, I picked my way among the cots, keeping low until I had a better view of the stairs. I waited and then made a dash for the side of the stairwell. There was no following shot. Instead, there was another voice, a voice I had heard once singing on the bow of the *Lorelei*, raised to the heavens in a psalm of praise. "Who is this King of glory? The Lord of hosts, He is the King of glory."

I remembered how the song had healed us, a company of strangers divided and shaken by the calamity we had witnessed at Spoorwegen's Landing. But this time the psalm went on only a few bars and then cut off. Made anxious by the silence, I inched my way along the stairwell wall, pistol at the ready. When I reached the top of the landing, I heard nothing further and stepped into the hall. The corridor was empty and still. Then I heard it, barely audible above the din of the insistent rain. It came from the end of the hall. From Deborah's room. It was like the sighing of the wind, a rhythmic creak that came and went.

I slid along the wall until I could see through the barred window in the door. She was dangling there, twisting at the end of the rope she had slung over a beam, her bare feet still kicking spasmodically. I tried the door, but she had locked it from the inside. Bowing my head against the bars, I listened to the inane creaking of the rope against the beam. The sharp odor of gunpowder and kerosene came from the room. The detonation and furious burst of flame sent me reeling. The flames fed on the furniture and bedding Bridgett had piled around her. A ring of fire closed in on her, enveloping her in an incandescent husk, igniting her dress, her hair, racing up the rope from which she hung like her own unforgiven heretic. Smoke obscured the fire and billowed out the door. I went back down the hall, sick with anger that she could have done this to herself, that I had been too late, and that there was nothing I could do.

>—⊚

I rode back to the gorge as if the relentless furies that had driven Bridgett Hannover to madness were clawing at my coattails. The air was thick with the downpour, and I knew it would not be long before the valley flooded. It was already a muddy swamp abandoned even by the rats that had nested in its sickly yellow coils. I could only hope that my engineer had kept to his post, ready to cast off. The stone steps that led down to the mooring were all a blur, and I slipped during my descent, cracking my kneecap against a rock, so that I had to limp aboard the *Lorelei*. I called out for Devadatta, but there was no answer. My cry was picked up and elaborated by the stony walls of the gorge that towered above me.

Using the railing for support, I limped back to the engine room only to find it empty. I went forward and climbed past the passenger deck to the top. The rain drummed a tattoo on the wheelhouse roof. Through the water-streaked windows, I could see almost a quarter of a mile up the gorge, its rolling current swollen and choppy with monsoon rain. Just above the mooring, the little waterfall churned with white water and debris.

When I left the wheelhouse, he was standing before the whaleboat with a carbine pointed at my forehead. Like me, he was drenched and bedraggled, and there was no mistaking the grim set of his jaw.

"Drop the sidearm, Ulysses."

"What have you done with my engineer, Fahey?"

"No harm to his black hide that a headache won't cure."

I placed the Navy Colt on the deck and kicked it away. Fahey lowered the carbine slightly but kept it pointed at me. "Now, I'm no mind reader like our friend Diem, but I'd nevertheless wager Miss Deborah Rand has entrusted you with a certain memento. It's my job to relieve you of the article. Mayhap that canvas bag you've got over your shoulder contains the very item I'm looking for." He held out his hand. "Let's have it."

My hand went to the shoulder strap but no further. "If it's hard tack and dried fish you're craving, then welcome to it."

"I'm in no mood to be toyed with, Vanders. You've been with her, I know that much. Why would the bitch coldcock me if she didn't have other plans?"

"Yes, I saw her in the forest. She's not coming back. That's all I know."

"That may be so, but our Deborah is too good at her job not to deliver the goods. Whatever she learns ends up in the hands of Charles Brooke, bleedin' rajah of Sarawak. And it's my bet she'd entrust with you with her treasures. Whatever treasures she may have on offer," he added, as if we shared some dirty secret.

"What's this all about?"

"I'll leave you to figure things out. Drop the bag and kick it over to me."

I raised my hand to the shoulder strap. "Let's say we might be able to strike a deal. Reward me with a few answers first."

Suspicion darkened his eyes. Then the grin returned, the indulgent grin of a bully inclined to tease his prey. "Why, it's easy enough to see with the proper squint. I told you from the first that John Bull was my devil. And your Rajah Brooke is the devil's own."

"So you've been working for the Dutch all along."

He greeted this discovery with a smirk. "They pay well. And on delivery."

"Then how was it you ended up in the Kuching jail?"

"It's an easy enough thing to land in a jail, Kuching being easier than most. When you met me, the value of my coinage had been spread about by my employers in Batavia. They knew that British public opinion—the conscience of the world, except where their own barbarism is concerned—might compel some action to aid the mission at Light of the World. The Dutch also suspected that one of the missionaries was a British agent. The last thing they wanted was a damned British expedition into the northern Sumatra highlands. The British didn't want to pick a fight with the Dutch, either. Seeing as the English use our White Rajah Brooke as a go-between, and since Brooke has a hankering for a steamship . . . Well, you can see how the thing worked out. Brooke put me on your foray to ensure its success, seeing as he and I had enjoyed some amicable business dealings in the past. Our rajah wouldn't know, of course, there was a fox in the henhouse, especially when he thought he owned the fox." Fahey made a slight, mocking bow.

"So Brooke had it all planned out that you rescue his agent. Clever of the Dutch to make him think they wanted you for the hangman."

"Cleverer yet to place a steamboat in your anxious hands. You were so keen to turn pirate."

"And the orders from your real masters, the Dutch—what were they? Find and murder the spy? So the world remains ignorant of the oil fields the Dutch have discovered in Mamaq territory?"

"Oh, she took you up into the highlands, did she?" The look in Fahey's eyes sealed my death warrant.

My only hope was to stall him until I might somehow gain an edge and make a dive for my revolver. "Spoorwegen worked for the Dutch, too. He must have known who you are. And you two were alone in the forest when he died."

Fahey shrugged. "Mr. Spoorwegen and I also had some business dealings in the past. He recognized me, even in his addled state. What a lovely favor I did the man." Fahey looked up into the sky, the thick raindrops splashing against his face, plastering his boyish curls against his scalp. He anticipated any move I might make. I did not doubt he was inviting it. "What drove him mad? They all become mad out here, that's a fact. It's in the wind, it's in the rain, it's in every tree and beast. It's in the ghosts of the place. Yes, and it seeped deep into the soul of our Deborah Rand."

"Yes, it has. She was compelled to play out her roles. To keep herself alive while she was among the Mamaqs. And to keep herself alive while she tried to figure out which one of us had been sent up the river to murder her. Bridgett Hannover made that point very forcefully. But for a different reason."

"Playacting?" He looked at me darkly. "She was on a thrill with the role she had chosen—as queen of the Mamaqs. Do you not think she fell in love with it?"

"To stay alive. And to save lives."

"To judge by the blackened villages up and down the Asahan, she was very convincing. Indistinguishable from the real thing." Fahey took a step closer, forcing me forward to the bow. "I'll tell you something else, captain of the *Lorelei*. I think her hands ran red with blood, and I think she held them up to the sky and shrieked her praises to the gods who had given her such power. Raw and naked power. For such a one as Deborah Rand, that's what she craves. Black Mary is as real as those oil-soaked idols we found. Black Mary, my friend, is the idol come to life."

"I think I hear the voice of a man outwitted by his foe. And the woman he loved."

He laughed at his grand practical joke. "A convenient excuse to string you along. Oh, I wanted Deborah Rand, all right. I wanted to find out what she knew. And then I planned to send her straight to hell. Damned sorry I was to miss my chance. Perhaps you'll do for recompense." The gloating smirk suddenly went sour. "What's that sound?"

I swallowed hard. I had been watching Devadatta's silent, painstaking progress as he crept alongside the whaleboat. He was nearly in position to leap on the Irishman. "I hear nothing."

"No, listen." Fahey pointed ahead and up the canyon. "Ahead. That moaning sound."

"Thunder, that's all."

"And the end of this banter of ours," Fahey snarled. "You have something I want."

I patted the bag at my side. "It's only her diary. That's what she gave me."

"Her diary!" His eyes narrowed on some brightening thought. "So that's it. Give it here."

I lifted the bag over my shoulder. The moaning sound grew in intensity, an ominous roar as it swept closer. I knew in that instant the meaning of the terrifying sound. I kept my eyes on Fahey, but I could sense Devadatta was nearly ready to make his move. One moment more . . .

One moment more, and the look on Fahey's face changed from one of triumph to one of horror. Devadatta made his leap. The impact knocked the carbine out of the Irishman's hands, and he dropped to the deck. I turned on my heel to see the thing boiling down the canyon, a white chaotic flux, howling with its own mad, wild power, unstoppable, its arms racing down the walls of the canyon with but one impulse—to overwhelm.

The enormous wave, born in the mountains and kicking its way down the birth canal of the gorge, roared over us and into us. My fingers clamped over the handle of the wheelhouse door, and I was driven inside by the impact of the water. The inundation yanked *Lorelei* free of her moorings. Like a twig, she was borne down the crest of the wave, her sides scraping bare rock. I scrambled to my feet; my hands locked on the wheel, and I looked out the port side as the stern-wheel of my ship splintered against a granite spur and we were swung violently to the side. Water filled the wheelhouse, swallowed me completely, battered me about in its surge like a piece of debris, but I held on to the wheel until it came free.

～

There was salt on my lips. I licked it away. Then the touch of wood. I pushed the object aside and opened my eyes. She had huge brown eyes, kind and concerned, intent upon bringing the spoon back to my lips.

"Truly, he has had enough for now, Tiet," said a familiar voice. "Leave us alone with him." The brown eyes withdrew. Beyond, there was light and movement, but as if seen from beneath the water, distorted and magnified into willowy shapes.

Then there was a pair of black eyes, keen and curious, a rattling sound, and a hand on my brow. I reached out for the hand, but it was gone. Then a different pair of dark eyes, worried eyes, a very large nose, and very large ears.

"Devadatta . . ."

"There is a recognition, Master Kung. The captain has come around."

More clatter. Footsteps. I sensed there was one fewer person in the room. I could see the ceiling. Nipa leaves fitted over wooden scaffolding and a carved molding that went around the eaves, strange shapes and dancing figures. I was looking into the dark eyes attached to the ridiculous nose.

"This makes things most perfect, sir," said my engineer soothingly. "This is an auspicious day that sees Captain Ulysses Drake Vanders of the Regal Sarawak Navy returned to us. We are pleased. We are most highly pleased."

I tried to sit up. An arm supported my back.

"Truly, you should take it easy upon yourself, Captain. You've been away from us for seven days. That is a long time to be wandering among the shades."

"The *Lorelei,*" I exclaimed with a flash of realization. "Fahey . . . you jumped him."

"All in good time, Captain, sir."

"A wall of water came down the gorge, Devadatta."

"Oh, it was more like a house, or a mansion, or a palace of water. It carried us downriver nearly to Bahal, which is our present location."

"We are with Radjah Dulah?"

"You might say there has been a slight alteration of governance. If you'll recall—and tell me if this is too taxing—Prince Bandarak had a lieutenant of the Crocodile Boys named Vanda."

"Prince Bandarak . . . and Vanda." I struggled into an upright posture. I looked around at the carved columns, the polished teak floors. Steps led into the house, bottles of colored liquid hung from pegs that had been carved into stylized animals, the hornbill, the tiger, the boar. Ceramic pots and jugs filled one corner, where a Batak girl was stirring something over a low flame. "Do you live here, Devadatta?"

"Everything that I have is at your disposal." The engineer smiled, as ever, all teeth. His turban was much more ornate than I remembered, white cloth bordered with a gold edging and a curious brooch, a ruby peacock, or so it seemed, pinned near the peak. He wore Batak pantaloons as well, very crimson, and an embroidered vest to match.

He gave me his wiry strength as I rose unsteadily to my feet. "Please to be steady, sir. I would not overdo things on the first day of your revival."

I felt a wave of dizziness and brought my hand to my forehead, my fingers exploring a bandage that encircled my brow. "What is this?"

"That bandage holds a healing salve made by Master Kung himself. Perfect for a nasty knock in the head."

I took a few halting steps out into the baffling world. The streets and lanes of Bahal were muddy tracks. A broad yellow parasol seemed to come out of nowhere and covered our heads as we walked in the rain.

"Take me to the river, Devadatta."

"Most unadvisable, sir. The sight of it will only arouse the most painful memories."

"I must go down to the river."

While we made our way to the landing, flanked by a crowd of curious onlookers who bowed as we passed, Devadatta explained the "slight alteration of governance" that had transformed Vanda into the new regent until Prince Bandarak returned to claim his throne.

During the prince's absence, the radjah's consort, Seowan, and her lover, the war chief, Ingit, decided to seize power by murdering Radjah Dulah in his sleep. Their plan might have succeeded, except the queen mother, Iruweh, got wind of it and alerted Vanda. He gathered a small group of loyal warriors who waited outside the royal bedchamber and cut down Ingit and Seowan as the assassins entered. As an added measure of security, they beheaded a few of Seowan's more ardent supporters. Unfortunately, Radjah Dulah died of a heart attack in all the commotion. Since Iruweh lacked another son but had a spare daughter, one who had been expressly molded to carry out Iruweh's every whim, the queen mother arranged a match between Vanda, hero of the hour, and the spare.

It seemed the spare daughter had been waiting for the arrival of such a hero, one who could elevate her to first lady of the land. The wedding feast lasted three days, at the end of which the spare promptly banished her mother for being a meddling old crone. At a stroke, the new queen had prepared the way for a new line of rulers who would spring, it was hoped, from Vanda's loins. The royal couple seemed to be working most assiduously to that end, it was Devadatta's opinion, since hardly anyone had seen them since the wedding. Order had been restored to the throne, and the Batak people all sang the praises of their new radjah. Oh, and there was one other little matter.

"It seems that in the new political climate," Devadatta continued, "a number of government positions had become vacant."

"Is that so."

"Most particularly, the post along the line of prime minister for
the Lake Toba Bataks."

I looked about me at the respectful onlookers, bowing, their
hands pressed together, mumbling blessings and words of goodwill. I looked again at Devadatta's flamboyant turban with the
ruby peacock.

"So it seems I have lost an engineer."

Devadatta presented a long face. "And I must say farewell to
the seafaring life. That is a hard blow. But it does nothing for
one's dharma to mope about. Besides, as Sancho Panza was called
to duty, so am I, although I am not governor of an entire island,
at least not yet."

We had arrived at the river dock. I looked about forlornly for
some trace of my lost steamship. The dock was empty, and a
solitary crocodile boat floated in the middle of the stream, two
men poling fore and aft. Standing amidships, his hand raised, oracle and bronze gong at his belt, was the diminutive figure of
Master Kung.

"Where is he going?"

"After his master, Diem, most assuredly."

"After Diem! Diem, if he is still alive, which I doubt, is in the
mountains, pursuing Deborah Rand."

"Oh Master Kung knows all this. He knows that Diem is completely ignorant in the ways of love, having had one misfortunate
infatuation in all his life."

"What are you talking about?"

"Kung believes Diem's malady to be that of love and nothing
but love for that crazy Deborah Rand. So he is off to find his
master and cure him of that malady. His work is finished here.
He has cured the town of the epidemic, and you of a cracked pate.
Radjah Vanda wished to offer him the post of chief guru of all

the Lake Toba Bataks, but he would not have it. His first duty is to his master, the man to whom he owes his life. And Diem is very much alive, though sorely deranged, according to the oracle."

"I wanted to thank him."

Devadatta raised an ornately carved staff of office in farewell to his friend. "He knows you are grateful. He has left more of the medicine for your wound."

I felt my head again. "What happened? Where is *Lorelei*?"

"I am afraid, Captain, that you are very much out of a job. I was hoping that I would not have to bring this news to you until you were very much better."

"She was *riding* the crest of that wave, damn it!"

My former engineer shook his head in commiseration. "Aye, and so she did, through the gorge, most miraculously, but when the wave set her down—you know that pile of rocks at the head-land about two miles north of here. That's where *Lorelei* landed."

"On the rocks."

"On those selfsame rocks. Most assuredly."

"Lost?"

"Lost, yes, most sadly. Along with Mr. Fahey, whom I know we shall not overly mourn. Indubitably. Broken. Smashed up. Sunk in the mud. But one thing, Captain! Her smokestack, though crumpled like a hat, rises most defiantly out of the turbid waters. You would be proud to see that."

"Lost."

"Perhaps it would not be such a good thing for you to see that. At least not until you are much, much healed."

L ost!"
  I heard the word explode through the paneled office door. It was followed by a string of agitated mutterings and blunt oaths, roundly expressed. Followed by an ominous silence.

Then the door swung open, and a Sikh orderly in white uniform, red turban, and gold braid stepped out and bowed. I rose from the cane chair in the anteroom, a bit unsteadily, since my knee still bothered me, but the pain seemed to dissipate entirely at the sight of Miss Irene Burdett-Couts, all shimmering in the bare-shouldered surrender of a white satin gown.

"*Captain* Vanders." She held out her hand. "You have no idea how anxious we have been for your safety."

"But here I am, safe and sound," I replied with a nervous smile, the smile of the doomed. Yet no one could feel more keenly the failure of my mission and the disaster that had befallen *Lorelei*.

"Yes, safe and sound and looking all too thin and worn." Her green eyes roved over me with a nurse's solicitude. "We shall have to do something about that."

"I am fine, really, Miss Burdett-Couts ..." Now that the reckoning was at hand, I struggled to find the words. "Regrettably, however—regrettably, not only am I several weeks late—"

The lady waved her hand. "No need to go over any of the

details now, Captain. Resident Townsend, who met your fishing boat when you sailed into Sarawak waters, has given us the gist of things. Rajah Brooke is most anxious—"

"Let me not clap eyes on the miserable son of a bitch." The door slammed.

"The rajah is a trifle on edge this morning." She lifted her eyes as if she had weathered many such squalls. "But be not discouraged, especially if . . . You will excuse my directness, Captain—but you *did* bring it with you?"

I tapped the canvas bag under my arm.

"Good." With that word of encouragement, she slipped inside the paneled room again. More expostulations, hurried exchanges. Again an ominous silence.

The door swung open. Again the turbaned orderly bowed. Irene Burdett-Couts waved me forward with her fan.

Charles Brooke, the White Rajah of Sarawak, was standing at a table to the side of his desk, his sleeves rolled up, his fingers black with grease. On the table was the model of a ship's engine that I had seen on my last visit to the great man, some ages ago.

"Irene says I should give you tuppence of my time," he grumbled, not looking up. "In spite of the fact that you have dashed the fondest hopes and dreams of the Regal Sarawak Navy."

I swallowed hard and looked about, hoping to find some support from Irene Burdett-Couts, but her glance was averted as she poured brandies from a decanter. I had the odd feeling I was on a stage, an actor cast, not by chance, in the role of the fool. As if to confirm my suspicion, the rajah's orange-breasted sunbird stared down at me from its perch in the corner, its head cocked as if waiting for me to perform. Even the manic long-nosed monkey in the opposite corner had ceased its incessant rounds in its gilded cage to stare at me, one paw folded over the other. All the creature needed was opera glasses to complete the sophisticated pose.

"Well," growled the rajah of Sarawak. He stood up and faced

me, his side-whiskers standing out like a hedgehog's challenge.
The glower was not quite as intimidating as I thought. Or perhaps
I was not as easily intimidated as I had been two months ago.

"Captain Vanders brings us word from our dear friend," Irene
said.

"Yes, our dear friend," Brooke muttered, wiping his hands on
a towel offered by his orderly.

"It's her diary, sir." I held out the bag, which Burdett-Couts
took as she handed me a brandy.

"Her diary?" Brooke shook his head as if this might be a
shrewd observation.

The lady unfolded the book from its oilcloth.

"I'm afraid some of the pages are waterlogged but not entirely
illegible. We had a wild ride down the Asahan and—"

"And that's where you lost her," said Brooke, his voice starting
to rise.

"Charles, let me look at this." Irene paced back and forth, flipping through the pages. Her dark ebony hair was coiled in ringlets
that flowed down her back and framed her face. She slapped the
book shut and, holding it against her breast, gave me the most
startling look. "It's in cipher. The one we devised together. Miss
Rand has done her work well. Very well." She opened the book
again. "She lists the number of platforms, production figures,
stockpiles. Names. Number of personnel. Charles, our friends in
Britain will love this."

For once Brooke looked ambushed. "They will?"

"Worth its weight in gold. Or diplomatic perquisites. Or steamships . . . Take your pick."

"You did say steamships, Irene?"

"Oh, two or three, I'd wager."

The mood of Charles Brooke lifted perceptibly. He wagged his
finger at me. "You know, a young man like Vanders here instills
a certain confidence."

"A report in cipher," I said with indignation as the realization took shape. "That's what I was sent to bring back to you, wasn't it? The wretched jottings of a spy."

Irene looked over at Brooke; his attention had returned to the miniature engine. Her gaze shifted back to me, a gaze at once guarded and a shade imperious. "In a word, yes, Captain Vanders." A sly smile. "But no ordinary one, sir. Deborah Rand's talents once graced the New York stage. One demented theatergoer, I'm told, tried to stab her, so real was her Lady Macbeth. Her Cordelia made stockbrokers weep. Men find her intoxicating, but she's a dangerous perfume. As you've no doubt discovered."

I did not rise to the bait. "Deborah's Rand career embraced one role you and Mr. Brooke did not anticipate. She became queen of the Mamaqs. She's with them now."

The steely smile did not leave Irene's face, although there was a hint of surprise in her beautiful green eyes. "Oh, our Deborah will come 'round. She always does."

"You don't care who gets ruined in the process, do you? Bridgett Hannover's life was destroyed by your agent. She hanged herself in a godforsaken outpost at the edge of empire, bereft of husband, child, and at last even of her reason."

"Yes, and the misfortunate Ameses," Brooke muttered. "A terrible loss. Naturally, we had hopes you would have been able to bring them out." He looked up at me sharply. "Certainly you don't think—"

"Of course Captain Vanders knows better," said the lady. "This tribe, the Mamaqs, murdered them."

"Then tell me who murdered the Mamaqs," I said, stung by their indifference.

"Policy." Brooke snorted. "What else do you think?"

"I've been to their lands, their former lands—with Deborah Rand. The Dutch sank their oil drills into the earth and struck despair. Such policy led to slaughter up and down the Asahan River."

"Let me demonstrate something to you, Vanders." Brooke held up a clear flask containing a molasses-colored liquid. He poured it into a tiny tank connected to the ship's engine on the table. He took a match from the table and, opening a valve on the side of the engine, struck the match. There was a flash, a poof of smoke, and Brooke tripped a lever. Immediately, the engine began to turn a connecting rod that in turn spun a wooden wheel. The wheel whirred along until there was a popping sound and the mechanism froze, followed by a gray plume of smoke that slithered from the exhaust.

"It needs work," said Brooke, rubbing his hands with satisfaction. "It needs work. But technicians and scientists are on the problem. And they will find the solution." He held up the flask. "This is the solution, Vanders—oil."

The orderly handed him a fresh towel. "Petroleum. Kerosene for the light-hungry masses. Oil is becoming the light of the world. But only for now. The future holds a different purpose for the stuff. The problem is in refining petroleum so that it will make an efficient engine fuel. Such a fuel will revolutionize shipping. It will transform navies. It will decide how the wars of the future will be fought. And the winners of those wars."

"There is still plenty of coal in the world," I reminded him.

"Coal is an archaic fuel," he replied, as if I had overlooked the obvious. "As a sailor, you know the stuff is bulky, inefficient, and unreliable, so dirty it's the absolute bane of machinery. Filthy stuff. A clean-burning petroleum fuel, however, that's a different story. A ship could carry a lot more of it, ending the reliance on coaling stations throughout the world. Ships will run faster and farther, and warships in particular will be able to strike targets that are now out of reach. Our government—and the governments of our allies—needs to know where the great petroleum deposits are. And they need to make plans to use those assets in times of crisis."

"You mean seize the oil assets of other governments."

"Seize! Another archaism, Vanders. We are entering a new eco-

nomic age—one in which deal making, not force, is the primary instrument of diplomacy. The Dutch and English will reach some
accord."

"And if not?" I think I must have been determined to be stubborn that day. Then again, I had just taken another measure of
Charles Brooke, rajah of Sarawak, and found it was in accord with
a certain Irishman's of my late acquaintance.

Brooke plucked at his drooping mustache. "The British have
already amply demonstrated they can take the Indies from the
Dutch whenever they choose."

"Then the Dutch had better keep their powder primed."

Brooke stiffened at my remark. "I detect a note of asperity,
Captain, and it's one I don't like. I still plan to pay you for your
services, if that's behind it. I have already signed the check. Irene?"
Brooke held out his hand.

Brooke's comely minister-without-portfolio brought over a
leather-bound accounting ledger, handing him a pen as she opened
the cover. With a dismissive jab, he signed the draft. She held out
the check with an encouraging smile. "I'm sure you'll agree it is a
generous sum."

A generous sum it was, and it made me bristle. "Is this supposed to buy my silence, Mr. Brooke? Or is this the payoff I receive
for playing the dupe? You deceived me, sir. I had no command.
It was all an illusion, from beginning to end." The piece of paper
trembled in my hand, and though my impulse was to tear it up
and toss the pieces in the rajah's face, something stayed me.

"You *are* ungrateful." The raven-haired assistant glowered as
if at a petulant child.

"Let me handle this, Irene." Brooke thrust his hands behind
his back and strode to the veranda that overlooked the bustling
port of Kuching. He stood there for a moment, and when he
returned, his irritation had changed to pensiveness. "Listen, Vanders—we both lost something and gained something by this adventure. True, I was not entirely candid from the start. There are

times when secrecy must be exercised, especially when large matters are at stake. But that does not make you a pawn, and that does not turn your accomplishment into an illusion. Your experience was very real, I think."

"Yes, very real, Mr. Brooke ..." Once more, I saw the shimmering blue wings of a delicate butterfly soar over a stream that led down the daring days and weeks of my adventure to the image of *Lorelei* bravely churning up a black-water river. I felt the solid tug of the wheel in my hands, the pounding of the engine beneath me. I saw Sweelinck lounging on the commandant's desk, and Devadatta leaning his grinning face into the rosy glow thrown off by the boiler, and the golden Iskandar leading a charge on a bony nag. I saw Diem lifting his mirrored snuffbox, and I felt the brush of Deborah's lips against mine. Perhaps it had all been the stuff of a dark fairy tale, as Deborah had said, but none of it was make-believe, any more than the check I held in my hand. I had earned every penny of it. Brooke was right. The command may have been illusory, but the experience was not. From this a real command would, in time, appear. I folded the check and slipped it inside my coat.

The White Rajah was back at work on the little brass engine, adjusting a miniature flywheel. "Irene, I'm sure Mr. Vanders is anxious to return to his ship." He looked up at me with something approaching a smile. "Captain Kepple felt your loss keenly when he sailed to Singapore some weeks back. Fortunately, the cutter that brought you to Kota Baru, HMS *Renown*, sails on the morning tide. You can rejoin your comrades, for the *Siren* is still refitting in Singapore. I'm sure you're anxious to return to your former berth—first mate, wasn't it?" He tapped his forehead. "Oh, and while I think of it. Do you have that commission in the Regal Sarawak Navy about you?"

"I'm afraid it was lost—in the waters of the Asahan."

A dark cloud settled over the features of Charles Brooke. "Yes, *your* commission and *my* damned steamboat!"

I looked over at Irene Burdett-Couts, who had placed my empty brandy glass on the sideboard. Somehow the look of sympathy had drained from her dark eyes now that she had her hands wrapped around Deborah Rand's diary. Business was business, after all, and ours was at an end.

"It is finished."

The dawn was breaking outside the windows of my cabin, the harbor unusually still under billows of cumulus tinged pink and gold, receding in stately procession like sails over the horizon. Along the wharves, strings of electric lights still burned. I blew out the kerosene lamp on my desk. The porcelain bottle of palm wine stood on the green blotter next to the record I had written of our journey up the Asahan River.

"Captain." There was a rap on my cabin door. "Captain Vanders, sir?"

"Proceed, Mr. Radhakrishnan."

My first officer set a tray on my desk. A steaming pot of coffee, biscuit and butter, the morning edition of the *Straits Times,* perhaps only two or three days old, and a slim yellow envelope.

I plucked up the telegram and, rising from the desk, held it up to the daylight streaming through the stern windows.

"Do you think it is—?" my officer began anxiously.

"By heaven, it had better be." I opened the envelope and quickly slipped the message into my pocket. "It is," I confirmed. I went over to the sideboard and drew two fresh sherry glasses. "Mr. Radhakrishnan, I would be pleased if you would join me in a toast. The hour is odd but the event momentous."

"With pleasure, sir," he said. "I think," he added uncertainly.

I presented the porcelain bottle and splashed a dram of the stuff in each glass. "It seems that Mr. Fairfield has finally stopped pacing his office in Aberdeen. He has made a decision. We'll be packing our seabags soon, Mr. R."

"The *Phoenix* is to be salvaged. That's the decision, isn't it?"

"She is to be salvaged."

"I am sorry to hear that, sir." I could see the thick line of worry beginning to knot his brow. When a young man stares at reversal, it seems his life is dashed.

"To the future, Mr. Radhakrishnan. For you have a bright one ahead of you."

My officer held up his glass. "If only I knew what it is to be, sir."

"There was more to Mr. Fairfield's message. He likes the idea of your studying at the new marine-engineering school in Hong Kong."

"Really, sir!"

"I believe you can count on it."

"Then I have you to thank for that, Captain."

"No, your own abilities, sir. Will you drink to the future with me?"

"This is palm wine," he said appreciatively after draining his glass. "Very fine."

"Oh yes, most unusual, for it is infused with the spices of memory and days long gone."

"This is the gift brought to you by that old boatman, isn't it? You know, I thought I had half imagined him. Especially after he vanished so suddenly."

"I was thinking the same thing. The man I remember could play sea shanties on a mouth organ with a fine fancy. And he could read the future with an oracle of wands."

"You knew him, then."

"Oh, we shipped out once. Long ago. If it was that man . . ."

He put down his glass. "With your permission, I'll see to the duty roster, sir."

"Yes, by all means." His hand was on the door. "Oh, and Mr. R. . . ." I felt a sudden impulse to tell him about an engineer I once knew. I could almost see him standing at the young officer's elbow, grinning at me with an elastic smile, a skinny little fellow with big ears and nose and a turban piled on his head. Tucked under one arm was Mr. Bulfinch's *The Age of Fable*, and under the other, the marvelous tale of Sancho Panza and Don Kixit.

"Sir?"

"I knew an engineer once, the finest I ever sailed with. A fellow from Travancore. He was shanghaied by a couple of pirates and ended up a virtual mikado of a remote Sumatra tribe."

"Truly, sir?"

"Truly, Mr. Radhakrishnan. A tale of raw human courage overcoming adversity. Remind me to tell you the story sometime."

"I will, sir."

Alone in my cabin once more, I went over to the frame mounted on the bulkhead. Even this many years later, the colors of the Golden Sura were as vibrant as the day I found her. More accurately, the day she found me . . .

After I had healed in Bahal following the loss of *Lorelei*, Devadatta, now self-styled prime minister of the Bataks, had arranged for a party to escort me down the Asahan so that I might rendezvous with a Malay fishing vessel bound for Kuching. The return was far less eventful than the voyage upriver. We made the delta in two days, just in time for the transfer. While my canoe was approaching the fishing boat, a butterfly with blue-black wings flitted out of the dense line of mangrove and, dazzling in the sunlight, flew from boat to boat until it landed on my forearm. There it came to rest, and there it stayed. And there this wondrous Golden Sura expired. It was as if the enigmatic island of Sumatra had left me with a parting gift.

My only regret after I returned to Kuching was that I had

missed Alfred Wallace by a week. He had left for England, never again to return to the archipelago where he made his momentous discoveries in evolutionary biology. We have kept in touch over the years, but I never did tell him the full story of the *Lorelei*. The Golden Sura mounted on the bulkhead has always been his promised specimen, but I must confess that with the passage of time, it has been harder and harder to let go of it. But I may yet; he is now eighty-eight and very much alive, living in England. And it seems there is yet other business between us. . . .

⮞⊂

It was time for morning inspection. As I buttoned my jacket, I turned over the *Straits Times* and skimmed the front page.

The leading headline was still in my mind as I stepped out on the quarterdeck, nodded to the bosun, and strolled down the deck of finely fitted oak, breathing in buffets of the chill November air. The doleful clangor of the salvaging yards was fitting accompaniment to my mood as I surveyed this graceful wooden vessel once more. I paused at the mainmast and followed the unwavering line of Washington fir as it rose to meet the sky with its topgallants, its stays trimmed to its sides, its yardarms bare of canvas. With a strong following wind, the *Phoenix* could make seventeen knots, her keel nearly dancing on the water. I once made the run from Singapore to Sydney in just under two weeks. She was a spent corsair now, shorn of her finery, ready for a final order and last rites.

With the stroke of a pen, Mr. Fairfield in Aberdeen had sealed her doom, but he was only reacting to the death knell tolled in the news. Coal was out and oil was in. The first lord of the British admiralty, Winston Churchill, had issued the order to convert all Royal Navy vessels to oil, a declaration made possible by the recent merger of British-owned Shell Oil with the Royal Dutch Petroleum Company. This guaranteed the Royal Navy with supplies of energy, at least to Mr. Churchill's satisfaction. Other navies would be swift to follow, and the final stage in the transformation from

F HIGHLAND   Highland, Frederick, 1945-

Ghost eater.

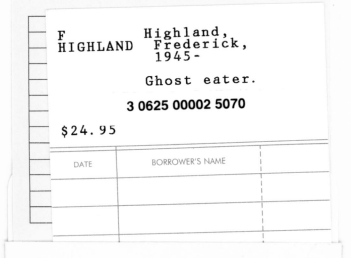

F HIGHLAND   Highland, Frederick, 1945-

Ghost eater.

3 0625 00002 5070

$24.95

DATE	BORROWER'S NAME	

sail to steam would be complete. The last of the wooden merchant ships would be sent to the auction blocks and the salvage yards, relics of an archaic age ruled by the wind, sacrifices to the Great God of Oil. Oh, there would still be sailing ships to ply the more arcane trade routes. For a while, at least. And a few clippers and brigantines would be preserved like dockside mummies for a penny tour. I was put in mind of that demonstration of oil-powered steam Charles Brooke had attempted in his office when I returned from Sumatra. He is rajah of Sarawak to this day. I wondered with what enthusiasm he would greet the admiralty's announcement. Recently, I read a little book by Sir Charles in which he warned that colonial competition and a Europe bristling with modern armies could only lead to the catastrophe of a world war. I knew some who thought his isolation in Kuching had made him an eccentric crank, out of touch and slightly mad.

I took my full measure of the *Phoenix,* circling her decks several times in memorial pace. Soon it would be time to summon my skeleton crew and give them the word that our skeleton ship had been condemned to the Kaohsiung scrappers so busily banging away across the harbor. I would review our long association and remind them that they could take pride in having served aboard the last of the three-masted barques doing business in the South China Sea. Then I would pack them off for a day of drink and riot in the dives of the city while I fulfilled Mr. Fairfield's instructions for final disposition of the ship, and wired funds from my personal account to the registrar at the marine school of engineering in Hong Kong.

I put my hands on the wheel of the *Phoenix* as she rocked gently at anchor. The wheel of the *Lorelei* was forever getting a kink in the steering line, I recalled.

"It is finished." The faded letters written on that calling card, barely legible, bore distinctive flourishes. I had seen that hand before. In a diary.

I did not know what chain of events had brought Master Kung

to my ship with a last, enigmatic message from Deborah Rand. I will probably never know. She had deceived me and perhaps even played me for a fool, yet the beautiful British spy and Sakti of the Mamaqs had left me with something that far outweighed the lie— a life renewed. And though the world may be an idle dream, as Devadatta claimed, it was no illusion that I had once danced under the moon with the elephants of Samosir and the queen of changes herself.

My thoughts went to that jolly boat with the yellow canopy, bobbing across the harbor to the City of the Dead. I saw the mute helmsman with the ravaged face, and I saw the teak coffins carved with the mysterious effigies and curious towers and dancing elephants.

"We shall meet again when it is finished," she had said.

And so we had.

sail to steam would be complete. The last of the wooden merchant ships would be sent to the auction blocks and the salvage yards, relics of an archaic age ruled by the wind, sacrifices to the Great God of Oil. Oh, there would still be sailing ships to ply the more arcane trade routes. For a while, at least. And a few clippers and brigantines would be preserved like dockside mummies for a penny tour. I was put in mind of that demonstration of oil-powered steam Charles Brooke had attempted in his office when I returned from Sumatra. He is rajah of Sarawak to this day. I wondered with what enthusiasm he would greet the admiralty's announcement. Recently, I read a little book by Sir Charles in which he warned that colonial competition and a Europe bristling with modern armies could only lead to the catastrophe of a world war. I knew some who thought his isolation in Kuching had made him an eccentric crank, out of touch and slightly mad.

I took my full measure of the *Phoenix,* circling her decks several times in memorial pace. Soon it would be time to summon my skeleton crew and give them the word that our skeleton ship had been condemned to the Kaohsiung scrappers so busily banging away across the harbor. I would review our long association and remind them that they could take pride in having served aboard the last of the three-masted barques doing business in the South China Sea. Then I would pack them off for a day of drink and riot in the dives of the city while I fulfilled Mr. Fairfield's instructions for final disposition of the ship, and wired funds from my personal account to the registrar at the marine school of engineering in Hong Kong.

I put my hands on the wheel of the *Phoenix* as she rocked gently at anchor. The wheel of the *Lorelei* was forever getting a kink in the steering line, I recalled.

"It is finished." The faded letters written on that calling card, barely legible, bore distinctive flourishes. I had seen that hand before. In a diary.

I did not know what chain of events had brought Master Kung

to my ship with a last, enigmatic message from Deborah Rand. I will probably never know. She had deceived me and perhaps even played me for a fool, yet the beautiful British spy and Sakti of the Mamaqs had left me with something that far outweighed the lie—a life renewed. And though the world may be an idle dream, as Devadatta claimed, it was no illusion that I had once danced under the moon with the elephants of Samosir and the queen of changes herself.

My thoughts went to that jolly boat with the yellow canopy, bobbing across the harbor to the City of the Dead. I saw the mute helmsman with the ravaged face, and I saw the teak coffins carved with the mysterious effigies and curious towers and dancing elephants.

"We shall meet again when it is finished," she had said.

And so we had.